FIELD OF FIRE

BY ZOE SAADIA

Obsidian Puma
Field of Fire
Heart of the Battle
Warrior Beast
Morning Star
Valley of Shadows

The Highlander
Crossing Worlds
The Emperor's Second Wife
Currents of War
The Fall of the Empire
The Sword
The Triple Alliance

Two Rivers
Across the Great Sparkling Water
The Great Law of Peace
The Peacekeeper

Beyond the Great River
The Foreigner
Troubled Waters
The Warpath
Echoes of the Past

Shadow on the Sun
Royal Blood
Dark Before Dawn
Raven of the North

FIELD OF FIRE

The Aztec Chronicles, Book 2

ZOE SAADIA

Copyright © 2016 by Zoe Saadia

All rights reserved. This book or any portion thereof may not be reproduced, transmitted or distributed in any form or by any means whatsoever, without prior written permission from the copyright owner, unless by reviewers who wish to quote brief passages.

For more information about this book, the author and her work, visit www.zoesaadia.com

ISBN-13: 978-1520714653

AUTHOR'S NOTE

"Field of Fire" is historical fiction and some of the characters and adventures in this book are imaginary, while some are historical and well documented in the accounts concerning this time period and place.

The history of that region is presented as accurately and as reliably as possible, to the best of the author's ability, and although no work of this scope can be free of error, an earnest effort was made to reflect the history and the traditional way of life of the peoples residing in those areas.

I would also like to apologize before the descendants of the mentioned nations for giving various traits and behaviors to the well known historical characters (such Axayacatl, Moquihuixtli, Teconal, Chalchiuhnenetzin and others), sometimes putting them into fictional situations for the sake of the story. The main events of this series are well documented and could be verified by simple research.

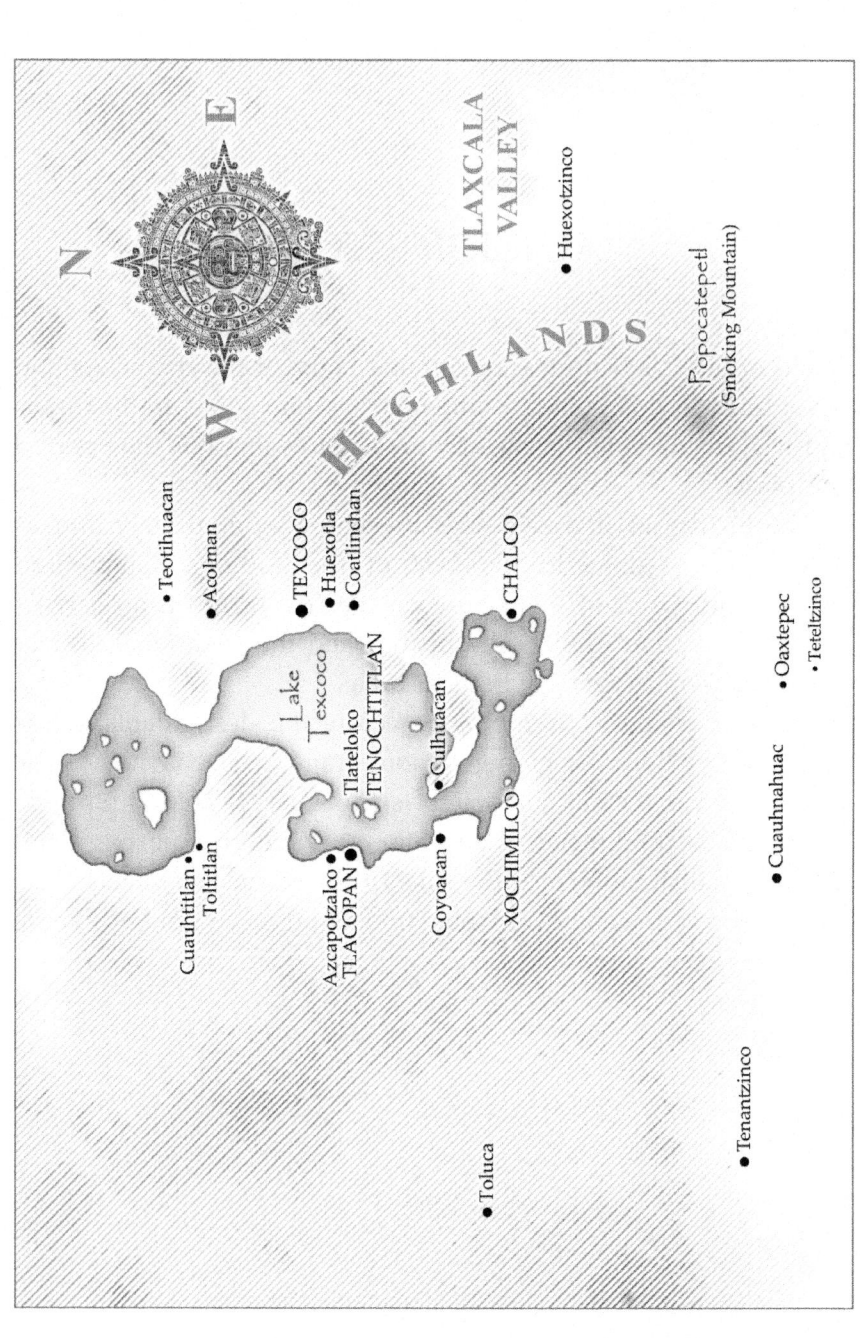

CHAPTER 1

*Tlatelolco,
1473 AD*

Tlemilli had a hard time restraining herself from breaking something. That prettily painted vase with annoying patterns; it stood upon the narrow reed podium, tempting her. She had actually left the cushioned mat in order to snatch it, then stopped herself, admiring her own self-restraint. It wasn't wise to antagonize them further by breaking more pottery. She had been driving them all mad as it was, Father's wives and their various serving maids, even the slaves.

Grinding her teeth, she stomped back toward the padded alcove, all colorful covers and embroidery. To administer a kick to one of the cushions helped. Planting another before risking admonishment by a farsighted maid, she watched it slip away and onto the tiles of the floor. But was it annoying, this prohibition to leave the women quarters. She couldn't even wander the Palace's gardens anymore. What a bore!

It had been more than a market interval. No, two by now. Well, one and a half. It was no market day. Still, she felt as though a whole lifetime had passed, many dry and rainy seasons since the day of the contest, the wonderful freedom of it, the most exciting of adventures. She had rarely left the Palace's grounds before, knowing every knoll and shrub in it, every single marble of every mosaic, every corner and every bench – oh, but did she know all those by heart.

When younger and just having moved to the Palace upon Father becoming the Emperor's adviser, she had been expectant and thrilled. What possibilities there were to sniff around forbidden grounds! She would wander those beautiful gardens for days, pretending that it was a forest, straight away from Tlaco's stories – her old personal maid had those in abundance – hunting insects and small animals, imagining that those were mystical creatures, with her being a powerful goddess, or a courageous huntress, half human, half jaguar, maybe, or any other entity she cared to admire on a given day. It was thrilling to think of herself in the middle of this or that wonderful legend, the stories Tlaco had in many twenties, telling her tales since Tlemilli could remember, the ones she demanded every morning and every evening, even now that she wasn't little anymore.

These days, Tlaco was old and ailing, unable to perform her duties properly. However, Tlemilli had adamantly refused every new personal maid that they attempted to press on her, even at the price of making them angry. Two of the stupid fowls, Father's second wife and his favorite concubine, went as far as complaining to him in person, nagging about the intractability of his daughter, but she had stood up even to this formidable man, claiming that Tlaco still did her job perfectly. They all knew she didn't, even Father himself, but luckily, he had been too busy, waving his nagging spouses and their petty complaints away. He had more important matters to attend to, as back then, two summers earlier, he had already became the new Emperor's Head Adviser. A more important job than keeping track of his numerous wives and daughters, and the commoners who served them. There were too many female offspring in Father's family and too few sons. He had enough frustration to face on that score alone, without being involved in the petty squabbling between those same shrilling females.

The only daughter who had brought satisfaction to him, earning her keep, was Citlalli, the sweet, beautiful, good-natured Emperor's wife – Chief Wife these days. The nicest person of them all, in Tlemilli's private estimation. Citlalli did not visit their side of the Palace anymore, but Tlaco's stories made up for this lack.

As long as those were forthcoming, she didn't mind imperfectly laundered clothes or badly served meals. Tlaco was part of her life ever since she could remember, Tlaco and Citlalli. But now both were away, one in the kitchen area, taking care of the midmorning meal, and the other in the Emperor's bed, taking care of their father's ambition.

Was Citlalli more of a tool to Father than a favorite daughter? The question kept nagging ever since that thrilling afternoon with that boy. He and his dubious Tenochtitlan friends and their troubles were all to do with Father and his work against the neighboring island's scum. She knew it before too, in the habit of sneaking around and eavesdropping on everyone, out of boredom rather than true curiosity. But now it all made her wonder. That boy had such fear of Father and with good reason, apparently. It was a terrible sight, when Father was hitting that other boy, held from both sides and helpless; it haunted her ever since. It was a bad thing to do, and why would Father do this?

Unable to stay still, she sprang to her feet, rushing toward the opening in the wall, the view it offered painfully boring, the same colorful mess of flowerbeds and carefully trimmed trees, with birds chirping in the treetops, unable to shut up. She wished she had something to throw at them. Like that sling he had clutched in his hand, the sling and the glistening round missile, so perfectly smooth, inviting to touch. Had he used it in the end? she wondered. And to what effect?

Back then, while talking her way up the incline, anxious to keep Father's attention, she didn't dare to glance toward his hiding place, of course. But now she regretted it. The chance to see him shooting his sling was worthy of a fleeting peek, wasn't it? That and the possibility of finding out if he managed to free his friends in the end. She didn't know even that. Father was too angry with her to answer her questions, had she dared to venture even one. Not on the same afternoon, when he didn't manage to make sense of her jumbled explanation and protests of misunderstanding. He didn't expect anything worthwhile from her anyway; no one did. However, later on, the next day, when someone had told on her, Tlemilli, let the Head Adviser know that his daughter had been barely present at the Great Plaza, sneaking away from the royal dais, spending her time gods-know-where, such unladylike behavior, she was in for real trouble as, suddenly, for the first time since she had been born, Father paid attention to her, clearing his busy day for a private conversation; interrogation, really. But did he get angry, barking those questions! Where had she been and with whom? How had she found herself running around the shores of the Great Lake, unsupervised, interfering with his activities?

Frightened to a degree, she bore his barking demands with enough aplomb, but when he lost his temper and started to scream, summoning his servants in order to demand the execution of her favorite maid to begin with, she had lost her spirit altogether, bursting into most shameful tears, begging to spare Tlaco, telling it all to him, every tiny detail. Which sent his rage straight to the skies, but by this point, she didn't care. To save the woman who had raised and taken care of her since she could remember, telling her amazing tales and listening to her charge's silly ones, was more important than anything. That boy was nowhere near the Palace or the Plaza to get hurt, or hunted down, or so she hoped.

And now, five – no, six! – days later, here she was, a prisoner in these same women's quarters, not allowed to go anywhere, not even the Palace's gardens, not even the relevant classes in *calmecac*, something she hated with all her heart but now found herself missing. Oh benevolent Coatlicue, mother of all gods!

Outside the opening in the wall, the sun was blazing happily, unrestrained. Like in the tale of Smoking Mountain from the Eastern Highlands, whose peak was easy to spot on a bright cloudless day even from the Palace's gardens. Both mountains were towering out there on the mainland, telling their tale of two lovers separated by jealousy and lies, to be reunited only in death, in the shape of two white-topped peaks, after the desperate girl had killed herself in order not to be given to another and her lover, finding her dead, doing the same to himself. A sad story, but a beautiful one. Tlaco told it differently from time to time, but they always ended the same. Well, of course they would. The mountains were there for everyone to see and behold. She always envied the warriors who were sailing toward the eastern shore, usually on behalf of annoying Tenochtitlan and its projected expeditions of conquest, and as much as she disliked the obligation of her city to obey the wishes of their pushy neighbors, she knew that she would hop into one of the sailing canoes given half a chance, if only for the opportunity to see both legendary mountains from close up. The tale had a ring of finality to it; still, for her, it had a different ending. The girl didn't have to give up and kill herself before her lover found her. She might have put up a fight or something.

By the distant cluster of trees, her eyes spotted a movement. At this time of the high morning, not many people were out strolling the gardens. The noblemen were busy with politics, courts, and meetings, and the noblewomen with their looms and their gossip. Some of her half-sisters and cousins of a relevant age would be escorted for their daily lessons in *calmecac*, some for the classes or services in the adjacent temple. If only she could have sneaked out together with them! Typically, she hated both the school and the temple training; however, now she needed a pretext. Somehow, in some way, she needed to get out and try to find that boy, to leave him a message. Maybe through the annoying filthy-mouthed commoner that kept clinging to him, if she managed to find this one. It was dangerous for him to be near the Palace, trying to keep his promise. Maybe later, but not now, not when Father knew all about him.

The man she had spotted, a short heavyset individual clad in a bright non-descript cloak, was pacing back and forth, exuding impatience. There was something about his pose, the furtiveness of his movements. Her instincts of an experienced eavesdropper told her that he might rather wish to be elsewhere, eager to have his meeting – what else could it be? – done and be over with. She contemplated going out through the wall opening whatever the consequences. It didn't look like a high jump.

"What are you doing?"

The annoyingly melodious voice made her almost topple over, perching on the windowsill, balancing there with an effort. She clutched the wooden plank tighter.

"Are you out of your mind? Look what she is doing!"

"Nothing out of the ordinary," was the first girl's showily loud reply. She didn't need to see the speakers, two stupid half-sisters of hers, empty-headed, coy, deceptively demure, giggly things, the contestants for the title of the best-behaved fowls in the world. A bore.

"What are you up to now, Tlemilli?" asked the older one, all sensibility and prudence, her tone that of a responsible adult tired of another child's antics.

Tlemilli rolled her eyes. "Nothing!"

"Why are you perched up there like a bird on the branch of a tree?" piped up the younger one, barely eleven summers old, an annoying thing, playing at being grown-up like her perfection of a sister.

"Because that's what I want to do." This time, she snorted loudly, incensed, yet at the same time grateful for their interruption. It wasn't a wise thing to do, to go out of the window and after being forbidden to leave the girls' quarters unless escorted by someone who wasn't a servant. Even Tlaco wasn't trusted anymore. Poor Tlaco.

"Whom are you spying after now?"

"None of your business."

The older girl snorted in her turn. "Leave her alone, Sister. She is the strangest thing in our world of the Fifth Sun. I wish the Adviser decided to remove her from our quarters."

The Adviser? To call one's father a father was apparently not in the line of grown-up behavior. This one was nearing her fifteenth summer, over the temple and *calmecac* training, and lording it over everyone, fluttering her eyelashes, hinting that the real grown-up matters were waiting for her now, beckoning out there.

"He will be removing you faster than me, you empty-headed heap of fat," said Tlemilli calmly, used to their confrontations, not opposed to those. Father's brood of shrill female snakes was exceptional, with his collection of wives being no better. Citlalli was the only worthy person, her only full sister too, but it had been close to three moons since she had left their quarters, moving to occupy the main wing of the Palace instead. A great honor on one score, a glaring disappointment on another. It was nice to have a readily spoken word of protection or encouragement. Citlalli was one of the oldest and greatly respected on all counts. "He will marry you off the moment he finds a stupid enough person to ask for you."

The delicately plucked eyebrows arched. "He will never be so lucky as to get rid of you in the same way. Not even the most meaningless of the Emperor's advisers would be prevailed upon into taking such an ugly heap of bones with the filthiest temper ever. Not even a tradesman from the marketplace with ten illiterate wives. Not even the filthiest slave from the kitchen houses!"

The younger girl was doubling over, all agog with delight. "Yes, yes. Not even the slaves who clean our rooms!"

Tlemilli felt like throwing something at them. "Shut up, you stinking, ugly snakes, both of you. Shut up!"

"See? She is even speaking like commoners. Shut up and all that. They say you were running around the Plaza among the commoners on the day of the contest." The older girl's face glowed with unconcealed satisfaction. "One hears that you did all sorts of things unworthy of noblewomen or even their personal maids. Which wouldn't surprise any of us, those who are forced to tolerate you all our lives. But maybe this time, you did take it too far. Father locked you up now. Maybe next time, he will prove even sterner. I hope he gets rid of you and not through a hastily arranged marriage." A fleeting glance beckoned the younger girl. "Come, Little Sister. Let us find worthy company to spend our time with, before a young thing like you gets corrupted in here."

Tlemilli searched her mind frantically. "You are nothing but a stupid, ugly, mean-tempered turkey," she shouted toward their disappearing backs. "And you smell of excrements straight away from the chamber pot."

"And you..." began the younger girl, turning back gleefully, ready to return measure for measure, but her sister's palm closed around the embroidered sleeve, pulling with force.

"Come, little one. Don't answer this commoners' slime."

The sound of their sandaled feet echoed down the hallway while she struggled to keep her balance on her narrow perch, refusing to come down out of sheer protest. Commoners' slime! Just who did they think they were, these two stupid turkeys? And what did they know about what happened there on the Plaza, or worse yet, on the lakeshore? Were they the ones to tell on her in the first place, the moment she succumbed to the temptation of sneaking down the dais upon seeing that boy anew? He looked so frightened, so desperate back then, running pell-mell, with no clear direction, with no one to pull him and yank like the man he had stood with before. What was he involved with? And where were his friends at that time, the pushy commoner girl and the other two? Back by the lakeshore already? What were they searching for, what were they seeking?

The room was quiet once again, a blessing. She peered at the trees where the suspicious man was pacing before. There was no one there now, but further down another pathway, she could see Father's unmistakable cloak, his regalia of the Head Adviser on full display, such a beautiful headdress, radiant green, rustling with the slightest breeze.

Quailing inside, she slipped over the windowsill, giving her actions not much thought. Father was up to something, that much was obvious, and she needed to know what it was. Maybe it had to do with this boy. Since that scary scene and the vicious dressing down, she kept trying to spy after Father in particular every time she managed to spot him, a few times through the last three days. He never talked about what happened on the day of the contest, but she still hoped he would. Maybe this way, she'd know who this boy was and where he came from. Or why he didn't come as promised. Couldn't he sneak into the Palace for at least a very short time? He promised! And it wasn't that difficult to sneak around here, was it?

The touch of the damp grass and the soggy ground on her bare feet made her wince, freeze for a heartbeat. Such a strange sensation. Not entirely unpleasant but not the most comfortable as well. Oh, but she should have paused to put on her sandals. Fond of walking around the inside rooms barefoot, liking the sleekness of the floor's chilly flagstones, she never stepped outside without appropriate shoes wrapped around her feet and her ankles. The servants could do it so quickly, so efficiently, to tie the multitude of straps and make the wear fit comfortably. Unlike the sandals of that boy! Grinning, she remembered how loudly his crude maguey soles flopped on the cobblestones, how they hampered his step every now and then. He seemed to be having a hard time with it, and at one point, he looked as though about to kick off the stupid rags for good. To do what? To go around barefoot? A wild idea! And yet, somehow, it looked as though he could manage that particular feat.

Stepping carefully, her senses on the new sensation, she slipped toward the line of the thicker trees and their relative protection. The moving figure wasn't where she had spotted it earlier anymore, but she knew where the newcomer would be heading if wishing to whisper something into someone's ear. The mosaic pond behind the main wing, where the artificially planted trees were denser, allowing a freer movement. She had listened to many private conversations in this corner of the Palace's gardens.

Revived by the pleasure of moving around unwatched and unhindered, she slunk into the dimly lit pathway, smiling to herself, careful of jutting stones and other hurtful pieces that made it their business to stab her unprotected toes. The clamor of another relatively secluded area brushed past her ears, making her roll her eyes in disgust. The Palace's noblewomen's favorite place of gathering when wishing to spend their time outside, all those chatty females, her various cousins, half-sisters, or just fellow unmarried noble girls, with the same dreary weaving and embroidery threads, glued to their looms, gossiping – a bore! However, it could give her a perfect excuse. She was allowed in the women's hall, wasn't she? That overly decorated chamber padded with cushioned mats and alcoves, podiums and even reed chairs, spinning tools and stashes of *amate*-paper, sharpened coals, colors and brushes, even columns to tie one's loom to comfortably. Everything to make the female heart flutter in delight. Disgusted, she used to avoid passing anywhere near this place unless forced – an often enough occurrence. Yet now it was her only possible shelter.

Pausing, she listened to the usual quarreling sounds pouring out, marring the clarity of the high morning air. The filthy-tempered Tenochtitlan's whiner, for sure, lashing at her maids, or her fellow wives, or other hapless victims. She was such a moaner! Even though, since the great competition, the displaced would-be empress had been remarkably quieter, more self-contained, judging by the lack of the usual morning noises. Did the event on the Plaza change her life in a way too? She remembered the annoying fowl sneaking plenty of glances from her royal dais, staring at *him*, that battered, haunted boy, seeking him out. What was her thing with him? She should have asked him that. Oh, but she had to find the way to return to this grass-covered incline or the alleys they had run together, or at least the Central Plaza. What if he was trying to keep his promise, but she wasn't there to help him along?

The voices broke upon her unexpectedly, with the pond still nowhere in sight. She stopped dead in her tracks, her heart pounding. Father's voice was impossible not to recognize, his way of twisting certain words, as though not in a hurry to let them out of his mouth, as though tasting them. Her limbs tingled with familiar excitement, their trembling threatening to give her presence away. If caught eavesdropping on Father now, she would be done for, this time for certain.

"Moquihuixtli sent the previous envoys without my agreement." Father seemed to be enraged already, raising his voice before remembering the clearly clandestine nature of this meeting. "But was he trying to send more delegations without consulting me?"

"No, no, Honorable Adviser." The other voice sounded more frightened than agitated, stumbling over his words. "No, the Emperor wouldn't do anything of the sort."

"Then why has this last envoy gone out without my knowledge?" Another stern accusation. She could imagine Father's converser quailing. "Why wasn't I informed of the futile attempt to approach both partners of their so-called Triple Alliance? How could this have happened?"

Something was tickling her heel, crawling beside it. Tlemilli clenched her teeth in an attempt to remain still. Father's wrath was scarier than silly creatures unless a snake or a spider. She slanted her gaze, worried.

"I don't think it was done on purpose, Honorable Adviser," the man was muttering, anxious to convince. "The Emperor trusts you with his life and his *altepetl*. He wouldn't wish to act without consulting you."

"But he did!" exclaimed Father, again forgetting to talk quietly. "Tell me about this delegation. Who was leading it? Who was instructed to do the talking?"

She tried to shake off the spider without moving, flexing whatever muscle made her ankle work, getting nowhere. It had such a round, fat body, and so many small, disgustingly hairy legs. But to have her sandals back on! The man kept talking for a long time, without Father interrupting; a novelty.

"So, Tlacopan was firm in its refusal, the junior partner in the Triple Alliance, yet Texcoco did not commit itself firmly for either side. Interesting." Oh yes, he did sound interested. But what were they talking about, and why couldn't they move on and reach the damn pond, allowing her to retrace her steps safely, to run back into the security of the inner rooms. From spiders to enraged fathers, she didn't want to face any of that. "The death of Nezahualcoyotl, their famous *cultured* ruler, did change things, didn't it? And not for the worst."

"Yes," agreed the other man, clearly placating. "His heir is young and timid. With him, Tenochtitlan will have less stern of an ally."

Another pause full of agreement. She breathed with relief as the hairy legs stopped tickling her heel. Instead of those, now ants were having their go at her toes. There must be a reason people weren't going around barefoot.

"Tenochtitlan's emperor is as young and more impatient, even if he isn't timid. Not that one! And yet that would-be great ruler might be unbalanced easily, maybe even removed. Without the advice of old foxes like Noble Tlacaelel or the old Texcoco ruler, he is vulnerable, prone to making mistakes." Father was orating now, forgetful of his lack of proper audience or an appropriate podium to stand on. Tlemilli fought her grin down. "Still, it wasn't wise to approach his official allies, the members of the Triple Alliance. Moquihuixtli made a grave mistake." The air hissed loudly, clearly drawn through clenched teeth. "He should have waited patiently, should have consulted me. His meekness and lack of confidence will be the end of us, all those erratic decisions – one moment the great ruler with no need of an advice, the other imploring and needing help like a little boy." Again, the raising voice. She tried to focus on her muddied toes and the ants running there busily, greatly content. "We can't best Tenochtitlan on the battlefield, not yet. We need committed, strong allies. And time. And good strategy." A brief pause ensued that made Tlemilli sick with impatience. "I sent envoys to Toltitlan and the neighboring towns. Unlike the Eastern Highlands, they will receive our swords and shields with open hearts. But Moquihuixtli will ruin it all with his impulsive moves, approaching Tenochtitlan's formal allies, of all towns and *altepetls* of our Great Lake. What silliness!" Another dour pause. "I bet it's his former Chief Wife making him do stupid things. Maybe she puts something in his food. I wouldn't put it past her. She is well capable of such treachery. The despicable over-indulgent rat should be executed for infidelity or any other appropriate accusation. He isn't man enough to do even that!"

Tlemilli felt like nodding this time. Oh yes, Father had been right about that. And wouldn't it be great fun to see the execution of the fat fowl, to hear her complaining about the unworthiness of the process by which her slimy neck was snapped, commenting on the lack of cleanliness of the strangling cord or its lack of refinement. The fight against a wild fit of laughter turned harder.

"I bet Tenochtitlan knows everything about those stupid delegations to Texcoco and Tlacopan by now. And about their outcomes as well. Such a futile action! And the one that puts Axayacatl on guard." Something swished, bouncing off the nearest tree trunk. A thrown stone? "While my envoys in the north and the east did bring us allies, without Tenochtitlan's awareness at that." Another brief pause ensued. "Come to think of it, we should not neglect the southern shores as well. The Lake Chalco dwellers are proud people, and they must still remember their glorious past, not so far removed from now, eh? They might wish to avenge themselves against the grandson of the emperor who has crushed them so soundly."

"Oh yes, Revered Adviser!" The man's excited exclamation made Tlemilli almost jump, forgetting Father's audience for a moment, with him orating for so long and with no interruptions. "The Chalcoans might wish to join our case with true zeal."

"Organize that delegation at once." Father again sounded calmer, deep in thought. "Do not involve our Emperor. He'll know in due time. His Tenochtitlan love has spies all over the Palace and the city, and still he refuses to get rid of her properly. Or at least to send her back to her brother. Claims it would be tantamount to a declaration of war. As though sending envoys to this same annoying *altepetl*'s allies, asking to rally with us and against it is not tantamount to the same thing!" Now he was almost spitting with rage. "From stinking commoners to even high born *pilli*s – mere children, imagine that! – sniffing around our plazas and shores, spying on us, eager to report our activities and competitions. Oh, but this woman has no shame! And when I lay my hands on her filthy spies again, they won't be sneaking away from me, not this time. They'll be begging to be put to death after I'm through with them!"

Forgetting the ants, Tlemilli fought for breath, her heart fluttering, refusing to organize into a proper beating. It was a struggle to get enough air. Oh, but Father didn't forget. He was still angry about it all, and should that boy try to find her, like he promised he would…

"The fact that Tenochtitlan might hear about our competing warriors was taken into account, Honorable Adviser. You said so yourself."

"Yes," grunted Father, quieter again but refusing to be pacified. "Wandering commoners who didn't bother to return home from the previous day's markets, yes. There was nothing unlawful in what we did, nothing inappropriate. No declaration of warlike intentions, even though Moquihuixtli did get carried away with his speech. That man is not subtle enough and his lack of patience is appalling." A loud snort shook the afternoon air. "But to plant outright spies, sniffing around with no shame or disguise, little *pilli*s of her own family? Oh, she'll pay for this. She and her entire *altepetl*, from the young hothead of their emperor to their unrestrained noble youths, untamed beasts every one of them."

Oh mighty Coatlicue! Tlemilli sucked in her breath, desperate to get away from where she was and fast. If she dared to move, she would have leaned against the supportive bark of a tree, her limbs jelly.

"That little beast Ahuitzotl! No wonder the boy carrying such a name turned out to be so obnoxious, so loathsome, a perfect member of this entire brood. But how this royal fowl Atotoztli keeps giving birth to son after son, like a commoner or a village peasant and not Tenochtitlan's noblewoman, the daughter of the previous Emperor. Disgusting!" The angry flow stopped momentarily, for a lack of air, Tlemilli suspected. The royal fowl Atotoztli was Tenochtitlan's current Emperor's mother, wasn't she? But who was this obnoxious Ahuitzotl?

"And his cronies," Father went on, apparently needing to talk, to vent his frustrations. Well, she didn't mind that as long as she was hidden and away from it all. And if he kept talking about spying boys, then he might tell what she wanted to hear, in case he knew more than she did. Her three days of stalking him might have paid off in the end. She held her breath. "Mere *pilli*s that should be in school, not spying around, sticking their noses where they shouldn't." Another heavy pause ensued. "The first one knew more than anyone, the beaten commoner that he was. But for the outright betrayal!"

More direful cursing. So many colorful words. She tried to will away her trembling. She wasn't in danger, even if caught. He wouldn't hurt his own daughter. Or would he? He looked as though he might back then after the competition. And he certainly meant to execute Tlaco! She held her breath again, this time more scared than curious.

"Keep your ears open, and spread more people around the marketplace and the wharves."

"Oh yes, Honorable Adviser. I've already done that, but I'll double the amount of our men here and next to the causeway."

"In Tenochtitlan too. Send people there, to wander around the markets and wharves, even the plazas. Hear what they are saying, have them reporting on the locals' mood."

There was a brief pause.

"What about the tunnel?" asked the man quietly.

"Leave it as it is. The dirty commoner is the only one who knows about it. If only they remembered his looks! The useless pieces of rotten fish kept him for an entire day and now they can't even remember what he looked like. All beaten and dirty, they claimed. Well, mud and blood in moderate amounts don't cancel people's looks!" A longer pause ensued through which Tlemilli didn't dare even to blink. "Oh, but I know who might remember! Why didn't I think of it before?"

And then her heart was making wild leaps inside her chest, while her instincts told her what it was before her panicked mind did.

CHAPTER 2

"Not long now."

The groan of the pimpled youth in the priestly garment made Miztli grin. Bypassing two smaller pyramids tucked on the outskirts of the Central Plaza by diving into a small passageway between those and the ball court's wall made their route somewhat shorter, but not by much. Ten paces spared, maybe twenty. For himself, he preferred to take the main routes, to stroll those until reaching the middle of the Central Plaza, as then it would open to one's eye in all its glory, with the Great Pyramid blocking the sky. Five, no, six dawns since seeing it for the first time and still he couldn't get enough of this view, had to fight the urge to stop and gape and hold his breath in marvel. So much might and beauty and power concentrated in one place, such an overwhelming sensation.

Every time he had been sent out on various errands that included the need to carry large loads – but was Axolin harping on that! – he would be most eager and thrilled, because such missions meant going out and coming back. It was not difficult to deliver massive bundles of either food, utensils, or firewood, no effort at all, in fact, even though firewood, and sometimes uncomfortably long and prickly fir branches, were no joy to carry; too cumbersome, poking one's sides no matter how tightly one would attempt to tie them together in the most compact of bundles. Back in his village, he was used to gathering firewood aplenty, sent out along with other children, picking the driest and the oldest of sticks, bundling them to make it easier to take home. Some older people would invest in making perfect bundles, strapping those to their foreheads, in the fashion of professional traders. Yet of course, back in the village, such meticulous investment was not necessary. There was plenty of firewood everywhere, close enough to home to enable one to have a quick run back and forth instead of bending under cumbersome burdens.

Even when working in the workshop, responsible for huge stocks of firewood to make the braziers work, he didn't have to go far in order to obtain this most important ingredient. Just around the corner, the man with wild hair and a twisted scar disfiguring his face was offering piles of branches from the mainland for sale. And as much as old Tlaquitoc might have wished to spare unnecessary costs, he couldn't send his slaving apprentice to the mainland all by himself, not the foreigner who didn't know his way around; and the rest of the family members could not be bothered.

Well, in the noble establishment called *calmecac* and the temples adjacent to it, it turned out to be quite different. The veterans and various priests running the school made it their point to push everyone into equal labor. A glaring lack of distinction between highborn and less noble elements inhabiting that school, and in the place that was supposed to be the snobbiest of them all, taking care of the best city youth's educations, rearing future statesmen, great warriors, leaders, even emperors. They said that the current Emperor attended this *calmecac* and not such a long time ago. This ruler's count of summers was not so far from the first twenty. A wonder!

Still, they would send him out more than the rest, but it didn't make him feel as though he had been ill-treated. There were classes he was not required to attend, plenty of those. In fact, the lessons he was expected to show his face at along with several other *calmecac* boys were fairly few and far in between, mainly the training upon which they were all made to practice with *atlatl* and *tlacochtli*, a fascinating device in itself and something he craved to be able to handle.

Sometimes a training sword was thrust into his hand, nothing but a mid-sized club, a longish stick with not that much weight to it. Father had a massive roughly polished cudgel back home and it was so much heavier and more impressive. However, those training clubs were not to be looked down upon, he had been informed by both his *calmecac* accomplices. The real thing would be as large or larger, adorned by up to ten razor-sharp obsidian blades.

"See the weapon that could stand up to the real obsidian sword!" Necalli would exclaim, deeply offended. "There is no such thing in the world, just none!"

"*Atlatl* is lethal enough and it shoots from a great distance. And so does a sling."

"If you wish to stay away from the battle, shoot from a safe distance and engage in no glorious hand-to-hand and take no captives, then you can stick with your stupid sling and discharge your *atlatl* until your hand falls off. No warrior will come out of you with that attitude. Only a cowardly peasant!" The *calmecac* boy was waving his hands in the air, both the good and the bad one, his wounded limb still bandaged, exuding an unpleasant odor. It became badly inflamed on the evening of their interview in the Palace and for a few days he had been missing, taken away to be treated either in the temple or at home; they hadn't been told where or informed as to his situation.

Not allowed to leave the school's precinct, there was no way for them to know what was going on, until young Ahuitzotl became aware of their predicament. Then they had come to know that their friend was on the mend, not dying and with his arm still intact, even though he was feverish for some time, his blood boiling and his wound stinking in a bad way. Still, after a few days of ointments and brews, he was getting better, expected to be back at school, his punishments not canceled. A good sign. Dying people were not to be plagued with discipline matters, were they?

Besides this only clash that left him more puzzled than offended and taught him to keep his thoughts to himself, as those boys, so down-to-earth sometimes, so loyal and friendly, were thinking in incomprehensible ways, his days in the school were mostly pleasant, the demands easy and minimal, the benefits great. When Necalli was away and recovering, he and Axolin spent enough time together, doing various chores, sorting or cleaning training weapons when required, sweeping floors in various rooms, arranging stacks of *amate*-paper covered with symbols he couldn't decipher but wished he could, working in kitchen areas. This was all part of the punishment for being absent without permission. Every student was to be engaged in the joys of being worked into exhaustion, Axolin would inform him, but not in such exaggerated amounts. There was a limit to one's being worked like a cheaply bought slave, but the school authorities thought there wasn't.

To this, Miztli listened with his grin of puzzlement barely covered. There was not much sweat in the tasks they were required to perform. He had worked harder even back at home, let alone at Tlaquitoc's workshop. The noble boys were nothing but pampered cubs, not always as tough as they looked, even though when in trouble, Necalli proved his worth above any reproach. However, now he was wiser than to sound such musings aloud. When Axolin fumed about him, Miztli, being sent out to bring in firewood twice a day like a common slave, he would shrug and go out, happy to do that. The alternative of being forced into one of the classes with priests and their intricately connected sheets of *amate*-paper covered with glyphs was too terrifying even to start considering it.

For the last two days, Axolin, back with the good grace of the authorities and his workload reduced to an acceptable minimum, was spending a considerable part of his mornings in those classes. And so did Ahuitzotl. A possibility that terrified Miztli more than the prospect of even going back to the braziers did. But what would he do with those colorful paintings? What did they see in those books, deciphering their meaning with such ease and no visible effort? However, the priests seemed to be as uneager to shove his face into the rustling stacks of papers, preferring to have him running around, doing their errands. A bliss!

"At long last!"

The pimpled apprentice was wiping the sweat off his forehead, glancing at the opening under the temple's stairs, wistful. His load was noticeably more slender and with no thicker branches and stakes, and so was the cargo of the third youth, another temple trainee. Their water flasks were also in Miztli's charge and carried by him, now thankfully emptier than when they had set out. Still, both his companions looked as though about to faint.

"Here or up there?" he asked when they kept lingering, enjoying the shadow the massive staircase was casting.

"We can use the corridor, can't we?" The hopeful glances they exchanged made him wish to snicker. Then the first one frowned with decisiveness. "Go up there, commoner boy. Bring them your cargo and ask about ours."

He didn't roll his eyes at their lack of subtlety, not wishing to antagonize any of them. Skinny, pimpled, and undeveloped, those youths came from noble families, future priests, and whatnot. Axolin warned him against making the temple servants mad, even novices and apprentices. Although it was obvious that they hoped he would deliver his cargo, then would be sent to call them in, taking a part of their burden as he did. He didn't mind. Those youths didn't try to order him about as Tlaquitoc or his sons would; just attempted to shift some of their chores on him.

Why were they all acting as though he wasn't an outsider, beneath everyone here, calling him "commoner boy" but not acting accordingly? Five dawns in this establishment and he still hadn't come closer to understanding any of it, his fear that old Tlaquitoc would be able to come and claim him back into slavery fading, turning less acute than in the beginning, yet still there. Through the first night here, snug on the most comfortable mat he ever slept on, surrounded by the breathing of other boys, so many of them, an entire hall padded with sleeping forms, he hadn't dared to close his eyes, afraid to wake up back in the airless reality of the melting room and slavery, his and his family's ruined future. What if he had fainted and just dreamed this entire day? What if, like back in the temple of the tunnel or Tlatelolco warehouse, he was just unconscious, not aware, full of a false sense of security, mistaking a dream for reality?

Well, five nights later, and the dream didn't break, making no more sense than before but convincing nevertheless. They were too real, those people, too vivid and lively, too vigorous in their activities and exchanges, the *calmecac* boys and their teachers and supervisors, and the priests of the temple, each day in their company stranger than the previous one, more fascinating. So different from the workshop and the wharves, the marketplace, or even his brief rushing along Tlatelolcan alleys and squares.

Tlatelolco!

His stomach would constrict every time he remembered, every time someone said that word. How to do it? How to sneak southwards and across the causeway? How to send her word in case she remembered too? Did she?

"Oh, isn't that our popular commoner?"

The exclamation tore him from his reverie, made him nearly jump out of his skin. Already near the top of the staircase, he halted abruptly, trying to see against the fierce glow of the early afternoon sun. The figure atop of it was silhouetted darkly, swimming before his squinting eyes. No chance to shield those, not with the stupid bags occupying his hands. Still, he thought he recognized the voice, nothing promising.

"They were looking for you all over, commoner wonder. Where have you been?"

He pushed his way up, trying to make it look like an easy walk. Even though blinded by the sun, it was still not difficult to recognize the annoying one named Acoatl, so broad-shouldered and tall, towering near the entrance, the chest laden with pottery looking like a toy with no weight in his massive hands. The best ballplayer in the school, useless in all the rest, or so Necalli had claimed. They had a clash with this one on his, Miztli's, first night here, before having enough time to find the mats designated to them. Other boys crowded them too, some staring, some asking questions. The tale of their adventures made its way quickly and practically everywhere, not only Necalli's and Axolin's unauthorized running away of two days, but also the Emperor's involvement in it, apparently, and the unclear status of their mysterious guest. But did they all gape at him!

He tried to pay the stares no attention, exhausted beyond reason, confused even worse, afraid but desperate to hide it, still hungry after a spare meal. Apparently, the school authorities made a point of not feeding their pupils to bursting, unwilling to encourage the tendency of indulgence. Or so claimed Necalli, full of his usual banter and jesting observations, reassuring more than solemn promises would. Still, this same Acoatl made the *calmecac* boy lose his good-natured attitude and fast, especially the broad boy's way of carrying on about punishments and the future of those who had pissed off the authorities, all these looming possibilities of disgrace, thrown out of school and whatnot, picking company with marketplace filth, disgracing the entire school with it. At this point, Necalli was growling and hissing, spitting half twenty curses per heartbeat, threatening balefully, especially about the remarks concerning the commoner elements of their company. Which didn't impress the massive Acoatl, half a head taller than Necalli and wider in his shoulders by a whole palm. Still, when the two antagonists were stopped from beating each other blue by Axolin and the others, not fancying collective punishments for brawling in the sleeping quarters – it seemed that everyone would get punished for that – the taller boy took the direful threats to heart, or at least some of it. Through the following days, he didn't seek to bother any of them, throwing an occasional remark toward Miztli but not trying to make it into an outright confrontation, not even through the days when Necalli was missing. Still, it was no joy to be around that one, especially now, standing considerably lower and with no one in sight but two skinny priestly apprentices down the stairs.

"Where have you been?" repeated the boy, stepping onto Miztli's path, blocking his way if only partially. To bypass, he would have to steer to his left, admit defeat. And what was to stop this one from stepping in the same direction, forcing his victim into more shameful dancing around?

"Isn't that obvious?" he retorted, stopping in front of his adversary, only a landing lower but not about to be budged. "Let me pass."

"Go around, revered emperor," was the angry response. Well, at least this one wasn't amused or condescending anymore. Still, the thought of how easy it would be to push him into rolling down the stairs made him worried. To what length might the annoying rat go in order to prove his point?

Desperate not to blink against the sun that was thankfully not so strong here, the shadow of the temple helpful, dimming the fierce glow, Miztli didn't move, staring at the hated face, its features prominent, the muscles upon massive arms bulging.

"You are looking for a good beating, market boy," growled Acoatl finally, moving a length of a finger away. "One day, not far away from now, I might oblige."

Miztli said nothing, just squeezed through, his heart beating fast. What a rotten way to finish a good day. Or to have such a stupid *pilli*, a barking dog out to prove himself, in a place full of normal boys, distant and not overly friendly but cordial, indifferent, not interested in him at all, everyone but this one. What to do with any of it? If forced into fighting, how could he possibly do this without making the authorities throw him out and worse, back into the workshop, maybe, the slavery, the courts.

"Hurry up!"

The dimness of the temple was a welcome change, even though he couldn't see anything for a moment, his eyes having difficulty adjusting. Another silhouette eyed him, this one skinny in a typical way, clad in a long robe. One of the minor priests, a small army of those in this particular temple.

"Put the branches near the altar, in that pile over there. The bags, take them to the back room. Be quick about it. You need to return here in a matter of heartbeats." The man was nearing him on the run, waving his hands in impatience. "Oh, never mind, give me those flasks. I'll take care of them. You just hurry now." While Miztli still pondered how to go about releasing the strap that tied his main cargo to his forehead – not such a familiar arrangement, not to him – the man was beside him already, relieving his hands, helpful but unsettling in his fussiness. What was that all about?

"Put the branches there. Don't unpack the bundle. Just drop it here. Hurry!"

Perturbed, Miztli tried to be as efficient as he could while dealing with the annoying strap. They surely didn't want him to drop the whole thing. Those fir branches were no firewood; no one wished them broken or cracked. That much had been impressed on him.

"Come, come. Hurry." The harangue continued, annoying more than a buzzing mosquito. The man was even hopping around in a similar way. "Oh, you need to change your clothes. Your cloak is appalling, so dirty. Oh oh!"

Free of the prickly bundle, at long last, he stared at the priest, blinking. "What… what am I supposed to do now?"

"Oh oh oh!" The man seemed as though about to start tearing his hair out, the way his hands went for the uncut matted mess. The priests of this huge temple puzzled him, some of them so richly dressed, so invested; others reeking and unkempt, their cloaks dark and unwashed, their hair a mess but walking the same beautiful halls, holding themselves with much dignity. "You need to run back to school and change your clothes. Oh, but you need to do it in a matter of mere heartbeats. Oh!"

More hair-messing activity. Miztli found it safer to just stare.

"Where are the other two?" Another priest neared, this one of the neatly dressed kind, his cloak long and crispy, sporting no patterns.

"Down, down the stairs. Honorable Priest," muttered Miztli, thrown out of balance even further. He was supposed to report their whereabouts, wasn't he?

"Why aren't they here?"

He found nothing to say to that, but before the panicked sensation prevailed, the first priest, unconcerned with anything but his, Miztli's, dubious appearance, broke into more frantic babbling. "He must present himself before Tecpan Teohuatzin. He must do it in a hurry. But he can't, oh, he can't appear before the Honorable High Priest looking like that. Oh…"

The other man nodded thoughtfully, not perturbed like his fretting peer. "Honorable Tecpan Teohuatzin wished to see this boy, yes," he said slowly, his gaze appraising, slightly kinder than before. "But it happened some time ago, so there is no harm in another delay. Send someone to bring him a clean cloak. Meanwhile, I'll inquire if the boy is still required to present himself and when it would be most convenient." The thoughtful eyes focused on Miztli. "Send someone with him. Have them make him change his clothes and be back here in the blink of an eye." Another frowning hesitation. "Take him yourself. Use the corridor behind the Beautiful Serpent's statue. It'll save you some time."

Another quick exchange ensued, to which Miztli listened uneasily, his puzzlement growing along with the nagging worry. The High Priest wished to talk to him? No, it couldn't be true. What could such a revered person wish to ask him or tell?

His upset escort waved him on impatiently, demanding to hasten his step. He did so, relieved to be heading in the direction that didn't involve the main entrance, chancing encounters he didn't fancy, from that filthy brute Acoatl to the priestly apprentices forgotten under the stairs. Also at this time of the day, the afternoon lessons might be already over, and if he managed to get away from his nervously tottering guard, he might be able to find Axolin or Ahuitzotl and tell them about all this, to have their advice or reassurance. If only Necalli had still been around. Ahuitzotl promised that the *calmecac* boy would be returning to the school on one of these days, hale and healthy. The royal rascal seemed to have inexhaustible sources of information. He had even tried to find out about Chantli and her situation, but in this, he had no luck whatsoever so far. The neighborhoods near the marketplace and the wharves were beyond the Palace boy's reach. And so was his knowledge concerning Tlatelolcan affairs. His brother, the Emperor, did not talk about anything of the sort, forbidding his family members to bring up this subject at all. Their mother, reported the boy, was beyond any regular state of rage.

As expected, some of the students were pouring in, as smeared and as sweaty as he was, coming from the direction of the ball court. About half twenty of those, none of them familiar or smiling. Miztli hastened his step, keeping close to his escort, sneaking glances around.

At the vast courtyard, the priest motioned him to stop. "Wait here."

He watched the dark garment disappearing into one of the

adjacent one-story buildings behind the mosaic pond.

"Workshop boy!"

The loudness of the familiar exclamation made him whirl in surprise, his excitement piquing. Necalli, thinner and paler than he remembered, definitely more haggard looking than in the midst of their Tlatelolcan adventures but sparkling with confidence as he always did, waved from the other side of the pond, squatting there along with a few other boys, busy sorting what looked like a pile of firewood.

"Come over. Where have you been?"

Despite the slight flash of irritation at the repeated questioning – but was everyone on his way, friend or enemy, going to be demanding detailed reports of his day's activities? – he rushed forward, his elation winning.

"So, wandering man." Not bothering to get up, his arm out of bandages but looking mangled and still badly inflamed, Necalli beamed with his unshakable vigor, radiating a sense of wellbeing not in accordance with his thinned looks. "I see you managed to survive our *calmecac* so far. Not bad, I say. While I was busy battling bad spirits, you were busy having a good time, eh?" A wink came with a light nod toward the others. "Have you been treated well enough?"

He nodded, wishing the others would disappear, swallowed by the earth or gone in any other creative or regular way. There was a clear message behind the question, light bantering or not, he knew, grateful. This one was reminding his peers that he, Miztli, was not to be harassed or mistreated.

The priest was waving from the other side of the pond.

"What does that one want with you?"

"He... he wants me to go back there, in the temple..."

Necalli's eyes flickered with understanding. "I'll walk you there."

In another heartbeat, he was back on his feet, light-footed and bouncy, his expression and movements conflicting with the paleness of his features.

"Are you well now?" asked Miztli, relieved to be away from the chilly presence of the others.

"Oh yes, better than ever." The *calmecac* boy grinned, winking again, with conspiratorial glee this time. "Had a nice bout with the other worlds. They said I was talking to the spirits, but I swear I don't remember any of that. If it wasn't my mother who claimed that, I would have thought they were putting me on."

"Ahuitzotl said you were recovering. He said not to worry."

"Did you?" The boy's grin lost its mischievous quality, flickering with momentarily unconcealed friendliness. "Bet you worried because there was no one crazy enough to join you on your next crazy adventure."

Miztli could not fight his grin from showing. "From what I hear, it is you who looked up all those crazy adventures. Not Axolin and not even Ahuitzotl."

"Oh, that one." Necalli burst into an uninhibited fit of laughter, attracting the attention of everyone around, even the waiting priest. Dropping his voice, he snickered again, covering his mouth, his eyes still twinkling. "I certainly didn't want him to come with us, but it was difficult to argue with that little beast. And when backed by Chantli…" His merry mood fled as suddenly as it came. "Did you have a word from her, or maybe that no-good Patli?"

Shaking his head, Miztli put his attention on the priest, whose squinting eyes were dark with displeasure. "I told you to wait here, boy!" The narrowed eyes brushed past Necalli. "And you, young man, go about your business."

In another heartbeat, he disappeared into the low building again.

"What was that all about?" demanded Necalli, his pointy eyebrows climbing high, threatening to meet his hairline.

"He said I'm to meet the priests out there in the main temple, maybe even the High Priest himself," muttered Miztli. "He dragged me here in order to change my clothes."

"Tecpan Teohuatzin? It can't be!"

"I… yes, I think it's a mistake too." He peered at his friend, his anxiety sudden and overwhelming. "I don't understand what they might want from me."

"Maybe something to do with the Emperor and your

connection with him." Necalli was chewing his lower lip in a familiar manner, his frown deep, banishing the twinkle. "Were you called to the Palace again?"

To merely shake his head in response helped. The thought of another interview in the Palace made his knees go weak.

"No? Strange." The *calmecac* boy's forehead creased even deeper. "They sent for me last afternoon, the moment I could stand straight. Back to the Palace and all, but not in that pretty hall. Just a side room." The twinkle was back. "Offensive hospitality, I say."

"What did they want from you?" asked Miztli, his mouth suddenly dry.

The handsome boy shrugged. "More of the same, I'd say. When I saw that none of you were there, I knew that he just wanted to hear what we went through separately, to get more out of us. Thought he had interrogated you without me as well, you and Axolin. Certainly that rascal Ahuitzotl." Another shrug. "He is a formidable man, the Emperor. But not difficult to talk to, not too intimidating."

"Intimidating enough for me," muttered Miztli, not reassured. To be interviewed by the Emperor alone, with no reassuring presence of this same Necalli, his readily delivered help every time he had stammered too badly – oh no, there was nothing good about that prospect.

"He did ask a few questions about you, wanted to know if I could back that pretty story of yours about the Tlatelolco competition." The twinkle was back, too pronounced to miss. "It was quite a tale what you told out there in the Palace. Like a storyteller, starts with the dramatic and then straight into politics and outlandish games and behavior. Left us all hanging on your words, even the Emperor. Made me sorry for missing all that."

"You wouldn't enjoy the kidnapping part."

"Who knows?" The challenging eyes flickered, then clouded. "I planned on sneaking away on my way back, maybe detouring through Patli's school, asking him about that workshop of yours." The cloaked shoulders lifted. "It didn't happen, but this afternoon, I'll be off, finding answers. You aren't confined to the school anymore, are you? Axolin says he was allowed to go out on the day before, even though he preferred to stay." The fleeting wink flickered conspiratorially. "I think he is afraid, doesn't want to face his family and all. His father is one demanding old beast. He'd go hard on Axolin if some of this story leaked out."

"And yours?" His curiosity arose despite his mounting uneasiness. But why did the Emperor ask questions about him? Why did he have to try and verify his story?

The *calmecac* boy waved his hand in the air, dismissing the notion. "Mine isn't that strict. He never forgets to look at all sides of the problem and he says that a good warrior needs a fair amount of enterprising thinking. Not instead of self-control and bravery and obedience, that is, but still. My father is a great man." The large eyes sparkled. "He was a great warrior until he was wounded too badly to go on fighting. He made his way into the ranks of the nobility through great deeds. And I'll tell you something he told me, but keep it to yourself." As though about to share a secret, he leaned closer, dropping his voice. "One can't achieve great accomplishments, do true feats of bravery, if he isn't prepared to act independently sometimes, to think for oneself, to gamble or do whatever is necessary. This is not the way to take captives or to lead warriors. Obedience alone is not worth that much." His eyes sparkled again with an unconcealed pride. "That's what my father says. And he knows. No one better."

Forgetting his uneasiness, Miztli found himself listening, mesmerized. "Your father sounds very wise."

"He is! You can be sure of that."

"You are lucky to have such a man for a father."

And to have him close by, not days of traveling away, he added in his heart, the longing returning, forgotten through these past five dawns, pushed aside by wild happenings.

"Oh yes, he was the best—"

The jittery priest was back, more nervous than before, tossing a new crispy cloak and a loincloth into Miztli's hands. "Change fast and be out in a matter of heartbeats."

They exchanged glances, unsettled.

The ball court seemed to be transformed, even though he had seen this wonder for the first time only on the day before, when Axolin and the others had been taken to train there. Not allowed to join, he was instructed to watch most closely by the stern warrior who had led the training, running the boys all over the vast enclosure, demanding and challenging with merciless persistence.

Ahuitzotl was the one to keep him company back then, along with some other much younger boys. Royal family brood, his chatty companion had explained. Only the older boys were allowed to train, those who had started the military lessons. Usually city boys, those who came from the neighborhoods adjacent to the Great Plaza, those who had seen fourteen summers or so. But he, Ahuitzotl, would be joining them all very soon, customary age or not.

"My brother promised," the boy had claimed hotly. "He promised most solemnly! He said I'm tall and strong enough to start. He said he'll show me some of the moves himself."

The Emperor? wondered Miztli, remembering that the thickset reticent man who had been present through the interview in the Palace was reported to be another full sibling of his current royal company. Happy not to be forced to run the perfectly swept, flattened ground, hit by the ball or yelled at when the hurtful contact didn't happen, he still found himself drawn into it gradually, wishing to go down there and try his luck in the end. It looked simple enough, especially when that annoying Acoatl was the one to take the ball on – then it looked like no work at all, the need to balance the heavy rubber on one's hip or an elbow, to make it stay in the air and away from the ground. Back in his village, there were no rubber balls to practice such bouncing, even though everyone knew that in Oaxtepec or the distant, so very important Cuauhnahuac, there was a court with players and serious games.

Approaching the walled enclosure now, he wondered uneasily,

following his jittery guide, doubtful. What was expected of him here? Why was he rushed to the ball court in such a hurry, clothed in a new crispy cloak and even a new loincloth? The noise coming from behind the low wall let him know that people were playing there, probably *calmecac* boys, judging by the time of the day – mid-afternoon, oh yes, that was when they had been taken here on the day before this one. No wonder there were very few boys at the school grounds now. Why was Necalli exempted? Because of his hand? It was difficult to imagine the energetic youth sitting on the tribunes high above, watching calmly. Not this one!

"Follow."

The small opening in the wall peeked at them discreetly, containing sounds of the game itself rather than the clamor of the tribunes. Nearly stumbling, as the priest pushed him in quite unceremoniously, close on his heels, jamming himself in as well, Miztli swallowed various rude exclamations that popped into his mind, looking around instead, his uneasiness growing. To observe the court from the height of the tribunes, watching it spreading far below his feet, was one thing; to feel it closing on him from all around was quite another.

From the relative safety of the walled corner, his incredulous eyes took in the men, nothing but blurry forms of glistening muscled bodies leaping ahead and along the continuation of this same sloping wall and the one opposite to it, amassing under protruding rings, then spreading out again, single-minded in their purposefulness, very determined. No training youths, his instincts told him. Frightened, he pressed deeper into the unevenness of the wall.

"Wait here and don't move. Not even a tiny step away." The priest was glaring at him, more forceful and even more threatening than his previous demeanor suggested. "You are to wait here. Is that clear to you, commoner boy? You are not to go anywhere until summoned."

"What am I to do here?" he asked, too unsettled to observe customary politeness. He was not to ask questions, of course, however the prospect of being abandoned in this strange unseemly place, hidden from the tribunes and the main side of the field, yet so exposed and unprotected made his mind panic. "What... what am I supposed to be waiting for?"

The priest's lips tightened. "The Revered One may wish to grace you with his presence. Now stay here and remember your manners."

The people on the tribunes shouted as though one man, which together with a mighty thud of the rubber ball not far away from the wall he was huddling against, drew Miztli's attention to the activity on the field somewhat against his will. The man nearest to his corner, a wide, well-proportioned type of solid muscle and force, hurled himself toward the descending rubber, inserting his body between the plunging shadow and the perfectly flattened gravel at an impossible angle, keeping his balance by a miracle, it seemed. Before the unnatural tilt had an upper hand, making the player falter, the ball bounced against the wall, evidently touching one of the marks, ricocheting off of it.

The people on the tribunes shouted as loudly as the players upon the field.

"Well done, brother!"

It wasn't easy to recognize the Emperor, stripped to a mere loincloth and lacking in even the most basic of jewelry, his body as muscled and as sweaty as the rest of the players; still, there could be no mistake at the reverence the others paid to the speaking ruler. Pressing deeper into his safe corner, Miztli just stared.

The man upon the ground leaped onto his feet nimbly, displaying no discomfort, even though his shoulder and upper arm seemed to be rubbed into a mix of dust and some blood.

"Nowhere near your previous throw, Revered Emperor," he called with an easy familiarity, displaying no special deference or awe. "This mark won't give our team but one additional point."

"We were near losing that point and another one, the way I saw it," responded the Emperor with a laugh. "The Chief Warlord's team would have had it unduly easy."

The man this comment was addressed to grinned with the side of his mouth. He was impressively tall, towering above his peers, even the Emperor, his limbs sinewy, long, and sturdy. None wore protective leather or helmets, leaving their bodies exposed to the possible ravages of such rigorous exercise. Fascinated, Miztli found himself gaping in wonder.

"Shall we proceed?" The Emperor shielded his eyes, glancing at the man who was poised at the middle of the field, holding the ball with both hands, apprehensive somehow. "The Master of the Game, what are you saying?"

"One point in favor of your team, Revered Emperor." The man with the ball hesitated. "Are you ready for another round?"

"Are we?" But again, it was easy to see that the impressive ruler was glancing sideways, toward the tribunes or maybe the side of the field and the low walls now adorned with many heads, the curiosity-consumed crowds perching upon those, pushing each other.

The memory of Tlatelolco surfaced, bittersweet in its vividness. But were the violent crowds eager to climb anything higher than a pavement in order to see better that vast spreading plaza. The nobility upon the dais had had it unfairly easy, yet Tlemilli cared nothing for the offered advantage, appreciating it not at all.

To banish the painful knot in his stomach, he glanced at the tribunes and the dignified crowds seated there, not many but enough to have the stone parapets covered with heads. Was it a game or just training? To keep his thoughts occupied, he squinted, seeking the familiar figure of Ahuitzotl. The young *pilli* would not miss out on something like that or let them avoid inviting him. Unsettled, he saw that none of the *calmecac* boys seemed to be present, not even one.

"Let us refresh before we continue." The imperial voice overcame the clamor of the shouting audience easily, with not much of an effort. Rubbing his hands one against another, the Emperor nodded curtly, indicating small army of servants that was rushing down the passes between the two walls, carrying trays and clean cloths. The Master of the Game strolled toward his corner, rolling the ball easily on his outstretched arm.

Miztli took a hesitant step toward the tempting proximity of the opening he had been pushed through before. The priest, where was he? Why didn't he stay to wait with him, to explain should challenging questioning ensue as to his right to be where he was, at the same field the Emperor was playing with his nobles, of all things!

"Come, come." As though to allay his gathering panic, the man was back along with two others, all nervous and ill at ease. The sweaty hand locked round his elbow, pulling him urgently, with not enough force to make him sway. "Here, hurry!"

The passageway that appeared out of what seemed to be a solid wall from anywhere but a close-up observation did not look like a tunnel because of its spaciousness and the generous illumination pouring in through the evenly spaced openings adorning its side. The moment they stopped, Miztli pulled his hand away sharply.

However, before the priest had an opportunity to scowl or reprimand, a figure shadowed the opposite opening, unmistakable in its tallness and prominence, the grandeur of its bearing. His shoulders covered with a brilliantly bright cloth now, his oily hair askew but in a becoming way, his skin flushed with a healthy glow, the Emperor came closer, arms linked across the broadness of his chest, his expression light, holding a grin. Not a cold or foreboding statue of the Palace's hall. Anything but!

"Is it not our adventurous foreigner?" said the man in a familiar reserved voice in which amusement was flickering, not attempted to be hidden.

"Revered Emperor," whispered Miztli, awed. With no imperial regalia and no decorations, Tenochtitlan ruler looked even more foreboding, so exceptionally well built, so towering, the scars upon his chest and his sides standing out, narrow twisted lines, brighter in coloring, drawing the eye, telling stories of battles.

"Wait for me outside." The inclination of the royal head indicated both his nervous escort and the hovering servant with a tray. Numbly, Miztli followed the drawing-away priestly garment with his gaze, his ears noting the calls of the noble players, as light and as unconcerned as the boys of his village, enjoying their well-deserved break under the steady hum of the tribunes' occupiers somewhere above their heads.

"Well, young commoner with a spectacular name," said the Emperor when no silhouettes shadowed both openings, letting the light stream in unrestrained. "I've heard that you've been doing not so badly in our noble establishment for youths."

Miztli swallowed hard. "Yes, Revered Emperor."

The man shook his head, his lips twisting again, this time in a one-sided grin. "Don't be that intimidated, boy," he said conversationally and as though meaning it. "You served me well until now and I believe you will go on doing so. My youngest of brothers is fond of you and so are your friends of our noble families. Which makes one wonder, given your more than humble background." The wide shoulders lifted in a shrug. "There must be something about you, your personal qualities, your possible inner strength, maybe; something that those boys must sense in you. Ahuitzotl is not the easiest *pilli* to get along with. Trust me to know that rascal well." The smile disappeared, replaced by a thoughtful frown. "Well, Tenochtitlan rulers, my illustrious ancestors, valued outstanding qualities in their subjects, nobles and commoners alike. And I don't intend to be different on that score. Therefore, do not be fearful or humble, not unless you have a reason to feel this way." The piercing gaze was suddenly not easy to stand, boring at him, penetrating. "Is there anything related to your Tlatelolcan adventures that you remembered omitting sharing?"

Even to merely shake his head came as an effort. To struggle not to drop his gaze, to keep staring into the contemplative depth, turned out to be another battle. He did so despite the sweat breaking over his back.

"Good." The intensity of his gaze lessening, the Emperor nodded with surprising lightheartedness, again deep in thought. "If so, you may find your new venture into our neighboring *altepetl* of interest." The amusement disappeared all at once. "What I want you to do, young IztMiztli, is this. Cross the causeway with no delays. Do it before the sun has left our world tonight." The thoughtful eyes narrowed. "Go to the house of Honorable Tepecocatzin. I trust you will find no difficulty locating the dwelling of such a prominent noble, even if your brief visit there did not leave a lasting memory as to its whereabouts." Another pause ensued, however briefly. "You will be given a note to present the nobleman with, to prove who you are and let him know what I want him to know. Do not – I repeat, do not – let your message reach anyone's hands but his." The gaze boring at Miztli turned stonier. "Whatever it takes, you will deliver your message to Noble Tepecocatzin and no one else. I trust you to be brave and clever enough to succeed. Is my trust misplaced?"

His thoughts rushing about in no semblance of order, he just nodded again, then licked his lips. "I... I don't know where this nobleman lives."

The strong eyebrows knitted in displeasure. "You've been there before. According to your claim, Lady Noble Jade Doll had met you there."

Oh, the elderly noble and his shed? His thoughts cleared a little, even though not his possible destination. But how was he to remember his way to these premises after being dragged there while unconscious? Still, there was the following morning and a few twisted alleys he and his kidnapper had to trace before reaching the Plaza.

"I... I'll find Noble Tepecocatzin," he said hurriedly before his newfound confidence left him again, put to test under the Emperor's suspicious gaze. "I will find him and give him the note, and I won't let it reach anyone else's hands!"

The wide forehead cleared a little. "Bring his answer to me, preferably a written one. Stress on him the importance of a written answer."

"Yes, Revered Emperor." Again, his back broke in cold sweat, remembering the last exchange that included no titles among his mumbling. Oh mighty deities!

"That is not all, young commoner." The Emperor's gaze softened again, filled with a hint of the previous amusement. "You will have to deliver another message, this time a verbal one. You will find no difficulty talking to my revered sister, our Lady Noble Jade Doll, will you? This is the main part of your mission. The communication with Tepecocatzin is just the side one." Again, only one side of the thin mouth was climbing up, leaving the other one motionless, a twisted mask. "I can send plenty of messengers to our Honorable Tepecocatzin. The communication with him and his likes presents no difficulty. But it is not so when the matters concerning my sister come to the forefront. Her location, her temper, even her loyalty, true loyalty, presents us with a challenge. She wouldn't trust random messengers and her ways with the people of humbler origins are erecting an additional barrier. But," the grin turned yet more uneven, "for some reason, she had taken a fancy to you, turned helpful for a change, going to great lengths in sending you back with reports on Moquihuixtli's dubious contests. A wonder." The wide shoulders lifted again, even if briefly. "So, being her choice of a messenger, you will just have to carry on with this task."

Again, he found it imperative to lick his lips, overwhelmed with this flood of demands and revelations, this sudden chattiness. "I will do as you wish, Revered Emperor." That came out surprisingly well. He breathed with relief.

"If successful, you will be rewarded." Again, the crooked grin was gone, replaced with a sterner gaze. "You will be instructed as to your further action, provided with necessary means." The thoughtful gaze did not thaw. "Be careful when finding your way into the Tlatelolco Palace. Do not underestimate those who are acting against us. You've tasted their ruthlessness, but it may be not limited to that." Another nod. "Bring me answers and be quick about it. I'll expect your return before the next dawn."

The imposing figure was gone, disappearing in the blazing light of the outside. In a short while, he could hear the man's voice, powerful but not imperial or distant, addressing his partners in the game, an undisputable leader but also one of them.

Dazed, he stared at the polished stone of the wall, the dull thuds of the rubber resounding against it, telling the story of the renewed game. Or maybe just a training session. Which one?

For a heartbeat, he listened to those, then just as silhouettes blocked the entrance through which the Emperor disappeared, a new realization dawned, making his stomach jelly. The Tlatelolcan Palace! He would be required to enter that place, delivering messages to the haughty princess by whatever means, and after he had been musing about it at nights, devising wild schemes, each more improbable than the other, impossible to even try to implement. And yet he had promised, and she must have been waiting, restless and impatient, pacing in her typical jumpy way. Oh mighty deities, but now that he might be helped into the Palace, expected to sneak around and seek Tenochtitlan's princesses, and with this elderly Tepecocatzin maybe interested in helping him...

Oh yes, the elderly man was bound to help, to make sure his, Miztli's, verbal message, whatever it was to be, reached the princess. He was involved as heavily, judging by the hastily organized night rendezvous involving a beaten commoner with nothing but a few famous names to mention. And then, slipped into the Palace, who was to know if he detoured on his way to the haughty princess?

CHAPTER 3

To slip away from the house became a true possibility when Tepiton, Mother's favorite house helper, twisted her ankle while tidying up Father's workshop. It has been another busy day that saw all the men of the family, even her ten-summers-old little brother, slaving there until the sun went down.

The temple's order of wonderfully thin glittering sheets – plenty of those along with other golden mixed ornaments – being received formally, to be delivered in good time before the ceremonies of the next moon, the load of work soared to the skies, and just as the village boy disappeared with no trace, vanished into the thin air. The speculations about his fate were many and various, not all of them favorable or optimistic; far from it. At least half of their household wished him a slow, torturous execution in whatever court he might have been judged and for whatever crimes, with her eldest of brothers being very vocal about it too. A bother!

Even outside the workshop, Miztli's absence was felt most acutely, because Father was now requesting Mother's personal slave's services to tidy the workshop after a day of work. Before that, the village boy was the one doing most of the tidying up, leaving to the slave only the actual cleaning. A sensible thing to do, was Chantli's silent conclusion. Why couldn't her brothers move the chests and the braziers out of the way, or arrange the tools as those should be arranged? This was the reason why Tepiton sprained her ankle. The poor woman had stumbled over a pile of ceramic forms and an annealing hammer that shouldn't have been there in the first place. What negligence! However, it freed her, Chantli, after a mere three dawns of confinement. Someone had to be sent to the marketplace instead of the limping maid; someone who couldn't be employed in the workshop. What luck!

On the first day, full of tearful promises that she would be back as soon as her chores were completed, not detouring by any possible distraction, temptingly loud scandal, or just to gossip with her girl friends, she had indeed bartered or bought everything that had been required and had run home as though all the creatures of the Underworld were after her. However, the next day and the following one had her relaxing. The family was too busy to pay her movements much attention, authorized or not. Even Mother, swamped with housework now, was not on guard as she might have been.

So now, three days later and armed with the list of edible goods she was to bring back home already in her basket, most of it, weighing her down but only a little, she huddled at the corner of the main marketplace alley, walled and paved and always a source of entertainment, with two of her best girl friends Quetzalli and Xochi, clutching baskets of their own.

"Those *telpochcalli* boys are something, I'm telling you," Quetzalli was carrying on, her prettily round face flushed. "I was passing by the backyard of their school on my way here, and they were training there, waving their silly sticks. You know those things, all sharpened edges, as though those were real spears. Silly!"

"Not silly," protested Chantli, her stomach twisting at the thought of training boys. Did they have a backyard to practice up there in *calmecac* too? Were they allowed to try real weaponry? "They have to train with something, you know? They can't let them kill each other with real spears!"

"Of course," called out Quetzalli tersely, wrinkling her nose in the silliest of manners. "But they are waving those things with such pride, such excitement. One might think that those were gifts from mighty Tezcatlipoca himself, with magical qualities and all. Not just branches one can find near the stalls of the firewood sellers in piles."

"But what did they do, sister?" interrupted the third girl, all eagerness and curiosity. She was a cute little thing, all curves and dimples, fitting her shortened name Xochitl, the Flower. "What made you so angry with them?"

"Oh that." Quetzalli rolled her eyes showily, acting for the benefit of the passersby, her laughter ringing prettily, spreading over the crowded street. "What do you know, sister? Their calls and shouts can be heard at the Great Plaza at the very least!" The decorated neck of her *huipil* rustled as she jerked her shoulders petulantly. "I suppose their teacher was nowhere around. They have it unfairly easy, our district's *telpochcalli* troublemakers. I heard that the school on the other side of the marketplace is run most strictly, with the boys not daring to sneeze without their teachers' permission."

Chantli made a face, out of patience with her friends, both of them. Too giggly of late, too silly. They had been best friends since she could remember, and it was always great joy to play and laugh and sneak around, spying on the marketplace vendors or their customers, imagining all sorts of adventures, enjoying themselves. Even though, recently, Quetzalli could talk about nothing but boys, laughing embarrassingly loud every time one would pass by, with Xochi following suit, adoring. So silly and obvious. Or maybe not so silly. She had done it herself too, hadn't she? It was just that after Tlatelolco, such giggling and eyelashes fluttering on the marketplace or near their local school, or the main square of that other larger neighboring district with a mosaic pond seemed like something childish, a stupid thing to engage with. There were more serious matters waiting out there. Like plotting nobles of the neighboring *altepetl*, their violent, unreasonably nasty behavior; or the village boy's miserable situation and his mysterious disappearance. Was he alive? Well? Treated with kindness? Was he truly dragged to the Imperial Court?

Then there was Father, so irritable and gloomy, so unreasonably angry all the time now; not the man whose nearness and conversation she used to enjoy whenever she could. Also, the *calmecac* boys; another worry. Were they punished too badly, not allowed to leave their school at all anymore? And if they weren't, then why wasn't Necalli trying to find her, to see if she was faring well. He said they would have to meet again, all of them, he said, to discuss the Tlatelolcan affair and its possible implications, but when he said it, he was looking at her, that much she remembered, deep inside knowing that he was trying to find an excuse to meet her again. Her stomach felt hollow, heavy inside.

"And then what did you do?" Xochi was asking, agog with curiosity, almost dancing. "What did you tell them?"

Chantli forced herself to concentrate, her ears picking up the sound of raising voices in the smaller alley, where the food sellers were offering their ready-made goods alongside other mats loaded with fruits and vegetables. Female voices, high-pitched and angry. Nothing new. Still, she peered in that direction. "What's going on out there?"

Xochi wrinkled her nose in a bad imitation of Quetzalli's cuter expression. "Some fowls are yelling at other fowls."

"They are doing it with so much spirit!" She listened to the growing shouts of too many women shrieking at once. "Will they start fighting? Let's go and see!"

Quetzalli produced another coy grimace out of her seemingly unlimited arsenal, such studied expressions.

Chantli suppressed the temptation to sneer. "Come!"

They followed her, as they usually did. It was always her leading, exploring, or just looking around, finding entertainment. She had an unerring nose for it, or so Xochi had claimed. Well, maybe her friend had a point there. Back under the Tlatelolcan causeway, she had also insisted that they must look around that neighboring city, find clues to Miztli's possible whereabouts. Logic said that he wouldn't be there, still alive and well, and even if he was, they didn't stand a chance of finding him – that was Necalli's reasoning, wasn't it? – but in the end, she turned out to be correct. Miztli had been in Tlatelolco and they did manage to find him, and just as the matters turned truly desperate. Her instincts had been right yet again! Shaking her head against the welling sense of unwarranted triumph, she hastened her step.

"I must be going back home soon," Quetzalli was complaining, balancing her basket on her shoulder, pouting. "Second Mother has my loom loaded with threads. She keeps nagging about my laziness. Even Father is tired of hearing her carrying on. She is such a witch, this woman. So ugly too!" The girl rolled her eyes prettily. "Won't be caught with a single decoration on her colorless *huipil* or, gods forbid, a jar of cream for her ugly face. And if someone mentions indigo while washing one's hair, she'll be fainting but only after lecturing one to death on good morals and such. Even Father is fed up with her high morals!"

Against her will, Chantli giggled, knowing this family well, the stone-worker from the end of their alley, like Father, another prominent member of the craftsmen guild, but unlike Father, sporting two wives, the last one a recent addition, a young, delectable-looking fowl. "He isn't suffering, sister. His Chief Wife may be a hard-hearted witch, but there's the Third Wife to keep him happy. And she looks nice too."

Quetzalli's snort rolled down the walled alley, overcoming its clamor, the shouting women at the far edge of it gathering quite an audience, yelling at the top of their voices, waving their hands.

"She may be looking nice to you from far away, but that little snake has her tough side. She thinks she is so important, lording it over us all, as though she is much older than me and my sister. Think about it! I've seen nearly fourteen summers and my sister is fifteen. We are women, not little girls. But do you think that this new toy of Father cares? No! She thinks that being a wife puts her above everyone besides her chief peer. What gall!"

"I saw her yesterday at the square with the mosaic pond," contributed Xochi, eyes on the clamor they were approaching rapidly now, hastening their steps. "She was doing laundry, gossiping with no pause for breath."

"So much like her!"

"How old is she?" inquired Chantli, perturbed with a mere possibility. What if Father took another wife? Would she have to tolerate some young presumptuous fowl at home and on a daily basis? Well, even if it happened, Mother would still be alive and there to shield her and her brother, unlike Quetzalli's mother, dead for quite a few summers by now. Poor Quetzalli!

The subject of her musings was waving her free hand in the air, this time in a natural manner. It was obvious that the topic of the pushy third wife made her forget her aspirations to look pretty on every occasion. "Less than twenty summers, you can bet anything you want on that. Just a few summers older than me and my sister. But does it stop her from scolding us as though we were little children? Only this morning, she was carrying on about how we never clean the porridge off our plates properly or put our eating bowls back in place. As though there are no slaves in our house to do that. Imagine! Just recently, Second Mother bought another girl to help around the house, and now we are just overcrowded, but at least one doesn't have to clean the house anymore."

"If only your mother were alive..."

As though eager to drown her words, the yells from the congregation at the edge of the alley raised, shouting in the same vein and worse. Flying insults were not new to particularly busy market corners, but today was no market day and the afternoon time warranted calmer procedures. If anything, the vendors should be busy packing, counting the earned goods or cocoa beans if someone was lucky to get paid by the most coveted currency, the noble people's means of payment.

"Go away, you stupid good-for-nothing," someone was yelling. "Take your stinking carcasses back to your stinking Tlatelolco!"

The crowding backs didn't let them see properly, so many waving hands and jumping up and down shoulders. They tried to push their way closer.

"You go away, you filthy cheater. You pushy snakes from your stinking would-be great *altepetl*, you are nothing but jumping-up piles of excrement, all of you!"

The visitors, obviously the offended Tlatelolcans, were giving back measure for measure. Chantli's interest piqued. Tlatelolco again. But why was it haunting her, why did it seem as though everyone spoke about nothing but that other island city, their petty claims to equality and demands of fair treatment. As though they weren't treated fairly so far.

"Look who's talking; the great Tlatelolcan conquerors."

This drew plenty of healthy laughter from all around, but a fair chunk of the crowd seemed to be comprised of the offended visitors as well, all those women shoppers. Spotting a low wall behind one of the stalls with baking tamales, Chantli pushed her way toward it. But it was impossible to see a thing in this agitation!

"You good-for-nothing piece of work," a hefty fowl with a huge arrangement of baskets piled in her massive hands and upon her arms was yelling. "You cheated me, you filthy snake. That maize isn't fresh. You Tenochtitlan snakes are nothing but cheaters, all of you. Liars and robbers, that's what you are!"

Satisfied with her semi-elevated perch, Chantli motioned at her friends, both girls having difficulty navigating their way in the gushing lake of thrusting elbows and limbs.

"Go away, go to your stupid little island. You all are no better than stinking foreigners from the taken villages. You should thank our Emperor for not making you pay us a tribute. A heavy one!"

"Yes, yes!" concurred a healthy part of the crowd, but the others shouted in indignation, the offended guests.

"Behold those who are talking so carelessly," yelled one of the men, a construction worker, judging by the dusty state of his hair and his eyebrows. "Soon you all will be talking from the other side of your mouths."

"Oh yes, they will be made to pay." This came from the hefty shopper, her fleshy parts trembling, shaking with rage. "Soon they will be coming to our marketplace crawling, selling their limbs and their inner parts."

"Oh yes, soon our warriors will make them talk differently!"

Something about this last exchange made Chantli shiver. They sounded so convincing, those silly words, the people who said them so passionate and as though meaning what they said. For some reason, it made her think of the Tlatelolcan ruler and his speech, standing on his elevated litter as though on a dais, addressing the surrounding crowds in a rolling, well trained voice. She had been busy thinking of their way out back then, worried about Necalli and Ahuitzotl, with Miztli trying to steer them away, her and his foul-mouthed noble fowl who couldn't fight her way out of a crowd of babies, the useless stick that she was. Still, the words of the Tlatelolco ruler stuck, echoing what had been repeated just now, even if in a less flowery manner.

Tenochtitlan folk were returning insults twice as loud and viciously, three times more colorful and at an enviable speed. No one listened to anyone anymore, and the pushing around began to turn violent. She could see Quetzalli and Xochi shoving their way out and away in a practiced manner. They all knew the signs. Relatively safe on her high perch, she contemplated staying for a little longer. Watching marketplace fights could be a great entertainment, unless caught in the middle of it. The thought of the visitors pitted against the locals made her wish to stay. It might turn out to be more fascinating than a ball game with both teams coming from some areas torn by war or just recently conquered. Such games had an additional layer of spice that regular games missed. And so would be this brawl.

Again, she sought out her friends with her gaze, both safely away, back at the farther side of the alley and gesturing. If she didn't get out now, she might need to perch on her wall until the brawl was over, either won or, more likely, separated by warriors and the marketplace court's authorities.

Still hesitating, she shivered all of a sudden, feeling the gaze before locating its owner. A tall man, as skinny as a copper string, was studying her with his eyes narrowed to slits and his expression reflecting no amused adoration she was used to seeing in strangers' faces if they stared at her, quite a few through the recent summers. However, not this one. The man's frown was direful and the painful concentration of his eyes was disturbing. It was as though he was trying to recognize her, like a distant acquaintance, some unpleasant encounter he was attempting to recall, to place her face with her name.

Perturbed, she took her eyes away, yet not before noticing him talking to a heavyset man next to him. Her stomach knotting, she glanced at her friends, who were still waving, motioning more vigorously now. Oh yes, she had better catch up with them before they lost their patience and left without her. The man in question was still staring, and so was his companion, oh mighty deities!

Without thinking, she slipped off her perch and onto the opposite side of the low wall, where the crowd of people seemed to press with less vigor, rather listening than trying to contribute, blissful onlookers. Pushing her way through, her heart beating fast, threatening to jump out of her chest, she tried to think logically. Why would someone bother to single her out and in such a non-flirtatious way? Who and why?

The smell of sweating bodies enveloped her, their pressing touch unpleasant, urging her instincts to seek her way out more urgently. It must be nice to be tall and broad like some of the men or boys, to be able to just push one's way through.

The flying insults peaked, both sides sparing no threats now, promising dreadful things. Nothing out of the ordinary for the marketplace frequenters. But for the staring men, she might have been amused, still safely out of the possible fighting zone. Why would this man gape at her so? He didn't look familiar, not in the least. Was he Tlatelolcan? Did he remember her from their adventures there? But who and why, and anyway, she had been apprehended by the warriors back then together with Necalli. Not by marketplace scum.

"Chantli, come!"

Just as Quetzalli's shout and her waving hand directed her toward more familiar parts and the regular crowding with no densely jammed bodies and breaths, a hand locked around her arm, jerking her to a stop. Surprised, she wavered, fighting for balance, puzzled for a moment. The skinny man towered above her, truly too tall for his unimpressive girth, thin to the point of sticking-out bones. Aghast, she just stared.

"It's her," he was saying, staring closely but evidently addressing someone else. "I'm sure it is."

"How..." began his companion, another familiar face from the crowding Tlatelolcans, but by now, she regained her thinking abilities, enough to yank her arm away, to pull violently with her entire body. His fingers fought not to let her slip, not caught by surprise. Still, she was as insistent, disregarding the painfulness of the struggle.

"Get away from me!" she yelled, mainly to draw attention of the people around. It wasn't like no one ever tried to harass her before. Not as bluntly and with such glaring lack of beforehand flirtatious talk, but still, men could sometimes grab a girl by force, to try to make her stay and flirt with them. On the marketplace, it was not out of the ordinary.

"Let me go," she went on yelling, struggling to break free, panicked at his insistence. "Get your filthy paws off me!"

People around began paying attention.

"Let the girl go, brother," said someone with a laugh. "You can't just pick them like prettily round tomatoes. Certainly not such delicious things."

"Get away from her." This time, it was a female voice, shrill from the marketplace haggling.

"I'm not—" began the man, still clutching on to her arm like a persistent mosquito, but now, emboldened with the ensuing support – displeased women with baskets and goods constituting the best of protection, more than amused men for certain – she kicked at his leg, reinforcing her struggle.

"Let me go, you filthy piece of human excrement!"

"Yes, get away from her!" This time, the voice was familiar and the presence next to her most welcome. Quetzalli, a veteran of similar harassments, probably much more than her, Chantli's, count, hacked her nails into the capturing hand, beating what it was connected to, quite skinny ribs, with her free fist. "Get your paws off her!"

In another heartbeat, her attacker was overwhelmed, his partner not coming to his aid, and the rest of the crowd against him. Rubbing her hurt arm with her free palm, her basket hanging precariously, threatening to spill its goods out, Chantli grabbed Quetzalli's wrist in her turn, pulling her friend away. The girl looked as though about to stay and give her, Chantli's, assailant a good piece of her mind.

"Come!" Anxious to escape, she pulled again. That man was not after her looks, that much was obvious.

The comments of the surrounding people melted away, drowned in the general hum of the fighting up the alley. Still, she ran on, until her friend began resisting for real.

"Where are you running, you crazy one? Xochi can't even catch up with us."

Only now she noticed the other girl, panting behind. The corner they turned was relatively quiet, not abandoned but not crowded as well. The food sellers were collecting their goods.

"What an annoying piece of meat this filthy rat was!" exclaimed Quetzalli, breathing as heavily as they all did. "I can't believe how he grabbed you and in front of everyone. What gall!"

As though it was better if she had been grabbed in a deserted alley, reflected Chantli absently, her heart pounding, thundering in her ears. "Let's get out of here!"

But this time, Quetzalli's eyes sparkled with challenge. "What a frightened mouse you are, sister. It's not like you can't show your face on the marketplace now. He was just a pushy man after pretty faces and curves. He'll be busy trying his luck with another fowl in a few more heartbeats from now, over his broken heart at your lack of cooperation." Laughing harder, she turned to Xochi, who had managed to catch her breath, leaning her palms against her half-bent knees, her round cheeks glistening. "He didn't even try to hug her or anything. Just grabbed her hand, and here she breaks out into this panicked flight."

"He wasn't after my looks." Pursing her lips, Chantli let the jab pass, too concerned to engage in this silly banter. "He is Tlatelolcan and he said he knew me. He has another man with him and they were both staring at me back upon that wall." She swallowed. "That's why I started to run away."

Quetzalli made a face. "Who was he?"

"I don't know. I didn't recognize him at all. He didn't look familiar." To wring her hands in the way she did seemed silly, so she pressed them to her mouth instead. "But it's all connected to what happened back in Tlatelolco. This man, he was one of the smugglers. I'm sure he was!"

Xochi was making faces as well. "Why would they be after you, sister? What did you do out there in Tlatelolco?"

Chantli felt her shoulders lifting on their own. To tell her friends about her Tlatelolco adventures was tempting, very much so. Under regular circumstances, she wouldn't have hesitated. Oh, she would have recalled it all and more, regardless of their willingness to listen even. Although, of course, such a tale would leave them breathless anyway. Still, this time, something held her back. They would not understand, neither the eagerness with which she went on exploring missions with boys she didn't know – noble boys, of all things, *calmecac* pupils! – nor the following night and day, in the tunnel or on the lake, with Tlatelolco nobles and smugglers alike, plotting and being violent, unreasonably brutish, even with the offspring of Tenochtitlan royal family. Oh, but she still needed to understand what happened there, what truly happened, how it all was connected to the possible trouble with the neighboring city-state that some people were talking about. If only Necalli came to talk to her, or that unruly boy Ahuitzotl. Even Patli, back in his *telpochcalli* for the last two days, might prove helpful at answering some questions.

"Let's get away from here," she repeated. "They are still yelling there, and if their fighting spreads, we'll be stuck here and... Let's just go."

This time, they nodded readily. "Don't take it that hard, sister," Xochi was murmuring, repeating herself. "You are not yourself, you know that?"

She let the silly remark pass. "We'll walk you home, Xochi," she offered instead, thoughts on the route ahead, by the far edge of the marketplace and then the district's main square and the school adjacent to it. The boys would be training outside or even let out for their evening home-visiting, and then there would be opportunities to talk to her cousin and ask him questions.

"What did you do out there in Tlatelolco?" inquired Quetzalli when the clamor of the food alley faded behind their backs, replaced with the usual marketplace hum, the vendors beginning to collect their wares. "You said nothing about it except that you were punished and weren't allowed to go out at all. What did you do to earn such confinement? Must be something dreadful, sister." The girl's eyes sparkled gleefully. "We always tell each other everything, but now you are being secretive. Which makes one think, you know, all sorts of wild thoughts." A wink. "They say your foreigner cousin was missing from *telpochcalli* for days as well, and just as you were missing, eh?"

Appalled, Chantli gaped for a heartbeat. "It was nothing like that!" she cried out, embarrassed to feel a hot wave washing over her face, coloring it into glaring hues. "Oh, how could you think something of *that* sort?"

"I'm not, sister." Now Quetzalli was positively glowing, evidently happy with the effect. "I said nothing. You were the one to assume things and change colors while doing it. You should see your face now. The setting sun glows less than your cheeks."

"Oh shut up, just shut up!" Whirling away so sharply her head reeled, she took in the vastness of the square plaza, with its mosaic pond glimmering in the afternoon light, sporting the colorfulness of its intricate adornments. People crowded it as always at this time of the day, strolling or hurrying about their business, plenty of passersby, enjoying the last of the sun.

"But you are touchy, sister," Quetzalli was saying, evidently offended now. "There is no need to yell at the top of your voice. If you are that touchy, maybe you better go home, relax with your loom and your..."

The rest of her friend's phrase was lost on her as her eyes took in the figures coming out of the alley they had left such a short time ago, walking hurriedly, in a rush. Not the stringy man or his friend, but somehow, they made her heart leap in fear. Those were not regular people done with their business for the day or out on an afternoon stroll, four in all; sinewy and somehow furtive, they reminded her of something or someone. Had she seen them before? Where?

"What now?" Quetzalli was asking, exasperation in her voice.

She wished her friend would shut up for at least a little while. But she didn't need the silly thing to carry on and on, drawing people's attention to them. Behind her back, the clamor from the fence that separated the school from the rest of the vast square was deafening, heralding either the outside training or, more likely, the break in the activities of the day. She shot it a furtive glance.

The men slowed their step and were talking between

themselves, arguing, waving their hands. One of them, a nondescript type of an average width and height in plain-looking clothing, was glancing at the tented area where the courts were held throughout mornings and afternoons. Out of instinct, she scanned this corner of the plaza as well. There were plenty of people there, strolling or talking, eating fresh tortillas from one of the nearby mats with cooking facilities, enjoying the shadow the stretched maguey cover provided. Nothing untoward there. She saw the newcomers scanning the area once again.

"We better go before the boys start spilling out of their school," Quetzalli said, not moving a limb, her baskets balanced prettily on her thrust-out hip, enhancing its elegant pliancy. "I can't stand their bragging and chattering. I've had enough of that for today."

"Have you?" Xochi's laughter rang again too loudly, attracting attention, if frequent glances of a group of congregating young men, construction workers judging by the dustiness of their cloaks, were any indication. No smugglers those, thanks all the great and small deities.

"I want to see my cousin, in case he is stuck at school and not allowed to go home."

"Still punished, that one, eh?" Quetzalli was sneaking glances toward the hubbub of the fenced yard as well now.

"I don't know. He didn't come home for the past two evenings." Chantli shrugged, glad to discuss someone else's blunders, her eyes drifting toward the nondescript men. They were still talking, more relaxed now. "Either they didn't let him out for spending so many days away from school, cracked head or not, or maybe Father told him to stay in and think about all this, learn good measures."

"Your father isn't that scary. Even with you, he kept it up for barely a few days. Think about it, sister."

"But she is his daughter, not a nephew," protested Xochi. "It's different."

Chantli couldn't help but giggle. "It's worse. Father is tougher with any of us than he is with Patli. He seems to have a soft spot for this one, for whatever reason. And I don't even know if he is the son of Father's brother or sister or whoever. He didn't let us ask questions about it. Just dumped Patli on us and demanded we treat him as a family." She shrugged, glimpsing the sinewy men beginning to move toward the stand with tortillas, all of them beside the one who was scanning the tented area with less and less patience, turning whichever way. "Which is strange if you ask me. Although Patli is not a bad person or anything."

"Maybe he isn't his nephew, you know," drawled Quetzalli, her lips twisting suggestively, eyes on the boys who were trickling through the opening in the fence, heading out in pairs and groups, some on errands, some for the desired outside; easy to tell who was who by their poses and the enthusiasm of their movements or the lack of it.

Chantli made a face. "I thought about it too, but it isn't likely. Father is not the type to cherish memories of long lost loves from the past and the fruits of it. He wouldn't have bothered if Patli was his son. Besides, he is of nearly my age, and back then, Father was already running his workshop, with no time to travel out there near the City of Gods, make love to local women, and leave them heavy with children."

"Maybe she was from here and he just sent her out there for some reason." Laughing prettily, Quetzalli turned her head away from the nearing group of boys. They were boisterous and loud, obviously not burdened by further school chores, out and up to no good, ready to enjoy their free time to the fullest. "That would explain some things."

"You have a great imagination, sister. I don't think..."

The sinewy man was passing by, hurrying toward the tented area, presenting Chantli with the sharp outline of his profile, silhouetted against the glow of the afternoon sun. She felt her insides freezing amidst the flood of frightful memories – *the heavy odor of the lake, the rustling of the reeds, the groaning of the causeway's beams, the heat of the torch thrust into her face, the profile of her interrogator as the man whirled at the yelling Ahuitzotl, this same eagle-like nose and the sharp curve of the chin, the heaviness of the slapping palm.* Paralyzed with fear, she followed him with her gaze, his back broad, crisscrossed with muscles, scarred in places, his paces long and forceful.

Beside her, the girls were still chattering, giggling with their usual showiness, acting for the benefit of every possible admirer.

"Look at this one!" Xochi's voice gained a conspiratorial tone, turning considerably lower. "That boy, by the fence, near the opening. The one who is trying to peek in!"

"No local boy that," observed Quetzalli, dropping her voice as well. "What is such a bird doing here? Is that a cotton cloak he wearing?"

Chantli paid their chattering no attention, her eyes glued to the drawing-away back, her heart beating madly. The man reached the tented area and was waving his hand, signaling someone. She tried to make her mind work.

"It is cotton, it is!" Xochi was gushing excitedly, her voice rising to squeaking tones. "And look at his sandals, all the way up to his ankles and with so many straps. But what sort of *pilli* is that, sniffing around our *telpochcalli*, looking for trouble?"

"He'll find it soon enough. Look how those boys are studying him." Quetzalli sounded unduly excited as well. "Shall we ask for his purpose here?"

Absently, Chantli glanced at the topic of their conversation, taking in the fence and the life gushing around it, many of the boys already spreading along the square, dashing away to enjoy their well deserved freedom. Only a few were still lingering, coming in or out of the narrow opening, talking between themselves, shouting.

The intruder her friends were discussing with such avid interest was lingering near the entrance, not daring to proceed but looking as though pondering that possibility, trying to peek in without being too obvious about it, his cloak flowing self-assuredly down his broad shoulders, its patterns and hues glimmering with aplomb, of the best quality, just like she remembered from before Tlatelolco, his hair collected proudly on the top of his head, in a warrior-like fashion.

Her heart leapt once again, this time bringing her insides back to life rather than freezing them.

"Necalli!"

Behind her back, she could hear the girls' shocked silence.

CHAPTER 4

There could be no mistaking her scream. Neither did the sight of her rushing toward him mislead him, oblivious of the crowding people, all those *telpochcalli* boys and others flooding the dismal square, staring at him as though he was an exotic animal put on display.

Admittedly, no people of his class frequented the squares and the plazas that dotted each Tenochtitlan district, twelve in all these days as opposed to the original four, the founding districts existing since the island city was not the capital of the world but just an independent *altepetl*; important yes, but not overly so. They didn't teach this in school, the less glorious history of the pre-Tepanec days, but Father was a great man for a reason. Aside from being a brilliant warrior and an outstanding leader, he had a gift for storytelling, which, combined with his love of reading old books and accounts, made the evenings spent in his company an unparalleled pleasure. As a child, Necalli had cherished those times most of all, when Father would limp toward the patio after the evening meal was removed, making himself as comfortable as he could, given his bad leg and his awfully scarred backside. The servants would rush to bring out a well-oiled torch and then refreshments and drinks, mostly well-brewed *octli*, accompanied with reading material. However, when he, Necalli, was around and smaller, Father didn't get to enjoy much reading on such evenings, because he would come and snuggle beside him and they would talk for a blissfully long time about old Tenochtitlan. Nothing but a stinking island, Father would say with a conspiratorial grin, cane-and-reed houses everywhere and a pitiful avenue for a marketplace, with a low pyramid to tower over a dismal palace and the Mexica people going around, as proud and warlike as now but humbled perpetually, looked down upon.

It was difficult to believe that, but Father showed him old books to prove his claims, accounts of old wars and some calendars and tribute collectors' reports. He collected those, cherishing every old scroll, paying plenty of cocoa beans and cotton mantles, more than they could afford sometimes, to Mother's reproachful remarks. He had a passion for reading and learning by himself and not through someone else's interpretations. One learned to read for a reason, he would say, and why not trust one's own eyes and abilities to understand instead of relying on others to do the same for you? People did not always wish to say the truth, not even the schoolteachers. And so he would tell Necalli about Tenochtitlan's less glamorous version of history, not to reduce his pride in their ancestors, he was careful explain, but to enhance it. To build a glorious city out of nothing gave more credit to those who did it than the assumption that it was always there, rich and powerful and safe, reducing its founders' work to nothing outstanding. Oh, but was it good to learn from Father and not from *calmecac* teachers about such matters!

Hiding his smile, he watched her bearing down on him, as unstoppable as a gust of wind on the stormy night, graceful even through such an unseemly rush.

"I can't believe you are here!"

Her shout bounced off the walled area, spreading in their immediate vicinity, attracting attention. Over his brief spell of euphoria, he saw people glancing at them, a group of youths as well, just out of school and babbling. Not a promising sight, not without his friends around and ready to come to his aid; nor with this overwhelming sense of tiredness creeping on him again, appearing so easily since those two dawns following their Tlatelolco adventures, when his blood began boiling and his wounded arm began to hurt for real. It was good to be hastened back home and into his family's care back then. Mother knew how to make one feel better with plenty of ointments one of her slaves specialized at making and plenty of special foods that hastened one's recovery if for no other reason than by making a person wish to go on living in order to consume more of the delicious fare. Still, this bout of sickness did leave him weaker, a state of affairs he tried to ignore, almost successfully.

"It's good to see you, Chantli," he said, eyeing the lingering youths coldly, answering their stares, hiding his misgivings. If worse came to worse, he would put up as fierce a fight as he could manage. There was no way around it.

She halted at a respectable distance, clearly aware of their surroundings as well now. More so than him, probably. These were her "fishing grounds." He wanted to chuckle at the thought, remembering her boasting this dubious knowledge when he had assumed the commoners of Tlatelolco were fishing in the reeds.

"What are you doing here?" Her eyes appraised him with open pleasure, their curiosity unconcealed. And their excitement.

Encouraged, he grinned at her. "I was just walking by. Enjoying the sights."

Her laughter trilled a little too loudly. "Something worth looking at?"

"Maybe." He shifted uneasily. "How about we go somewhere else, talk where it's less crowded?"

"Well..." He saw her eyes drifting past the chattering youths, darting toward the plaza-like square, turning haunted. "Yes, but... you see..." Her gaze was back upon him, dark with concentration. "I think I saw, over there, where the food stalls are... there was this man..."

"What man?"

"I think, I think he was one of the men, the men from that tunnel, down the causeway." Her eyes turned imploring. "The one who had attacked me and Ahuitzotl. The man you... you hit. I think it was him."

He felt it like a blow in his stomach, the mere memory squeezing his entrails, let alone when spoken aloud. "How could you recognize him? It doesn't make sense. It was dark, and he... he fell, and was, was motionless..." The words trailed off, annoyingly helpless. He clenched his fists hard. "Do you think you saw him around here? Did he... did he recognize you?"

She looked as though about to take a step back. "No, no!" The vigorous shake of her head made her neatly braided hair jump. "He didn't see me. He was over there, by the stalls with the food." He looked in the indicated direction, her arm delightfully trim, the pointing finger delicate and long, noble looking despite the broken nail and the coarseness of its skin. "Then he rushed away, toward the tented area over there." The glittering eyes were upon him again, narrowed with concentration, fully immersed. "He was looking for someone, scanning the plaza several times. So I think he rushed there to meet whom he was looking for. He looked eager enough." The frown returned. "Also, there was this man back in the marketplace, in the walled area. He tried to grab my hand and pull me somewhere. My friends thought he was just trying to get somewhere with me, but I think he was connected to all these, somehow. There was a brawl there, you see. The Tlatelolcan women yelled hard and they were fighting with our local fowls. There was much agitation, and..." He watched her teeth making a mess out of her lower lip, a pretty sight as her lips were delightfully full, outlined boldly. "I think this man who tried to grab me was connected to this Tlatelolcan mess. He didn't look like someone after a pretty face."

He tried to digest this flood of information, his thoughts difficult to organize with her so near and so lively, his eyes noting the details, the gentle curve of her cheek, the shadow her thick eyelashes were casting upon it, the soft glow of her skin peeking from beneath the flowery embroidery of her simple bright *huipil*, so glossy, inviting to touch, to wonder how it would feel.

"Wait, tell me more—"

"Say, Chantli, won't you introduce us to your friend?" The girls burst upon them from the same direction Chantli had appeared earlier, walking prettily, balancing their baskets in a showy manner, both pleasing the eye, all dimples, curving in the right places, their eyes appraising him, holding no shame.

"Oh... yes, er... I..." Chantli blinked, funny in her sudden bewilderment. "Yes, well, this is Necalli. He... he came to... to..."

Her words died away almost naturally, trailing off.

One of the girls, prettier and shapelier than her friend, smiled slowly, enigmatically. "It's a pleasure to meet you, Necalli." Her eyes appraised him openly, glimmering, provocative. "You must have a spectacular full name."

He grinned at her, used to this sort of flirtatious talk from the marketplace fowls through his frequent excursions there with other *calmecac* boys. Why would one go to the marketplace but for something like that? They weren't quick to let you have your way with them, those marketplace girls, but they certainly weren't shy about flaunting their looks and the possibilities those offered. But for Chantli's obvious embarrassment and the awareness of being here alone and unprotected, he might have enjoyed himself.

"So you know our Chantli." Another pointed scrutiny. "She said nothing about such high company. Not a word."

"Stop that, Quetzalli," demanded the girl, finding her tongue at long last and apparently a great deal of her regular forcefulness. "Necalli is a friend of Patli. And yes, he is my friend too. And we... we must go now." She made a gesture as though about to grab his arm, then evidently thought better of it, tossing her head instead, signaling.

The one called Quetzalli, definitely a pretty bird, but not in Chantli's league, neither in looks nor in her blatant flirtation, raised her eyebrows high, her smirk unconcealed. "What are you so agitated about, sister? What are you afraid of?"

"I'm not afraid of anything," began Chantli hotly, then fell silent again as the youths chattering next to the school opening began drawing nearer, their walk purposeful, not just drifting. Necalli's sense of wellbeing evaporated.

Pressing his lips tight, he watched their set faces, their eyes narrow and dark, promising no good. His hand sneaked toward his girdle on its own volition, the long obsidian knife tucked in there safely, Father's cherished gift. If worse came to worse, he thought, shrugging inside. Encounters with *telpochcalli* boys were never a pleasant experience, the rivalry between districts schools well known and nourished, their mutual dislike of the prestigious *calmecac* coming to an outright hatred and hostility. He'd never wandered the less well-off districts alone before.

The girls fell silent as well, turning to watch the nearing youths. Chantli's saucy friend rolled her eyes pointedly. "What district you are coming from, rich boy?" she asked quietly, with no previous coyness or tease.

"What does it matter?" he countered, not pleased. Marketplace fowls were allowed to flirt but not to patronize, most certainly not that.

Her eyebrows climbed yet higher, but now it was Chantli's turn to lean toward her friend, the clearness of her forehead creased, her whisper holding urgency. "Necalli attends *calmecac*, out there near the Great Plaza, you know, and—"

"He does not!" The third girl was staring at them, wide-eyed. "Not *calmecac* surely. Only noble *pillis*—"

"Use your eyes, Xochi," the other girl cut her friend off quite rudely, her eyes narrow, full of attention. "I suppose you want me to distract the boys, eh?" Now her gaze was on Chantli, flickering with challenge. "Let you two scamper off unmolested."

"Unmolested?" But it was outright offensive, the way this lowly fowl assumed she could get him out of trouble. "No one will manage to molest me and get away to tell the story. I'm not afraid of that lowly bunch! They are nothing but stupid commoners with no sense and no training. I can handle them and they'll be crying for their mothers before I'm through with them."

It came out well if their expressions were to judge, three pairs of wide-open, glittering eyes, highly expectant. For a moment, they made him believe that he would actually manage, something a brief glance at the nearing youths and the confidence of their step shattered quickly. But to have those girls go away somewhere, not to watch him getting that beating. Chantli especially. She would try to interfere, to help out. Oh yes, he knew her well enough by now. Still, it would be unseemly, and under such circumstances, inappropriate. It would take off his dignity as well. He felt the smoothness of the antler his knife's hilt was made of, reassuringly glossy, pleasantly solid, absorbing the warmth of his palm, brimming with it.

"Necalli, please listen." She was peering at him, leaning closer, attempting to hold his gaze. "It's not the time. The fight will draw attention, make those people out there look," her head jerked lightly, indicating the crowding near the small pyramid and the buildings surrounding it, "and if they are, you know, if there are Tlatelolcans among them, or those who are involved..." Her eyes were peering at him, anxious to convince. "Let Quetzalli distract those boys while we go away. She can do it so easily, and no one would even notice. Please!"

Her nearness was distracting, that gaze of hers, urging and imploring, familiar from their Tlatelolco adventures, something he missed the most since saying their farewells at the edge of the causeway, this comradeship and the tickling sensation in his stomach or maybe his limbs, this apprehensive expectation, as though promised something wonderful, not a solid promise but a lure. Maybe yes, maybe no. But what was it?

"I can't just scamper off," he said, gathering his strength back with an effort.

"You are not scampering. They didn't even challenge you yet, you eager warrior!" This came from the aforementioned Quetzalli, a saucy thing. "They are just walking this way."

"They'll be here soon enough," he muttered, afraid of this line of reasoning. They might have a point there, and wasn't it the best of solutions to retreat before the trouble began, to regroup somewhere, or return when stronger, not weakened by illness and with ever-loyal Axolin by his side and maybe some others. The workshop boy certainly, such potential there. Then the *telpochcalli* troublemakers would think twice before trying to do something stupid.

"Not if we go the other way," Chantli was saying, beaming now, her smile one of the widest, another familiar sight, the best of them all. "I'll owe you plenty for this, Quetzalli." Momentarily, her palm locked around her spicy friend's arm, pressing it warmly. "I'll repay you, I promise. As soon as I can. You are the best, both of you!"

Another grateful beam, and she beckoned him toward the other side of the fence, the next corner close enough, offering the unknown. Slightly dazed by so much decisive efficiency, he followed, almost against his will. It was not like he was escaping a fight, he reasoned. That other girl was right. He hadn't even been challenged yet.

Behind the roughly carved wooden planks, a few alleys spread, leading to the tented enclosure, offering shade.

"That man, he went somewhere here," she whispered, pressing against the wooden planks, losing some of her high-spirited firmness.

Necalli was still busy watching their backs. But this Quetzalli girl must have been good at distracting their possible following. No wonder, really. With such looks and spunk, that girl would make a blind person pause.

"Let's blend over there," he muttered, beckoning toward the shade of the tent.

"But that's where that man—"

"We'll worry about it later," he said, taking hold of her arm without thinking, pulling her along. Her wrist was warm and delightfully smooth against his palm, just like he remembered. But why would she change in a mere five or six dawns? It felt like a lifetime had passed. He tried to collect his thoughts. "This man can do nothing to us in this crowd, even if he recognizes us, which I doubt. It was dark, and..." For the life of him, he couldn't bring himself to talk about what had happened under the causeway, not yet. Even when recalling his adventures to Father, trying to be truthful, to a degree – even then. "Let's worry about it later."

Oh, but it felt good to be surrounded by people, even if commoners who smelled like the end of the busy day. He pressed her closer, pushing their way through. In the heart of the tented area, people were squatting on mats or on the dusty pavement, some gossiping, eating snacks, some tossing colored beans, busy with the game of *patolli* upon a crudely drawn gaming mat, shoving wooden figurines, betting on the outcome, the players, and the onlookers alike. Absently, Necalli glanced at them.

"Do you see him somewhere?"

She shook her head, her brow creased thoughtfully. The smile threatened to sneak anew. But he missed her company, didn't he?

"Why were you following them on your own? It's dangerous

and you know it. These people are capable of terrible things. You should have let us know, any of us. What about that cousin of yours? Isn't interested in any more running around, is he?"

She made a face, following his lead away from the game and toward the crowded pond, crudely tiled and shallow, connected to the water construction that supplied this vital necessity all the way from the mainland to the multitude of similar pools and reservoirs. There was no lack of fresh drinking water in Tenochtitlan, with no one forced to drink the muddy waters of the lake, even though Father said that it was not exactly the case before the Tepanec War, before the independence.

"Oh, Patli is not that bad," she said, walking beside him easily now, waving her hands. "But he was at home for a few dawns, until his head healed, and then he disappeared back at school. I think he is not allowed to leave, as he hasn't come back for three evenings, including this one." Her happiness dimmed again. "That's why I came here. I wanted to talk to him, ask about you. You and your friend, that is. I thought that maybe he kept in touch with you somehow."

The glow was spreading again, warming his insides. So she came here because she wanted to ask about him. Not to run around with her friends or flirt with *telpochcalli* boys. He fought his smile down with an effort.

"We are good, both of us. Axolin is walking quite straight by now, barely limping if at all. And my arm, oh that one gave me some trouble, but now it's good and healthy. Presentable." He waved the limb in question, relatively clean now, with no smelly fluids and no swollenness or exaggerated pain. "Ready to use in fighting. No trouble there."

She brightened visibly. "Oh, I worried about your arm so!" Slowing her step, she turned to face him, leaning toward the slightly smeared bandage. "Did they punish you back in school? Did they go hard on you?"

He grinned at the memory. "They were about to crack the hardest on both of us, yes. When we appeared there on that evening, all drubbed and beaten and smelling like commoners after a whole market interval of fishing, they almost fainted with rage, raving for half a night, promising hair-raising punishments until the world of the Fifth Sun ended. The stories of the previous four worlds' ruinations looked like nothing compared to their promises." To retell this night in such a deriding way felt good, liberating. But this one wasn't a pleasant memory. "I wonder how you managed not to hear their screaming. They must have been hearing it out there and across the causeway. That Tlatelolco nobility, you know, that vile, ugly, stinking Teconal, he must have heard our *calmecac* teachers' screams and I'm sure it did him nothing but good." Another one that was a pleasure to deride, a scary memory. "It was such a lively night."

She was all eyes now, laughing and gaping at him at the same time, an impossible combination. "How did you manage to survive all that?" she breathed in the end. "I mean, didn't they stick to their threats, whatever they were?"

"Oh well, they tried to." Pleased with the effect, he eyed her, enjoying the sight. The unreserved excitement suited her best, making her beauty shine and his stomach flutter in most thrilling of ways. "Our *calmecac* teachers are known for sticking to their threats and worse. But..." Another pause, to enhance the effect.

"But?" She seemed to stop breathing, her eyes like two round plates, huge and not daring to blink.

"But for the Emperor's interference." He shrugged nonchalantly, as though disappointed with the lack of dramatic ending. "They didn't dare to go on threatening people whom our Emperor relied upon. After that first visit in the Palace, it was all back to normal. Or, well, most of it." He shrugged again, pleased with her continued gaping, such a dumbfounded expression. It was difficult not to laugh in her face. "What happened? Did you see a huge water serpent? Where?" To pretend to look around was to overplay it. He made do with a simple smirk.

"But how? It's impossible," she muttered, then her face brightened, losing most of its unbecoming bewilderment. "Ahuitzotl! I knew it. *That* boy." Her smile stretched wider. "He talked to the Emperor, didn't he? Made you all invited to testify."

Beckoning her to resume their walk, aiming to reach the stall and the mats offering warm tortillas, his hunger sudden and explosive, always like that since the recovery, he grinned. "Something of the sort, yes." But was she arriving at her conclusions and fast.

"And how was it? What did the Emperor look like? How is it to talk to him? Scary?" There was no stopping her now.

"It wasn't that bad. He is an interesting person, our Emperor. An impressive type." To downplay his initial trepidation and sometimes an outright fright felt good again. As though there was nothing special about being received in the Palace, allowed to talk to the mighty ruler that not many were permitted to even look in the eye. "I liked him. He is a good man. Great warrior, they say, and now, after meeting him, I believe them. He is a worthy leader." The memory made him chuckle. "Your workshop boy was having a hard time. The Emperor wanted to hear his story as ours wasn't that impressive, and he kept stammering, forgetting the proper address and all that. It was hilarious! He kept talking to Tenochtitlan Emperor as though he was a *calmecac* teacher. No, not a teacher! His workshop craftsman, your father. No proper titles. The Emperor had to remind him of that 'Revered Emperor' bit. At this point, I thought that boy was going to bury himself in the pretty mosaic of the floor. He was so flustered." Again, the laughter was turning difficult to defeat. "The Emperor said, 'Forget your bad manners, commoner boy, I'm after your knowledge now, so just tell it all and stop stammering.' That was beyond hilarious. I had the hardest time trying not to burst into the loudest fits."

But Chantli's eyes were again rounding to enormous proportions. "Miztli was brought before the Emperor too? To tell his story?" she muttered, incredulous. "He... he was brought to the Palace?"

Now it was his turn to eye her in puzzlement. "Yes, I just told you that. Why are you so flustered? He was more involved than all of us put together, was in the thickest of it. And believe me," he exhaled loudly, beyond silly joking around as well, "if you heard his story, you wouldn't believe what he has been through. And how filthy this Tlatelolcan mess is." To drop his voice became a necessity, just in case. "It might come to a war with that filthy little island. Ridiculous as it may sound, but I believe Ahuitzotl now. That *pilli* knows what he is talking about, and the Emperor is very closemouthed, of course. He doesn't betray his thoughts with a word or expression, but he was eager to hear what that Miztli-boy told him, every word, especially about that tunnel with weaponry, and that stupid contest of theirs. He didn't dismiss any of it lightly. He called me for more questioning later on, on the day before this one, and he sent our workshop boy back to Tlatelolco just now."

To lean closer and whisper into her ear became a necessity, a pleasing one. She smelled of fruits or maybe of sweetmeats, something with honey or flowers, musky, sweetish, and hers alone. He fought the urge to pull her into his arms like back on the accursed Tlatelolco shore, after the terrible night.

"He sent him back there?" she gasped, moving away in order to see him better probably. For some reason, it annoyed him.

"Well, yes. It's a secret and not to be shared with anyone, so don't scream about it at the top of your voice." He tried to push this unreasonable irritation away. Why would he feel bad about her wishing to see him better? "Axolin pried it from Ahuitzotl. Trust our pushy *pilli* to sniff such an undertaking out before it happened and then to rush to share. He likes it that now we treat him as one of us. A presumptuous beast." The smile was winning, overcoming the momentary resentment. There was no way around liking that Palace's boy. A law unto himself, a true beast.

"But Miztli, is he in danger now? What did the Emperor think of him? Did he try him in the Imperial Court?"

"What court?" He tried to see her expression, not an easy fit with people pushing all around, eager to make their way toward the food offerings as well. It made him wonder if he had enough means to pay. A cocoa bean should buy them both tortillas and maybe a handful of crispy *chapulin*. "The workshop boy is in a good shape, pampered in *calmecac*, taught to use weapons. He doesn't have to be taught that in our school, you see, but the Emperor insisted that he is to be kept in *calmecac*, even though he doesn't attend regular lessons yet." Another glance at the crowded stall rewarded him with a view of large pot balanced on stones, placed above a raging fire, offering steaming tamales as well. His stomach reacted violently. "Still, the Emperor was impressed enough with his shooting skills, so he has old Yaotzin, our schoolmaster, training him with all sorts of different weapons, and in the meanwhile, he sends him out on various secret missions like this one. A perfect tool." He shrugged, a little envious. "I wish he would decide to use me as well. Because of the stupid hand, I was left out!"

But she kept staring at him, her eyes refusing to return to their natural proportions. "Miztli is training in *calmecac*?"

"Oh yes; training, living, eating, sleeping. Being sent to fetch firewood and other necessities. More often than the rest of us, or so Axolin says. He was definitely after one such raid on the mainland when I met him this afternoon."

She was shaking her head hard. "I can't believe it. Miztli in *calmecac*? It's beyond understanding!"

But now her continued astonishment began wearing on his nerves. "What do you and your family have against this one? He is a commoner from a forsaken village, a peasant, yes, but he is a good person with plenty of courage and skills. In *calmecac*, they accept gifted commoners. Even your cowardly cousin was considered. So why not the workshop boy?" Glancing away, he shrugged. "The Emperor saw his worth. Only your greedy father wanted to sell him into slavery against every law and custom."

She bridled right away. "My father has nothing to do with it. He made him work, but he was always fair to Miztli. And he was concerned when that boy had been taken away by the warriors. He worried about him. He did!" she added hotly, flushing against his pointedly climbing eyebrows. "He made me retell everything that happened to us in Tlatelolco because he wanted to know what trouble Miztli had gotten himself into. It shows that he did care, and that he wanted to help."

But was she being naïve on purpose? "Do you know what he wanted to do to him for being absent from the workshop through these few days?"

She eyed him from beneath her brow, like a petulant child would. "What?"

"Nothing good. Or lawful!" The smell of the tamales was distracting and so were her chiseled cheeks, flushed and more defined now, such a pretty sight. It made him wish to end the silly quarrel. But why were they always arguing, getting angry with each other? "Forget it. We don't have much time. I must be back at school before midnight rites, and I'd better have proof that I've been spending some of this evening at my father's house. So..." The corner of her mouth was tugging with a smile and it made him wish to laugh for no reason. "Come, I'm dying of hunger."

"Me too," she admitted readily, in her typical straightforward way that now pleased rather than embarrassed him. "And I'd better return home soon as well. I had been punished too, so you know. You are not the only one to suffer the consequences and no Emperor came to intercede for me."

"He should have," he said with a laugh, propelling her forward and along the low wall of the temple's pyramid. "You've been—"

The man he almost bumped into looked familiar, coming from the other side of the stone wall, hurrying alongside it. Necalli stopped dead on his tracks. The memory of the well-defined profile with its prominent, slightly misshapen nose surfaced, impossible to mistake. This and the man's arrogant, proud bearing of a highly ranked warrior, even though his clothes disclosed nothing, a regular cloak with no special insignia or embroidery, no distinguished adornment. Still, no mistake. He had seen this one at the patio of their *calmecac* only this afternoon, when the sun was still very high in the sky, strolling in the company of a priest from the adjacent temple, and then later on, standing at the opening of the wall just as he and Axolin and two other boys were hurrying through it, happy to be outside and away from yet another school day. However, this time, this man's company was one of the teaching veterans, looking atypically nervous, furtive in a way. Oh yes, this was what caught Necalli's attention back then, he remembered, the teacher's lack of usual stern watchfulness, as much as the guest's marked disinterest, exaggerated in a way.

Even now, the school visitor still looked arrogant and sure of himself, but obviously on guard, watchful, maybe even eager, halting at the edge of the crowd, scanning the pushing people, his height an obvious advantage. What was he looking for? Wayward students? For good measure, Necalli pressed against the corner of the wall, catching the girl's hand to stop her progress.

"What?" she asked, not attempting to free herself, the touch of her skin as pleasing as ever, distracting.

"This man," he muttered, not taking his eyes off the object of his worried attention, half expecting to see the schoolmaster materializing next him. "He was in our school and on our way outside..."

Instead of the schoolmaster's broadly built silhouette, a stringy-looking man was approaching the warrior, watching him intently, as though waiting for a signal. The tall warrior's eyes narrowed, and he glanced at the same direction, then brought his arm up as though to touch his forehead, a small piece of *amate*-paper clutched between his fingers, tied by a crimson string, catching the eye. Reassured, the stringy man pushed forward, now flanked by two more tough-looking types.

He could hear Chantli gasping, her hand tightening around his bandaged arm, hurting it. He jerked it away without thinking. "What in the name—"

"That man... him again!" she whispered, pressing close, her breath tickling his ear. "That man from the marketplace. He is here!"

"Where? What man?"

A group of passersby, traders judging by the bundles tied to their foreheads and hanging down their backs, pushed past them, interrupting their view. "Move along. You are blocking the way," one of them said peevishly, bestowing an impatient glance on Chantli. Briefly, Necalli stared him down, too preoccupied to get angry with the lowly trader for real.

"That one, the skinny one; oh, it's him!" Chantli's whispering kept pouring into his ear, unpleasantly hot and urgent. "That's the man, the man who tried to grab me back on the marketplace... It's him!"

The stringy one halted before reaching the warrior, tossing something toward his companions, glancing around as though sensing their scrutiny. In the corner of his eye, Necalli saw the stranger from their school doing the same. Without thinking, he pushed himself and the girl backwards, pressing against the crumbling stones, his heart pounding.

"Which one?" he breathed into the thickness of her braid that was now stuck between him and the side of her face, obstructing. "The skinny one?"

She nodded so vigorously, the braid struck him across his mouth, making him wish to laugh. There was a nice smell to it, something spicy and strong, sweetish in a way.

The man from the school was shifting impatiently, shooting the lingering group furious glances. When he turned around and dove into the next alley, the scrawny one and his followers rushed to catch up. Necalli didn't hesitate, pleased to feel her following at once, with no indecision.

The alley was crowded, not as badly as the square but with enough flow of people to let them blend. It wasn't easy to keep the non-descript cloak in sight without being too obvious about it, but the first time he lost sight of it and began cursing quietly, Chantli was motioning with her head, indicating an especially thick congregation of people, traders and other busy commoners, talking between themselves. Behind them, the foursome they were following was disappearing into another alley.

"You are good!" he breathed, appreciative, steering her around the crowding commoners.

She beamed at him, pleased with herself. "The skinny one is impossible to miss. I'm watching him."

"What did he do to you?"

Her frown overshadowed the smile. "He tried to grab me back on the marketplace. Quetzalli and Xochi helped me to get away. They said he was just trying to have his way with me, but it didn't look like anything of the sort. He said 'it's her' or something and he looked surprised, gaping at me in no playful way." Momentarily out of breath, she paused, following his lead but determined to say her piece. "It was just as our marketplace fowls were fighting the Tlatelolcan scum. It was strange too, all their yelling and brawling. The Tlatelolcan women were screaming about us getting our comeuppance and soon. It sounded out of place, you know? Not the usual marketplace squabbling."

He watched the new alley spreading before them, fairly deserted but for a few hurrying women with baskets. Of the people they followed, there was no sight.

"Come and be the quietest."

She made a face, but he could feel her following dutifully, her footsteps rapid upon the dusty gravel. The alley ended dishearteningly soon, just a narrow pathway, nothing more, with blank fences of simple patios on either side, spreading their shadows.

"Where..." she began, but he pressed her fingers with his, signaling to keep quiet.

To retrace their steps toward the hubbub of the other side felt curiously safe; still, he kept pausing, listening intently. From one of the patios, the voices seeped out. Against his better judgment, he put his ear to the densely tied planks.

"I'm not going as far as the Chalco shores," a voice rasped, muffled by the thick vegetation clinging to the high fence. "—silly and unnecessary – they can't ask that of us—"

More voices joined the vigorous protest, those muffled and difficult to understand. He pressed his ear closer to the rough wood.

"No one is asking you to go anywhere," said a calmer voice, someone standing next to the interwoven branches they were pressing against, or so it seemed. The *calmecac* visitor, Necalli knew, having not heard this man's voice before, but somehow certain of this conclusion. The self-assured words could not belong to the marketplace scum. "You will wait at the road to Acachinanco. Tomorrow with dawn, you will arrive there and you will not leave until receiving word."

A clamor burst at the other side of the alley, bearing down on them, heralding trouble. Or so Necalli's senses told him. Tearing his face off the fence, he glimpsed a group of youths, boisterous and animated, looking familiar in no promising way. In another heartbeat, he felt himself leaping into the narrow gap between the nearby fences, somehow guessing its existence, dragging her after him, surprising them both on this count. The rough wood tore at his skin, but he kept squeezing, pleased with her following, uttering no sound. But she was incredible, this girl, wasn't she? So responsive!

In a heartbeat, they were surrounded by a wall of green, not thick or dense but still a cover, bearably prickly. He tried to listen through the insects' insistent buzzing.

"Toltitlan is a more logical place to meet." That voice sounded clearer coming through the greenery instead of the woven barrier. "Why wander out there in the gods forsaken swamps of Acachinanco?"

"Because that is what expected of you!" rasped the warrior, obviously angry. "You are paid to do what you are told, not to ask questions!"

Outside, the youths' voices were drifting away, the loudness of their talk disturbing. What if these people came to explore the source of the noise? He could feel Chantli tensing, covering a gasp. What in the name of every possible deity did she...

Then the question came to an abrupt halt as his gaze took in the tiny form of a little girl standing behind their backs, pressing against the nearest wall, staring at them, her eyes huge and round, widening with surprise.

"Hush, little one," Chantli whispered, reaching out with both hands, palms upwards, imploring. "We will do you no harm. Please?"

Aghast, he held his breath.

CHAPTER 5

It was strange to see Citlalli without the splendor of the imperial wife's regalia, not hidden under beautiful diadem and sparkling bracelets. In a prettily adorned cotton blouse and a long embroidered skirt, she looked thinner than Tlemilli remembered, too delicate, somehow frail. All those dimples and soft curves, where did those go?

Having not seen her sister since her elevation three or more moons ago, glimpsing the imperial wife on various official occasions only, Tlemilli blinked, surprised and somehow unsettled. There was something strange about her radiantly beautiful, cheerful, light-hearted sibling; something different, unsettling. Her beauty was still there, unarguably – the luminous eyes, the dimple of the chiseled chin, the softest glow of the skin, so creamy it invited touch – yet, something was not the same.

"What are you doing here, little one?" Citlalli's eyes widened in surprise, the bluish shadows underneath those deepening. "How did you get here?"

Tlemilli bit her lower lip, disappointed, even offended, by such an unenthusiastic reception. "I just... I was just passing by." She drew a deep breath, pulling herself together, determined to save the last of her dignity. "Father sent for me. This is how I happened to enter your exalted side of the Palace, oh Revered Empress. Those are nice quarters you got yourself here."

This made Citlalli laugh, the familiar lilting sound, so pleasant to the ear. Nothing artificial about it. Not like the chortles Matlatl was practicing day and night, aiming to please that exalted future husband of hers, stupid fowl.

"You haven't changed, you silly one." Shifting to make herself more comfortable, the occupier of the beautiful quarters pulled her loom closer, straightening the wide strap that was wrapped around her back. "Come, sit here, Little Sister. You can mind these threads, make sure they aren't twisting." A light sway of the graceful head sent the maid who had been squatting at the indicated place before away. Another one hesitated near a narrow podium laden with trays. "Out with you two. Wait outside. Oh, and bring refreshments. Tortillas with honey. You are still fond of those, aren't you?" Again, the familiar warm flicker.

Tlemilli breathed with relief, her smile ridden with guilt.

"Come. What else would you like to spoil yourself with, little one? Chocolate drink? With a touch of vanilla in it?" The glow dimmed again. "As long as you can, why not enjoy this imperial luxury? They don't serve that in our father's women's quarters, do they?"

Tlemilli tried to pay the disappearing smile no attention. "No, no vanilla. I like my chocolate spicy now. And my food too. The *molli* made of chili peppers. I ask Tlaco and she puts it in my meals and my chocolate drink. When she remembers, that is. She forgets many things these days." Her own mood darkening, she dropped on the indicated cushions, careful not to let the threads arranged in dangerously close proximity scatter and twist between themselves. "It's difficult not to let them see, the way she keeps forgetting things. They notice sometimes, and then I have to lie and claim that I was the one who forgot to order my meals or give my clothes to the laundry maids. They must think me simple-minded, those stupid, annoying lumps of fat." To snort loudly helped. It made her feel as though she had put the empty-headed gossipers in their place. "I hate them all!"

Citlalli's gaze saddened. "You don't get along with the lot of them any better now, do you?"

She tried to get away with a shrug.

"Oh, Milli, you are as lonely as I am." The fleeting smile tore at her. Citlalli was never glum or despondent. Sad sometimes, yes, like all of them, disappointed when unable to get something or go somewhere, hurt after a particularly nasty quarrel with their fellow half-sisters, a multitude of those. No, this was her, Tlemilli's, prerogative. Citlalli rarely got into quarrels. She was too nice of a person, too liked and admired, too even-tempered. Everyone loved her, even the Emperor. And yet, she didn't look happy or content now, not like back on their side of the Palace.

"You are lonely because you can't come visit us anymore?" Still careful with the precious threads, Tlemilli pulled her legs up, hugging them with her arms, leaning her chin on the perch her folded knees created. They never managed to wean her off her favorite, frowned-upon pose. "Why would you miss those gossipy fowls? I would move to your side of the Palace any day, to order everyone about, get all the sweetmeats that I want, and have them take me out for the marketplace and wherever I wish every morning and afternoon." She exhaled loudly. "I wish I could go out whenever I wanted."

Citlalli glanced at the threatened strands, then lifted her gaze again, her generously folded mouth quivering, eyes dancing. "And that's what you think the Emperor's wives are doing, little one?"

Offended by such open patronizing, Tlemilli frowned. "Why not? If they are not at liberty to do all that, then what's the point of being an emperor's wife?"

Her sister's smile died away. "It's not as though one chooses to become the Emperor's or anyone else's wife." It came out bitterly, in an atypically defiant, almost daring tone.

Tlemilli blinked. "But it's nice to be the Emperor's wife, isn't it? It can't be not nice, or all those stupid fowls wouldn't be so envious of you."

Citlalli's generous lips pursed into near disappearance. "I would switch places with any of them in a matter of a heartbeat, Milli! With any one of them, just anyone. Send them here, into this nice set of rooms, while I would go to our old house near the Plaza. Or anywhere else, for that matter. The filthiest corner of the marketplace, if I had to." A moment of hesitation. "And I would have taken you along, little one. Only you! Keep you away from the Palace."

Astonished, Tlemilli watched the familiar, delicate features setting into a mold she had seen mostly in the obsidian mirror of the women's hall, a tall massive affair set in an exquisite golden frame, offering one one's likeness. Not a pretty sight in her case, all sharp angles and bones, the wide mouth too large, the widely spaced eyes out of place. No harmony in such a face and no calm, but to see such an expression on Citlalli's beautifully soft features was unsettling, to say the least.

"But I thought it was nice," she whispered, too disconcerted to protest for real. "I thought... I thought you were happy..." Holding her breath, she peered into the familiar face, seeking the old Citlalli, the lighthearted cheerful girl she had grown up with, the only person she loved and admired and followed since she could remember herself, spilling out her troubles and frustrations, sharing thoughts; the only person who could turn her anger into laughter and make everything right with a simple word or a hug. They had no mother like some others, but with Citlalli, it wasn't an important deficiency. "I thought you liked being the Emperor's Chief Wife."

The generous mouth quivered again, then the mask, the thinner, bleaker version of her sister, was gone.

"Don't look so frightened, Milli. It isn't that bad." The trilling laugher made her feel better. "You look as though I just turned into a scary serpent or an ugly frog. I shall tell them to bring in my mirror. That will scare you for good." The laughter died away, replaced by a thoughtful frown. That one was familiar, comforting, promising wise revelations or advice. "I'm not suffering here, on this side of the Palace. It has its bright sides and all. But," the tip of the pink tongue came out, licked the full lower lip, "it's not what they all think it is, the envy and politics, being always on guard, always striving to do what is expected. Well, let us just say, it is not something you would enjoy, and I'm not that different from you. You see, I do want to please Father, and the Emperor is a good man. He treats me well, and he likes me enough to visit my quarters more often than he does to his other, more prominent wife." A fleeting smile had again a bitter quality to it. "It pleases Father that the Emperor does that, and it's good, I suppose, good for Father's policies, good for our city, good for the general welfare of its people. But," the smile turned one sided, decidedly crooked, "but personally, it does not please me. I would rather the Emperor did not neglect his exalted Tenochtitlan wife, did not go against Tenochtitlan in such a provocative way. I may be just a young woman with not much wisdom or understanding, but I feel it will bring us disaster, our Emperor's conduct. Also, it pains me that because of me, he neglects not only his previous woman but also the child, the baby, his official heir. Father wants me to bear the new heir, and the Emperor keeps expecting that, but it still didn't happen and the wise women tell us that no baby would settle in the belly of a woman when she is pressed and unhappy, so no wonder no baby settled in mine as yet."

Tlemilli tried to digest it all. "They want you to have the Emperor's baby?"

The generous lips pursed again. "Yes. Father is angry with me for not conceiving. He says I let everyone down: him, the Emperor, the entire city."

"But it's not fair! How can he press you with something like that?" Unable to keep still, Tlemilli sprang to her feet, scattering the threads after all but not caring. "He can't be angry with you for something like that. And he must protect you should the Emperor grow angry with you about that. Maybe he doesn't visit you often. They say that a husband should visit his wife often enough, otherwise—"

"Hush, little one! You are screaming at the top of your voice." This time, Citlalli looked downright worried. "Calm down, Milli. Just calm down."

Tlemilli shut her mouth reluctantly. But how dared they? "You can't be held accountable for not conceiving!" she whispered stubbornly, needing to say that. "It's not your fault!"

"Yes, yes, I know, little one. Don't go into screaming fits. You are not on your side of the Palace." Citlalli held her hand out imploringly. "Sit back here. Do!"

Exhaling loudly through her clenched teeth, Tlemilli obeyed.

"You can't talk like that here, you just can't." Evidently relieved, her sister leaned back on her cozily arranged cushions, eyes still wary, gauging. Again, not a typical behavior. Citlalli was always so calm, so sure of herself. "For your own good, little one, do not mention Father or the Emperor at all, even back in your quarters. Keep away from it all, politics and intrigues, keep away from those as long as you can. Father won't be looking for a husband for you, not for a few more summers. Enough time to enjoy your life as it is, with no worries or obligations, no intrigues, no spitefulness. As long as you can keep away from all this—"

"Keep away from husbands, you mean?" Unable not to, Tlemilli snickered. "It won't be difficult in my case. But I did stick my nose in politics or whatever it is. I did make Father angry with me. And with good reason too. Not like in your case." Her mood darkened again. "He has no right to be angry with you. You are a perfect wife and the Emperor adores you. They all say that. How can he not? They talk about it day and night, you know, the stupid fowls, his wives and the girls too. Everyone! They talk about nothing but how he prefers you to that ugly Tenochtitlan turkey. They are so proud of you, but none is as proud as I am, and—"

Again, the imploring hand. "Stop that, Tlemilli! Stop talking about it so loudly. Just stop!" The gentle fingers locked around her wrist, heedless of the slipping loom and the messed up patterns. "Don't get offended, little one. I know how proud you are and how uninhibited. And I love you for that. But," the fingers pressed, "you can't speak that freely, not here. I'll make sure we meet somehow, somewhere; outside, maybe. I'll take you along next time I visit the marketplace. How about that? The very next market day, we'll ride in my litter, spoil ourselves with plenty of pretty things and some sweetmeats."

"Yes, yes, oh yes!" She had a hard time restraining herself from jumping back to her feet. "Yes, please, we'll do that. You promise?"

Citlalli's smile had all its old beaming radiance. "Yes, I promise. I should have done it before. It'll do both of us nothing but good, and they can't tell us not to, can they? We are full sisters and entitled to see each other." Then the smile dimmed again. "Why is Father angry with you?"

"Oh that." Tlemilli giggled, her previous predicament not marring her current bout of happiness. Oh, it was so good to be with Citlalli again! "I did some wild things on the day of the contest. Back there on the Plaza and then later on, on the shore. Oh, but it was just wonderful! I'm sorry you weren't there to see it. They say you were sick. Were you?"

Citlalli just shrugged. "What did you do?"

"Oh well. It was truly wild. I never did something as wild, and it was incredible." Her stomach turned at the mere memory, at the possibility of talking about it, telling it all aloud, savoring the sensation. "You see, there was this boy, just under the dais. He was... well, he was, I don't know, he made me watch him. He was so different, not like everyone." Her sister's widening eyes made her stumble over her words, searching inside her mind, never trying to articulate why she did watch him in the first place. Only the fact that she had to. "Well, I helped him to get away from the people who were after him. We huddled under the podium where they put the dais on and, Citlalli, you wouldn't believe it, it was so good, so interesting, just amazing. He... he was different. You would think that too!"

Her sister's eyes were like two round bowls by now. "You were huddling with a boy under the podium on the Plaza?"

"Well, yes, but it's not like we did something bad." Disappointed with the reaction, Tlemilli rushed on, needing to tell it all now, craving to do so. "He was fleeing from people, Father's people, as it turned out, and I helped him to find his way to the shore." She fought down the urge to embellish, to boast that it was easy to find that shore, that she had done so with no trouble. "We started to wander a bit, but in the end, we did find it. Well, everyone was rushing this way at some point, and then, when his friends got in trouble with Father's warriors, I helped them, made Father go away. And then, well..." She shrugged, pleased with her sister's unbecoming stare and the atypically gaping mouth, but unsettled too. When told out loud, her story sounded wild, implausible, unreal. But for Father's continued interrogations, today's questioning as well, she might have assumed that she had dreamed it all up, this day and this boy and all the wonder of running around the city. "He promised to come back and find me, you see? But I don't know how he can do it, get into the Palace and all that, and with Father eager to know what he looks like now."

"You've been out there, outside the Palace? And with someone Father is looking for?" Citlalli's eyes kept growing wider and rounder, turning the size of plates for serving fruit. "You... you interfered with Father? And he caught you doing this?" Even her voice climbed to unbecoming heights, turned funnily squeaky.

Tlemilli fought the untoward wish to laugh. "He didn't catch me at first. I went to draw his attention away, and it worked. He left that other boy he was beating and went with me. Back to where everyone was, the orating Emperor and all. He didn't suspect a thing. He paid me no attention." Leaning forward, she pressed her palms to her chest, eager to convince. "He didn't suspect a thing!"

"But then what happened?"

"Oh well, then, you see, someone told on me. I bet it was the fat turkey. Back on the Plaza, she had been watching that boy too, making faces at him, signaling." She frowned. "He never told me what it was. We had no time for that. But when I think about it, I remember that I noticed him because she had been watching him too. Making nice faces, smiling even. Imagine that haughty fowl smiling at people. I've never seen something like that happen, but she had been playing with those fat lips of hers when watching that boy. You see? That was why I noticed it all." Another shrug seemed to be in order. "I was bored. The contest hadn't started yet."

"Noble Jade Doll was signaling the boy on the Plaza? The boy Father was after?" Like always, Citlalli was arriving at her conclusions and fast, separating important information from less relevant bits.

"Yes, she was. She certainly looked that way. And Father was glancing at her with much interest. I noticed that too. And then he followed her gaze and his face lit like a torch that had too much oil in it. Puff, like that!" She flailed her hands in the air, hitting the fallen loom in the process. "So the man who was with this boy got all frightened and he began dragging him away, but then that boy came back, all panicked, running like a madman. And well, at this point, I helped him. We hid under that podium. You know, the longer one, where they put the imperial dais for the ceremonies. The Emperor was making speeches just as we huddled underneath it. It was so funny. I never had a better time in my life!"

Citlalli's palms were cold and a little clammy as they wrapped around her wrists, forcing her hands down, gently but firmly, with much authority. "Calm down, Milli. Don't yell and don't wave your hands, unless you want us to be interrupted." The liquid eyes moved closer, dark with concentration, willing her into a more reasonable mode of thinking, as they always did. "Now tell me. You said Father was angry with you because of this. You said someone told on you. Tell me exactly what Father accused you of? What punishment did he threaten you with?"

To feel Citlalli so close and involved made her calm immediately, as always. Shutting her eyes for a heartbeat, she tried to concentrate, inhaling her sister's smell, something sweetish and spicy and tickling one's nose.

"Father wasn't truly angry with me back on the shore. He was fuming, of course, as those boys that he caught were from Tenochtitlan, noble boys sniffing around, or so he kept muttering, very angry with them. There was this girl, you see? An annoying fowl who fell on us out of nowhere, just as we were hiding again, that boy and I, and he was busy thinking what to do. This girl, she came crying for help, talking about other boys who got in trouble. One was called Necalli, and the other Ahuitzotl. But did she keep carrying on and on, using their names, yelling quite stupidly, demanding that he do something. So we went out and down the shore, and there they were, two boys, one held close and interrogated by Father and the other, a smaller one, kicking and cursing like someone possessed. Father was beating the older boy, slapping him, I think. It was scary to see." She tried to move away, to escape the penetrating gaze. The loom was still between them, gaining some of her attention. "Anyway, that boy, he got a sling by then. A warriors' sling, a pretty thing, you know? I never saw one up close before. It was woven so tightly, like the things on our looms, but its middle was not woven at all. Something solid, like our shoes. And that ball, you see. He just picked one up. There were so many of those. The warriors were going around, picking them up. Some were cracked badly—"

"Tlemilli!" The gentle hands shook her lightly. "Tell me what happened then."

"Oh then, well, he was going to shoot at them, I think. So I told him I'd go down there, talk to Father, take him away. He was so very grateful, Citlalli. He looked at me really intensely, you know, like he wanted to tell me things. But for that other annoying fowl, he might have." To take her gaze away and back toward the overturned loom became a necessity. She pressed her interwoven fingers tightly. "When we were in that crowd and jostled so badly, everyone pushing and shoving, hurting bad, he... he was protecting me and not that other fowl, and then down there on that slope, well, I think he wanted to stay with me, but he had to help his friends, and the stupid girl kept nagging him about it." The patterns of the unfinished fabric blurred. "So he picked up more stones, in addition to his precious missile. He said he would have very little time to shoot as many of those as he could before they started running toward us."

"He wanted to shoot Father?" This time, it was Citlalli's turn to cry out, then swallow the rest of her words, her eyes again out of proportion with the rest of her face.

"I don't know. Maybe." Her own indifference with this possibility surprised her as well. But shouldn't she care about something like that? "So that was when I told him that I would go down there, talk to Father, take him and his men away. I didn't manage to take them all, but some went away with us. So I didn't fail, not entirely." The grin sneaked out on its own. "I told Father that the Emperor was anxious to have him close by when the winners of the contest were to be presented with their rewards. It was difficult to prove my lies as obviously the Emperor would wish his Head Adviser along in the end of the great ceremony or contest, wouldn't he? So he didn't stop to ask the Emperor about it, or even to wonder about the strange choice of the imperial messenger. He just dove back in and began making speeches and patting warriors on their backs."

"And then what happened?" Her sister was all ears now, like a child told a fascinating story, hanging on her, Tlemilli's, words as though she had been the most skillful storyteller. A novelty. Pleased, she paused to gain maximum effect.

"Did this boy shoot the warriors who remained?"

The good feeling evaporated. "I wouldn't know. Father kept me by his side for some time, then made the slaves take me away and back to the litters of the others, to their silly chatter and complaints. They were making faces, the stupid turkeys." She stifled a giggle. "The state of my clothes was not at its best by that time. I must have been quite a sight, the way they gaped at me. I was afraid they would faint from all this staring and I told them so. It's such a pleasure to get them shocked, especially that filthy Matlatl. This one thinks the world of herself and she doesn't reach your ankles in anything, neither looks nor manners. Such a stupid loud-mouthed turkey!"

Citlalli's eyes narrowed. "Does Matlatl give you trouble?"

Tlemilli just shrugged. "We fight a lot, yes. But she can't best me; she never does."

"Oh, little one!" The gentle palms were pressing her again, with much passion this time. "But back to what happened. How did Father find out? How did you get caught?"

She lifted one shoulder, not wishing to move out of her sister's sweet-smelling embrace. "Like I told you, someone made sure to let him know that I wasn't around our dais most of the time. So he called for me and demanded to know all about it." Moving away and back to her loom-staring, she traced one messed-up pattern with her finger. "He was mighty angry, like I never saw him before. Not with any of us, the girls, anyway. So that tells me that this boy did manage to free his friends and probably escape too. He talked about them only this morning, those 'sniffing-around *pillis*' as he called them, and about him, that boy, most of all." To study the overturned loom became a necessity. "I happened to overhear him." A glance at her sister reassured her. No anger there. Citlalli knew about her habit of eavesdropping on the Palace's dwellers, no one better. It had begun way before Citlalli had gone up in this world, moving to the Emperor's side, becoming unhappy as it turned out to be, a disquieting thought. "It sounds like those boys did manage to get away, you see. But I knew they would. He was so good, this boy, so... so reliable and good-looking. Of course he managed to free them all and make them escape."

"What was his name?" An almost motherly smile was playing on Citlalli's lips, annoying and reassuring at the same time.

"I don't know. I didn't have time to ask that."

"But you told me the names of the others."

"Yes, that other stupid girl was repeating their names over and over. Necalli and Ahuitzotl, Ahuitzotl and Necalli. As though one time to hear about them wasn't enough."

"Ahuitzotl?" Citlalli wrinkled her nose, her high forehead creasing even if slightly. "Isn't that the name of Tenochtitlan royal house's offspring?"

"I don't know. It's a mighty strange name. The Water Spiny One, the monster everyone hears about. Why would someone call a child by such a name?"

"Maybe his calendar suggested it. Maybe this name is what would give its carrier mighty powers in the future." Absently, Citlalli pulled her loom back into its rightful position, straightening its threads with her practiced fingers, her thoughts evidently elsewhere. "So Tenochtitlan is involved in our affairs more than we might wish to think it is. And Father knows about it and keeps a close eye." A sigh, then her sister's gaze concentrated back on Tlemilli. "You should keep away from all this, little one. Truly away. This matter is not for us to solve, even if some imperial wives think differently." Again, the bitterness. Tlemilli pushed away her frustration with not knowing this boy's name. It was such a simple thing to inquire, to ask. Why didn't she? "So Father questioned you about it? How did you get away?"

Her mood spiraled down once again, very abruptly. "I didn't get away. I had to tell it all to him, everything. He threatened to execute Tlaco. He meant what he said!"

Again, Citlalli was staring. "What did he do to you?"

She rolled her eyes, pleased with such a careless, worry-free grimace. "The obvious. Not allowed to leave our quarters and all that." A shrug came with the same ease. "I never believed I would miss going to school, but I began missing it at some point. The dreary *calmecac* lessons under the priestess, would you believe that I began missing that?"

Citlalli wasn't to be sidetracked. "But you've been sneaking around all the same. You said you overheard Father this morning."

Sharp Citlalli. "Well, yes." She attempted a winning smile. "You know me. I was bored."

Her sister's grin put her worries to rest. "Yes, I know you, little rascal." Then the open concern returned. "You are here without permission! You sneaked here. Oh, Tlemilli, he will be livid when he hears. And I won't be able to protect you!" On her feet now and looking unseemly agitated, the young woman waved her hands. "We must bring you back quickly, without drawing attention. And then somehow make sure none of the girls told on you. Oh!" One of the palms was pressing against the soft mouth, the fine upper teeth chewing on it. "We must find a way to prevent him knowing that you got away. And you must promise me – promise and swear! – that you will be more patient now and won't sneak away again, not until—"

"Wait, Citlalli, wait." To jump to her feet in her turn was a relief. "Wait, you didn't hear me out till the end. I didn't sneak away now. In the morning, yes, I did. But not now. Father sent for me not long ago. He sent for me himself, most officially. He wanted to ask me more questions." She peered at the unbecomingly worried face, eager to convince. "He sent for me and brought me here, to this side of the Palace. He wanted to ask me about that boy again, wanted me to describe what he looked like. In detail! But it didn't go badly, because I was prepared this time, you see? I wasn't caught unaware. I had time to prepare before he sent for me."

The memory of the high morning surfaced, making her shiver again, the dread that had crawled up her spine just as the ants did to her bare feet as she had listened, the realization that it was her that Father meant to question, to learn of his looks; the way she had run back madly, anxious to be in the girls' quarters first, before being sent for, anxious to provide no evidence of her sneaking around, the signs of it smeared all over her legs, those sticky lumps of earth. And then being sent for just as Tlaco was massaging her feet after soaking them in a bowl full of pleasantly warm water, clucking with her tongue, admonishing silently but not about to let anyone know. Everything in the nick of time, before the other girls began pouring in, eager to retire for the mandatory midday rest. Well, Father's messengers apparently cared nothing for the ladies' custom of resting, so she had been rushed here, to this side of the Palace, afraid but prepared, not about to be caught in her lies and thus made to share her true observations. If he didn't remember what this boy looked like, then anyone's description would do. She wouldn't be the one to refresh their memories, not when it came to this boy.

"What did you tell him?" Citlalli was peering at her closely again, her forehead creased worse than before.

For some reason, it made Tlemilli pause. Was she telling too much? Were there things in which her sister, the Emperor's favorite wife, should not be involved? For her own good, that is.

"I... I didn't tell much. Just the things he already knew." A shrug came with difficulty. "He didn't seem to care."

Citlalli's carefully plucked eyebrows were sliding up. "It's not like Father to let you off that lightly."

Tell me about it, she reflected, remembering the refreshments her sister had ordered upon her arrival here. Wasn't it the time for those to be served? The honeyed tortillas, oh yes, she wouldn't be opposed to such a treat now.

"You see, Father told the maids to take me back after he was through with me, but then, just as we reached the main staircase, one of the royal fowls fell upon us straight away from her royal litter. That open thing, you know, just a seat with no curtains." Against her will, she snickered. "Oh, she was such a sight! Elderly and as dry as an old berry but laden with so many bracelets and necklaces. I kept wondering how she managed to move around at all. I swear, I couldn't stop staring. So she scolded me for gawking, then demanded the maids – my escorts! – to get busy with taking her things. She had litter-loads of those; must have emptied the entire marketplace. So I was left with no escorts, and so seized on my chance and bolted away, to try and sniff out where you have been living, oh Mighty Empress."

Citlalli was laughing hard now, pleasing Tlemilli greatly. Oh yes, like the old times. It always made her feel good, clever and witty, the ability to make her perfectly accomplished, well-mannered sister laugh in an uninhibited manner. Not many could do that. No one but her, for that matter.

"What if we go out and stroll those pretty gardens of yours?" she asked, still raiding the clouds of well-being, not wishing a good day to end, not yet. "You can take me around before they banish me to our ignoble side of the Palace. Please! Oh please, Sister, please."

Citlalli's expression was changing again, from startled surprise to open doubt. It was a funny sight.

"Just like that?" The young woman's frown was almost painful, her glance at the open shutters and the soft afternoon light that seeped in subtly, delicately, almost haunted, as though she had expected the Underworld nightly spirits to line up there, waylaying her coming out. "At this time of the day?"

"Why not? It's not even dusk yet. Oh please, please!"

"I don't know." But there was still open doubt in the arching eyebrows, in the helplessly blinking eyes.

Tlemilli caught the cool palms in hers. "Yes, you do. You do know and you do want to. Please, Sister, please. We never go out together now, so only this time. Please!"

The hint of a smile twisting the full lips let her know that she had won.

CHAPTER 6

Even though it was already near dusk, the insects were still as much of a nuisance as always, buzzing around, assaulting his bare arms and back, annoying in their persistence. Eyes on the neatly paved alley, so wide three people could stroll alongside it side by side, or so it seemed, Miztli clutched his *huictli*, the short digging stick used for ruffling the soft earth, its touch familiar, bringing thoughts of home once again.

Through the last market interval or more, he hadn't thought about his village, not even briefly. Which was a novelty. Back in the workshop, he had all the time in the world to think about home and his family, miss them all dreadfully, every single aspect or memory; however the last market interval left him with no time for any such musings. His first misadventures here in Tlatelolco, then the following days in *calmecac* kept him too busy. And not that he had much spare time now. Not even close. Still, the familiar acting of tilling the soil brought back the memories in force. But did he do his share of digging and seeding, weeding and watering, tending their family plots of vegetables and other growths. The land wasn't theirs, but the fruits of it were. At this time of the season, they must have been collecting some of it already, beans probably, and maybe the first maize. Father wouldn't be free to go down the mines, not for a while. Were they missing him back home?

"Over here. Work this part of the ground." The man next to him, a squat tired-looking type of indefinite age, sweating profusely, pointed toward the nearby tree, one of many, a row of beautifully slender giants adorning the pathway, guarding it. "It needs to be weeded, so don't start with that wedge of yours as yet."

Obediently, Miztli shifted toward the indicated spot, managing to do it without getting up. Short term and pretended as his new duties as a Palace's gardener were, he didn't want to tire himself more than necessary. The day was long and demanding as it was, from the usual morning *calmecac* chores, to the mainland ceremonial wood collecting, to the hastily organized rush across the Tlatelolco causeway, the search for the dwelling of the old noble Tepecocatzin, the uneasy interview, the hastily hatched plan, and now this, digging in the Palace's magnificent gardens, pretending it was his only purpose. Oh yes, it was an eventful day, to say the least.

The clamor of the nearby pond drew his eyes back toward the pathway. Such a pretty avenue. So wide! Again, he tried to calculate how many men could go alongside it without jostling each other. Three, at the very least; maybe four. Unbelievable! He watched an open carriage progressing alongside it, carried by four sturdy men. Oh yes, they didn't look as though fighting for space. A glance at its passenger reassured him that this one was of no interest to him; still, he found it difficult to take his eyes off and back toward the ruffled soil. So much sparkling jewelry. And why would a person wish to be carried along those beautifully arranged gardens? Weren't those made especially for the pleasure of walking? The other nobles who had passed by seemed to understand that.

"Don't dig around here. Just pull the weeds out."

The man who had supervised this small army of gardeners, dressed nicely in a clean cloak and sandals, unlike the rest of them, drew closer, lingering, unsure of himself. Clearly, he didn't know what to make out of the additional worker that was cast on them out of the blue and just as their day was about to end, along with the demand to work as long as necessary, into the evening if need be. Oh yes, they weren't grateful to him, those tired, sweaty people. Miztli felt a light twinge of guilt. It wasn't fair that they were made to work longer because of him and his dubious mission.

He sighed, remembering his conversation with the elderly dignitary, all dignity and cold grace.

"So this time, you carry more important communication, boy, do you?" The washed-out eyes measured him coldly, radiating an open doubt. "The Emperor himself sent you, you say?"

It proved again challenging to collect his thoughts. "Yes, he did."

"Honorable Elder." That came out curtly, a sharp reprimand.

Miztli swallowed. "Honorable Elder."

"That's better." The chilling eyes left him, came to rest upon the podium laden with papers and bowls of coals and brushes inside those. "Open the shutters wider, then bring me the message you carry. Be quick about it."

He didn't linger on purpose, but his anger kept gathering. The Emperor was much more approachable, a nicer person, insisting on no titles while dealing with important things. He was a person one actually wished to honor regardless of what the *calmecac* boys called a protocol, while this elderly noble seemed anxious to emphasize his status as opposed to this of his guest. As though he had played with ideas of ordering the noble elder about or talking to him like to an equal. Did they have time for any of this silliness?

"Did you read what is written here?" Another freezing cold inquiry.

"No."

"Can you read?"

"No."

The contemptuously twisted lips made him feel worthless. He clenched his teeth through another longer pause. This time, the man seemed to sink in his thoughts, concentrating on the task at hand probably instead of being busy with putting the unasked-for messenger down any further. A small mercy.

"The Emperor wishes you to talk to his revered sister."

Miztli just nodded. A good way of avoiding using honorific titles. No words, no need to honor anyone.

The eyes measuring him narrowed again. "You are insolent. I will let the revered person who sent you know about it." Another stony stare. "Commoners should know their place, even if persons of noble blood entrust them with special missions." The grizzled head shook. "I shall send you into the Palace, disguised. You will deliver your message and memorize everything the princess might wish to relay in return. Will you manage to do that? Last time, you were stammering and, but for the noble Jade Doll's patience, no one would have listened to what you had to say. You would have failed your Emperor and his faithful and noble servants."

"I'll remember, Honorable Elder," promised Miztli, tired of this game and aware, knowing that he depended on the old man's will now. The Emperor trusted him to return, carrying words of reply, important messages, maybe. The man who had come to instruct him after the Emperor returned to his ballgame was clear about it. Every word was to be memorized carefully, every little detail. Oh yes, it was obvious that the happenings in Tlatelolco were monitored closely now, but the dwellers of the neighboring city were not to become aware of that. Not a difficult conclusion to arrive at. And then there was this opportunity, a gods' sent gift. To be smuggled into the Palace and by the people who clearly knew how to do it, who must have done it plenty of times before; oh no, he didn't dare to count on such a stroke of luck, assuming that the royal beauty would be coming to the elderly dignitary's house again, like through the first time. Back then, the woman had come in the eye of the night, unconcerned with convention. So what was to stop her from rushing out again in order to receive her revered brother's word, this time a real one, not a faked, desperate stammering. And then how was he to sneak into the Palace? By what means? He had promised and it had been more than five dawns.

On his way toward the causeway and across it, he had racked his brains, trying to devise a plan. Maybe after the interview with the princess, somehow. Would he manage to convince her, to talk her into taking him along? Say that the Emperor wanted to receive a written word instead of verbal one? But she could have written her note from the house of her nobleman accomplice; she didn't need to bring him to the Palace in order to do that.

All those maybes and possible plans, and yet, here he was, arriving at his desired destination so easily, disguised in a perfect way. A gardener? Oh well, they needed people capable of tending the earth even in those huge sprawling *altepetl*s, didn't they? Those wonderfully vivid flowers and carefully trimmed trees, such a lavish celebration of radiant aroma and coloring, like the splendor he had glimpsed back in Tenochtitlan's Palace. No haughty nobles took care of those, digging in the fertilized soil, turning their aristocratic noses away from the buckets with human waste, the ones that were collected each morning from every house, to be carried into the fields and make the earth become richer, more generous with its fruit. The thought alone made him snicker.

Another open seat drew his attention, appearing at the far end, carried by sturdy litter-bearers. He narrowed his eyes, remembering that this was the same direction the young woman who had brought him here had disappeared quite a long time ago, sneaking him in through the back gate, drawing no unduly attention. Stripped of his clothing, left with a loincloth and little else – a somewhat forgotten sensation – and not even sandals he had grown used to through those last five dawns of *calmecac* life, he was now uncomfortably aware that this was not how one should look while strolling better parts of the city. Also, it was challenging, the need to pick up one's step, avoiding treading on especially sharp gravel or islands of broken pottery that adorned some of the alleys. Apparently, sandals made him forget how to walk properly. A bother.

Concentrating on his task, ruffling the earth but carefully, pretending more than actually hoeing, he glanced at the open palanquin again, hopeful it would carry the haughty princess. How was she intending to talk to him here? A highborn lady could not stop to chat to a commoner digging in the earth, could she?

"Don't just stare, boy!" This came from the supervising gardener, towering above him again, tense and ill-at-ease. "You can't explain your—"

Now he noticed the warriors, a whole group of those, passing by, talking in loud voices, their spears clattering. Palace guards! Aghast, he caught one of their gazes brushing past him, lingering for a heartbeat. With an effort, he took his own gaze away, making it drop toward the flattened earth. What was he to do with it? The digging stick felt slick in his palm, slippery and uncomfortable to hold, the heavy scent of flowers all around overwhelming, yet now a threat. He fought the urge to leap onto his feet.

You are here to work these gardens, his mind repeated again and again, not very convincing. *You came here to work this land. Like the rest of those digging-around people tending to those flowerbeds. You are here legally. You didn't sneak in.* Still, his back was covered with sweat and the folded note tucked in the small bag alongside with his sacred obsidian puma burned a hole in his side. What if they searched him? What if they found the message? What then?

More voices were nearing, more feet drifting past. The warriors were still there. He could sense their presence, their voices like flying missiles, words shot as though from slings. But to have one such ready at hand now. Either the wonderfully professional shooting device, his spoil from the previous adventure here, lost in the old Tlaquitoc's workshop, or at least simpler straps he was made to practice with in *calmecac*, still better devices than the ones he could lay his hands on back in the village. But for the opportunity to recover his rightful spoils. The deceitful craftsman had no right to keep it, no right whatsoever.

"Oh that pool, I don't know. It looks pretty, but the fish would be better off swimming the Great Lake."

The familiar husky voice made him jump, the thoughts of the lost sling or the nearby warriors scattering like spilled out beans. Blinking against the last of the sunlight, he tried to see through the multiple silhouettes, all those moving around forms. The palanquin, again rather an open chair, adorned with cushions and decorated embroidery, was nearing, forcing the people to edge away. The warriors mainly, as others didn't crowd the paved avenue, just strolled along. All of them but her, the Tlatelolcan girl, the force of nature, so easy to recognize, her jaunty way of moving, waving her thin arms as though determined to hasten her progress, lively and clumsy and agile at the same time – an impossible combination – pleasing the eyes in her outlandishness. He caught his breath.

"I definitely live in the wrong side of this Palace," she went on in her lovely rush that he remembered so well. "Think about this pathway, the width of it. I can lie across it and no one would have to complain and ask me to move away. Or step over me. It's *that* wide!" A giggle. "I shall try it, you know. Just to see what they do."

The bubbling flow stopped all of a sudden, cut by the gasp of her companion, a tall, beautifully dressed woman in an intricately cut *huipil* and high-soled interwoven sandals, sparkling turquoise and metal ornaments aplenty. Much gold in addition to copper in those decorations, with maybe some rare silver powder thrown in, he reflected randomly, staring at the dazzling wear, the most available sight from his observation point upon the ground, partly shadowed by the trunk of the tree and the low hedge.

"We... we better go the other way. Come by the flowerbeds."

Their followers – a few equally agitated women, maybe maids or attendants – shifted uneasily, their eyes on the nearing palanquin. The warriors turned to watch as well. He fought the urge to jump onto his feet no longer. No, it was too daunting to crouch like that and not even in the thickest of shrubs, half out and at the mercy of everyone's passing glance.

"What? Why?" From his bettered point of view, he could see Tlemilli resisting her companion's pull, not struggling to free her hand but maybe about to do so. It was easy to predict some of her reactions. Despite his mounting worry, he felt the smile blossoming. But she didn't change, not even a little bit, did she?

The palanquin was already upon them, halting its progress, pausing as though not certain as to the advisability of stopping for good. It was easy to see its bearers' visible hesitation. The tension among the strolling the path grew in proportion.

Feeling his own stomach tightening into a stone ball, he watched the woman upon the cushioned seat, unmistakable with her extraordinary beauty and the freezing quality of her gaze. The memory of Tenochtitlan Palace surfaced, the cornered sensation of being interrogated by the Emperor's mother, interrupting the conversation, so cold and cutting and threatening, so pleasant to the eye. Oh yes, there was much likeness there.

"Greetings, Honorable Sister." There was no mistaking this voice either. But did he remember its melodious lilt, the clearness of its ring, again the coldness, now more pronounced, as cutting as the winter wind. "Have you been enjoying the evening stroll?"

The woman by Tlemilli's side shivered ever so slightly. "Greetings, Honorable Sister. It's a pleasure to see you." Her voice betrayed no agitation or fear, as melodious, even if higher in tone.

"The pleasure is all mine," answered the Tenochtitlan princess, her smile positively freezing.

Amidst all this, he could sense Tlemilli beginning to turn around slowly, as though in a trance, moving with her entire body. When her eyes encountered his, they were much larger and rounder than he remembered, two huge glittering pools, unblinking.

Time stopped for a heartbeat, or maybe more – he couldn't tell. As mesmerized as she was, he stared back at her, taking in the paleness of her chiseled cheeks, and their sharp angles, more pronounced than he remembered, the wide mouth slightly open, as though it froze in the process of trying to say something, lips definite and dark red, drawing attention but for those eyes, so large, so widely spaced and tilted, like a drawing of a mystical creature. Oh yes, that was that, he decided numbly, his mind refusing to concentrate on the problem at hand – her eyes and all the rest of her, it belonged to some mystical creature out of ancient paintings, some sort of a goddess. Which one?

"I didn't know you were fond of strolling these gardens," the Tenochtitlan beauty was saying somewhere out there, outside their private circle of staring, her words muffled, reaching him but barely, bouncing off, her politeness exaggerated, at least to his ear. There were plenty of undercurrents there, oh yes.

He saw Tlemilli's eyes beginning to return to normal proportions, not turning more regular, not hers, but losing their dazed expression. The wild joy that flooded in made his own stupefied senses snap back to life. His danger signals up, mixing with most ridiculous splash of excited relief, he tried to stop her possible crying out by bringing his hands up, both of them, either imploring or ordering her to keep quiet.

It helped, if partly. Her leap toward him stopped in midair, or so it seemed, with only the upper part of her body tilting but her legs still glued to the ground. At least that. Her lips moved but no sound came. In the corner of his eye, he saw the maid who had brought him here and had gone to fetch the princess earlier hovering not far away, her pleasantly round face troubled, eyes wide, returning to the scene with the noblewomen briefly, then back to him.

"Our Palace's gardens are a lovely place to stroll." Tlemilli's companion's voice rang with perfect composure, no exaggerated politeness or hostility there, not a hint. "This near-dusk time is the best. Don't you think?"

"Yes, it is." The princess in the palanquin was nodding with matching aplomb, but her lips were pursed tight, taking some of her beauty away. "Even though the imperial wives' proper place is at their quarters and their looms, waiting for the Emperor to grace them with his visit. The most noble born among us or the less highborn ones are all restricted in the same way." The smile that flickered was small and it dripped poison. "We are lucky in one way, unlucky in another. Don't you think, sister?"

A part of his mind listened to this exchange, fascinated, noting the undercurrents. The rest of it was swept with indecision. To wait? To try and sneak away? To do what? His eyes returned to Tlemilli, noting her drawing toward him, slowly and carefully this time, no eager rushing out. The smile that tugged at the corner of her wide mouth was tiny, conspiratorial, her eyes reflecting it, flickering in delighted excitement. He felt it in his stomach, a powerful squeeze. To keep his lips from quivering back turned difficult.

"We cannot complain about our lot, Honorable Sister," the princess's adversary was saying, her tone still innocent and calm. "A woman's lot is never of her choosing. We rarely have a say in what we do, do we?"

He could feel Tlemilli's presence, so close, the warmth of her body and the brush of her velvety garment, the sleeve of her *huipil* rustling crisply, pleasant to touch but not as her skin would be. For a wild moment, he imagined pressing her to him with force.

"You came!" Her breath brushed next to his ear, tickling it. She was so very tall for a girl. "I knew you would!"

He tried to will his heart into less maddening pounding, his eyes darting around, noting the warriors, still lingering not far away, and the maids and others, so many, watching the noblewomen, listening to their pleasantries and well concealed messages or threats. Good. Tlemilli was leaning closer again.

"You should see yourself, looking so funny, all naked and covered in dirt. What are you doing here looking like that?" Her eyes flickered, so close he could see every fleck, every golden speckle in their brown depths. Her eyelashes were dark and long at their edges but strangely short in their inner parts. Was that what made her eyes look so strange? he wondered randomly, unable to take his gaze away. She was so near, as though already in his embrace, even though his hands were glued to his sides, not daring to move a fraction, not with all these people around them, the highest of the nobility and the beauty of their surroundings. And even without it. Would he dare to do... what? He didn't dare to even think about it.

"We can't talk here," he mumbled, his throat as dry as a neglected plot of land in the end of rainless moons. "I... I... Where can I find you later? Maybe... somewhere?"

She nodded most vigorously, not attempting to draw away, not even a fraction. But they'd all notice, wouldn't they? He didn't dare to look around, not anymore.

"Oh, but we do have our say in many things, little sister," someone was saying in a chilly, indifferent voice. The Tenochtitlan princess, was she still talking? Were they all?

Tlemilli was frowning thoughtfully, in the fashion he remembered too well from their Plaza adventures. It was impossible to follow her ever-changing expressions or to predict those. "I can't get out in the evenings. Not even through the wall opening." Her eyes turned dark with concentration. "But maybe in the morning. Oh yes, in the morning, I will certainly manage to get out and into the gardens. They won't watch me, and... yes, with the others out there in their *calmecac*, and me... Oh, it would be so much easier if I was allowed to go too, but... oh no!" Suddenly, her hand grabbed his, her fingers as smooth and as cold as he remembered, their touch making him shudder. "But you can't be here; it's too dangerous for you. Father, he made me tell, he wanted to know all about you, how you look, and what were you looking for out there, and... Oh!"

Her grip tightened painfully, while her other palm pressed against her own mouth, muffling the words as though trying to strangle them back in. He felt them cascading down his stomach as well, in a freezing surge. The silence around them became profound, enlivened by no additional speech. Not this of the two noblewomen, nor of anyone else, for that matter. Even the birds in the treetops seemed to muzzle their warbling. The world went unbecomingly still.

"Milli!" Tlemilli's companion seemed to come to her senses faster than the others, her voice still calm but commanding, just a little too strained. "Come here, little one. What are you doing out there by the trees?"

Tlemilli reacted by pressing his arm tighter, not about to let go. He felt their eyes, so many, boring at them. It was so eerily quiet now. He didn't dare to look around, to meet their incredulous gazes. His imagination was good enough to envision all that.

"I... I want to tell him something. I need him to do something for me!" Her words rang with surprising firmness, even though he could feel her so very tense by his side. That heartened him for some reason. Not her reckless bravery, but her plight. Like back down the Great Lake's shore, he knew he must help her out, must protect her somehow. And wasn't it his fault now?

He straightened his gaze to meet theirs, noting more passersby gathering around in an array of colorful garments and jewelry, some slowing their step, others hastening theirs courteously, tilting their necks to see better despite the attempted politeness.

"What is the meaning of this?" The Tenochtitlan princess straightened upon her cushioned seat, her forehead creasing in puzzlement, eyes flickering. When those shifted back toward her elegant converser, they had an unpleasant spark to them. "Is that your sister, Honorable Fellow Emperor's Wife? Huddling with slaves working the gardens and in the broad daylight?"

The other woman drew herself up with a start, her back, presented to them, tensing visibly, turning to stone. "My sister can speak to the servants if she wishes them to do something for her," she said stonily, with not a hint of previous cordiality, pretended or not. "Like any of us, other noblewomen, she is at liberty to do that."

The beautiful face was setting into a stony mask. "Maybe in your family it is acceptable to hold slaves' hands while asking them to do one's bidding, but it is not the custom with the royal family members. And being one such now, however temporary..." The full lips tightened again into an invisible line, taking much of its owner's beauty away in the fashion he remembered too well from the ghastly interview in the old nobleman's shed. "You would do better to extend the teaching of good manners to all your family members. Even your illustrious father can benefit from such lessons, come to think of it."

Some of the crowding nobles covered their gasps. Others looked pleased enough, the minority of the watchers. The warriors' faces were sealed masks, betraying no emotion. He could see their leading man motioning the rest, drawing away resolutely. Tlemilli's companion – could they truly be sisters; but they didn't look alike in the least – drew in a convulsive breath.

"My father is as impeccable noble as any of the Emperor's advisers," she said quietly, her voice trembling. "And so is my sister. She is an impeccable girl, with nothing to reproach her for."

"Except her recent escapades that made even our Revered Adviser roar in anger, didn't they?" The royal woman's smile didn't waver, turning yet colder, having a squashing quality to it. "There are no secrets in this Palace. And I'll tell you another thing, little imperial wife. Among true nobility, people of royal blood like our Revered Husband or myself, there are rules, certain unspoken rules, ancient customs and rituals, lines of accepted behavior, you see? Among true ancient families, people behave with a measure of true decorum. Something the newly baked elites such as your father, coming out of minor nobility circles, unaware of the true dignified ways, might wish to learn." Leaning back among her colorful cushions, the woman sighed showily, shaking her impeccable royal head. "No wonder this *altepetl* cannot measure to Tenochtitlan and the Great Capital's achievements."

That didn't go down well with the bulk of the listening crowd, but as the other woman drew another convulsive breath, biting her lower lip, Tlemilli came back to life all at once.

"Do not badmouth my sister or my father," she called out hotly, her head held high. "Tenochtitlan can teach us nothing but how to be pushy and nagging and overwhelmingly obnoxious. And crybabies too, carrying on day and night and doing nothing but complain. We don't want to learn that. Tlatelolco nobility can do without those fine arts!"

Her pale cheeks glowing dull red, the girl tossed her head yet higher, her palm still clutching his arm, tightening around it, as though seeking support. He pressed it in his turn, containing its trembling. But she was so brave, and what she said was good, even eloquent. Somehow, he didn't expect that of her, not a smooth speech.

It seemed that no one else did, judging by their expressions. They were all staring, but this time with a measure of surprised appreciation. Even the princess was gaping, even her own sister. In a corner of his mind, he felt a small surge of pride. The rest was busy with calculating their way out. How to take her away from them all?

"You are a strange little girl who understands nothing, not even the subjects and arts she is supposed to learn and understand." Tenochtitlan woman regained her ability to talk quickly enough. "Keep your thoughts to yourself, little girl, until you are much older and understand what you are talking about. If ever." The royal shoulders lifted slightly, making the exquisite bells woven from copper strings ring. "This is another lesson in good manners. Your lack of such strengthens my point."

The other woman stirred to life as quickly. "This is an unwarranted accusation. My sister spoke well and was not disrespectful. Her manners are not to be questioned."

The royal woman rolled her eyes. "Will I be forced into a debate on good manners here in the middle of the road?" she asked, bringing her perfectly groomed palm to her forehead in a showy manner, as though warding off a splitting headache. "Speaking of decorum and good manners." A light nod toward the litter bearers, who all this time stood in their place, holding the royal woman and her palanquin high above her less worthy audience. "Do proceed. I wish to enjoy the pool before the last of the light is gone." The hand came down again, indicating the maid who had brought him here. "Bring one of the slaves, that young one, to the pool as well. And hurry."

The crowding people began shifting as though awakening from a dream, breathing with relief, many of them. Were such agitated exchanges a rare thing in the Palace's gardens? he wondered numbly, still afraid to believe that it might be ending well, this entire scene, without him being dragged away by the warriors or her being scolded maybe or reprimanded or punished in any other way. It was obvious that what she did was wrong, unacceptable, from talking to him in such an open manner and in front of everyone, to picking fights with the Emperor's influential wife, her sister's equal in status or not. A glance at the other woman reinforced this conclusion. This one stood there so very pale, her gaze agitated, cornered, a beautiful woman too, but haunted, unbecomingly upset.

"Come, Milli." She motioned with her head, not moving from her previous spot, as though glued to it.

Tlemilli's hand indeed left his with readiness that disappointed him momentarily, against all logic or sense. Yet, what she did next had his heart racing again, wilder than before.

"What do you want with him?" she demanded, stepping in front of the palanquin that the sweating bearers began carrying again with obvious relief. "Where are you taking him?"

The royal woman turned her head briefly, already passing them by, her eyebrows, two perfect lines, arching. "And why would you wish to know that, girl?"

Tlemilli swallowed in a visible way. "I don't have to tell you that!" she stated, losing none of her fighting spirit. "You have no right to do something to this boy. He did nothing wrong!"

"And you are concerned with his fate, are you?" The question came out sweetly, too sweetly.

"Tlemilli!" This time, her sister headed toward them, determined.

Without noticing, Miztli found himself beside her as well, heedless of reason. "It's all right. I'm good, no trouble," he whispered urgently, straight into her ear, not caring how it might look but needing to reassure her, and to make sure no one heard his words. "I'll find you later tonight. I promise."

She seemed as though about to argue. He could feel it most clearly, reading her motions and expression as easily as some people read exclusive *amate*-paper scrolls. The realization made the warmth in his stomach spread, banishing the fear. To catch her gaze was not difficult; her eyes were seeking his anyway. A reassuring smile, willing her with his eyes, then he turned away, hurrying off toward the troubled maid and against all their stares. Behind his back, people were talking, the hum of their conversations low, delicate. No dominant female voices, no shrilling tones. He let out a held breath.

CHAPTER 7

Ahuitzotl was beaming. "Where have you been? What took you so long?"

Perching on the low wall that separated the ball court from the adjacent side of the Plaza, he looked exactly the same as on the day when she had come here asking for their help at finding the village boy, not even two market intervals ago, but a lifetime, it seemed now. So much had changed!

Back then, she had put on her best *huipil* instead of the everyday one and tried to make her hair look pretty. Still, here on the Plaza, she stuck out like a red tomato in a pile of green avocadoes, treated no better for her efforts to look respectable. While now, oh now, straight away from the marketplace and dressed accordingly, in the simplest maguey blouse and skirt, disheveled from all the running and sneaking around, eavesdropping on Tlatelolco scum, slipping through gaps in fences and huddling in prickly bushes, she didn't feel uncertain or frightened, not about to be pushed into mud and yelled at by irritable noblewomen in litters. With Necalli by her side, it felt as though she had every right to be here, on this magnificent sparkling Central Plaza, among all this grandeur and splendor. He would not let people humble her and make her feel like dirt, not him.

"She was punished too, you know," shouted Necalli, cupping his palms around his mouth to overcome the deafening clamor coming from behind the royal boy's perch. "Get down here, you climbing monkey."

As expected, Ahuitzotl made a face and didn't move a muscle.

"What are you two wandering there for?"

"But I truly must smack him one day. I must!" she heard Necalli muttering, drawing a deep breath through his widening nostrils, his lips pursed too tightly to help him with that.

She neared the wall hurriedly. "Come, Ahuitzotl. We need to talk to you."

Please, she added with her eyes, not daring to say it aloud, not with Necalli fuming by her side, getting angry with the intractable *pilli*. Such a familiar feeling. She felt her happiness welling. But it was back to their Tlatelolco adventures, it was! And did she miss it all through the dreary days of confinement and fear. Speaking of which, she would be better off hurrying for home soon. The dusk was nearing and the moment Father was back from the workshop and the baths, she'd better be there, all dutiful and nice. She pushed the nagging aspect away, pleased to see the royal boy skipping down the steeply placed stones with the agility of a feline creature.

"So did they punish you?" he asked, landing beside them with an elegant thud, breathing most evenly, as though having just stepped down the bench he had sat on before. "How?"

"You know, regular things. Not allowed to go out and all that." She shrugged, ridiculously pleased to see him. Even though only a little over a market interval passed, he looked changed, more confident and smug, less challenging than before, as though those few days had made him grow or mature. His clothes were again a celebration of colors and rich adornments, his hair arranged in an almost warriors' fashion but not quite; the shaven parts were missing.

"Girls always get it easier." The mischievous beam brought the Ahuitzotl she knew back, this challenging spark. She made a face at him. "Yes, they do," he went on, his eyes sparkling happily. "Not allowed to go out is no punishment. Ask him what he and Axolin had to endure on that first evening when we returned. You wouldn't like any of that."

"Stop bragging," interrupted Necalli, good-naturedly this time. "You didn't get any of those joys either. Royal *pilli*s never do."

But the boy's eyes glinted in pure contentment this time. "Can you imagine the future Emperor of Tenochtitlan and all provinces and tributaries and whatnot getting a stick to his backside. Not likely."

"Future Emperor of Tenochtitlan? Wake up from this dream!" Necalli's outburst of roaring laughter had a clear ring of authenticity to it, so much happy amusement. "It's not good for you to sleep with your eyes open."

"Shut up!" As expected, now Ahuitzotl was puffing up like an angered turkey, his good humor momentarily forgotten. "I don't need to fall asleep or wake up. I will be the Emperor! The most remembered too. Like my brother, or even better. And you, you will..." The angry flow of words stumbled for a moment, rather for lack of air than the lack of appropriately dreadful threat, Chantli surmised. "You will be nothing but a common warrior with a stupid club. Like the most dirty peasant. With no captives and no warriors' lock!"

Necalli was making faces but toward the end of the spirited tirade, his derisively twisting lips began pursing angrily. Hastily, she stepped between them.

"Oh come, you two. Stop that. Can't you spend one single heartbeat without yelling at each other? Please! We have important things to talk about. Stop that!" To order them into better behavior felt wrong, out of place here in the grandeur of the Great Plaza, and with her looking no better than a marketplace seller of food. She glanced around uneasily, the clamor behind the wall of the ball court shifting but not showing signs of subduing. Her confidence plummeted some more. "Please?"

They both glanced at her briefly, then at each other, then at her again.

"Oh well." Necalli's shrug was brief and one sided.

Ahuitzotl turned his face away, his lips twisting in a ridiculously similar manner, mirroring the *calmecac* boy's challenging expression. Was this why they never got along without twenty altercations being exchanged as they went, she wondered, suddenly amused. They were too much alike in their nature, their attitudes, their tempers. Boys!

"Listen," she went on, addressing Ahuitzotl's stubbornly half-turned profile, encouraged by her realization, feeling so much more mature and sophisticated than them. "There are things concerning Tlatelolco that we ran into this afternoon, Necalli and I, things that maybe your brother, the Emperor, needs to hear, you see? You can talk to him, can't you?"

"I can talk to my brother whenever I like," was her answer, muttered through a stubborn frown.

"Then you must listen to what happened out there on the marketplace."

He shrugged sullenly in response. "What happened on the marketplace?"

"We ran into that man from under the causeway, remember? The one who had captured us, you and me."

That got his attention at once. "That filthy piece of excrement? But he was dead!"

"Apparently, he wasn't."

"People don't die that easily," contributed Necalli, over his own spell of anger as well. Another similar treat to both of them. She hid her grin. "I hit him with a pitiful training sword and I wasn't even aiming to kill." He grimaced, as though brushing away an accusation. "It was dark and I was in a hurry. You two were making pitiful noises."

"We were not!"

They cried it out in unison this time, causing Necalli to fling his arms in a mocking defense. "Oh no, don't turn that united front against me." His eyes twinkled, difficult to resist. "I take it back!"

That boy! She fought down her smile, then turned to Ahuitzotl, anxious to divert him from another possible outburst.

"Anyway, this man and some other of his fellow smugglers, they are running around our marketplace, stirring up trouble, meeting with people. We happened to overhear one such meeting." She glanced at Necalli, surprised that he let her talk, not attempting to interrupt and take the lead as he always did, but he seemed to be away, deep in thought. "They talked about meeting other Tlatelolcans on the road to... to... What was this town called?"

Necalli frowned. "Acachinanco. This scum was to go now, or

tomorrow at dawn, and wait, presumably for another scum, on the road to Acachinanco. They spoke about Toltitlan as well, and even about sending someone to Chalco, but that our local smugglers didn't like, lazy corpses that they are. Too much walking or sailing, I presume."

She remembered them huddling in those prickly bushes, frightened and uncomfortable but thrilled by being together with him again, and even with their enforced closeness. She hoped he didn't mind any of that as well. He didn't look troubled on that count, did he? And oh, but was it good to feel his arms around her, pressing her close, enveloping, protecting. He wouldn't let the smugglers harm them again. He wouldn't even let any of them grab her arm like back on the marketplace, hurting it with the tightness of the grip.

Back then, swamped by those feelings and musings, riding the cloud of euphoria, she didn't truly listen to the plotting men, and so saw the girl appearing from behind their backs before he did. Then it was her turn to act, to try and reassure the frightened little thing, and thus, before the girl started screaming – evidently not reassured but only terrified into a brief spell of silence – they were squeezing out and away, to run down the pathways until their chests threatened to burst, heading here, into the more respectable parts of the city and then the glorious one through the allies only he seemed to know. She had lost her way in the maze he made them zigzag through too quickly to even try to keep count of turned corners and prettily paved roads.

"We must go to the Plaza," he had panted when they had paused briefly, both doubled over but in the best of spirits, their smiles smug. "Find Ahuitzotl... tell him about these people and their prospective meeting and what not."

"Where is this Acachinanco place, anyway?" she breathed in her turn, straightening up with an effort, eyeing their surroundings, vividly colored walls separating the paved alley from the evidently rich dwellings, many two stories high.

"What?"

"That road to Acachinanco they were talking about? Where is it? And Toltitlan? I think I heard that name before, but I don't know where it is."

"On the mainland," he said absently, scanning their surroundings, not the pretty walls and pavement, but the people hurrying past them. Making sure they weren't followed? she wondered, cursing herself for not thinking of that possibility as well. "The western side of our Great Lake and to the north. The Tepanec side."

That impressed her. "How do you know all this?"

He made a face. "They are hammering it into your head when you are in *calmecac*. Everything there is to know, and then some more. History, the lay of the land, laws; you name it and they make us learn it. And you better remember it all, or else." His shrug seemed to be laced with pretended indifference, apologetic in a way. "Well, one does need some of this knowledge. How can one lead warriors on campaigns not knowing even his own countryside and what towns are populating it and where they are located?" He winked. "Think about where such a leader will get his people to. Wandering Tlatelolco swamps, eh?"

The sensation of pride in him and his knowledge – but *telpochcalli* boys would never know something like that – welled. "You'll be a great leader! No splashing in Tlatelolco swampy shores for you."

He shrugged with one shoulder, clearly well pleased. "We'll see about that." His smile was so wide, so unguarded, it took her breath away, the open affection it held. Oh yes, he cared about what she thought, he did! He liked her believing in him. Oh, Coatlicue, mother of the gods! Before her heart went off its regular tempo, his grin widened and turned mischievous. "Until it happens, I predict there is more splashing in those particularly muddy waters in store for all of us. Eh?" Then he sobered again. "Let us hurry. Find Ahuitzotl, tell him to let his brother know."

"His brother the Emperor?" She felt the wave of misgivings returning in force. She didn't belong even in this pretty neighborhood, let alone out there on the Central Plaza, trying to talk to the Emperor. "We can't possibly bother the Emperor with our strange tales!"

"We won't. Ahuitzotl will bother him. The little beast has his ways."

"But the Emperor?" she kept repeating, feeling silly. "We can't. He is the Emperor!"

"That is a brilliant argument, Chantli." He laughed in her face, suddenly unbearably smug and haughty, another familiar treat, not missed at all, this one. "He is the Emperor, yes, the ruler of Tenochtitlan and all its provinces and tributaries, besides those who are trying to make trouble, like that filthy neighboring *altepetl*. He is interested in all this, believe me. Our Emperor is a great man and not too haughty to listen to all sorts of people. Witness your workshop apprentice." Again, he sobered, glancing at the thickening dusk. "Come, let us hurry. We'll find Ahuitzotl, tell him about this Acachinanco business, see what he thinks. The Emperor is training at the ball court and the little beast is sure to be there, invited to watch, if not to play." A chuckle. "I wouldn't put it past him to try and push his skinny ten-summers-old carcass straight into the Emperor's and his warlords' game. He won't be too shy to do that."

She shook her head at the memories, concentrating on the boys and their lively discussion full of too many unfamiliar names.

"Try to find the way to let your brother know," Necalli was saying, an urgency in his voice. "As soon as you can. Maybe before the next dawn, eh?" He wrinkled his nose in a somewhat embarrassed manner. "I know it's not much of a hitch to go by, but I swear it's important. It is! I feel it in my bones. This man from under the causeway and the rest of the Tlatelolcan smugglers. Even if we didn't manage to recognize any of them, they were Tlatelolcan smugglers. One of them tried to grab Chantli back in the marketplace, didn't he?" His eyes leapt to her, glimmering with excitement, with this lovely enthusiasm of his. So handsome!

She just nodded, bereft of words.

Ahuitzotl's face darkened at once. "Was this the man from under the causeway?" he demanded, very indignant.

She shook her head. "No, another one. Skinny type, neglected. Clearly some scum from the wharves. I didn't know who he was, but he seemed to recognize me for some reason."

To her tiny twinge of relief, Necalli stepped closer, standing next to her, protective. "You must stay at home for the next few days, avoid going to the marketplace or anywhere around there and the wharves."

She puzzled over this statement. "And how am I to do that when I'm being sent to the markets to buy things? Who would do this instead of me?"

Now they both stared at her. "There are slaves to do that."

"Ours twisted her ankle."

They still stared.

"You must have more than one slave," suggested Necalli somewhat helplessly, watching her in a wary manner.

She took her gaze away, embarrassed rather than incensed. He must think her family to be the worst of the commoners.

Ahuitzotl was the one to break the awkwardness of the silence. "My brother is still on the court. He didn't look in a hurry to return to the Palace. Was too happy to be able to get out and play." He rubbed his hands gleefully. "I'll try to catch him for a talk right away. Wait for me here, both of you. Or out there by the tribunes. Don't go anywhere."

His words lingered as his prettily embroidered cloak disappeared behind the corner of the low wall. They exchanged glances, puzzled.

CHAPTER 8

Citlalli's hands were trembling as she brought them to tuck an invisible tendril back among the elaborately done multitude of tresses.

"Why did you to do this, Milli?" she demanded, her voice having an unusually shrill note to it. "Why did you pick an argument with her?"

The last of the sun was sparkling off the polished statues adorning the wide alley, coloring those in richer hues. Tlemilli studied them, her heart still pumping. "She is such a poisonous snake, so pompous and presumptuous, so... so malicious! I didn't think she could be so nasty. She has no right to talk to you like that!"

Citlalli's lips twisted unpleasantly. "She can talk to me in any manner she likes, and my only way to counter that is to be polite and well mannered, to let her rudeness bounce off me, to push her into showing her true colors, true lack of dignity, her illustrious ancestry or not." The manicured fingers were tearing at the pins that held the tresses in place. "Half the Palace was listening to us!" Again, the shrill tone.

Tlemilli narrowed her own eyes, perturbed. "It was not half the Palace," she offered, feeling as though called upon to say something. "Barely ten, twenty people. Slaves most of them, servants." That brought her thoughts back to her own agitated worry. "She had no right to take that boy away like that and for no reason. He did nothing wrong!"

Citlalli's eyes were back upon her, narrow with fury, her hands jumping in the air, leaving the harassed pins and tresses alone.

"Until you threw yourself all over him, yes, he did nothing wrong." Her cheeks sporting unhealthy red, the young woman glared at Tlemilli, positively glowing. "Why did you do this? Why? It was most inappropriate, out of place, unseemly. It gave that poisonous snake such a delightfully easy excuse to spread her venom, to sink her fangs in!" The eyes were slitting into as thin lines as the lips were. "That's the same boy who got you in trouble back at the contest, isn't it? That's why you went to even greater lengths at making a fool out of both of us, surprising even the haughty Tenochtitlan snake into a mere stare. A barefoot naked slave, Tlemilli? Is that the best you could do? To throw your affection at a slave, land him into trouble with public displays of it, then yell about the unfairness of it at the top of your voice, diving into arguments with the Emperor's wife about it?" The embroidered cotton rose and fell along with its owner's angrily drawn breaths, such agitation atypical to noble Palace dwellers, let alone Citlalli. "Even the slave felt how inappropriate it was, trying to calm you down. Even that lowly boy."

"He is not a slave," muttered Tlemilli, hating to be reprimanded by the only person she loved and respected, hating the truth in her sister's words. "He is not naked and not barefoot. He was dressed well enough back on the Plaza, and he was no one's slave back then." She shrugged, addressing the easiest of issues. "I don't know what he did here and in such a state, but I'm sure he has a good explanation, and but for the fat poisonous snake, I would have heard it all by now." She bit her lips stubbornly. "He promised to come back and find me and he did this. That is why he was here now, disguised. Disguised! How else could he sneak into the Palace? They wouldn't just let him in." The brilliance of this explanation made her feel better. Of course he had to disguise himself, and he knew what he had been doing. He would find the way out of the Tenochtitlan snake's clutches. But she still needed to try and help him out. Citlalli was right on one count. It was her pouncing on him like that that exposed him and she needed to do something about it. "I'll try to find them, see where she has taken him."

A hand wrapping around her arm startled her. "Stop that

nonsense at once!" Citlalli stared at her wide eyed, her open shock overcoming the previous unusual bout of anger. "Milli, stop talking nonsense. You will go back to your quarters and you will put it all out of your head and just hope that the Emperor's Chief Wife doesn't try to use your silliness against any of us. Or that no one else who was present decides to sniff out this story." The grip on her arm tightened, not hurting but relaying the urgency of its message. "You must listen to me in this, little one. You must keep away from it all, this side of the Palace, the Emperor and his wives, and our father. Just keep away from it. And most of all," again the peering gaze, anxious, openly imploring, "keep away from this dubious boy. If there is more to him than the naked slave's appearance, then it's even more imperative to keep away from him. Maybe..." The once-again narrowing gaze shifted, turned thoughtful. She watched Citlalli's teeth sinking into her perfectly full lower lip. "Maybe Noble Jade Doll's behavior in this aspect has nothing to do with you. Maybe she needed to talk to this boy anyway, and if it is so..." Another scrutinizing glance, still deep in thought but concentrating rapidly, measuring her. "What did he tell you that made you change your mind? What did he whisper in your ear?"

The sense of uneasiness returned, just like back at the alley, the sensation of being out of her depth, an annoying feeling.

"He told me that he can handle it," she said slowly, for some reason reluctant to relate his words now, but not knowing how to avoid that. "He said that he is not in trouble and that he'll find me tonight. Again, that is. He had found me and but for the filthy snake..." The words trailed off under her sister's incredulous gaze. She tried to gather her senses. "He is not bad and not involved in anything. In anything connected to this Palace, that is. Back in the city, he was involved in something, yes, but it has nothing to do with anything here, your Noble Jade Genitalia, or anyone else really, not the Emperor or Father..."

Again, the words began to die away in an annoyingly helpless manner. But he had everything to do with Father, he did! Back on the day of the contest and with those Tenochtitlan boys whom Father was beating down upon the shore, and him readying to use that sling in order to save them. Did he mean to shoot his missile at Father? She didn't ask herself that before. Why didn't she?

Her heart racing again, she tried to take her gaze away from her sister's scrutiny, needing time all of a sudden, time to think, time to understand. Oh yes, yes, he was so very afraid of Father back on the Plaza too, shooting terrified glances, running around in a panic, with the fat Tenochtitlan turkey seeking him with her eyes as well, signaling even, or so it seemed. Oh yes, she had noticed all that before her curiosity had made her leave the dais, and after they had been together, she had forgotten all about it. No, she did ask him, she did, but he didn't answer and she had been too busy enjoying the unexpected freedom, enjoying his company.

"What, little one? What are you thinking?"

She took a step back, freeing her hand without noticing it. "I... I must go. I... I will..." It wasn't easy to avoid Citlalli's attempt to recapture her arm. She had to jump quite a few steps away in order to do that.

"Where are you going? Milli!"

But she just waved at her sister, then turned around and rushed back down the alley. "I'll tell you later. I must..."

There was no time to explain, not now. The dusk was setting in firmly, and if she wasn't back in her quarters by the time it was dark, they would be sending servants to look for her, alarming Father's wives or, mighty deities, Father himself, somehow. He was too busy to keep an eye on his numerous daughters and their upbringing, but of late, he wasn't too busy for her in particular, and his wives knew it, nosy fowls that they were. Oh yes, they knew all about her transgressions.

Her heart beating fast, she forced her legs into slowing her step, the rare passersby, mostly busily hurrying servants with baskets and trays, glancing at her, puzzling. At this time of the day, so near the night, respectable noblewomen were in their rooms, lazing around, enjoying their evening snacks.

Well, not all of them, she thought, clenching her teeth, while listening to the voices coming from the pool. The fat Tenochtitlan fowl was out there, harassing that boy, asking him questions maybe. Questions about what? What did he do for these people? How was he involved? And on what side?

For the first time, she wondered about it. He had nothing to do with Tenochtitlan, did he? He lived somewhere here in Tlatelolco, maybe in some remote parts, remote enough not to know his way around the Plaza or the shores. And yet, the boys he was determined to free from Father's hold were Tenochtitlan *pillis*; everyone said that. And the annoying girl who kept nagging on him back by the shore, was she from Tenochtitlan too? And what if he…

She pushed the disquieting thought away. No, he wasn't doing anything wrong or harmful. He wouldn't! Oh, but did he look funny just now, with nothing but a loincloth and his hands and arms smeared with earth, and his chest so broad, glistening with sweat. A breathtaking sight, straight away from Tlaco's stories. A warrior, a hero on a rescue mission, too busy to care for appearances such as appropriate clothing. Not looking a simple commoner like the rest of the slaves around him, digging in the flowerbeds. No, not him! Warrior-like, that was how he looked, warrior-like and handsome. Also, he had been dressed properly back on the Plaza. Not as richly as the Palace's dwellers, but he did have this cloak and shoes – admittedly, very cheap-looking shoes, with no decorations and not even closed on the heel, but still. No, he wasn't just a commoner. He must have been more than that!

Knowing the royal side of the Palace less than the other wing, she slowed her step once again, reaching the spot where the previous scene had taken place. No gardeners spread in the dirt or under the trees and the flowerbeds now, and no quarrelsome nobles such as herself or the filthy Emperor's wife. Good. The sounds from the pool came through muffled. No voices of people laughing or chattering, but the regular sounds of water and its surroundings, the trees and the breeze, and the late birds still fussing, preparing for the night. As always, it soothed her, made her think of the forests near Smoking Mountain, the vastness and freedom that must surround it. It must have sounded just like that.

Another quick glance around, and she slipped between the flowerbeds and into the shimmering semidarkness of the trees, her mind calculating. Straight line, then a sharp turn to her left. That should bring her to the other side of the pond, or so she hoped. The sounds should guide her.

To kneel in the muddy earth spotted with flowers that spread all around the pretty pool with its handsome mosaic made him feel incredibly awkward. The flowerbed he pretended to attend was heavily scented, making his head ache.

The woman had made herself comfortable on the elegantly glittering step, watching the slick fish darting near the edge, waiting to be fed, maybe. It was so very uncomfortable to face her from the corner of his eye, to stay where he was despite the demanding questioning, following her instructions. It made sense for her to sit there on the edge of the pond leisurely, as though enjoying the view and the peacefulness of the abandoned place, and for him to work on unobtrusively, as though busy with his important task of weeding the flowers. Still, the challenging, almost hostile interrogation caught him unprepared, made him wish to face his possible enemy. Was the woman an enemy now?

"What were the exact words my brother used? Exact words!"

He took a deep breath, the evening breeze making him chilly, cold upon his sweaty back. "The Emperor, he told me to bring the message, the piece of paper. He said to find you and give you this, the paper that I gave you. He said to find you and... and talk to you, to listen to your words. Your messages, that is. He used the word 'messages'."

"Did he tell you to look up despicable Teconal's daughters, any of this disgusting brood?" That came out in a swish, like a shot arrow.

He said nothing, desperate to collect his thoughts, which were scattering badly, like spilled beans.

"Did he?"

"No, he did not." He marveled at the sound of his voice, so even, so tranquil. Inside his head it felt like a storm in an open field, with pieces of dry earth twirling and swirling in the groaning air.

"Then what is it? What did the ugly, skinny little snake want from you? Why were you talking to her as though you knew her?"

He clenched his teeth tight, the storm intensifying, darkening with anger. Oh yes, he remembered that same resentment when Chantli was talking about *her* in the same way. To swallow his words back and say nothing became an effort.

"Well?"

"It has nothing to do with the Emperor or anyone." Still this expressionless voice. Where was it coming from?

Even with his back to the woman, he could feel her stiffening with anger. "You will answer my questions, commoner, and you will do it with appropriate humbleness." The cutting words, as sharp as obsidian arrowheads, held an open threat. "Unless you wish to be brought before this same Teconal, or maybe my husband, the Emperor of Tlatelolco, with an accusation of spying on our city hanging above your head. How long will you survive, do you think? Longer than the first time?"

His heart was making strange leaps inside his chest, fluttering against his ribs in no particular order. To draw another deep breath became a necessity. "The Emperor sent me to deliver you his message and to bring any words you may wish to send him back. I did as he told me."

Now even his words were organizing too neatly. He wondered about it briefly, the sound of his last phrase. Like back in the Emperor's audience. Was it Tlemilli's magic again? For a wild moment, he considered springing to his feet and running away, to look her up before fleeing this accursed Palace and city, never to return.

"My brother may not know that you've been conversing with the enemy. Does he? Did he ask you to seek out that meddlesome, ugly little snake and give her messages too?"

This time, he did spring to his feet, turning to face the woman, unable to stay in his previous pose, prudence or not, not anymore, hating the sight of the beautiful face, the line of its pursed mouth repulsive, the nasty spark of the well-defined eyes adding to the unattractiveness. Speaking of ugliness!

"She is not an ugly little snake!" he hissed, the movement in the corner of his eye distracting but not entirely, his mind processing it somehow, despite the splashing wave of a red-hot fury. The maids and the litter bearers, he knew, without the need to glance at them. Ordered to keep at a respectable distance, they evidently did not take their eyes off their noble charge. Well, he didn't mean to harm this woman, only to run away from her poisonous presence. He took a deep breath, trying to calm the mad racing of his heart. "I came to deliver you the message the Emperor asked me to. I did as I've been told. Tlemilli has nothing to do with it." The thought rushed through his mind, making his stomach freeze. "She is not to be harmed. She... she has nothing to do with it."

The woman's eyes slitted into near disappearance. "You are telling me what to do, you filthy, naked, foul-smelling commoner? Oh, but my brother could not have sent such an impudent, ill-mannered, insolent peasant to me. It's all a ruse, a sham. It's my enemies' doing!" Her voice climbed to a shrill height. "I will have you taken away by the Palace's guards. I will have you executed like the last of the criminals. I will—"

He didn't stay to listen to any more shrieks, the burly litter carriers bearing on him, blocking the pathway or even just the vacant ground under the trees and beyond the terraces, so perfectly groomed and untouched, a last resort. His instincts taking over, he jumped over the low border, intending to cross the pool by running or swimming—it didn't matter. Just to get away from that woman and the unreasonableness of it all.

The touch of the cool water refreshed him, but the momentarily good feeling didn't last. Shallower than he thought, the slippery stones of the floor had him fighting for balance, crushing against prickly reeds, breaking them while scratching his limbs, the ducks scampering away, fluttering their wings in real panic.

As panicked as they were, he scrambled back to his feet, water dripping into his eyes, blinding him. The other side of the pool blurred not far away, not the farther edge but still a haven. He could not stay splashing in the exclusive pond, among the ducks and the fish until the Palace's guards arrived. The royal woman stopped yelling, but the stunned silence that came from the side he had left was even more discouraging. The servants were the only ones to chatter in high-pitched, agitated shouts.

Grabbing the nearest slab with the glittering mosaic, he pulled himself out, throwing his body over the slippery edge, paying no attention to its cutting touch. The pieces of glassy stone took pleasure at tearing at his skin, but he hurled himself upward and away, charging into the beckoning darkness, all amok. Just to get away from there! This place had no rules and no reason.

Behind his back, the voices were raising again, female voices. The wild suspicions surfaced, but he dove deeper into the grove, desperate to find the way toward the wall, any part of it. He was not a good climber, but the wall he had seen while passing the back gates on his way here did not look foreboding.

He tried to make his mind work. The haughty princess, what would she do? Call for the Palace's guards and point at the place where he had disappeared? Then they'd be tracking his steps, but if he had gone over the wall by that time, and if no one was there, and if—too many "ifs"!

He slowed down a little, trying to listen to his senses, to decide the possible location of the city out there, his only way of escape. How much time did he have? How long would this woman's servants take to reach the warriors, alerting them, making them chase him? And then what? Another threat of a court, a trial, an execution? But for what charges this time? And what if she was lying, bluffing like old Tlaquitoc did?

His mind cleared a little, weighing the possibilities. If put back in this dreadful Teconal's hands, to be tortured for information, he would indeed be forthcoming with plenty of it this time, much more than he could have yielded when first falling into this man's hands. But then he would be implicating the haughty Tenochtitlan princess as well, wouldn't he? Would she take this possibility into account before alarming the guards, making them chase him?

The thought made him slow his mad racing, look around more

carefully, shivering in the strengthening breeze, his hair dripping water, his loincloth soaked. The steady hum came from his left, the dim flickering of torches. The Palace! He darted deeper under the cover of the trees. So peaceful there, so quiet. An opportunity to relax, to think, to calculate his way out. Or try to do so. Over the wall and toward the causeway, but carefully out there as well, with the smugglers and other criminal element, so many involved and waylaying, serving this same Teconal. And then back to Tenochtitlan? What would he do there? He could not come to the Emperor with the tale of his aristocratic sister, the recipient of his messages, yelling and screaming, accusing him of every sin possible, setting Tlatelolcan warriors hot on his heels. The Emperor wouldn't be taking such a report kindly. And then what? What if he'd grow as angered, as indignant over his possible ties with the enemy? But Tlemilli was no enemy. She had helped him and he just wanted to find her and talk to her, to keep his promise, to enjoy her company, maybe. She was happy to see him. That much was obvious. To the Palace's nobility too, the haughty princess ahead of them all. Oh mighty deities!

The night insects were busy crawling around his wet, muddied feet. The sandals would be of help now. But had he grown used to this sort of wear!

He tried to banish the insistent mosquitoes, their buzzing annoying, interfering with his ability to think. Or to listen, for that matter. Were those footsteps? The rapid flapping, not even, not monotonous, the soft thumping upon the ground, hurried, agitated, unsure of themselves. No warriors these, and not men chasing someone. He peeked out carefully, his heart going disturbingly still.

Her silhouette was difficult to mistake, her slender, angular shoulders, the thin arms swaying as she went, as though helping her progress, not about to bottle her natural impatience. He remembered her running down the hill, so cumbersome and funny, and yet so determined, not about to give up. The warm wave was back, washing his insides. To intercept her took him only a few hurried steps, a hand held out, demanding to keep silent. Surprisingly, she complied, turning to face him with an admirable alertness, all senses and ears, animal-like.

"You got away," she breathed, leaning too close, her face nearly brushing against his, almost of the same height as he was when standing on her toes. Then her nose wrinkled in the funniest of ways. "What's this smell? Why are you all wet?"

He motioned her to keep quiet. "It's a long… long story," he whispered. "But I must get away from here, from this Palace. Do you know of a way to… to reach the wall, somehow?"

Her giggle was satisfactorily quiet. "Just like back on the Plaza, eh?" Then she sobered. "On our side of the Palace, it'll be easier. No one guards us too closely." A resolute motion of her head, leader-like and decisive, moved the dark air. "Come."

Indeed, just like back on the Plaza, he reflected, amused now more than panicked. But did she form a habit of appearing when he needed her most, her earlier pouncing on him and in front of the haughty princess notwithstanding. This was what actually landed him in trouble with the easily upset recipient of his message, but there was no point in thinking about it. Not now. Tlemilli was Tlemilli, living by different laws, and hadn't he been determined to find her anyway?

"Who is after you now?" she was asking, leading their way through the darkness, walking invisible paths, sure of herself, more so than out there in the city. "The fat fowl?"

He nodded.

Her snort was light, barely heard. "You said you were not in trouble when she dragged you away."

He shrugged. "I thought I wasn't."

A brief spell of silence had her slowing her step, studying him through the darkness. "What happened? What did she want with you?"

To roll his eyes felt like the best of courses. "Things. It doesn't matter. She is insane! And…" He swallowed, his stomach tightening in no pleasant way. "You must keep away from her. She really hates you, and… and she thinks you are involved, involved in something. In all those politics. And… and you must keep away from it all, and her."

She had stopped long before his heated tirade trailed off,

melting into the chilliness of the early night, leaning too close again, all eyes. "And you? How are you involved?"

"I..." He tried to look elsewhere, finding it impossible to tear his eyes off hers, her face outlined faintly, the sharpness of its angles softer in the darkness but still so very definite, unsettling and pleasing at the same time, a peculiar mask fashioned from obsidian or turquoise, a material so very difficult to work with, hence the edges. Like his precious talisman. His fingers wrapped around the small leather bag, feeling it out, encouraged by its touch.

"You didn't tell me back on the Plaza or down the shore. There was no time. But you must tell me now. You promised, remember?" Her gaze didn't steer, holding his, eyes huge and unblinking, trustful. "My sister thinks that I should keep away from you. She thinks you may be dangerous, working for that Tenochtitlan snake, maybe. But she is wrong, isn't she? You wouldn't do something like that. You are not against us, even if Father did something bad, treat you or your friends badly. You wouldn't turn against us because of that. You wouldn't help that Tenochtitlan snake. I know you wouldn't."

Oh, but she wasn't even asking. Half stating, half pleading, peering at him from too close a proximity, her breath warm upon his face, the gentlest of gusts.

"Father can be harsh sometimes, and he is scary at times, yes; but he has the best of our people's interest in his heart. He wants our side, our island to be independent and strong, as important and powerful as Tenochtitlan is, or maybe even more so." A brief smile twisted her lips, the old familiar mischief, gone again almost before noticed. "We can do it, you see? We can. Tlatelolco is as good as Tenochtitlan, better in some things. We aren't lazy or cowardly or unworthy. We deserve to be as powerful. More so! Don't you see it?" Again the smile, tearing in its openness and sincerity. "Tenochtitlan has all the provinces, so many towns and *altepetls* under their rule. Them and their allies from Texcoco and Tlacopan. They wouldn't join our war against them. But we don't need them. We are not a provincial town. We are their equals, and we can be better than them. That's what Father is trying to achieve. Don't you see it? It's a good cause, even if sometimes he does not pursue it especially nicely. Don't you agree?"

He was staring at her, mesmerized, his skin crawling in the most pleasant of ways, covered in goose-bumps, the pouring words caressing, making him wish to close his eyes and let her speak on without listening or needing to answer. As long as she stayed that close and kept looking at him like that, with so much trust and affection, so anxious to convince. To convince him of what? It didn't matter. Only the night mattered, and her nearness, and this all-prevailing sense of tranquility. That magic again.

Without thinking, his hand reached out and touched her face, curiously confident, as though knowing what it had been doing. It was so close anyway, and he needed to make sure she was real, not about to disappear in the mists of the night, melt there and leave, taking the spellbinding sensation away.

When his palms took hold of her shoulders, acting on their own, with no consideration to his will, it puzzled him for a fraction of a heartbeat, this confidence. But what was he doing? She was so pleasant against him, warm and smooth and pliant, curiously fitting, as though made to be held just like that. If only she kept talking. However, the breath of warm air on his face stopped abruptly together with the flow of her words. Only her eyes remained, wide open and dazed, breathless with expectation, still unguarded, still trustful. It made his head spin and his lips do something wild.

She tasted of sweetmeats, he discovered, something sweetish and bitter, or maybe spicy or hot. He didn't know, didn't care. The lightning like at the fiercest of thunderstorms was on, keeping his senses occupied, vitalized, acutely aware, animated. The fact that she didn't wince or pull away but kept absolutely still, her body pressing very close but her lips not reacting, letting his explore on their own, didn't help. It left him powerful and confused at the same time, certain in his demands, his right to hold her like that, but afraid. What if he scared her with this… this strange thing? What if she ran away, never to return?

The thought made the thunderstorm subdue all at once. But for her pressing so close, leaning against him, he would have jumped backwards. As it was, all he could do was to back away with his head alone. A silly motion. He could see it in her eyes, the puzzled inquiry, the frown as they opened abruptly, their bewilderment on display. Had she closed her eyes earlier? Had he? He couldn't even try to recollect.

It was difficult to tear his eyes off hers again, but just as he began to feel irritated, not knowing what to do or say, her entire face crinkled with laughter. Just like that. One moment mesmerized, or puzzled, or even about to get angry as well; the next this mischievous giggling, so typical, so out of place, like back on the Plaza or down the shore, impossible to anticipate.

"You just kissed me," she breathed into his face, beaming, her entire being radiating nothing but mischief, making him wish to laugh as well, taking misgivings away. "You did!"

"Maybe," he said, holding her tight, comfortable now, less afraid.

"Do it again!" This time, she looked like a child shown a trick, a toddler tossed in the air, squealing with fright, then demanding more. Not very enticing, but he felt like reaching for her lips again anyway, regardless of her demands, suddenly certain that the sensation of the thunderstorm would be back, as breathtaking as before, unable to fight the temptation.

Indeed, it had, and when her lips reacted, soft and welcoming, demanding in their turn, he felt the world around them going into a wild spin. But for them clutching each other, they would have fallen, he knew, not even trying to make sense of it all, swept with the wild current, letting it carry him away and into the wonderful unknown.

Out of breath, they stared at each other, panting, not laughing anymore. Her eyes were enormous in the sharpness of her pale face, so clearly visible, even in the moonless dark, staring at him with wonder. It made his head spin anew. But he needed to tear his eyes off hers. That would solve part of the problem. He needed to think, to make his mind work, yet it was impossible with her in his arms and looking at him like that, plain impossible.

"I need to catch my breath," she whispered in the end, pulling away and thus solving his problem, even if inadvertently. Which left him disappointed somehow.

He busied himself with an attempt to rearrange his scant clothing. Too scant. Now he wished to have that cloak he had left at the old nobleman's house out there in the prestigious part of the Tlatelolco neighborhoods, close to the Plaza and the Palace. The memory served to dampen his mood even further. But what would he tell that noble Tepecocatzin, or the Emperor himself later on? Oh mighty deities!

She was looking at him closely, frowning now. "What?"

"Nothing," he muttered, embarrassed by it all. "I... I'm sorry. I..."

Her face fell and she took a step back, bumping her shoulder against the dark silhouette of a tree. "It's the kiss. You didn't like it!"

"What?" Now it was his turn to stare at her, forgetting his brooding.

Shrugging, she turned away, her eyes boring into the ground, stubbornly at that.

"Tlemilli..."

She shrugged again, with one shoulder, like an offended child. The last of his misgivings petered off, replaced with a wave of amused confidence, such an unfamiliar feeling until meeting her.

"Stop that, you silly one," he said, taking hold of her shoulders, turning her around forcefully if gently, making her face him. "You talk crazy things."

A light push under her chin, his fingers lingering there, relishing the sensation, everything about her so pleasing, delightful to touch. Her eyes persisted at looking downward, even when the rest of her face couldn't. That made him laugh.

"You are the wildest thing I've ever met. Wilder than an ocelot and crazier than a coyote with a thorn in its paw. And as unpredictable as a monkey."

That made her giggle, eyes still persistent, going out of their way in order not to look up. "So many animals. What else?"

"A squirrel," he went on, pleased with his success. "A chatty squirrel."

"Oh!" Now her gaze leapt upwards, narrowing with ever-changing expressions. "All that? A chatty squirrel and a crazy monkey? Well, then you, then you are…" Her lips pursed and the wideness of her forehead furrowed like a wrinkled blanket. "You are a close-mouthed lizard. Yes, that!" she called out triumphantly, then pressed her palm to her mouth, looking around hastily.

For a heartbeat, they held their breaths, listening, the wind moaning stronger now, rustling in the nearby trees, muffling the hum of the outside life, the clamor a large body of people always created, however distant. It was difficult to believe they were still in the city, let alone the Palace, the imperial dwelling.

"Yes, you are that," she repeated, now in a dramatic whisper. "A lizard, sneaking around, popping up everywhere, telling nothing." Snuggled in his arms now, she shifted, then looked up again, more difficult to see in the hiding moonlight. "I never saw a coyote or a monkey, let alone a jaguar or something of the sort. Squirrels too. Are they as chatty as people are?"

He was hard put not to giggle, even though his thoughts were again scattering in inappropriate ways, his body trying to take the lead again, her nearness distracting. "Yes, they are chatty. Like you. Or maybe less, but not by much."

This time, her elbow jabbed into his ribs. "I make up for your inability to talk. Someone has to."

He fought against his laughter no longer.

"See?" she went on, triumphant again. "You can't talk. Only snicker here and there. And kiss." He could feel her smile spreading; a smug affair, he could bet his life on that. "That you can do. But you stopped. And then you talked, but only a little. Enough to inform me about chatting squirrels."

He knew that she would feel the trembling of his limbs, the laughter impossible to hold in, craving to break through in a roaring outburst, making him do silly things. He pressed her closer, careless of the consequences. If they were caught huddling here, and with half of the influential dwellers of this royal residence hungry for his blood, they would be done for. He didn't care. With her, there was nothing inappropriate, no need to hide anything, words or feelings.

"Chatty squirrels are nothing compared to you," he informed her, holding her tight, enjoying her warmth. "They can't talk that much, and they surely can't kiss that… that nicely." Her eyes were again wide with expectation, hanging on his words as though he had been the best of orators. He searched his mind frantically, desperate not to disappoint. "And they are not as pretty, either. Don't have this sort of eyes. Like a deep lake on a sunny day, you know. So deep and clear, and calm, but not really. You don't know what is in there and it may be dangerous, but still you want to dive in and… and you know it's going to be good."

Inconceivable as it was, her eyes grew yet larger, widening to an impossible size, mesmerized, drinking in his words, absorbing them. Yes, those magical lakes, definitely; beckoning, full of promise, offering nothing dangerous – only good things. Her lips opened slightly, but just as he reached for them, another sound interrupted their paradise – cracking branches, footsteps creaking upon the gravel, voices ringing in the crispiness of the night. Not quiet or concealed, his senses informed him, somehow calming amidst the wild thumping of his heart that now burst into mad fluttering. Not of people creeping around, trying not to be heard. Someone was out there, a few men probably, but they walked firmer ground – an alley? – and they weren't moving like charging warriors or hunters on a path. He pressed her tighter, signaling to keep quiet.

The voices carried on, then died away. The creaking of the footsteps remained for a few more heartbeats. Then only the wind and the natural rustling were there. He dared to breathe once again, aware of her inanimate form, rigid in his arms, clearly afraid.

"They are gone," he breathed into her hair, enjoying its scent. Something sweet and spicy; something he had never inhaled before.

She nodded, clearly as alert and listening. He wondered briefly about that, the perfect stillness of her pose, the practiced ease with which she froze just as he expected her to make trouble. More puzzlement about the enigma that this girl was.

"They went toward the main wing of the Palace," she

whispered, her breath tickling his ear. "We can sneak in the direction of our side. The wall there is lower and not as closely guarded. There are some crumbling stones not far away from the women's hall, where the stupid fowls sit and gossip all day long." Slipping away from his embrace, she took his arm, back in the lead, in the familiar fashion of Tlemilli from the Plaza, decisive and sure of their course. "Let us hurry. One can't know who might be sniffing around here next and when they notice that I'm absent at such a time of the evening, those gardens will swarm with more guards and servants than you would wish to see in your lifetime." She pulled again forcefully. "Come."

The night seemed to be less thick, less oppressive as they reached the edge of the artificial grove and sneaked along another smaller pond, abandoned at this time of the evening. Thanks all mighty gods for that! Readily, he dove under the cover of yet another cluster of trees.

"Here it'll be only a short walk toward the wall," she whispered, out of breath and panting. The memory of her running down the shore, trying to keep up with him and Chantli surfaced, making him grin. She might have been good at sneaking and hiding – a natural thing, come to think of it, if anything he had learned about this girl so far could be an indication – but she was no runner, not her.

Another patch of moonlight, then the blissful darkness again, this time accompanied by a more distant hum, of the Plaza out there, he presumed. He tried not to let the thoughts about the outside world and what was expected of him there surface. Not now, not in the calmness of their night.

"You will find me again, yes?" she was asking, peering at him closely, in this typical fashion of hers, so childish and trustful. "Will you come back?"

"Yes, I will. Somehow." He frowned, trying to organize his thoughts like back in the heart of the Palace's gardens, missing their cozy privacy and the memory of those thunderstorms.

"You must, you know?" Her smile flickered, laced with a generous amount of mischief again. "You owe me that kiss, the one that got interrupted. And also," she made a face, "you must tell me about those squirrels and the coyotes with paws and ocelots. Did you happen to actually see any such thing?"

He nodded, glancing around, feeling dreadfully exposed, the noises stronger here, coming from all directions, intruding with force, reminding him that he had no right to be here. And neither did she. She said they would be combing these gardens if she didn't return to her quarters soon, didn't she?

"How? Do they have those things in the district where you live?" she was asking, oblivious of their lack of privacy or not caring. Knowing her, the latter assumption might be a certainty.

"No, of course not." Despite his mounting worry, he chuckled. "You won't find anything bigger than a rat in your cities, unless in the baskets of women heading for their kitchen. Then you'll hear plenty of yelping and barking, or cackling."

"Oh, one hears plenty of that from the kitchen areas as well," she confirmed, beaming again. "I love dog meat the best, better than turkey's, even though they say turkey is softer or whatever, kept for the imperial side of the Palace. So our side gets the leftovers of those same delicious turkeys, and if there is not enough, then we have to do with mere dogs." Her nose wrinkled comically. "When I was small, we had this cute little *itzcuintli* back in our old home, before the Palace, me and Citlalli, and no matter how tasty those tamales are, I sometimes think about it and feel bad eating those dogs."

He knew he had to hurry and leave, but like back on the Plaza, her irrelevant chattiness was most pleasant, soothing his nerves.

"I never ate a dog in my life," he confessed when she stopped momentarily, out of breath.

"Never ate a dog? How so?"

"Back in the village, we don't raise those things. There is no need. You could always go out and shoot things, rabbits and birds. An opossum, sometimes. But they are ugly and difficult to track!" He smiled at the memory. "And Father and other men would go out and hunt deer and bring plenty of meat sometimes, so we would have huge feasts. I miss that the most." He shrugged. "Deer tastes the best."

Her eyes were again widening beyond any normal proportion.

"You… where do you come from?"

He cursed his tongue for going loose on him like that. "Ah… umm… it doesn't, doesn't matter."

"Yes, it does." She caught his arm once again, as though afraid he would turn around and run away. Something he might have considered as of now. "So that's where you saw all those animals! You have been out there on the mainland?" The last sentence she breathed in pure awe. "I mean, you've been away from this island? You came from the mainland?"

He shrugged with one shoulder.

"Oh mighty deities! I knew it. I just knew it. That's why you are strange, not like everyone. Oh, you must tell me how it is out there. Have you been to the Eastern Highlands, where Smoking Mountain is? Have you?" She was pressing his hand hard, with all her strength, he suspected, breathless with excitement, her gaze clinging to him in pure wonder.

His embarrassment evaporated all at once. "Smoking Mountain, yes; one can see it easily, even from Oaxtepec, they say. It's beautiful, this mountain, and they tell plenty of stories about it and the other one, its mate, the Fair Woman. If you walk the woods to the east and a little toward your Great Lake, then you can reach them both in the end. But it's some days of walking, they say, and it's different in those highlands, difficult trails, scary highlanders." The memories swept him, bitter and sweet, bringing his longing for home in force. "It's beautiful out there in the woods. You would enjoy it there, you know?" The thought made him smile, banishing the longing, even if briefly. It was easy to imagine her skipping along this or that trail, tottering into an occasional brook, mainly by mistake, jumping over fallen logs instead of skirting those, clumsy and nimble at the same time, and happy. "You would like real woods, you know. And you could chat with those chatty squirrels."

Her beam was back, ten times more intense. "Will you take me there one day? When no one is chasing you or me or anyone? Will you?"

He just nodded, bereft of words, his stomach tightening in a hundred painful knots. "Yes, I will. One day."

She swayed closer again, her smile shining, as though he had given her a beautiful golden necklace or had taken her to all these places already. Impossible to do that, plain impossible. But did he hate that voice of reason, always there, nagging, ready to ruin his every dream. There was no way to do that. Or to enjoy more of her kisses and silly chattering. Back in Tenochtitlan, there were enough troubles waiting, enough challenges now that he had managed to anger the Emperor's sister. Oh, but he would have to think, to think hard, to come up with solution, or it'd be back to courts, executions, maybe slavery, the workshop, old Tlaquitoc. He pushed away the rising wave of familiar dread.

"Oh, Smoking Mountain," she was saying, her words spilling again in a breathless rush, pulling him off the brink as they always did, offering an anchor to grip and feel safer, able to deal with it all. "It must be so beautiful from close up, so powerful. Overwhelming, I would think. Don't you? Have you never gone at least a little close? How far it is? A day of walking? Two days? Father sent a delegation to Lake Chalco this morning. I overheard him saying that, and I swear I wanted to sneak away and into their canoes. To hide between those shields and the swords they were carrying." Her wink held all the mischief. "You know, those things they bring you when they want you join in their war. He said Moquihuixtli sent plenty of those all over, to Tenochtitlan's allies even, and that they turned him down, both of them. Father said it was really like the Emperor to do that, to approach Tenochtitlan's allies. But he is hopeful of the others, Toltitlan and Cuauhtitlan. And about Chalco! But I did wish to sneak away with one of the delegations all the same. Not because those Chalcoans or even the Texcocans would be happy to join the war on Tenochtitlan, but because it would bring me to the mainland and to Smoking Mountain. I truly must see it one day, I must!"

If the Eastern Highlands' volcanic peaks might be overwhelming in his estimation, her breathless tirade gave a whole new meaning to this word. Blinking, he tried to make sense of what she said. "Your father sent a delegation to Lake Chalco and those other towns? Why?"

Her slender eyebrows climbed high. "To join our war on

Tenochtitlan, of course. He wouldn't be sending them shields and swords just to make them feel good about themselves." Her wink held plenty of mischief. "Our warriors could use all this weaponry, don't you think? What would they wield when Tenochtitlan's hordes attack them? Kitchen spoons?" Her giggle trilled the night air. "I can imagine that happening. Even though our warriors would win anyway. They are so much braver and stronger than Tenochtitlan brutes, with so much more spirit. You saw it on the day of the competition. Wasn't it a breathtaking sight, all those flying missiles and spears? Still, weapons are the essential part, so of course our warriors would need those, and we are not as disgustingly rich as our annoying neighbors. We need every spare club or spear."

"They have plenty of clubs and spears tucked all over Tenochtitlan," he muttered without thinking, remembering the old ruined temple and the underground room full of such unexpected treasures. "Whole tunnels of those."

Her forehead furrowed once again. "Who?"

"Your people." He shrugged. "Your father. Your emperor. His warlords, or whoever leads his warriors. These people."

"My father has tunnels?" Her face began crinkling in the familiar way he grew quite fond of, the wrinkled nose and an uneven twist of the lips, one side of the wide mouth climbing faster than the other, much faster – but did this silly expression make his heart beat stronger. Then the lovely grimace stopped in midair, melted away, replaced by the widening eyes and the palm springing up, pressing against the suddenly gaping mouth. "The tunnel... and you... and my father said... but what, how..." Taking an abrupt step back, she swayed away with the upper part of her body, staring at him with painful intensity, as though trying to see into him. "You... you never told what you are doing, why you are here... You never said. But... but the Tenochtitlan fowl and my father, they are after you all the time, and you, coming here... Did you come from Tenochtitlan just now? Are you going back there?"

The enormous eyes blinked and it tore at him, the helplessness of this motion and her entire thought process again on display, arriving at her conclusions, fast but aloud, so typical, so Tlemilli-like.

"I have to go back, yes. I must," he said, taking a step forward, anxious to close the distance again. She was so helpless and he needed to comfort her, to make her feel better again. She didn't deserve that. Not her!

"You are spying for Tenochtitlan. Just like my father said!" That came out as quite a shriek, not something terribly loud but enough to shatter the silence of the night around them. "You… you are not what you say you are!" Thankfully, she lowered her voice, but her words clawed at him all the same, the open accusation, and her eyes, dark with disappointment, not adoring or laughing or teasing anymore, glittering with hurt. Not unknown but safe lakes, not anymore. "You are not what you say you are!"

I never said what I was, he wanted to tell her. *You never made me tell you a thing. I didn't lie to you.* But the pain in her face was too much to bear, to come up with truths and half-hearted explanations, or more appropriate lies. He wasn't out of danger himself, and should she keep on yelling at him that loudly…

His hands strayed toward her, acting on their own accord, eager to hold her, not to kiss or anything, but just to comfort. She looked too defenseless, too hurt, pathetically lost, like a child having her favorite toy taken away, expecting it to be broken before her eyes.

The hastiness with which she leaped away made his heart fall. She didn't trust him, not anymore. "You are with them!"

Then the distant clamor to their left intensified, became louder. A torch flickered somewhere, then another. He glanced at it briefly, his hands still outstretched, pleading, part of his mind urging him to bolt for the dark mass of the wall, to claw his way up and over it, the other one demanding to catch her and make her listen to him, even if by force. She must let him explain. It wasn't like she thought it was!

She stared at him like a small rodent surprised by a snake, aghast, beyond being terrified. A heartbeat passed, then another. The clamor grew closer and the voices, agitated voices of more than a few people, male and female, talking rapidly, spreading around those gardens, or so his senses whispered to him. No time for explanations.

"Please, Tlemilli," he whispered. "It's not what you think, it's just not…"

To bolt away and into the merciful darkness become a necessity. As he did this, he could see her still staring at him, a pale glassy mask, a terrified one.

CHAPTER 9

A touch to his shoulder jerked Necalli out of sleep, pulling him from a particularly cozy dream and into the reality of the spacious hall crammed with mats and sprawling figures, nothing but dark heaps of limbs. Blinking, he lay there for a heartbeat, trying to get a grip. The murmuring of deep breath and occasional light snoring was familiar, reassuring. He closed his eyes again.

"Necalli."

Another brush of the hesitant hand made him leap into a sitting position. In the darkness, it was difficult to see, but the figure squatting next to his mat did so haltingly, unsure of itself. Or so his instincts informed him, calming the momentary leap in his chest.

"What?" He tried to see better, the moonlight dim and not bright enough, seeping through the distant doorway.

"Can you… would you… would you come… out there?" A heartbeat of hesitation, a nervous shift. "Please."

He nodded readily, recognizing the uncertainty, the familiar faltering speech. "Where have you been?"

The silhouetted shoulders jerked upwards, bare again, adorned with no cloak. His mind registered it, momentarily puzzled. Then it got busy with picking up his step without tripping over his fellow students' sprawling forms. They were tucked so densely sometimes, all in one corner of the vast building. Why didn't the priests let them sleep all over this place? He remembered asking Axolin that on their first night here.

A brief glance back at the abandoned sleeping space rewarded him with the sight of his friend's form piled next to his mat. He wondered if he should wake Axolin for this as well. The workshop boy's sudden return, and just as they had been discussing this one's yet again mysterious disappearance this very evening warranted that, didn't it? Axolin would hate to be excluded. The tale of the afternoon adventures with Chantli crowned with a brief interview with none other than the Emperor himself, the quick work of Ahuitzotl once again, offended Axolin badly enough.

He snickered, remembering the ball court and Chantli huddling under the tribunes, openly afraid. When Ahuitzotl had dragged them across the wall and down instead of up the nearest passageway, the girl had lost the last of her lovely matter-of-fact aplomb. Which dimmed some of her natural glow, but somehow made him even warmer inside, reminding him of the Tlatelolcan shore where she had lost her confidence briefly, regaining it back only when snug in his arms, pressing close and making him think wild thoughts. Well, back on the ball court, the sensation was back, and when the Emperor, sweating, towering, impossibly impressive without the expected regalia and clothing, more amiable than he would ever imagined the Great Capital's ruler could be, neared, waving his numerous followers away and to the safe distance, all he, Necalli, could think of was how she would feel if he took her into his arms again – as warm and lively as back in Tlatelolco, or maybe even better now that they weren't all muddy and spent after a night in the lake? It was difficult to concentrate on the mighty ruler, and it worried him to a degree. But the Emperor himself seemed to be surveying the girl with his gaze, his eyes glinting with open amusement. It gave Necalli time to collect his thoughts, but he still remembered the opening phrase, addressed to Ahuitzotl, who was all agog with impatience, pushing himself forward as was his custom.

"But do you keep your net of young troublemakers and spies as diverse and as unconventional as they come, Brother," was the Emperor's final verdict before the impressive man's eyes left mesmerized Chantli, shifted to Necalli, became businesslike. "Tell me what you heard on the district plaza, young *pilli*, and try to remember every word."

And now, diving into the crispiness of the night, the moon still strong, uninhibited by clouds and wind, he thought again how wise the Emperor looked, how impressive, crisp and curt and listening, volunteering nothing, understanding everything, not above using people from all walks of life and not only advisers and warriors. Even youths like himself or the high-spirited royal *pilli*, even barefoot villagers like the workshop boy. Was this one truly sent back to Tlatelolco this afternoon?

"Where have you been until now?" he repeated, feeling safer to speak in loud whispering as opposed to the murmuring of the sleeping hall. The school courtyard looked peaceful in the moonlight, deserted for real.

"I... I must talk to you," his workshop companion whispered, looking around in an openly haunted manner, all nerves. Only now Necalli could see how neglected this one looked again, like back during their first meeting on the way to the tunnel or maybe even worse, with no cloak or shoes and his hair not even tied by a simple string, sticking up everywhere, caked with mud.

"What happened to you?"

The commoner glanced around again, as jittery as a cornered animal, ready to bolt away. "Can we talk somewhere where it's more... where it's quieter? Out there by the fence, maybe?"

Necalli's excitement welled. Oh yes, he was up to something, something big, maybe, something to do with his imperial errand. He tried to camouflage his anticipation with a nonchalant shrug. "If it's too noisy for you here." To lead the way toward the low barrier that separated the school from this side of the Plaza took him no time. "Now spill it out."

However, the workshop boy's eyes kept darting around, jumping between the peeling off plaster of the wall, the cleanly swept ground, and the dark courtyard they had just left. So much indecision!

Necalli made a face. "You crazy adventurer, you dragged me out of sleep and now you look like someone who would rather scamper away given the chance. Well, it won't work." He grinned widely, jabbing his elbow into the temptingly exposed ribs, smeared with dirt and sweat and whatnot, not pleasant to touch.

"I've had a busy afternoon too. Ask the Emperor about it. Your leisurely stroll around Tlatelolco is nothing to boast about."

A hint of a grin was his answer, a forced twist of the pursed lips. "How did you know I was in Tlatelolco?"

"I know everything, workshop boy. So just spill it out. Why do you look like a runaway slave, for starters? Forgot your respectable new clothes elsewhere?"

"Oh, that." The commoner glanced at his exposed torso, shrugging briefly with one scratched shoulder. Now he could see that his body sported enough of these as well, rubbed raw in some places.

"Were those violent Tlatelolcans chasing you again?"

A vigorous shake of the disheveled head denied that accusation, but the broad face was filling with misery and fast. "I… I was to sneak into their Palace. The Emperor told me to. He said to find his sister, that haughty princess, their emperor's wife. He wanted her to tell me things, to bring her messages back here. Written messages!" The frantic whispering rose as though there was a particular meaning to those messages being written. "He wanted me to bring back word from her."

"Oh, I see. Well, obviously, it's not easy to get into their palace. Not easier than it is to sneak into ours, I suppose. One can't just walk in and demand an interview with imperial wives, can one?" He tried to see his companion better, at a loss as to what to say. That boy was so obviously dismayed, so ruffled and upset, so troubled; even scared. "Even if you didn't manage, it's not something you should be worried about. The Emperor will understand. He should have sent you—"

"I did get into the Palace. It wasn't difficult." The troubled eyes clung to him, almost pleading. "That old nobleman Tepecocatzin, a haughty piece of work that one, he arranged the maid to take me there. He had a scroll from the Emperor, the one I brought him. He read it, and he wasn't excited about it, or about me – he hated me from the first time, didn't trust me. But he made one of his maids take me straight into the Palace, just dropped me in as one of the slaves working the gardens. It was so easy. We just went in through the back gates, me and that maid. No one even asked a question."

"Oh, that's neat!" He tried to take it all in. "That explains your slave-like appearance, wild boy. Better than anything else, I would say." To grin as widely as he could seemed to be in order, the attempt to encourage, his companion's welling misery too obvious again, on full display. What went wrong? "So you got in and then what happened?"

"Oh well, then that maid went to look for the princess to let her know I was digging there in the mud, full of messages and all that. And… and…" The eyes dropped to study the spotless ground again, the youth's massive palms clutched together, making a mess out of each other.

"And? What did our royal Jade Genitalia do when she found you there in the mud?"

That brought the anticipated chuckle. The eyes were back upon him, glittering wildly. "She is all of that and more. The filthy snake of a woman! Stinking genitalia, yes!"

Now it was Necalli's turn to stare, taken aback by so much unexpected anger. "What did she do to you?"

But the eyes peering at him lost their angry spark, filled with misery again. "She yelled at me, threw all sorts of accusations. About me being a stinking commoner and not trustworthy. And other things. She was supposed to tell me things, useful things. Like about that competition back then. To bring information to our Emperor as he asked. He wanted to know what is going on in that Palace, I suppose." The broad palms came up, facing the dark sky. "Instead, she yelled so loudly, with so much hatred that… that in the end, I just bolted away because her men were starting to run toward us. Those who carry the chairs, you know. Where the nobles are riding."

"Litters?"

"Yes."

Necalli tried to take it all in. "She was yelling at you in the middle of the Palace and had her litter-bearers chasing you? It doesn't make sense."

The wide shoulders were again lifting in misery. "It was in the depth of the gardens, by the pond. Pretty secluded. That's where the maid had taken me after, after the princess arrived. She ordered the maid to take me there, while she spoke to… to other noblewoman. And then, then…" Another speaking attempt trailed off into nothingness.

Necalli tried to make sense out of it. So the Emperor sent the workshop boy to seek his sister out and ask for more information. A logical choice, as this one had already been used by the haughty princess before, hadn't he? But then she started yelling at him out there in the middle of the enemy lair, accusing him of… what? Betrayal? Lack of loyalty? Humble origins? Well, she knew this boy was anything but a royal *pilli* before, didn't she? And why would he seem disloyal all of a sudden and just as the Emperor himself had sent him?

"Why did she snap at you like that? What did you say?"

Another shrug. The stubborn stare drilled holes at the ground.

"You are not telling it all to me, brother. You are hiding something. And you know, I can't help you if I don't know what you did." He jabbed his elbow at the inanimate figure again, trying to encourage. "You are always like that, closemouthed, more listening than talking. I noticed that about you. But it won't do now, workshop boy. You'll have to tell me exactly what happened." He shrugged at the continued silence. "I won't tell anyone, I promise. Not even the Emperor when he'll be asking about the cheeky villager who dared to piss off his precious sister with a vulgar name."

This time, the haunted gaze came back, the chuckle an almost imperceptible sound. "She is vulgar, she is, whatever that means. She is the filthiest!" The air hissed, drawn forcefully through the pursed lips. He saw the decision flooding in, hardening the wide features. "She has her reasons to suspect me. In a way. You see, there was this girl. She is the daughter of that filthy adviser Teconal. Not the first daughter, the one who took their emperor from Jade Genitalia and pushed her from the high seat of a chief wife."

"Oh yes, everyone heard of that scandal. The marketplace rocked with gossip when it happened. It was just as the winter moons were over." He forced his mind to focus on the issue at hand. "So what did this Tlatelolcan lusty fowl have to do with you and your love quarrel with our Noble Genitalia?"

The village boy ran his hand through his disheveled hair, his face twisting in a painful grimace. "No, it was not because of this one. Even though this one is mighty pretty, all curves and flimsy draperies." His face fell again as he drew in a breath resolutely. "There is another daughter, young girl, a wonderful person. I… we got along well last time, and she… she helped me to get away from the Plaza when they were shooting slings. She… she is the best girl ever, the best of company, and, you know, she is funny and good and I didn't know she was Teconal's daughter in the beginning, and when I knew, it was too late, and she helped me tremendously. She helped us all. Back there on the shore, she drew this same Teconal away, so I would be able to start shooting that sling. You know, when he was holding you there on the shore."

That was one memory Necalli didn't cherish. It still made his insides shrink with anger and dread he didn't care to admit. The knife pouncing toward his eye, or that haughty Tlatelolcan scum hitting his face, backhanding him as though he had been a slave who behaved badly. The mere memory made him go rigid with fury.

"She did so much for me, for all of us, and she was the nicest, the best of company," his companion was rushing on, apparently oblivious of the lost audience or indifferent to it, in need to talk. "And well, I wanted to find her when I was there in the Palace. I promised her and I had to. I didn't know if she wanted me to keep that promise, but I wanted to. And then, then she found me all by herself, like the first time. That's so much like her. She is like that, a whirlwind, like a mighty river, can't be stopped. Like a storm. But a good storm, not a deadly one. She is so forceful but naïve, just a child sometimes, unprotected. I didn't want to hurt her. She… she assumed things, said I was a spy, and yes, I know I was, am spying, yes, but it was not against her. I would never lie to her or do something to hurt her. But she thought that I did."

The gushing flow stopped, more from the lack of air than anything else, Necalli suspected. He tried to slam his mind into working. The longer the workshop boy talked, the less sense he made with his jumbled up story. Who was this girl whom he apparently liked that much, didn't want to hurt but somehow managed to? And how did it all connect to the Emperor's now angered sister?

Acting out of instinct, remembering how Father's heavy palm would rest upon his shoulder, pressing it reassuringly every time he was confused or troubled and needed to talk, he reached out, clutching the muddied limb, pressing it tightly. "Wait, tell it all in some order, man. Don't carry on like a girl overwhelmed by her first reception in the Palace's hall." Amused by his own comparison, he grinned. "You sound like one of my sisters when they were younger and acted up about everything. A silly lot."

The stare, then the agitated gaze calmed a little. "Go jump—"

"Shut up and go on with your story. We haven't much time. Any moment, a sleepless priest can fall on us, or some of the boys wander out. And where are you supposed to be anyway? Reporting to the Emperor? What did he tell you to do after you are back from your Tlatelolcan excursion?"

The recently gained spark drained off the haggard face. "Yes, the Emperor. I have nothing to tell him, nothing to report. Only that his sister grew mad at me and threw me out of the Palace and just as he needed me to act rationally, to bring news back here. And I don't think he'll thank me for making such a mess out of this mission. I think he would sooner throw me out of here as well, back to the workshop or courts or whatever happens to people who make royal family members angry with them." Again that breathlessly rushing speech.

Necalli pressed the slippery shoulder harder. "Wait. Stop panicking. Nothing happened yet, and I still need to hear what exactly occurred in that filthy Tlatelolcan Palace. You either tell it all calmly and in the right order, or go jump into the lake yourself. Eh, village boy?" He winked nonchalantly, but his stomach kept churning with excitement, wishing to hear it all, sensing his chance to get involved and for real, not just silly eavesdropping out there on some petty district square with some stupid smugglers. "Go on. Spill it out in an orderly manner. So that other girl, the one who left such a lasting impression on you, she was there too?"

The distressed eyes flashed then shifted again. "Yes, she was there. And she picked a fight with the princess because she thought she was ordering me away to just spite her or her sister. I mean, they were nasty to each other, those two emperor's wives. Our Tenochtitlan fowl was outright mean. The other one answered nicely enough but with all the implied nastiness underneath. You know how it can be sometimes with people, when they say one thing but mean to relay another…"

Necalli grinned. "Yes, I know. I have two sisters. You get to learn everything about double-talk and veiled threats when you have more than one female at home."

A fleeting grin was his answer. "I only have brothers."

"Lucky you. But back to your story. What happened in this Palace's garden with the pretty royal fowls by the pretty royal pond?"

The high forehead creased again. "It wasn't by the pond yet. Just on that long alley, very pretty and paved and so wide I think half twenty people can walk it without jostling each other. And Tlemilli, she saw me there and she didn't care how inappropriate it all was. She rushed and talked to me and kept talking until the royal women stopped badmouthing each other. They were all so appalled by what she did, and the rest of them." The boy shivered visibly. "There were warriors there and many other people. I didn't know what to do. But then the Jade Genitalia stopped that quarrel, even when Tlemilli tried to interfere. She wouldn't have let her take me away, not her; she is so loyal!" The anguish was filling the dark eyes again, too visible to miss. "But I told her it's all right and she listened, so the maid took me away and toward that pond, where it was really secluded. So I wanted to get this mission over with, but that woman turned as vicious and as unreasonable as a nest of snakes just woken from their winter sleep. And I… I couldn't help it, couldn't make her calm down and listen. It was hard to talk to her with me stuck in the mud, pretending to do something there, to weed flowers or whatever, but it was scary with her getting all angry, hissing behind my back. I told her that the Emperor sent me and that he is worried about her and all that. She likes to hear that she matters to them, that spoiled royal princess, but she wouldn't calm down and she talked bad about Tlemilli, truly nasty and at some point... Oh, I don't know, I couldn't stay like that, kneeling there in the mud, and with my back to her. I thought she might attack me, maybe. No, it's silly, right? But somehow, back there... and I couldn't let her talk like that about Tlemilli. I had to make sure she left her out of it. She is so naïve and so brave and she doesn't understand what they are doing, her father and that princess and everyone. They are so cruel and not caring. They are ruthless and she doesn't understand that..." Another pause ensued, followed by loudly drawn breath.

"So what did you do?"

The eyes dropped again, scanning the dark ground with exaggerated interest. "I told her to leave Tlemilli out of it. To forget all about her."

Necalli found himself staring, beyond wonder at this point, trying to imagine. The pretty Palace's pond and the Emperor's wife – chief wife! – a sister of another mightier ruler, the renowned beauty, so very noble and haughty, the most illustrious ancestry to this one, impeccable from both sides, two great Tenochtitlan's emperors for grandparents, brought up in the Palace, married off beneath her only because her emperor was ruling an *altepetl* with no provinces. To think of such an exalted lady being told what to do by a commoner boy digging in the mud and in uncompromising tones was hilarious, beyond a joke. But did he remember how this barefoot naked wonder made him and Axolin angry back in the tunnel, sounding his mind so readily and with no misgivings, completely inappropriate when talking to a higher class than himself, in this village boy's case everyone being higher than him, even the filthy craftsman who had made him slave at the braziers. To think of that one ordering the haughty princess about made the struggle to keep wild laughter in nearly impossible.

"You... you are beyond it all, man," he guffawed, trying to keep quiet, failing miserably. "Something rare, out of the storytellers' tales." The pair of indignant eyes was boring at him, piercing the darkness. "Stop staring at me. Tell me what happened next." A stubborn silence was his answer. "You crazy piece of dog meat, just get on with it before I go back to sleep and leave you to sort it all out by yourself. To go and order more nobility about, eh? The Emperor himself, why not? Go tell him what to do and whom to talk to." He snickered again, then brought both arms up, palms forward. "All right, all right. Just go on. What did the lovely princess do? Ordered to have you fed to the fish in the pond?"

This time, the thundering silence was interrupted with a reluctant snicker. "Close to it. I had to dive in to get away from her litter-men."

"You dove into the Palace's pond?"

A wary shrug.

"You aren't real. I'm starting to think I'm dreaming you up."

"Go jump in—"

"Yes, the lake, I know. You need to enrich your cursing vocabulary." He forced his mind into sobering. "Look, this is a mess you got yourself into, yes, but it's nothing we can't deal with. We'll think of something." He glanced at the sky. "We have still a considerable part of the night left to think of a solution. The Emperor won't expect you to fall on him in the middle of the night with your troublesome report. Do you know what he wanted to hear about Tlatelolco? Did he say anything? An indication?"

The workshop boy shrugged. "There is serious trouble brewing there, one can see that without any reports. They are bubbling out there in Tlatelolco and the Emperor knows it. I bet he has plenty of spies there and I bet they are watching us as closely."

Necalli made a face. "He doesn't look unduly worried. This afternoon, he was busy playing a ball game with his nobles. Would the ruler who was afraid of the war with the neighboring city play ball leisurely on a sunny day? I would say he would be busy making speeches, instead, preparing his warriors and inspecting his arsenals."

"Unless he wishes to appear this way," muttered his converser, as though to himself.

Necalli felt his own interest piquing again. "Why do you think so?"

The wide shoulders were again lifting in a familiar manner. But this one was shrugging with every second phrase. No wonder he didn't talk much, that village boy. A deep piece of work, come to think of it.

"Come on, spill it out."

"I don't know, I didn't think about it, had no time for that. But he seems very wise, very sharp. There is no way we see something he doesn't. Do you know what I mean?" The attentive eyes were clinging to him, lifted briefly from their troubled misgivings. "He was playing that ball, yes, but he took time to sneak away and talk to me privately, making sure no one listened. Stated his business curtly and briefly, with no possibility of misunderstanding. Sent me to spy on that town, pass messages. Does it not mean that he is very much aware of what is going on and that he is on guard, and maybe knows how to deal with the trouble too?" This time, the expected shrug came accompanied with lifting hands. "What if he tries to put them off guard or something? Make them look down on him and so make mistakes. I don't know."

Impressed, Necalli glanced at the dark courtyard, remembering his own interview with the formidable ruler. "Well, he did take time off the game to listen to us this afternoon as well. Like you said, all crisp and curt and matter-of-fact. He wanted to hear everything we overheard from this gossiping Tlatelolcan scum. So maybe yes, maybe he does know what he is doing. I wonder what he did about that Acachinanco road."

"What road?"

"There was this scum out there near one of the plazas, where Chantli lives, probably those same smugglers from the tunnel and under the causeway. She recognized one and she said another one tried to grab her hand. He didn't look familiar, but she said he acted as though he knew her." He frowned. "I told her to stay at home for the next few days, not to wander about and chance the trouble like you got yourself into last time." This came out well, such grownup responsible words. Would she listen to his demand? That was another question. He didn't hold his hopes high. The smile, too warm and too private, threatened to sneak out on its own. He turned to scan the dark square once again. "Anyway, those Tlatelolco smugglers talked about going to Chalco, or rather their unwillingness to do that. Then one man, a leader clearly, told them to wait on the road to Acachinanco and not to move from there until meeting someone, their envoys, I'd presume." Now it was his turn to shrug. "The Emperor was interested in all this, enough to pause in his ballgame. Or maybe he had just finished by then and was on his way back to the Palace anyway."

The workshop boy was all eyes now, listening as though afraid to miss a word. "Where is this Acachinanco located? What is it? A town?"

"Yes, a stinking town in the east, on the mainland. Near Toltitlan."

"They've been sending some weaponry to Toltitlan and Chalco. The Tlatelolcans, that is."

"What weaponry?"

"Swords and shields."

Necalli found himself staring. "Who told you that?"

He watched his companion's face close abruptly. "No one. I just heard it."

"Where did you hear it? Who told you? I promise not to tell anyone!"

Another painful hesitation. "Tlemilli."

He felt like gasping. "Teconal's daughter?"

The frown deepened. "Well, yes."

"Wait, let me get it right. Teconal's daughter told you that Tlatelolco had been sending swords and shields. Specifically those things, yes? Not anything else. She said swords and shields?"

The discomfort of his companion grew most visibly, expressed in the protectively hunched shoulders, in the way his entire body swayed backwards, as though trying to escape the sudden interrogation. "She said something like that, yes. What's wrong with that?"

"Don't you know?"

"Know what?"

"What swords and shields mean?"

The silhouetted head shook negatively. "What does it mean?"

"It means that those who send such particular offerings invite the recipients of those gifts to be their partners in war." The words hung in the night air, making it heavier, more difficult to breathe. "And so now we know what those people would wait for on the road to Acachinanco!"

"What?"

"The answer. If the swords and shields were received, then this same Toltitlan is in, with the filthy Tlatelolco and against us."

He heard the workshop boy drawing in a sharp breath.

"Toltitlan and Chalco, you said? Did she mention any other cities, towns, villages? Any other names?"

"No, she did not." The boy's voice picked a terse note. "And you promised not to tell anyone!"

"But we must. It's important. The Emperor must know!"

The pair of wide-open eyes neared his, peering from the darkness, piercing it with the intensity of its stare. "No, he doesn't. Or even if he does, it will come to him from someone else. We will not be using her knowledge, not a word of what she said!"

For a heartbeat, a silence prevailed, not comfortable or friendly as before. Necalli's mind raged impotently, bound by his promise, longing to tell its recipient to go and bang his head against the wall. What stupid insistence. To keep important knowledge because it came from this or that source? Knowledge was knowledge, nothing to deliberate about. You either tell or you don't, but for better reasons than stupid loyalty to one who said it, especially if there was no way to prove where it came from anyway.

"You are a thickheaded commoner to insist on something like that," he said in the end, frustrated. It would be so easy to tell this one to go and kill himself or do whatever he wanted, left alone to explain to the Emperor how miserably he had failed, to face the consequences. If the Emperor suspected him of double loyalties now, as his sister certainly did, and judging by the way the stubborn villager behaved now might be truly the case, then his prospective slavery in the workshop would look like warriors' paradise compared to what would happen to him. The royalty were not famous for their mercy or the slowness and lack of harshness in their judgment.

For another heartbeat, he stared into the dimly lit, by now familiar face, taking in its wide, satisfactorily prominent features, pleasant to the eye despite the mud and the bruises, the broad lips pressed tightly, determined, the deeply-set eyes matching, stern and unblinking, unwavering, unafraid. Strong, loyal, trustworthy, and a friend, as ridiculous as it might sound. Just a village boy from a meager, gods' forsaken province that no one even heard about, a barefoot commoner with no family, no protection, and yet a friend now. How strange.

"Forget it," he said tiredly, at a loss as to how to proceed. "I don't understand your insistence in this, but have it your own way. Keep your secret from the Emperor and everyone and let someone else get the glory of revealing this plot. Like you said, he is an exceptionally wise man, our Emperor. He probably figured it out all by himself or will do it soon enough." He shrugged. "I don't know what he'll do to you for making his precious sister mad, but let us hope it won't be something scary. I don't know how to help you in this when you refuse to see the obvious. Oh well." Shrugging, he began to turn away, hoping he wasn't overplaying it, knowing that if allowed to go back to his mat and his cozy blanket, he would never, never manage to fall asleep, not with all these revelations buzzing inside his head and the missed possibilities driving him positively mad. *Come on, you stupid villager*, he thought, *stop me already*!

"Wait." It came out quietly, like a gust of wind.

"What?" He forced his muscles to stay still, not to turn back too readily. "I'm dying to fall asleep. There is not much of the night left, you know."

"Please." This time, he did turn around, rewarded with the view of a painful frown, such a contorted grimace. "I... what did you mean when you said that I refuse to see the obvious?"

Necalli forced a shrug. "It's easy. The Emperor sent you to

bring him information, to report any unusual happenings. Well, you did this. You went out and brought back some priceless knowledge of the enemy seeking allies and all that, sending official declarations and envoys to at least two important enough regional centers, especially Chalco Lake's dwellers. Don't you see it? You did precisely as the Emperor told you. So why would he be angry with you? Think about it. It doesn't matter how you gathered your knowledge. Only that you actually brought it and that it is good."

The wide-open eyes were filling with comprehension. "But he told me to talk to his sister, to reassure her and bring her word back to him."

"Who is to know that what you say now isn't coming from her?"

The frown was tuning painful again. "She would tell. She won't be backing my lies, and those are lies, they are!"

"She is not here, you simple-minded villager. She is out there, in Tlatelolco, not able to communicate with her brother and family but through people like you. She can't get an audience with the Emperor tonight or tomorrow or any time soon. You, on the other hand, can and will. So whose word will the Emperor be listening to, eh?"

"Yes, but later on, when she does manage to come here. If that Moquihuixtli throws her out or if there was a real war with that town and Tenochtitlan conquered it. She will be back here, telling what truly happened."

Necalli felt like snickering again, this time wholeheartedly. "But one can see that you haven't been to school, any school, in your entire life, brother, or you wouldn't have worried about something that may or may not happen in the future. Worry about today. You are in trouble now. Until the Emperor meets his spoiled, arrogant, annoyingly loudmouthed sister that is clearly getting on his nerves as much as his revered mother does, many things may change, in your or her or the Emperor's or this city's life. In school, you learn to think like that and get away from your transgressions as best as you can, lie your way out and not to worry about the future until it happens. In your current situation, it's even more intense. Today matters more to you than some future day when some vengeful princess may wish to badmouth you. Think sensibly, man."

And if that didn't convince the simple-minded peasant, then nothing would, he decided, watching changing expressions chasing each other across the broad, dimly lit face. The moonlight was fading. Heralding the end of the night? He glanced at the sky, hopeful.

"Well, what do you say? We can't huddle here until the dawn comes."

A haunted glance faced him again. "What do you think we should do?"

"Go wake Ahuitzotl, disturb our royal *pilli*'s precious sleep." Necalli stretched, trying to conceal his welling excitement. "Ask him to try and find the way to get us into the Palace now, wake the Emperor without making him wish to cut our hearts out right there on the spot, but to hear what we have to tell him instead."

"And we say that his sister told me all that, about Chalco and Toltitlan?"

"Yes, we do. And don't you go all red in the face or stammering or worse yet, trying to blurt out the truth about offended princesses, or anyone else, even that Fire Girl you are so fond of. Once you start lying, you stick to it. Is that clear to you?"

Even through the thickening darkness, he could see the flashing anger, the familiar resentment. "I know that. I've lied before in my life." The broad shoulders lifted again, in a lighter motion this time. "Just not to the mighty Emperor."

Necalli felt his own laughter brimming, threatening to spill out. "Me neither, truth be told."

CHAPTER 10

The sun was beating down on them, scorching the dusty road and the thirsty trees that crowded its edges. Nothing but a relatively narrow track, not a main road, either paved or otherwise visibly maintained, reflected Miztli tiredly, his limbs heavy, head pounding with exhaustion and lack of sleep. The *calmecac* boy claimed it would bring them to their destination where the roads from all three towns, Acachinanco, Toltitlan, and Cuauhtitlan, would meet at a large crossing point the stupid Tlatelolco smugglers managed to overlook.

They either didn't know this terrain well enough, claimed Necalli, cocky and very sure of himself now that he was again in the lead; or maybe they just didn't care, stupid amateurs that they were. He had tried to convince the imperial warriors into sending some of their people here, or at least into letting them go and "sniff around." However, the Emperor's men, a closemouthed, tough-looking, alert group of people, more scouts than warriors with their brief, forceful movements and their faces sealed, already not happy about the need to have a pair of school boys trailing along, were out of patience with Necalli's suggestions and his attempts to stay around after the smugglers had been identified by the *calmecac* boy who was the only one to know what they looked like in the first place. This was the only reason they had been allowed to enjoy this sightseeing trip on the mainland instead of a regular school day. But did the prospect alone make Necalli glow with happiness!

Blinking the sweat away, Miztli wiped his brow, remembering the night. Such a blur of events and sights. The occurrence in

Tlatelolco Palace he had tucked deep into his mind, not daring to take it out for a reflection, not yet. Maybe not ever. The noble princess, so mad, so unreasonable, yelling at him there by the pond, looking as though not above attacking him with her own hands, those perfectly groomed sharpened nails, strangely attractive in her fury, a wild jaguar. And then her, Tlemilli, a safe haven, as always, wonderful and bubbling with life and this lovely chatter of hers, hiding in his arms, letting him kiss her, not embarrassed in the least, not uncomfortable to demand more kisses. But weren't the girls supposed to be difficult about those things?

Back in his village, some of the local pretties certainly liked to flaunt their looks, making boys talk about them, and *this thing*, the kisses and all the rest. But of course not many had the courage to actually try and do something about it, approach the girls with more than a cocky talk or teasing catcalls. Yet, here was Tlemilli, all pliancy and warmth, snug in his arms as though there was nothing more natural in the whole world of the Fifth Sun to do than to let him kiss her and laugh about it and discuss it between the two of them in the most comfortable of manners. What a thrill! It was so good to be with her, so wonderful and fulfilling, exciting and relaxing all at once, if there was such a combination, but then the talk of the politics got in the way again, and he didn't see the danger until it was too late.

Clenching his teeth against the painful memory, he forced his eyes to look upon the road, hating it, the dry brown earth and every shrub upon it, every broken log, and most of all, the annoying flapping of the gods' accursed sandals, such an irritating sound. They spared his feet the encounter with thorns and gravel and sharp branches and stones, yes, but they also rubbed his skin into painful sores where the straps were fastened around his ankles, reducing the advantage the sturdy soles gave. It hurt to walk in this way and they did nothing but walk since before dawn's break. A bore!

The *calmecac* boy's sandals were like those of Tlemilli, covering his foot up to the ankle, supporting it. A wrong turn of thoughts again! Tlemilli hated him now, as much as the haughty princess, maybe more. She thought he had betrayed her, and she had been right about that too. He almost groaned aloud at the pain in his stomach, so intense, like a real blow. He had betrayed her, he had! Not back in the Palace, maybe, not in the way she thought he did. As though any of it was of his choosing! And why did she imply that he concealed something from her when all the time since their first meeting it was she who did all the talking, not him, she who had assumed things, never bothering to ask him outright.

However, it didn't matter, because back in Tenochtitlan and the *calmecac*, he did betray her, oh yes. Whatever Necalli said, it was a betrayal. He had used her words, the things that she had told him about her father, the knowledge he could not have learned from another source to justify his using it. He had used her information, given to him in all innocence, without intent, and by doing this, he had betrayed her in cold blood, with enough forethought and preparation – a true betrayal! Distraught and at his wits' end, wild with panic and lost, yes, but it didn't matter. He could have kept silent about those swords and shields being sent to all sort of places, but he didn't. He had told Necalli and then let the *calmecac* boy persuade him into carrying this information on and straight to the Emperor, into using it for his own, Miztli's, good. A true cold-blooded betrayal. But for the possibility to take it back now, to return to that night and refuse, not to let his friend wake Ahuitzotl.

"Not long now," Necalli was saying, panting, fairly out of breath. Under other circumstances, Miztli might have reflected on it with a good inner feeling, for his breath was all normal and only a dull headache behind his temples reminded him that he hadn't slept for the entire night. Still, as it was, he just nodded, not tearing his eyes off the ground.

"They will be sorry for not listening to us," went on Necalli, apparently oblivious of his lack of audience. "Those smugglers are stupid. No wonder they are still waiting, getting angry and dying of thirst. You'll see that I've been right about that place being a wrong one. You'll see."

"I will not be the one to go down hard on you for going here instead of returning to school," muttered Miztli, incensed. Why was this one nagging and nagging, justifying yet another independent enterprise. The warriors, who had used their eye-witnessing skills, sent them both back the moment the lingering Tlatelolcans, two skinny neglected types lounging upon the side of the road, were recognized. The *calmecac* boy was sure enough about one of the loungers, so the warriors spread all around, slinking behind the bushes, attracting no attention, like true scouts. Back then, Miztli had found himself watching with some interest, lifted out of his general gloom, even if briefly. Still, when attempting to stick around, something that Necalli tried to do quite forcefully, not picking outright arguments with the impatient warriors but fairly close to doing something like that, suggesting all sort or ways of using them and their skills, they had been told off in the most uncompromising of manners. They were to run back to Tenochtitlan and their school, hastily at that. It was the end of the matter. Even when Necalli tried to claim that the scum they were watching had picked the wrong place, as some of the traffic ensuing from the towns like Toltitlan or Cuauhtitlan was using a different route, the big crossroad somewhere to the east of here, he had been told off most rudely, with no patience at all.

"But they are waiting on the wrong road, the Emperor's people and the smugglers alike," had claimed Necalli, halting as soon as they achieved enough distance to talk with no need to whisper. "They are waiting on the road to Acachinanco, yes, but they are not supposed to receive messages from that particular town, are they? Their messengers will not be coming from there, if your Tlatelolcan Fire Girl could be trusted. And if so, then this Acachinanco place is of no consequence to them, only the road to it, and between the two roads, they need the one that leads to the other two towns as well, the ones that received swords and shields."

That was as good an argument as any. Against his will, Miztli felt his interest stirring. "And we will help by going to this other road how?"

The *calmecac* boy waved his good hand nonchalantly. "I don't know. We'll see. Maybe we'll spot the people who are supposed to meet the stupid smugglers. Maybe we'll find out the other way." Narrowing his eyes, he tried to smash an insistent fly. "One thing is certain. I'm not crawling back to school now, knowing that those thickheaded warriors did all the wrong things, watched the wrong people on the wrong road. When they come back with nothing, it will make us look bad, you and me. The Emperor will be mad. He had left his sleep in order to receive us, to listen to us and hear us out and organize that party to the mainland. Think whom he will be angered with the most if it comes to nothing? Not the snotty warriors!"

Miztli shuddered at the very thought, then shrugged off the splash of renewed panic. There were too many ways to make the Emperor angry and he was tired from all this, his mind reaching its limit of coping with such an avalanche of happenings and of living on the edge. After betraying Tlemilli, he stopped being concerned with such petty matters like angered rulers or their haughty sisters or anyone really. Who cared for any of this when all he wanted was to crawl somewhere quiet and fall asleep, and forget all about it somehow?

"That map should be good for just those areas, I would think." Pausing briefly, Necalli reached for the small leather bag he had tied to his girdle along with an impressively large obsidian dagger, its blade long and vicious looking. Not his Tlatelolco trophy, reflected Miztli, remembering the knife the *calmecac* boy had paused to pick up before scampering away from the accursed shore. Back then, it made him ashamed that he didn't think to do it himself, and now he wondered where the Tlatelolcan knife was. "We must be somewhere around here now."

Curious in spite of himself, he came closer, peeking into the unfolded piece of *amate*-paper the youth was holding close to his eyes. As expected, it contained a scary amount of drawings, some painted, some just crudely drawn lines.

"We left them somewhere there," Necalli was musing, tracing some of the lines with his finger, bypassing a pretty painting of what looked like a crouching dog or some other sort of such animal. He hesitated, then slid his finger up the page and somewhat to its left, as though about to head toward the next painting with the clear head of an eagle in it. "We should be close to here. Very close now. No point in going further if we don't run into this crossing of roads soon."

Miztli just shrugged, wishing his companion had put the silly painting back and began walking again. It was getting hotter and the wish to kick off the annoying sandals, followed by the fluttering cloak, grew with every step. Soaked with sweat, it did nothing to make him feel better besides blocking the breeze that blew from time to time.

"You are not much help, man." Necalli peered at the road ahead, then back into his precious painted piece. "I could walk here all alone and exchange the same amount of words with myself. What's eating at you? It's annoying, your gesturing or just murmuring single words in reply."

Miztli rolled his eyes, not caring. "What do you want me to do? Tell you a story?"

"What?" The *calmecac* boy glanced at him, his scowl deep. "You annoying piece of dung, you can try to be helpful for a change, you know? Not just trail along. It's annoying, that gloomy face of yours. Could have bolted back for Tenochtitlan and school if you are afraid to wander about, doing useful things."

"I'm not afraid," cried out Miztli, his anger sudden and splashing with force. "You are the one doing stupid things, not me, and still I'm here, am I not? And if you think you lost your way and got us wandering here for nothing, you can talk about it quietly, without screaming fits. I got enough blame from everyone for everything; I won't take any more dung talk from you!"

Breathing heavily, he glared at the familiar face, ready to evade the first blow and to deliver one back, welcoming the confrontation. It didn't matter if he got hurt or not, as this boy was probably as good with his fists as he was good with everything else; witness the wariness with which even brutes like the ball-playing Acoatl treated this one. Still, he didn't care. It was too much, this last day and night, and in a fight, one at least could hit something, taking his frustrations out, as opposed to the helplessness of being one to betray the only person he cared about.

"Shut up, you stupid lump of stinking peasant meat," Necalli began hotly, but the voices from behind the curve of the road made him fall silent, then turn his head with obvious concern. Against his will, Miztli listened too, even though his nerves were still stretched, still trembling, his eyes on his companion and the long-bladed knife that was dangling in dangerous proximity to his right unwounded arm.

The voices stayed where they were and, without coordinating their actions, they dove toward the nearby bushes, then slunk along, their hearts pounding. The men who were squatting on the fallen logs scattered across the wide clearing with more tracks spilling into it appeared to be armed heavily, their girdles burdened with clubs and spears besides the customary knives, more than one on each side. Holding his breath, Miztli stared at the glittering piece of glossy black on one of the spears, like his talisman in coloring but so much more choppy, dangerous looking, more than Necalli's knife that looked as though made out of single piece, polished into relative smoothness. More like his sacred puma.

Involuntary, his fingers strayed toward the tiny bag, tracing the general outline of the treasure it held. Through those last *calmecac* days, he had had neither time nor enough privacy to take out his talisman and hold it properly, to feel its smoothness and strength. In school, he was afraid to flaunt it in case someone managed to steal it from him. That same annoying Acoatl, maybe. He wouldn't put it past the hatred-filled piece of excrement, even an attempt to take it by force.

He forced his eyes back to the dangerous men, their talking loud, overbearing, carrying on above the rustling greenery, the obsidian of their spears reflecting the fierce midmorning light. Necalli's elbow made it toward his side, light but insistent.

What? he inquired, moving his eyes alone.

Those men, indicated the shifting gaze, back upon him as quickly. *That's them.*

As though he couldn't figure it out all by himself! And why would such dangerously armed men sit here in idleness otherwise, irritated and glancing around, talking rapidly, with no calm of a well-deserved rest if they had been on the road for a long time, starting their journey with dusk, maybe, like traders did. Like the people of his village did, at any rate. But maybe the dwellers of the mighty capital were different even in that.

What do we do? he inquired, moving his lips with no sound, sensing his companion's atypical indecision.

The depth of Necalli's frown could rival a stormy night. He stifled a chuckle, now in the thick of it, actually beginning to feel better – efficient, useful, doing *something* – motioning with his head toward the road they had come from, still stretching to their left, peaceful. The sensible thing was to slink back and run all the way toward the smaller crossroad they had left both the warriors and the smugglers, to see if there was no change in their situation, to let the Emperor's men take it from there.

You go. There was no mistaking the intent of the sway of Necalli's head.

Miztli shook his own forcefully, afraid that such vigorous motioning would give away their presence. Of course they should remain together no matter what, either by going or by staying. There was no point in splitting and why would these people leave if they were to wait for the stupid smugglers who had managed to miss the correct meeting point?

Necalli was signaling with his eyes again, very insistent. Miztli rolled his eyes, then tried to explain by moving his lips alone. *Either together or not at all*. He wasn't leaving the *calmecac* boy all by himself here. It was too dangerous and unnecessary. Also the Emperor's warriors they had left behind were not likely to listen to him, the commoner. Come to think of it, he should be the one staying to keep an eye on this crossroad, with the *calmecac pilli*, a more respectable person in the eyes of the Great Capital's dwellers, rushing to alert their previous escorts. Speaking of efficiency.

Necalli was burning him with his gaze, shaking his head vigorously, indicating the narrow track they had used to get here. *Go now or I'll beat you real bad later on*, the furious glances promised.

He turned his head away, scanning the squatting men,

pretending indifference. Let that one fume all he liked, the presumptuous *pilli*. They either go together or they stay. Because that was what he decided to do right now. They couldn't go on piling missions on him, ordering him about, and he was messing it all up anyway, even when he tried really hard. The spasm in his stomach was back, as painful as before, every time he remembered. How did it come to him betraying her, *actually* betraying?

Through the faint sound of his own grinding teeth, he could hear the *calmecac* boy moving about, creating much noise. Making a point of crawling away, going about his new mission all alone? He didn't have time to ponder that as, in another heartbeat, the bushes parted with too much force, as though spread by the gust of a stormy wind.

His senses on guard, somehow ready for such a development, he rolled away in time to avoid the crushing touch of a solid wood, something heavy, smashing into the ground where he had been a heartbeat earlier, splattering muddy dirt. Hurling himself up and away, he had managed to scramble to his feet, spending a heartbeat glancing around, seeing the *calmecac* boy avoiding a similar attack of a heavily tipped club in his turn. This one was just like Father's back home, he noticed, darting away from a renewed assault, the club back at it and pounding, relentless, like a cooking spoon in the cooking area, eager to smash an insistent pest.

Faltering upon the slippery ground, he darted toward the relative protection of a nearby tree, needing a respite from the relentless pounding, cursing his sandals whose straps chose this very moment to go lose on him, making him fight for his step in addition to the stupid staggering, lurching to and fro, trying to escape. Until now, people of the Great Capital and its neighboring island made a habit of chasing him, yes, trying to capture and then recapture and use him for their own needs, but no one was so determined to just kill him off.

Near his projected destination, he stumbled on another loose strap, then went down for good, meeting the earth with an unseemly loud thud. Mud went splashing all over, spraying his eyes, but the sensation of his chaser staggering nearby gave him courage, pushing the panic away. Relying on his senses rather than his vision, he kicked viciously, feeling his partly bare feet connecting with something – a pair of legs? The marshy thump that followed was music to his ears, his clearing vision reinforcing the hopeful assumption. His attacker was on the ground, struggling to get up, his club lying in the mud, temptingly unattended.

He didn't think it all through, not even for a heartbeat. Not following the man's suit by trying to get up at all, he threw himself toward the coveted possession, part rolling part bouncing off the swampy roots, like a rubber ball of the royal court.

Somehow, the man guessed his intention, flinging himself toward the fallen club as well. However, a fraction of a heartbeat gave Miztli a clear advantage, this and his newfound agility, which caught him by surprise. He was never held to be particularly quick of movement or nimble. So where were those reactions coming from?

The touch of the club felt good, pleasantly round, well polished and fitting, as though made for his hand. With no time to explore this new sensation, he twisted away but wasn't quick enough to avoid being grabbed or, rather, fallen upon. The man was heavy, forceful; and angry.

Pressed into the uneven ground by a considerable weight, he panicked again, kicking wildly, wriggling with true madness, pushing the strangling hands away, the club hindering, still clutched in his sweaty palm. To smash it against something, *anything*, seemed like the right thing to do. He did so with every grain of strength he possessed, not much by now, with all this thrashing in the mud. Still, it made his attacker pause, stop, even sag against him. Another suffocating feeling. To push the struggling limbs away became easier for some reason.

In another heartbeat, he was on his feet, gasping for breath, blinking against the sweat stinging his eyes, the club still there, grasped too tightly to leave his hand, maybe not ever. To wield it felt good, somehow natural. The man upon the ground stopped struggling and went still.

For some time, Miztli just stared, then dared to rub his eyes with the back of his hand, his mind refusing to take in the sight of his rival, just a heap of limbs, crumbled in the mud. The sounds of struggle were still there, interrupting the peacefulness of the woods, but those did not belong to their side of the clearing, of that he was sure now. His senses told him so, soothing, whispering, the sight of the crimson sprinkled around helplessly spread limbs fascinating, so distinct against the richness of the brown and green, strangely appealing.

Shakily, he rubbed his forehead and his face, then became aware of the shouting accompanied with cursing and familiar-sounding thuds. The *calmecac* boy! The thought rushed through his mind like lightning, bringing his numb limbs to life. In another heartbeat, he was racing back toward the road, his heart pounding, the club gripped tightly, reinforcing his resolve.

Upon the crossroad, two passersby jumped out of his way, gaping at him in open dread. Traders, judging by the bundles tied to their foreheads. Both managed to keep their cargo intact, scampering into the bushes to his left, disappearing there. He paid them little attention, his eyes darting toward the open ground and the two figures that were fighting to keep another one in place, all three upon the ground, thrashing there in a similar fashion to his previous bout with the clubman, he suspected.

To tell the *calmecac* boy apart was easy, the edge of his well-cut cotton cloak and relative slenderness of his limbs helping, preventing the confusion. Also his position, pinned down by the other two, struggling viciously, but still at a clear disadvantage. His rivals seemed to be as burly built as the man who had chased him, scary types, worse than the smugglers from the Tlatelolco causeway, well fed.

He hesitated for enough time to pick up a stone, his eyes measuring the distance, very little of it, calculating. As one of the men turned around, alerted by his senses, maybe, or by his ears that might have informed him that this was not one of their peers returning, he hurled it with all his might, returning to clutch the precious club, ready to charge. In the corner of his mind, he did wonder how he came by this knowledge, of when to shoot and when to attack on foot, like warriors in stories. Father did let him hold his club, oh yes, even to wield it in the privacy of their patio, but he never made him practice or told stories about it, so he didn't even know if Father participated in wars, ever. People of their village just didn't seem to be warrior types.

The man that his stone crushed into collapsed with expected readiness, to lie upon the ground with his limbs jerking madly. Having taken the missile straight in the face and from such close proximity, one couldn't expect any other reaction. Spending no time glancing at the fallen enemy, his confidence soaring, the club feeling wonderfully light in his arms, so very fitting, Miztli rushed forward, pleased to see the other man already on his feet, his own club up and ready. A true fight, just like in stories!

The *calmecac* boy, he noticed, scrambled up as readily, thoroughly dirtied and scratched but otherwise seemingly unharmed. Good! He didn't have time to muse over any of it. The other man's club was crushing against his, pushing it backwards and into his face with a force he couldn't counter. So much strength! He twisted away from his own weapon's range, fighting for balance, losing it rapidly as the heavy tip of the other club bounced off his shoulder, paralyzing it for a moment with the intensity of the pain, shooting all the way to his elbow and into his stomach even, piercing.

The ground was harder than back in the woods, hitting his side with force, adding to the confusion. His instincts made him lurch away all the same, but somehow he knew that he wasn't quick enough, not for this adversary, a better warrior than the first one, lethal in his unerring assault. Desperately, he brought his arms up in an impotent attempt to stop the descending club, his own nowhere near his reach now – where was it? – his eyes unable to see, blinded by the glow of the high noon sun.

One heartbeat, then another. His heart was pounding deafeningly, drowning the rest of the sounds. When another heartbeat passed – twenty in his case, the way it was racing – he dared to roll away, then struggled onto his feet, the understanding dawning. The *calmecac* boy; he must be in need of help again!

Indeed, they were locked in a funny way, two dark silhouettes against the blinding glow, dancing as though in a strange ritual, their limbs interweaving. Only after much blinking, he realized that Necalli was hanging on the man's massive back, refusing to be shaken off despite the violent efforts, hence the hopping around and flailing arms and elbows. And the thundering curses; oh, but those truly made the air shake.

The *calmecac* boy's arm, locked around the sinewy neck in an uncompromising grip of a jutting elbow, didn't look as though about to slip despite an occasional shove that managed to reach his ribs yet did nothing to deter him from his perch. This time, Miztli didn't pause to pick up the fallen club. His fist hurt as it crushed into the violent man's belly, but not as much as it did connecting with the upper part of a jaw, next to the temple, just like Father taught him. In fist fighting, he did have some training.

In a heartbeat, it was over, with their adversary crumbled upon the ground and the *calmecac* boy scrambling to his feet frantically, in a real hurry, having gone down with his persistent rival as well. Miztli paused to catch his breath, his heart still thumping, still trying to jump out of his chest. His whole body shook and his limbs felt as though they were made out of straw, like *petate*-mats, not a reliable support.

"Are you all right? You look quite a sight." Necalli was staring at him, wild-eyed, himself a sight with blood smeared all over his mouth and one of his eyes swelling rapidly, in no proportion to the rest of his face.

Miztli stared at him for another heartbeat.

"Stop staring and help me." Businesslike and as though it was all in a day's work, the *calmecac* boy knelt by their crumpled enemy, pulling at his torn maguey cloak, pushing the limp body with his other hand, not very successful. "Help me!"

"What... what do you want to do with him?" asked Miztli, blinking in confusion. But for the stupid trembling to go away! And what if Necalli saw it? Oh, but he probably did. He bit his lower lip hard, trying to force his limbs into stillness.

"To tie him up, obviously. And the rest of them too. They'll be up and about in no time, way before we reach our people." Impressively purposeful, Necalli wiped the blood off his mouth, but it kept trickling from his split lip, brilliantly red, rich in coloring. "That man out there, the one who went after you, is he dead or something? Where is he?"

A shrug made him feel better. "I don't think he is dead. Just out cold, maybe, like those two."

"This one is not out cold." For the first time, his companion seemed to lose some of his good-natured aplomb, glancing at the first fallen man warily, not rushing to check on his condition, the dark spot under his head tucked face down in the dusty road still growing, not a sight one might wish to deal with, so much blood. "If the other one is in the same condition, then I'm not sure your rivals are about to live to tell their stories, brother." The now-uneven eyes leapt up, measuring him with an unconcealed appreciation mixed with somewhat amused suspicion. "Are you sure you are telling us all about you and your past? Do all your fellow villagers shoot slings like veterans and wield clubs with so much spirit and skill?"

"I didn't wield that club with any skill," muttered Miztli, pleased and embarrassed at the same time. But how did this one come to such a wild conclusion, assuming that he did what he did on purpose and not out of panic and a desperate need to survive? "He got me and but for your pouncing on him like that, he would have pounded me into a tortilla." He grinned at his own comparison, feeling better by the moment, the trembling gone. "A well rolled tortilla, made out of the most pounded dough."

Necalli was guffawing in his typical uninhibited manner. "They tried to do the same thing to me." He shrugged, his good humor evaporating. "They were one too many, with that hulking piece of excrement so terribly strong. I felt like a toddler, hanging on him, trying not to let him throw me off him." Another shrug. "Let's get busy tying them, then scampering away before the filthy Tlatelolcans and the Emperor's warriors, for that matter, leave that other crossroad for good."

Nodding, Miztli knelt in his turn, putting the remnants of his strength into the attempt to roll the massive body off its cloak. Oh, but that one was a hulking piece of excrement, indeed. What did they eat out there on the western side of the Great Lake? The fallen club beckoned and he pulled it closer to himself, thinking of its owner, maybe coming back to his senses now, maybe already rushing here. Well, they truly had better be gone.

"What's that?" A rolled-up piece of *amate*-paper slipped into the dust as he propped up the limp body with the last of his strength, preventing it from rolling along with the pulled-away cloak, the yank of his *calmecac* companion forceful, disclosing no sight of exhaustion or hurt.

Letting his burden fall back, Miztli busied himself with picking up the scroll. As expected, it was covered with glyphs, hastily drawn symbols, not painted or elaborated, just sketched.

"Let me see!" His companion was studying the cheap material, probably pondering how to make a rope out of it, presumed Miztli, eyeing the obsidian knife from the *calmecac* boy's girdle with envy, now out and ready, glittering in the fierce sun, reflecting it.

"It has drawings."

"I can see that, you brilliant scholar. But what do they say?" Squinting, he tilted his head as though trying to see the message with his good eye, probably the case. "Oh wonderful," he cried out after some poring over the drawn symbols. "Swords and shields and all. Just like you said. Tremendous!"

"What does it say?" muttered Miztli, not happy with the reminder of this particular information he had brought.

The *calmecac* boy's eyes glinted with triumph as he brought his arm up, victorious. "It has been accepted, the swords and the shields." He waved the paper before Miztli's eyes, then sprang back to his feet, his excitement spilling. "The proof. We have the proof for our claims now, whether those lowlifes get away or not. Written proof! What can be better than that?"

Miztli just nodded, overwhelmed by so much efficiency or such swiftly arrived at conclusions.

"And now let us tie that one, even if loosely, and hope that his companions, your victims, are too dead to come to his aid until we are back. And if not," another happy grimace, "we have their love letters, don't we? Come, help me out. We'll cut it in a few ribbons and hope it'll hold on."

CHAPTER 11

Tlemilli watched another persistent fly land on the tip of her toe, beginning to walk up it briskly, its tickling not unpleasant. Unwilling to move, she blew at it from the side of her mouth, her curled up pose making the distance minimal. Still, the fly stayed, undeterred, bent on its exploring journey up her bare foot and toward the sticking-out bone of her ankle, as though there was something of interest there. She blew at it one more time, then let it be. It didn't matter. Nothing did.

Since last night, she had been here, curled in the alcove she had made her own, in the small side room where the girls would eat their midmorning meal sometimes, or meet for gossip if they didn't feel like going to the more luxurious but more crowded women's hall. This was their private haven, but she rarely spent her time here. Until now. Now it felt good to be encompassed by the brightly painted walls, the security of a close space, the alcove relatively private if one cared to face its inner side, with one's back toward the passing servants and girls. Not a bad place at all.

Tlaco was fussing about it since the early morning time, trying to force her charge out and into the baths or bed or gardens, claiming that her punishment, her confinement to these rooms might be overlooked. She could eat her meal outside, the way she liked. The midmorning meal, the main meal of the day, was well on its way, with most of the Palace already replete, certainly the dwellers of their wing, and why was she huddling here like a statue in the alcove? And would she please turn to face her? And what was wrong with her, what had happened? And wouldn't she like to go to bed now, after such a sleepless night, and hear the story, the new one, something she never had heard before? Such desperate means made her heart go out toward the old woman, but she wouldn't move. She couldn't. Not even for a story. Especially for this!

For what would a story do but remind her, make her stomach cramp dreadfully and her chest struggle for air, just like it happened several times through the night. Back in the dark gardens, it had caught her completely unprepared, this strangely suffocating feeling, when even her nose would refuse to cooperate, clogged as though she had been sick all of a sudden, and that dreadful sensation of everything falling apart, tearing from inside out the moment he melted into the night, as though he never had been there at all. The tears that followed felt salty upon her tongue, and they surprised her, made her feel silly. She was not like those stupid fowls who would howl and cry upon slightest of provocation and even without it. The girls looked so ridiculous when they did this, but then the suffocating wave that kept welling inside her would take her attention away, a scary wave, surprisingly painful. It was like to fall on one's stomach, something that happened to her once or twice, the most unpleasant thing. So while the small army of servants with torches, all agitated and upset, had fallen on her, asking too many questions, hastening her away, fussing as though the end of the world just happened, she had missed most of it, engrossed in the dreadful feeling that kept coming back throughout the fuzzily dark, desolate night.

However, now it had been warm and sunny, and she felt that if she kept absolutely still, didn't move or talk or think, then maybe the dreaded wave wouldn't return. It was too scary and she wasn't sure she would be able to withstand it again.

"What is she doing now?" someone was asking, an annoyingly familiar voice. The stupid barking little dog, Matlatl's full sister. "Why is she like that?"

"I don't know." Another voice, one of the others, not the lady-perfect, thanks all the small and great deities. "Come."

When the little baggage was dragged away, Tlemilli breathed with relief. If only Tlaco would follow suit. But the worried woman did not.

"Come, little one." The wrinkled hand was pulling at her shoulder, gentle, insistent. "Let us take you to the baths, have you clean and relax. Then a good meal, your favorite tamales, with ground young dog. Not the ugly turkey. Please, little one."

But Tlemilli just shook her head, not trusting her voice not to break in the silliest of manners as it did before, when Tlaco had managed to corner her into talking. No more risking that. She turned her attention to the plaster peeling off the alcove's corner. Another familiar sight. She had studied it since the light came up. It looked like a lizard, those small, tiny, crawling cracks.

"Please, stop that, little one. Please!"

The sound of light footsteps, more than one pair, distracted them both, heading up the corridor just outside the women's quarters, where the patio and a row of narrow gardens separated it from the suites of other noble advisers and their families. Tlemilli's heart leapt. In another heartbeat, the pair of gentle arms was enveloping her, pulling her into their blissful warmth.

"What is it, Milli? What is it?"

She didn't resist this time, tucking her face into the beautiful patterns of the soft cotton, inhaling the delicate aroma, something sweetish but not overly so, soothing, comforting. The tears were back, clogging her nose, impossible to arrest.

"Come, little one. Tell me what happened." Citlalli's voice had an unusually agitated ring to it, not like her normally measured singsong speech. "Oh, little one!"

She snuggled yet closer, afraid of the tears and the sensation of falling down the black pit, but less so in the fragrance of her sister's warmth. Citlalli would not let her fall too deeply.

"Is that about this boy?" The whisper brushed past her ear, a mere breath of air.

Sniffing loudly, desperate to clear her nose, Tlemilli shrugged with one shoulder. "It's not. I hate him."

The movement Citlalli made indicated her glancing up briefly, scanning the room. There were maids there, Tlemilli's ears told her; not only Tlaco. Citlalli's escorts, probably, and maybe some others. Their filthy stupid half siblings would be drifting here soon enough. It was not every day the Emperor's wives paid them a visit.

"You need to calm down, Milli. You must!" Again, the warm whispering, the urgent one. "We can't talk here. You must calm down and come with me."

The thought of leaving the safety of the familiar warmth and scent made Tlemilli shake her head in a vigorous refusal. However, Citlalli was already pulling her up, gentle, uncompromising, steering them both away from the coziness of her hiding place. Tlemilli resisted but only for a little while.

"Bring us wet cloths." Citlalli's voice had an authoritative ring to it; now it was the Emperor's wife speaking. "And something to eat; a snack, not a meal. And be quick about it, Tlaco. You two, help her along."

Overwhelmed by so much brisk efficiency, Tlemilli let herself be pulled out and away, facing the floor stubbornly. She must be a sight, after the whole night of crying and no sleep or food or anything, and this after an evening of running all over, worried about *him*, trying to help, then huddling there in the depth of the gardens, safe in his arms, delightfully cozy. He had such a nice smell, of fresh earth and that pond he had to dive into in order to get away from the Tenochtitlan snake, or so he had claimed, his smile wonderfully shy, unsure of himself. Why did he have to run away from the haughty princess? she wondered all of a sudden. Wasn't he spying for her and on her filthy capital of the world's behalf, presumptuous nonentities that they were. He was, wasn't he? But if so, he shouldn't be in trouble with the foul-mouthed fowl.

The suffocating sensation was back, making her chest tighten painfully. It didn't matter, any of it. He was from Tenochtitlan, the enemy, working against her people, actually working against them, not just living in that other filthy *altepetl*. And yet, he said he had come from Smoking Mountain or somewhere around it, with all those animals he promised to show her.

"Come, little one. Let us dry those tears." Citlalli's hand was sliding down her cheeks, caressing, the touch of the wet cloth relatively pleasant, brushing away the tears, even though the new kept coming. No, it was hopeless. She could sense her sister's tension, the impatience there, attempted to be hidden but not quite. "Just come with me. We'll have them bring us refreshments to my suite."

She let the delicate hands steer her toward the opening and into the corridor, refusing to face those who stared, quite a few fowls by now, not only maids and an occasional male servant. The sun was strong at this part of the morning, shining generously, kind. It always was. She felt her numb, taut skin stirring back to life. A fleeting glimpse rewarded her with Citlalli's worried face, glaringly pale in the fierce golden light.

"Maybe I should send for my litter. You shouldn't be walking in such a weakened state."

Tlemilli shook her head, the vigorous motion making her vision swim. Clenching her teeth, she willed the dizziness away. "I'm good. I don't need all this fussing around. I just wanted them to leave me alone. That's all."

A momentary silence prevailed, interrupted by the regular noises of the high morning, the chirping of the birds and of the royal fowls in the women's hall.

"What happened last night, when you ran away from me, Milli?" This came in a sterner voice, demanding an answer. Citlalli was as delicate and well mannered as Tlemilli was wild and turbulent and unruly, but inside, her sister was made of a harder material than people credited her with. This was why their numerous half-siblings never sought to pick fights with her. Growing up together, they couldn't help but to know.

Tlemilli swallowed. "I don't want to talk about it!"

"You must." Citlalli's fingers wrapped around her wrist, arresting their progress along one of the narrower pathways, perfectly swept and embedded with flowers. "You may not understand the seriousness of the situation, little one, but you pushed yourself into something you shouldn't have neared and now I must know what is happening with you in order to help you extricate yourself. This is serious, Milli, more serious than you or even I can imagine. We may be facing a war!"

"Yes, I know that." Forgetting her private misery, Tlemilli

peered at her sister, noting again the paleness and the dark shadows under the luminous eyes. "That pushy island, they may want to war on us, but they will never manage as much as to make us sweat. They will never—"

"Stop talking nonsense, Milli!" This came out sharply, like a breath of a chilly wind. "They will manage to make us sweat and worse. You don't know what you are talking about, but you are not such a child anymore, and you can't make things happen by the sheer power of your will. Even if you have a great deal of it, much greater than they are prepared to tolerate in a girl of a noble birth." A warmer note crept in, however briefly. "You thought it all to be a thrilling game, little one, a relief from boredom. I know how your mind works. But it is not so. Father is angry with you now and suspicious, and the Emperor's Chief Wife too, judging by what this woman shouted at you yesterday in the gardens." The worried eyes bore at her, flickering with unbecoming anxiety. "And now I find you crying your heart out, you who never knew how to shed a tear. And your maid claims that you've been up all night and refused to eat or sleep or even leave that alcove. When she came to my quarters, all nervous and trembling, I got the scare of my life, Milli! I thought something happened to you." A sigh. "And now I know that something did. And you must tell me what it is, little one. All of it. To the very last word!" Another stern command.

Tlemilli shivered, unused to such prying into her affairs, and from ever-considerate Citlalli at that. Father might have ordered her to tell it all, shouting and threatening, maybe even turning violent like back then on the shore, with those boys. But Citlalli never demanded confessions.

"Did you go to see that boy when you ran away from me?"

To shrug in response felt appropriate.

"Milli!"

Startled, she stared at the atypically agitated face, twisted and less beautiful than of yore. The anxiety did not suit her sister, she reflected, troubled but more puzzled than afraid. "I don't want to talk about it."

"You must!" The air hissed as Citlalli drew it in sharply, the decorations of her lavishly embroidered *huipil* jumping along with her rising and falling breasts. "Listen, little one, listen to what I say carefully. It's important. Not only to me, your sister and a person who is concerned with you and your wellbeing, but also to our *altepetl*, its leaders and citizens, everyone around you; the Emperor and our father. Think about it, Milli. Our father seemed to be concerned with the spies from Tenochtitlan." A brief grin stretched the generous lips, surprisingly playful, almost conspiratorial. "I'm sure Father sends spies to Tenochtitlan as well, and I'm sure his people are more efficient than theirs are. But," the smile disappeared, replaced with a thoughtful frown, "the fact remains that people are spying against us as well, and the Emperor's Chief Wife is suspected. Well, naturally. Her loyalty should be with her people as much as ours should be with ours." A tiny puzzling smile twisted the generous lips. "I pity her. In her situation."

"Pity?" cried out Tlemilli, forgetting her qualms and misgivings. "No, you can't pity that poisonous snake. This woman is the most foul-tempered beast and she deserves everything bad that I hope is going to happen to her. Everything!"

But Citlalli was shaking her head sadly. "Don't waste your time wishing bad things on people. It may come back to you and you most certainly won't deserve it."

"But this snake—" began Tlemilli hotly, then stopped herself, desperate to impress her sister with lucid, grownup thinking. "This woman is bad, all bad, with no good side to her."

"Maybe, but think about it. She is married to a ruler who wishes to make war on her brother, another ruler. She mothered a baby who is both rulers' close relative. What would you do if you were her? Think about it."

"I would start by being nice to people!"

Citlalli's smile was back, wide and not patronizing. "That's a good start."

Pleased with such open approval, Tlemilli wrinkled her nose. "And then, well then, I suppose I would think hard, choose my loyalty."

"Unless you don't have a choice." The smile was gone again.

"She didn't have any more choice than I did, little one. No more choice than you will have when your time comes." A shrug. "She may not survive this war, but I'm sure she is worried about her baby the most."

"Well, I worry about my sister and my *altepetl*. I don't care for foul-mouthed snakes or their babies! Tenochtitlan should not force us into war in the way it does. You know it as well as I do."

"It is not that simple, little one." Suddenly, Citlalli's cheeks lost the last of their coloring. "The Emperor spent last night with me. He came earlier than usual and stayed very late. You see, he likes spending his time in my suite, dining and resting and talking. Sometimes he can stay well into the night, composing poetry or reading it. He seems to enjoy that, and my poems please him. But last night, he hardly touched the food, or the scrolls. Or even me." The pale cheeks blushed momentarily, then drained of color once again. "He is always nice and chatty, you see, but this time, this time, he talked about... about our stance with Tenochtitlan, about his policy toward the Great Capital, or rather our father's policy. He said it outright – your father's policy! But he didn't sound as though accusing me or our father. He talked about it as though it is an accepted thing. He was careful to point out that he trusts his Head Adviser and doesn't doubt his wisdom or the advisability of his strategy. He said it in those very words! He does trust our father, you see?"

Tlemilli just nodded, surprised with her sister's openness. Citlalli was the one to keep her thoughts to herself. "He trusts Father's policies but is not happy with them?"

The young woman's sigh held a measure of sad acceptance. "Something like that, yes. He doesn't seem to be convinced as our father is that if it comes to war, Tenochtitlan will not squash us like it did with the rest of the world. I mean, think about it. When you take a step back and away from our father's grand strategy of surprising the enemy with one swift blow in its heart, you are left with the fact that Tenochtitlan is enormously rich and strong, and that it subdued all *altepetl*s, towns, and villages around our Great Lake and further inland, that there is not a single settlement that does not pay them or their so-called partners in the Triple Alliance tribute. When you look at it like that, you can't help but notice that we are just an *altepetl* with no provinces, a thorn in their backside, maybe. We are the only ones who pay them not a single cotton cloth, not an item of food. We are not obliged to supply men for their building projects or warriors for their campaigns. And we are here, sitting in their backyard, on almost the same island as they are expanding theirs so rapidly there will be no need of a causeway soon. A perpetual reminder; maybe a lure. They humbled so many lands and places. What's to stop them from humbling us with all the power and resources they have? What's to stop them, Milli?"

Citlalli's words were gushing out as though she was the one in a need of a talk, more than the Emperor even. Tlemilli held her breath, her head reeling from tiredness, but in a bearable manner, not about to fail her step. Which would be embarrassing, to faint in the middle of the gardens, on the way to the royal side of it, if that was where they were heading. Did Citlalli intend to conduct such a conversation in her richly furnished suite of rooms, where only on the day before she was throwing fits when she, Tlemilli, merely mentioned the Emperor or Father or less successful imperial wives?

"They can't humble us, Sister," she said, somewhat at a loss. "They are no mighty deities or legendary heroes from stories. They are just an island city, exactly like ours, but with vile tempers and annoyingly haughty ways. That is all. Father knows what he is doing and so does the Emperor, even if he doubts some of it sometimes." The shadow of the main stairs beckoned, together with the aroma of the midmorning meal spreading all around this wing of the Palace. "Let us go—"

"Tenochtitlan conquered every land, every town and village, every empire, alliance, or *altepetl* around our Great Lake and far beyond it. Does that tell you nothing?" Citlalli stood in the middle of the wide alley, as stubbornly as a child refusing to go home. About to throw a tantrum? wondered Tlemilli, vaguely amused. It was not often that her perfectly accomplished sister lost her sensibility and just as she, Tlemilli, was full of practical suggestions and reasonable thinking. Come to think of it, it had never happened before.

"Well, they can't conquer us!" she offered, unsettled.

"Because Father wants to surprise them with that night attack? What if it fails? What if it doesn't go as planned, his nighttime surprise? With your friends who are spying on us, irritating Father, how can you be so certain that Tenochtitlan doesn't know what is going on and is ready and prepared?"

What nighttime surprise? wondered Tlemilli, a part of her mind curious, the other part angry. The spying boys! But she didn't need to be reminded of that!

"If Father says that his attack will work, then it will work," she muttered, staring at the uneven stones lining the alley, wishing to conceal the tears. They were again springing too readily, with no regard to her will. That boy did spy for Tenochtitlan! He didn't even try to deny it. Oh no, he was nothing to her now, a reminder of her silliness, nothing more. But was she stupid to help him back upon the Plaza, bothering to ask not a single question as to his purpose, not a word of explanation! He had needed it back then badly, oh yes. And he was interesting and good looking, and nice, and different, like no boy or man she had seen in the Palace or the Great Plaza where they had lived when she was smaller. He had such dark, deeply set eyes, so thoughtful even when troubled, so absorbed and then all of sudden intense, powerful, deep. He had seen things she never saw, animals from the stories and Smoking Mountain and maybe it was just the beginning of it, this mysterious knowledge. He *was* different!

The pain was back, as intense as when he had left, melting in the darkness, his eyes pleading and his hands stretched toward her but not about to embrace her once again, to try and explain, maybe. His flight told it all, didn't it? Proclaimed his guilt beyond any doubt.

"I don't presume to claim a deep understanding of Father's or the Emperor's plans," Citlalli was saying, oblivious of everything but her own agitation. One good turn. It was not like her sister to be that flustered or open with her thoughts. Or blind to the plight of others, for that matter. However, this time, it was a blessing. She didn't want to return to the topic of her personal unhappiness, to answer more questions about that boy. What was his name anyway? Why didn't she bother to ask him at least that?

"I think you understand it all very well," she prompted, pushing her misery away with an admirable effort, pleased with herself. He was guilty, he was! But what if he wasn't? "That nighttime surprise, what is it? I didn't understand it too well when they talked about it." An innocent blink. She had no idea what this nighttime thing was.

Citlalli waved both hands in the air. "There is nothing to understand. Father thinks that if we managed to sneak our warriors into Tenochtitlan tonight, place them around important places, like plazas and wharves, encircle Palace and storm it, and get rid of the royal family, then this *altepetl* would crumble and put up no further fight. Then we'll be the leading island and they'll be the backyard tributary." The delicate shoulders lifted slightly. "It sounds good, yet too simple to my unsophisticated female ears. They are no backward village, those conquerors of the world. They can't be caught so shamelessly off guard. And what if they do know what we are planning, with all the spies and doubtful loyalty of some of the imperial wives? The Emperor says that Tenochtitlan is being watched, so we would know if they were suspicious. He said their emperor was playing ball with his nobles the day before, unconcerned and unheeded. But somehow, it doesn't reassure me, Little Sister. Somehow, those observations make me more worried instead. And I know that I'm just a silly young woman and our father and the Emperor do know what they are doing, and yet..."

This time, her sister's shrug held so much misery-filled helplessness that Tlemilli's heart went out to her and she hurried to wrap her arms across the fragile shoulders, heedless of people around them.

"You are not silly, Citlalli. You are the smartest of them all! And if you are worried, then there is good cause." Her mind rushed ahead, overwhelmed. "But will they truly try to invade Tenochtitlan at night? This very night?" The implications kept mounting, making her head reel, not from hunger or exhaustion this time. "But how? They'll need plenty of warriors, won't they?

Even if the surprise works."

And *he* would be there in Tenochtitlan, surely; exposed to this danger. She shivered again, her thoughts racing. How to warn him, how to make him aware? There was no way to do that, and why would she, when he had run away without an explanation, guilty of what she accused him of? But he said it was not what she thought it was, and his eyes were so anxious, so intense. He didn't want to go and leave her like that, and but for him doing it anyway, she would have relented, would have let him explain. Oh yes, she would have. Now she knew it beyond a doubt.

"I don't know how they'll go about it. The Emperor didn't talk about details, only about this surprise attack and how the omens are actually against it. He said every omen he saw recently points at a disastrous outcome. There was an old man in the Palace's gardens, near the kitchen houses, speaking to a dog, being answered back. He said he saw it with his own eyes, only on the day before. And then, on the same day, the magnificent turquoise mask that hung in the main hall, on one of the walls – you must have seen it on this or that reception – well, it started to moan in a sorrowful way. He had heard it with his own ears, he said." The young woman's voice trailed all of a sudden. "It got broken. When he told the servants to take it off."

The suddenly shifting eyes made Tlemilli understand, reading her sister's expression easily, when allowed. The mask didn't get broken. The Emperor wanted the ominous relic to shatter and be gone.

"Well, if the omens are all so bad, why won't he call this night sortie off?"

Citlalli shrugged helplessly. "He can't. It will look bad, don't you think? To advisers, and warlords, and everyone. Will show weakness." A sigh. "Father is very forceful, even for the Emperor. It's not easy to stand up to Father when you don't want to do what he wants."

Tlemilli just snorted in response, the memory of the recent interrogations making her skin crawl. If the Emperor was preparing to inform Father that he wished to change his adviser's strategies and plans, she wouldn't have liked to switch places with the mighty ruler, not even for a heartbeat. And yet, a surprise nighttime attack on the mighty neighboring *altepetl*? But how? Wouldn't their warlike, always victorious neighbors be ready? Not an innocent village them, like Citlalli had said, having plenty of warriors inside the city, with no immediate campaigns to keep their emperor and the best of his veterans busy elsewhere. How was Father planning to overcome this hurdle?

And then it dawned upon her. The tunnels! *He* was talking about tunnels dug all over Tenochtitlan, full of weaponry, he said. And Father was talking about tunnels when referring to this boy in particular. *Oh mighty deities, please help him to remain safe!*

She pushed away the wave of sadness again. The nighttime attack, better think about this thing, safer! The tunnels, yes, what a perfect solution. Sneak people in innocently, then arm them only when safely in. Brilliant! But Father was so wise, so farsighted.

"They might manage nicely with that surprise attack," she said, mainly to make Citlalli feel better. "Father prepared it all very well. He has stashes of weapons all over their filthy island, so all he needs to do is to sneak in enough warriors and I'm prepared to bet my life on the fact that he thought it all through very thoroughly." Again, the painful misgivings were sneaking in. *He* looked so haunted when she began accusing him, so lost. Not guilty in the least, just aghast, dismayed, disconcerted. His eyes told her that he wasn't guilty of the things she accused him of, even though his mouth refused to offer a word of reassurance, something she needed badly, she realized now, desperately. Just one word, to say that no, he wasn't spying for Tenochtitlan, that there was a reason for him being there and involved, another different reason, and she would have flung herself back into his arms and would not let him go, the servants looking for her or not. She would have rather gone over the wall together with him. Could she? The sudden thought made her knees go weak. Could she have done it, gone over the wall with him, and into the city or wherever he was going? And why-ever not? No one would miss her here in the Palace, no one but Citlalli, and Citlalli would have understood. And if so...

"Where did you get all this information, Milli?" her sister was asking, peering at her with renewed interest, even with a spark of the old familiar amusement, so very missed. "Through your usual eavesdropping? Who did you manage to overhear this time?"

"No, no, it's different," she breathed, needing to remain alone and to think; to think hard. How to find him now? How to let him know that she wasn't angry, not anymore? There must be a way to do that. A message! She must send him a message, but through whom?

"Milli, are you all right? You look as though you have seen a ghost!" Citlalli's eyes were very close, very worried. "You are still shattered by this night. And you still must tell me about it. Come. Let us take you to my quarters, have you eat a good midmorning meal, with all your favorite delicacies." Gentle hands steered her around, making her face the towering stairs, their glitter violent in the fierce glow of the high morning sun, hurting the eyes.

Then the motion stopped abruptly, as their hearts went still in perfect unison, or so it felt. Father's embroidered cloak and his headdress of the Head Adviser were impossible not to recognize, no matter how one might wish such a vision to be a mistake. Not a chance. He was watching them, standing midway down the wide staircase, his arms linked across the broadness of his chest, encased in glittering jewelry, his followers a few steps behind, hovering, like always. His expression was impossible to decipher, not from such a distance and when looking against the glowering sun deity, but it held no kindness and not even the usual aloof disinterest, not this time. She could have bet her life on it.

CHAPTER 12

This time, they didn't need Ahuitzotl to reach the Emperor. The warriors from Acachinanco road didn't mince matters the moment their captives were dumped in the courtyard of the temple adjacent to the Eagle Warriors' Hall. The lack of the heavily armed messengers from the second crossroad did not seem to bother anyone. They were too busy for that. Still, on their way back to the city, Necalli felt a light twinge of worry. What if the Emperor didn't believe their tale, not to its fullest? The men they had fought on the crossroad would have been a great help at proving their point.

Shrugging, he tried to push his misgivings away. What they brought would surely be enough, the original smugglers and the paper. It seemed to satisfy the imperial warriors back upon the wrong crossroad and while finding the correct one, with only one half-dead body present to strengthen their point, that of the man whose face the workshop boy had crushed with a thrown stone, hurling his flying missile with expected accuracy. But this boy was a wonder. So clumsy in some things, out of his depth and pathetically undecided at times, watching the world through those deeply set, observant, often cornered, haunted eyes, unpresumptuous but never knowing his place, never just following without asking questions or bringing forth arguments, yet so reliable, always there. Then at the direst of moments, the puma would come out roaring, surprising its owner as well, Necalli suspected, striking out and lethal, leaving dead or badly maimed bodies in its wake – witness that man with the crushed face. Everyone could hurl stones, but not to such telling effect.

Even the imperial warriors were impressed enough to comment on that, the quality of this hit. A pity he couldn't claim it for himself.

The rest of their "victims" were missing, the hastily tied man and the one the workshop boy managed to get rid of while taking the scum's prettily polished club, an achievement in itself. Had it been an obsidian sword, the commoner would have been made a warrior on the spot, Necalli suspected grudgingly. Or at least put to work hard in *calmecac*, honing his warrior's skills; not in this or that *telpochcalli*. If he or Axolin worried about the actual possibility of their protégé being shipped to one of the commoners' schools, they could put such thoughts to rest now. The Emperor clearly liked using his unusual tool, fascinated with the strange foreigner as much as they all were.

The Palace's wall beckoned, glaring in the strong afternoon sun. Hastening his step, Necalli touched the hurting side of his face again, willing the swollenness to go away. The bloated eye still pulsated with pain, refusing to focus and let him see properly, making the need to walk straight an effort. Oh yes, that was a mighty blow from that hulking piece of excrement. It was a wonder it didn't send him into the other worlds, like the workshop boy's fist did to this same offender later on. Another thing to puzzle over, or rather fish out of their exotic companion. Where would one learn to use one's fist to such telling effect? The commoner would have to share this knowledge. He owed them that much.

The thought of Axolin made him uneasy and, as they approached the narrow gate of the side entrance that the warriors headed for with no hesitation but were stopped and challenged with questions, he frowned, disliking the twinge of guilt, not a very familiar sensation. Axolin would be beyond furious by now, left out of the daring adventures, sanctioned by the Emperor himself this time, no unauthorized sneaking out of school. He would make a big deal out of it, maybe even stop talking to them, go and friend that annoying brute Acoatl, just to spite him, Necalli, for preferring the commoner wonder and his company. But he didn't prefer or choose the workshop boy ahead of his friend of two summers. Things just happened this way. Still, Axolin would refuse to be pacified with mere reassurances and promises of a better treatment. He knew that one well enough to predict the worst of reactions. Even though, deep down, he had to admit that it wasn't fair, and his friend certainly did not deserve to be left out and behind just like that. However, he had no time or patience to deal with Axolin's fits of jealousy, not now. He was too spent and hurt and swamped with revelations to add a moment of smooth-talking oratory to any of it, not with the looming war and the possibility of being involved, truly involved.

"Those two can't enter."

One of the men at the gate was eyeing them with open suspicion, his eyes squinted into near disappearance, face screwed with displeasure.

"The Revered One may wish to interview them," was the hesitant answer. For some reason, their imperial escorts seemed to lose half of their naughtiness and aplomb. It made Necalli uneasy. But wasn't this one of the revered houses of the highest military order they were trying to talk their way into? Inconceivable! He was too deep in thought to notice where they were heading before, assuming their destination was the Palace, an awe-inspiring place in itself, but not like the House of Eagle Warriors. One glimpse at the protruding heads of stone birds of prey adorning the wide staircase and the murals of warriors and serpents spreading along the walls, painted in vivid red, glimmering proudly, made his breath catch and his skin crawl.

"The boys?" repeated the man at the gate, incredulous.

"Yes, the boys." Their escorts exchanged flickering glances. "Those two beaten, wild-looking ocelots, yes."

The man at the doorway didn't join the covert chuckling. "They may wait on this patio, but this is the farthest they'll be allowed to step." His stormy gaze swept past them. "And only if you promise that the Revered One might wish to see them. Otherwise, they are out and you will be answering to the Chief Warlord himself. You personally!"

The smirking stopped, replaced with appropriate gravity again.

"Go to this bench and don't move a limb until you are called for." The curt nod of the leading man from Acachinanco road indicated the long, narrow seat adorned by murals reflected on the wall it was adjacent to.

Afraid that his companion might miss the significance of quick wordless reactions, Necalli motioned the workshop boy to proceed ahead, however to his relief, the commoner wonder did not argue this time, not like back on the accursed crossroad.

"I think they won't be rushing to chop our limbs off if we perch on that bench," he said after a while as their inhospitable hosts and noticeably subdued escorts disappeared in the semidarkness under the staircase, swallowed into its depths. The breeze was stronger now and the shadow the sloping wall provided most welcome, calming his fraying nerves. "Sit, workshop wonder. Don't stand here like one of those columns." The relatively small part of the nearby patio was adorned most lavishly with an intricate roof and four columns supporting it, decorated with stone ornaments of serpent heads and stone flowers. "They'll make one such out of you, carve you in flowers and put you out to support that roof if you keep standing here like a Palace's guard on duty."

The brief twist of his companion's lips was unmistakable, making him feel better. The stone statue came back to life, and not too soon. He didn't like solitude, certainly not when facing possible difficult encounters, about to be reprimanded, maybe, and whatnot, and the way the workshop boy was barely breathing by his side made him feel very much on his own indeed.

"What is this place?" Perching on the edge of their imposing seat, the commoner glanced around as though checking possible routes of escape.

"If I tell, you'll faint."

The glance shot at him held enough flashing anger to reassure him that his companion was not beyond hope.

"You really want to know?"

"Yes."

"Well, you've been graced with the entrance into the heart of one of the highest orders of warriors in this land. The Eagle

Warriors' Hall is equal only to the Jaguar Warriors' one on the other side of the Plaza. How about that? Not a bad location for your commoner limbs to tread."

The workshop boy's eyes were widening out of proportion. "The Jaguar Warriors?" he whispered.

"No, the Eagle Ones. The Jaguar Warriors Hall is on the other side of the Plaza, next to the Palace and Tezcatlipoca temple. And you better not mix these two. Our hosts might be offended." A wink seemed to be in order as his companion was beginning to look terrified again. "Relax, man. It's not that bad. The Emperor is probably visiting them, making inspections or orating before the best of his warriors. That's why they brought us here. To report to him. Like we were supposed to do anyway."

The commoner boy nodded, not reassured, his hands clutching onto his newly acquired club with much force, making his knuckles go white. Was he going to fight the most renowned force of the capital with his precious spoil of a weapon? The images that invaded his mind made Necalli wish to snicker out loud.

"Tell me where you learned to swing your fists so efficiently. It wasn't bad what you did back there on the mainland, that last punch; not bad at all. Sent that hulk straight into the dream worlds and he wasn't a weak, skinny type, was he?"

The protectively hunched shoulders jerked in the semblance of a shrug. "He came back to our world quick enough to disappear before we returned."

"That has nothing to do with your punch. He stayed out for long enough to let us get his messages, tie him up, and be gone." His amusement evaporating, Necalli busied himself with studying the carving of a four-petal flower next to his foot. That meant four directions of the world, he remembered, each for relevant coordination, dedicated to the deity responsible for it. "That filthy piece of rotten meat was huge, fat enough to be protected against regular punches. His jaw should have broken your fist instead of the other way around."

"I didn't hit him in the jaw."

"Where then?"

"Higher above. The side of the head next to the eyes, on the same line the eyes are. A person would collapse right away if hit there with enough force. My father said so, and he was right, apparently."

Necalli found himself staring. "Your father said so?"

"Yes."

"Your father should teach in *calmecac* if he knows all that."

A light snicker was his answer. He grinned in his turn, but fleetingly, his mind still racing, analyzing what had been said. If he could learn something like that, to hit with such accuracy, unerring, he would gain a certain edge over other boys and later on even his fellow warriors. To be able to send a person into other worlds with one's fists alone was not a bad ability, to be used when needed.

"Can you teach me that punch?"

"Yes, of course." His companion's eyes were upon him now, over their initial dread, observant again. But this one was a deep piece of excrement, saying little, listening much. "I never used it before. Didn't think I'd manage. You need to practice this thing, Father says."

"Didn't you?"

"Well, Father made me hit things here and there, but not in real fights. He said it's a dangerous blow, to use only if my life is threatened for real. Not in fights with other boys."

"Well, it was threatened this afternoon. And through our Tlatelolco adventures." Against his will, Necalli chuckled. "It must be very peaceful in your village or around it if you never used real punches before."

As expected, a shrug was his answer, the closing face and the clouding eyes relating it all. But it must be difficult to be so far away from home, in such a different place, surrounded by the grandeur of the Great Capital, its wonders and dangers and forceful ways. Did this one miss his gods-forsaken village?

"Well, if you teach me and Axolin this punch, we'll find a way to repay you." He made a face. "Axolin must be so very mad by now, but this will mollify him some. Bound to."

"Why would Axolin be mad?"

"To be left behind like that? Wouldn't you be mad if we

sneaked out on you in the middle of the night, went to enjoy all those *legal* adventures, and told you nothing about it?"

"I don't know." The workshop boy was frowning again. "Would you take me along if it wasn't me who woke you up last night?"

"Yes, of course. We are in this together."

The deeply set eyes were widening again. "We are?"

"Yes, of course. That's what friends do to each other, you know, but we've been lousy toward Axolin and will have to find ways to make it up to him."

"Yes." Again, his companion was looking away, back in his thoughts, troubled.

"What?"

"Nothing. I just... I didn't think, didn't think we are friends... like real friends..."

To chuckle at such silly mumbling helped to cover his own brief spell of embarrassment. "And what did you think we were? Lovers?"

That made the broad cheeks turn all sorts of glaring colors. "Go jump..."

A group of men dressed in plain cotton cloaks but with an obvious bulging of either swords or clubs attached to their girdles spilled down the wide staircase and toward the narrow side entrance they had been admitted through earlier, their bearing haughty, eyes watchful, scanning the surroundings in a practiced scrutiny. Clearly Eagle Warriors but for their outfits. Necalli forced his eyes down and away, anxious to keep his manners and make no blunders in such a place. When it became quiet again, with the men pouring out and into the adjacent alley, exchanging quiet words, he noticed that he held his breath.

"What are they up to?" he whispered, unable to keep quiet.

"Who?'

"The Eagle Warriors, who else?"

"Those were them?"

"Obviously."

Another spell of silence, then a smaller group descended the stairs, this one progressing at a slower pace, with clear deference, the warriors in the forefront wearing full regalia of beaked helmets but not their body armor of layered cotton soaked in salt and other extracts to make it harder for the obsidian to penetrate.

"The Emperor," breathed the workshop boy, clearly ready to go back to his terrified state of staring and stammering.

Necalli forced his own taut nerves to relax. "About time. He almost made us wait." To push his elbow into his companion's side proved a challenge when needed to be done carefully, drawing no attention. "Bad manners our Emperor has."

No chuckle greeted his words, but the tense limbs next to him relaxed imperceptibly. Good. More stammering in front of the Emperor, who was busy with his elite warriors, wouldn't do. The mighty ruler had enough on his plate, gathering sleepless nights and doing a great deal of running about, surely out of patience and in need of brisk, crisply spoken reports. And no, he wouldn't be letting him, Necalli, do all the talking, making it easy for everyone involved. The Emperor would wish to hear from both direct sources, just like back at that first audience more than a market interval ago, just like last night when the workshop boy was too distraught and miserable and afraid, and with him, Necalli, ready to speak for them both in the best of the orating fashion, yet stopped almost immediately. The ever practical Tenochtitlan ruler was not about to make do with secondary information, that much they had learned so far.

Both on their feet and hardly daring to breathe, they watched the group reach the neatly paved ground, splitting as they did so, the warriors turning to enter the dimness below the stairs and an obvious set of rooms spreading underneath it, revealing the tall figure of their ruler, himself dressed as imposingly in the headdress of a leading warrior and a cloak of vibrant coloring and glittering ornaments, the massive breastplate adorning his chest, blinding against the glow of the high sun.

Necalli felt his own vocal abilities about to betray him. But where were the warriors who had brought them here? Still huddling under the stairs, enjoying the coolness of the underground walls?

The magnificent feathers rustled as the Emperor turned toward the gates, his followers close by. Yet something must have attracted his attention. Or maybe it was the custom of scanning one's surroundings, noting if something was out of place. Two ruffled boys huddling in the patio of the elite warriors' sanctuary certainly were no ordinary sight. The wide palm came up to shield the narrowing eyes, sending more flickering lights reflected by the multitude of gleaming bracelets. A curt order, then another, and the Emperor's followers spread, some heading toward the opening in the wall, disappearing in it, some freezing at their previous spots, frowning in puzzlement.

"Well, this is a sight I didn't expect to see in my Eagle Warriors' Hall." The words rang with enough power to reach them, genuine to a degree, neither distant nor cold, or even displeased. "How did you enter these premises, young rascals? And in such a state!"

By now, he had closed the distance and so the last words came out more privately, spoken in no orating tones. Necalli took a deep breath, encouraged by the affable, somewhat amused scrutiny.

"We've been brought here to wait for you, Revered Emperor," he said, his voice unsatisfactorily squeaky, not manly enough. He cleared his throat. "The men you had sent to the mainland thought you would wish to interview us upon our return."

The Emperor nodded soberly, his forehead creasing, a clear hint of displeasure creeping in, unsettling Necalli's painfully gained confidence. "Where are they?"

"Oh, they... they went down there, under the stairs. They entered the halls under the staircase, Revered Emperor. I think they hoped to find you there." That came out in a pitiful rush. He drew a deep breath, but before worthier words came to mind, the man was already signaling his followers. In another heartbeat, some disappeared in the semidarkness of the staircase's passageway. The rest were sent back, to stand where they were until now, at a respectable distance but ready to do the mighty ruler's bidding.

"Now tell me what happened." Those words held a measure of clear impatience, yet the eyes of the man were not without its previous light amusement, as though expecting to hear something wild, even welcoming it.

"We went out there to wait at the road leading to Acachinanco, Revered Emperor," began Necalli, encouraged, pleased to hear his voice ringing clearly now, without stridency or stammering. "The smugglers from Tlatelolco were already there when we arrived, so the warriors you sent hid and they—"

The imperial hand cut the words short. "Relay the important parts. What happened with the messengers from Toltitlan? Did they arrive? Did they bring their answer?"

Necalli nodded hastily, collecting his thoughts anew, wishing the Emperor would direct some of this flood of questioning at the workshop boy, as was his custom. That would give him a piece of much needed respite.

"They brought messages, yes," he mumbled. "In writing. Your warriors, Revered Emperor, they have the scroll, they are keeping it, that is..."

An impatient gaze shot toward the staircase. "What does it say?"

He swallowed hard. "It says that the swords and the shields were accepted."

"By Toltitlan alone?"

"No." He licked his lips. "Well, there was a glyph of the neighboring Cuauhtitlan there as well. Both glyphs were present in the message... I think..." For the life of him, he couldn't remember what was in the scroll besides the glyphs concerning swords and shields. "We were in a hurry to bring the message, and to let your people know. Your warriors, that is; we were in a hurry to reach them and I only glanced at the scroll when Miztli found it."

He didn't mean to put the workshop boy on the spot by mentioning his name outright, but now that it happened, he felt a wave of relief surging through his limbs, easing his strained muscles, while the piercing gaze left him, leaping toward his companion, narrowing some more.

"You found the scroll? How?"

As expected, the commoner seemed as though he would rather

disappear under the polished stones of the pavement.

"Yes, well, I did," he muttered, quailing visibly under the penetrating gaze, clearly not noticing the amused, even somewhat good-natured glint. "It was just as the man we were fighting... when he went down and Necalli thought we should use his cloak to tie him... he tried to free it and then the paper; it just fell out, and I picked it up, because, because it might be important, and..."

The Emperor didn't seem to mind the disjointed mumbling this time, nor did he pay attention to the usual lack of titles. But did the wild commoner keep forgetting those!

"Whom did you fight, boy? And with what? That club?" The twinkle was more pronounced now, clear in the gaze resting upon the workshop boy's new weaponry.

"I... no, it was before that I used the club and then Necalli, he saved me by pouncing on that man..."

"Revered Emperor!" Their previous escorts appeared from under the stairs, looking worried, rushing toward them in an indecent hurry.

The Emperor's lips pursed imperceptibly. "Bring me the scroll."

One of the warriors fumbled with his girdle. Fascinated, Necalli watched the strong face of the Tenochtitlan ruler turning stonier. The contents of the message clearly did not please him, even if they didn't manage to surprise him.

"Where are the people who carried this message as well as the recipients of it?" The words shot out like flinty arrows.

"They are alive and bound, waiting to be interrogated."

A short nod. "All of them?"

The men dropped their gazes. "Except the two who had managed to get away," muttered the leading one miserably.

Nothing changed in the stony face. "Explain."

The warriors' spokesman licked his lips. "We were waiting at the place the Tlatelolcan criminals were waiting, Revered Emperor. However, there is another crossroad leading to the towns in question, and there I had sent the boys to watch and report to us if they saw something suspicious." Through another nervous pause accompanied with more wetting of lips, Necalli hid his contempt, incensed with such a distorted version of the events but relieved that they didn't have time to tell their side of the story. There was no need to make enemies out of warriors the Emperor used for secret missions, clearly important people, able and efficient, even if they didn't deign to listen to his, Necalli's, reasoning at first. "By the time we reached the place, only one man was still lying there, wounded badly enough to remain in the other worlds. We brought him along with the captured criminals from the first crossroad."

"Who had wounded him? How?"

"One of the boys." This time, all eyes went to them. "His face was caved in quite thoroughly."

Necalli licked his lips in his turn. "It was Miztli. He threw the stone."

The Emperor's eyes crinkled momentarily. "The shooter, eh? Forgot to bring the sling this time?"

The workshop boy blushed badly. "I didn't, didn't have a sling then, yes. Revered Emperor."

"I see." The man nodded thoughtfully. "What happened to the other two men?"

"He hit one with the club," ventured Necalli when the questioned hero fell silent once again. "But the man probably came to his senses later on. And the last one we managed to send to the other worlds, but he was clearly not dead, so we tied him with his cloak, but maybe the other one freed him when we were away."

A group of warriors was lingering nearby, again elite eagle fighters but clad in plain cloaks, while the amount of messengers waiting for the ruler's bidding to approach him seemed to grow with every passing heartbeat. The Emperor's eyes went to them, assessing, gesturing some to come nearer, indicating the willingness to listen to quick reports. Watching one of the talking men, Necalli tried to make his heart calm, realizing that in his eagerness to retell the happenings upon the crossroad, he had forgotten to use the proper title just like his workshop companion did.

"There is much activity, mainly near the wharves next to the old causeway, Revered Emperor," one of the messengers was gushing, clearly anxious to report his news. "Quite a bad crowding on the other side of it as well, as far as one can see. My people are sneaking all over their wharves, listening."

"Good." The Emperor nodded coldly, disclosing no emotion. "Keep watching their activities on both sides. It's bound to become worse toward sunset."

A curt gesture summoned another man, this time one of the elite warriors in a plain cloak. "Were your men spread out as I directed? Near the Tlatelolcan causeway and the wharves, but also the marketplace and each plaza, however small and unimportant?"

"Oh yes, Revered Emperor. I supervised their allocation myself." The man looked unbecomingly anxious. "And their disguises as well, their clothing and their behavior."

"Good." Another curt nod, but this one was warmer, holding clear appreciation. "They are not subtle enough, our neighbors, are they?" A rhetorical question no one attempted to answer. Necalli listened, afraid to breathe, lest it would remind the Emperor of their presence, to be sent away with a wave of the imperial hand. Oh, but this intricate planning and preparation was all to do with Tlatelolco, wasn't it? And yet, how and why? Why was the Emperor allocating people all over Tenochtitlan, disguised warriors and such?

"The tunnel with weaponry is watched most closely, I trust."

"Oh yes, Revered Emperor." The man allowed himself a light grin with the side of his mouth. "There has been much activity in those areas through the first part of the morning and on the day before. Not very well hidden either." Another hinted grin, gone as quickly. "However, they seem to be quiet since mid-afternoon. Which makes one wonder."

"They might be crowding that island under the causeway." This came from the workshop boy, a matter-of-fact observation, offered in a calm, thoughtful voice.

They all turned to stare, even Necalli. Accustomed to the foreigner's spells of impulsive talking and deeds, at the wrong timing most of those, his independent thinking and this momentary forgetfulness of the company well above his status, he still had to fight the wave of hysterical laughter down, watching the warriors' gaping faces. Even the Emperor was staring, frowning but in no direful way, more puzzled than angered. The village boy looked again as though about to faint. The stammering speech would be back now. Necalli gathered his senses hurriedly.

"There was this island under the causeway, Revered Emperor," he said, trying to cover as much of this slip as he could without sounding as insolent as his companion did, presuming to offer his opinion to the mighty ruler without being asked to do so.

"What island?" The Emperor's lips did not quiver in amusement, not anymore.

"Not far away from the wharves of the old temple. In the reeds. Maybe five, maybe ten times twenty paces away." He tried to calculate frantically, to remember how many paces they went before the monster attacked them and how many paces may have been left. "The tunnel led there and the smugglers seemed to make use of it, reaching the island by canoes, then diving into the tunnel, presumably."

"Why didn't you report any of that before?" Now the man sounded outright angry. Necalli quailed inside.

"Revered Emperor, it is my fault. I should have told about this island before, when telling... when telling about the tunnel and all." Again the workshop boy burst in, in a surprisingly steady voice, with almost no stammering. A wonder. "I can guide... we can guide your men there, by the way of the wharves. We can do it easily, can draw no attention. It won't be—"

The Emperor was already summoning more men. "Make the boys take you to the island under the causeway," he tossed at the second reporting warrior. "Take no more than a few men, dressed plainly. Do not show your eagerness in any way. You might be watched most closely around the temple in question." A cold gaze brushed past them, lingered for no more than a fraction of a heartbeat, contemplating. "After you have shown that place, do whatever the warriors tell you. Do not – I repeat, do not! – offer an argument or try to go on side missions of your own. You are not to be exempt from punishment even if you are successful and have the best interest of this *altepetl* in your hearts. Is that clear to you?" The freezing gaze moved away. "I value obedience as much as independent thinking. Do not mistake that."

Bereft of words, they just nodded.

CHAPTER 13

Quetzalli fell upon them while Mother was busy scolding her youngest for running around unsupervised and in such troublesome times. He was allowed to play on the patio, or even down their alley with his friends, but she had explicitly forbidden any excursions to the marketplace or the wharves, not with such unrest everywhere, so many rumors and talk.

"It is so strange out there!" Quetzalli had breathed, bursting into the main room, agog with excitement. "The marketplace is alive with men, as though everyone just decided to go shopping, not trusting their women to do that. Imagine!"

"What were you doing running out there, Quetzalli?" demanded Mother in the same angry tone she had used on Chantli's brother just now, still agitated and furious. "At this time of the day, you have no business running around the marketplace alleys. Your Second Mother wouldn't send you out, not this close to evening time."

Quetzalli made a face, one of those cute winning grimaces she had in abundance. "Second Mother would send me out at night if she needed something badly enough." Her shoulders lifted briefly in a sweetly apologetic manner. "It's not dangerous out there, just strange. The sun is still high enough to make one sweat like when bathing in *temazcalli*."

"When you are out of something at this time of the day, you come here and ask for it, little one," insisted Mother, a hint of amusement creeping in, unable to stand firm against Quetzalli's charm. No one could.

Chantli signaled her friend with her eyes – *in a little while*. Her loom still needed much attention, but she could claim a well-deserved break after completing a few more rounds of weaving, finish the pattern of yet another line of rectangles, use up most of the yellow and red threads. Oh yes, this could be claimed as an excuse, the need to go and fetch more maguey strings. Mother couldn't expect her to weave for all eternity.

She sighed, then motioned her friend to keep Mother busy and in better spirits than before. Quetzalli had a talent for things like that. Enviously, she shook her head. If only there was a way of making Mother relax her watch, trust her daughter like before the Tlatelolcan adventures. However, her previous day's escapades did nothing to improve her situation at home, with her barely managing to return with dusk, sweaty and disheveled, some of her baskets' contents missing. And how could it not, with all their running and creeping around? Well, who cared for the stupid baskets when the matter of Tenochtitlan's wellbeing was at stake, important enough matters to make the Emperor himself interview them, her and Necalli, make them retell their news.

Oh, but was it thrilling and dreadful and awe-inspiring, the Emperor so tall and broad-shouldered and imposing, so muscled and full of scars, so imperial but not terrifying; intimidating, yes, but to certain degree, possible to talk to. Necalli had done it so well, had spoken with so much confidence, deferential and earnest and matter-of-fact, speaking with so much presence of mind and clarity, reporting the happenings, venturing his own observations only when asked to. Did they learn how to talk to mighty rulers out there in his *calmecac*?

"It's not something one can point one's finger at. Everything seems normal when you go around. Just the amount of people on the streets, men instead of women, you see." Quetzalli's pouting voice tore her from her memories, the longing still there, the wish to drop it all and run out and find him and tag along on more exciting adventures. He had told her to stay at home for a day or two, not to chance any more marketplace encounters with the Tlatelolcan scum, but they had a hard time separating out there in the darkness of the alley after he had taken her back here, prolonging the moment, talking silly things, not daring to do what they both wanted, knowing it was not the time. Still she knew that the memory of that Tlatelolcan shore was strong in his mind, prevailing, as persistent as in her thoughts, and but for people still walking around and then Mother's voice coming from the patio, interrupting the semidarkness, invading their private world, they might have...

"Whatever is happening, it's better that you all stay inside," repeated Mother, crouching next to the cooking stones, feeding dry branches to the fire underneath those. "The men out there would start brawling and none of you want to be a part of something like that."

Quetzalli went on making agreeable noises, then slipped toward Chantli and her loom. "Punished again, sister?" she whispered, dropping on the vacant part of her mat.

Chantli rolled her eyes tellingly.

"Can you get away as far as your patio, at least?"

"When I finish this thing." She motioned at the stretched threads. "It won't take long."

"Well, hurry." Helpfully, her friend's nimble fingers got to work, arranging the colorful edges, offering the relevant ones.

"Thank you," breathed Chantli, then moved her head closer. "It was incredible yesterday, just incredible! But Mother was so very mad. I came back really late and the things in my baskets were missing."

"I saw your handsome *pilli* just now."

Her heart stopped at once. "Where?"

"Heading toward the wharves. Or maybe the causeway. Or our neighborhood, eh?" A wink. "Maybe he was on a mission of freeing you. He had an ample escort, you know."

Chantli tried not to let the threads escape, her trembling fingers unable to cope with them all of a sudden. "Who? Who was with him?"

"But you do care, sister, don't you?" Quetzalli's voice trilled, attracting the attention of both her mother and her little brother, still skulking after the scolding, making faces but daring not to argue. He was forbidden to go out without permission as well, until informed otherwise. Poor thing.

"I want to walk Quetzalli home, Mother." She heard her own voice ringing with stridency, holding no calm. "I'll be back in a matter of heartbeats."

The older woman's lips pursed. "I don't believe I can trust you to return right away, little one."

"Yes, you can, Mother. I'll be back in just a few more heartbeats, and I'll finish this cloth before it gets dark. It will be perfect. You'll see!"

"Why can she go out and I can't?" cried out her brother, the little rascal.

"I'm not going out! Just walking Quetzalli home."

"It's the same as going out," insisted the little beast, incensed over his own unfair treatment and thus turning vengeful. They usually got along very well, covering for each other when need be. "She was missing half a day and she lost her baskets and I was missing for only a little today, and it's not—"

"I didn't lose my baskets and it's not any of your filthy business what I do, you little monkey! You—"

But her heated tirade was cut short, as Acatlo, the eldest of their half-brothers and Father' right hand, burst through the doorway in the same fashion Quetzalli did such a short time ago but with none of the pretty girl's elation or flair. Just the opposite. His not unpleasant-looking face was screwed in a most direful scowl, and his eyes shot thunderbolts, glowing worse than the coals in the melting room braziers. Not a very familiar sight. Acatlo was gloomy and prone to anger, but not with such passion and heat.

"What happened?" Mother was on her feet now, staring, her hands dripping water and dough.

For a moment, the enraged man said nothing, breathing heavily, glancing around the room. His eyes grew darker when they rested upon her, but his gaze did not linger, sliding on toward the rest of his younger half-siblings. "Father wants you in the workshop, you lazy monkey," he tossed. "And you better start appearing there every morning. You are not that young as to not start putting in a real effort."

The smaller boy took a step back and toward his mother.

"What is this all about?" she demanded, frowning now. "If your father needs his youngest son's help and he sent you to bring him over, you don't have to make it sound as though he was avoiding his duties. Don't take your own frustration out on your siblings!" She motioned the smaller boy curtly. "Run to the workshop and help your father." Then her attention returned to her cooking facilities, but not before bestowing another direful glance at her eldest stepson. "Is there still much work in the workshop left for today?"

"What do you think, woman?" demanded Acatlo, his massive chest still rising and falling, smeared with so much soot he looked like a priest reading for a special ritual, when they used to paint their bodies with black dye.

"Don't be insolent," admonished Mother after peering at her stepson for another heartbeat. "Answer my question."

"Yes, there is much work to be done!" he breathed. "Like there always is since the unworthy piece of excrement from the dung-covered village scampered away to enjoy the life of the capital, may he break his both legs and arms and his neck and die painfully slow, covered in feces and—"

"Acatlo!" called out Mother, her cheeks taking the color of the setting sun. "Don't talk like that in the house and in front of the girls. How could you? Your father won't be pleased to hear the words you used!"

"Father won't be pleased to learn that the ungrateful rat is strutting out there, happy with himself!" he retorted, beyond caring, or so it seemed.

"What do you mean?" the older woman muttered as Chantli's heart picked up its tempo.

"Just what I said," he spat. "Courts or not, the filthy creature is out there, enjoying his life. I just saw him, going down to the wharves, all busy and purposeful, dressed in a cloak. Imagine that! The filthy piece of peasant excrement that he is!"

"But... but how... how could it be?" Now Mother looked unbecomingly taken aback, even frightened.

"If I knew, I would be dragging him here from wherever he is hiding. Or what would remain of him!"

"Oh, oh, your father... he won't take it well!"

The hefty man rolled his eyes, his heavy abrasive fists clenched. "We'll find out where the filthy rat is hiding. Father must make it his business to find out, to lodge a complaint with the local authorities—"

"He is not a filthy rat and he isn't hiding!" She heard the words coming out of her mouth and didn't regret them, not for a moment. Acatlo was always too tough with the village boy, even if Father wasn't, although according to Necalli, Father was also terribly unfair sometimes. Why didn't she ask in what ways? "You can't force him back here. He won't be slaving in the workshop, not anymore."

They all turned toward her, bereft of words for a moment. She could hear Quetzalli breathing by her side, all ears, afraid to miss a word or a gesture. Such juicy gossip! She didn't care.

"What do you mean, Chantli?" demanded Mother but in a small voice. Her eyes were disproportionally large, two gaping plates.

"Just what I said," she repeated, deep down afraid that she must have sounded ridiculously like her detested half-brother. "The village boy is learning in *calmecac* these days because the Emperor himself put him there. He has seen his worth after what this boy has done in Tlatelolco and he is now putting him where he rightly belongs, with boys who are trained to be great warriors!"

To see Acatlo's widening eyes and loosely gaping mouth was a sight worth seeing, even though it sent rays of apprehension down her spine, the tiny surge of fear she didn't care to admit. He was a violent man, her half-brother, and what if Mother didn't manage to stop him? He never hurt her or the little one, but it was only because they never crossed his path, never did something to make him angry. And because of Mother's watchful eye.

"What is that nonsense you are talking about?" he demanded in the end, his eyes still wide but his mouth closing, pursing ominously. "What are you blabbering about, you stupid girl?"

"I'm not blabbering and I'm not stupid!" she flared, beyond caring. "And the village boy does deserve a better life than slaving in the workshop, cleaning and melting and doing everything you don't wish to be bothered with. He was not a slave, but you made him into such, and now he is enjoying the life that he deserves and you just hate to admit that none of you can measure up to him, can make the workshop work in the way he did!"

"You stupid little rat—" he began, and she struggled to her feet, hindered by her loom and the wide strap that fastened it across her back, and her fear that he would reach her when she was still on the floor, defenseless, but Mother was already between them, spreading her arms wide, stopping her stepson with the sheer power of her will and the habit of obedience formed over half twenty past summers.

"Stop it, you two!" she cried out in the voice that they all knew well. Mother was a nice person, not very powerfully built, not like Quetzalli's Second Mother, such a hefty matron, but when she wished them to do her bidding, they all did, even overgrown brutes like Acatlo. "Stop this bickering over a person that is of no consequence to both of you. Go to the workshop, Acatlo, and I'll send you..." Momentarily, she stopped, as though rethinking the matter. "I'll bring you all your meals there in a short while. Now go. Go!"

Unable to see but her mother's back, Chantli knew that her eyes were willing the angry man away, radiating power that helped her raise this brood of four children, two of them difficult and not even hers. Getting to her feet with studied movements, she let her breath out carefully, slowly, her limbs unpleasantly light, not very responsive. Quetzalli's hands helped her out of the loom's strap, for which she was grateful, but then Mother was facing them again, with Acatlo storming out and away, and the penetrating gaze of the older woman making her struggle with the uncooperative tool more difficult.

"What is this all about, Chantli? What do you know about the village boy and how?" The generous eyes were now mere slits, boring into her, uncompromising.

"I heard about him," she mumbled. "Only on the day before. I didn't know a thing before that!" She pressed her arms to her chest, imploring, hating how her voice sounded, pleading and weak. "I swear I didn't!"

"Who told you?"

"The boy who was with us in Tlatelolco back then." To face the crude wooden floor felt safer now, better than her mother's piercing gaze for certain.

"Where did you meet him?"

A moment of heavy silence. "On the marketplace."

"She didn't," piped up Quetzalli, the most welcome of interruptions. "I was there, talking to that boy from *calmecac*, and when Chantli came along, he told us about your apprentice. He was going to tell it to me anyway. With no connection to Chantli." The girl paused demurely. "He is a nice boy. He is interested in me."

But Mother was not to be fooled that easily. "Were you with that boy in Tlatelolco, Chantli?"

She found it safer just to nod. "I told you about it all, Mother. Everything! Don't you remember?"

"Yes, I do remember, but you did not tell me anything about your intention to see any of these boys again, Daughter!"

"She didn't," ventured Quetzalli again. "I was seeing him yesterday, not her. And he was telling me about your village apprentice..."

"Stop that, both of you! The village boy is of no interest to me. But you, Chantli, are! And I will not—"

Another draft of air brought in her little brother in a hurry. "Mother, Mother! Father wishes you to come to the workshop!"

The older woman pressed her lips so tightly they lost most of their coloring, turning distinctly pale. "I will be back soon and then we'll have a good talk. Quetzalli, you better run home now, girl. Before your family starts to worry." A reproachful glare made them both quiver. "Chantli taught us all about how worrisome it is not to have a girl back at home after darkness."

In another heartbeat, she was gone, leaving them standing in the suddenly empty room, staring.

"That was a sight I could do without," breathed Quetzalli. "Your *nantli* getting all angry. I never imagined her capable of something like that."

"You didn't see it all yet," muttered Chantli, the reaction setting in, making her eyes water. "She'll go down hard on me now. They all will. I shouldn't have opened my stupid mouth. Who cares what that good-for-nothing Acatlo said about the village boy? It wasn't my business anyway."

"Was that what your handsome *calmecac* admirer talked to you about as you scampered off and around that corner? About your runaway apprentice? I thought it was all about kisses and whatnot."

"Oh please!" To wring her hands felt silly, such a pitifully helpless gesture. "It's not about that at all. There are troubles with Tlatelolco, real serious troubles, and that's what Necalli wanted to find out. And we overheard some people plotting and the Emperor wanted to hear about it. And that's why I was late to return home, but they are all watching my every step now and I don't... I don't..." Her voice broke and again she was grateful for Quetzalli's arm wrapping around her, supporting, encouraging. Not like Necalli's embrace would be, but Quetzalli was a good friend, even if silly sometimes. She was loyal and there when one needed her. "It's not fair, not just. I did nothing wrong and our city is in turmoil and maybe in danger too. Bad things are happening and I'm left out of it because my family keeps such a close eye on me. I wish I was in your place!"

Quetzalli was steering her out and toward the doorway. "Don't yell at the top of your voice, sister!" she admonished. "They are all close enough, you know. In the workshop. Just walk me home as you said you would. Your mother said nothing against it, did she?" The crispiness of the evening cleared her head, the breeze pleasant, soothing her nerves. "I shouldn't have jumped out with all this," she repeated, calmer now, trying to think. Would Mother talk to Father about it, about her suspicious activity with a *pilli* boy? And was Acatlo now an enemy, to beware and try to keep away from? Oh, but how enraged he was, how furious! To think that the village boy was at this one's mercy before, hurt. Did Necalli know what Father did to him as a punishment, before the Emperor's warriors took him away? She would have to ask him that. The thought of Necalli brought another question. "You said you saw him, the *calmecac* boy? Where?"

Quetzalli was squinting against the dancing shadows, deep in thought. "Not far away from here, you know? And come to think of it..." Another pause, not to tease, of that Chantli was sure. It was not like her lightheaded friend to be so thoughtful all of sudden, her teeth making a mess out of her lower lip. "Come to think of it, it may be the same sight your foul-tempered brother might have glimpsed. There was that other boy, yes, and he did look somewhat familiar, just a little, but I didn't give it much thought. Maybe it was your troublesome apprentice. I don't remember what he looked like. Never saw him but in passing."

"Where... where were they?"

"They hurried down that other alley, leading to the wharves and the causeway. You know, where the warehouses are." The girl's arm waved in the general direction of the Great Lake, the sounds coming from there familiar, regular shouts and yelling, thuds of heavy objects, of boats dragged up the shore or tied to the wooden planks, the typical clamor of the end of the busy day. Nothing untoward or worrisome. She tried to see through the grayish dusk.

"Only the two of them?"

"Oh no!" The exaggeratedly lilting laughter brought the other Quetzalli back, the lightheaded creature from the marketplace alleys. "If they were alone, I might have stopped to talk to them, you know? To your handsome admirer, maybe. Or the other one, as he looked nice enough." She wrinkled her nose. "For an uncouth villager, your apprentice was dressed as nicely as your love interest. School cloak and all that. Hardly a village boy."

Chantli pushed the familiar resentment away. Necalli wouldn't look at Quetzalli, would he? Not in the way he was looking at her, surely! She pressed her lips tight. "Who was with them?"

Quetzalli rolled her eyes. "Men. Warriors, I would say, even though they were dressed plainly, like the boys. Nicely but plainly. Still, they looked arrogant and dangerous. Not like the boys."

"Why would warriors take them somewhere? Why?" Oh mighty deities! The images of the Tlatelolco shore were back, washing her insides with the purest of dread. She grabbed her friend's arm, startling them both. "Did they look as though they were kidnapped? Were they resisting?"

Quetzalli was studying her with her forehead furrowed like a wrinkled blanket. "No, they didn't. Oh well, I don't know. I didn't look too closely. Those warriors, they don't make one wish to stop and stare, do they?" The pretty face crinkled anew. "Why would you think they were kidnapped?"

"Because this is what happened back in Tlatelolco!" She wrung her hands once again, her thoughts racing, helplessly confused.

"You were kidnapped to Tlatelolco?" Now even Quetzalli's eyes lost their regular proportion. "Is that what happened to you back then?"

"Not me, but them! Ahuitzotl and Necalli, they were kidnapped. And Miztli too, but that was on another occasion."

"Who is Miztli?"

"The village boy."

"Oh, what a nice name." Quetzalli snickered, then turned serious again. "They didn't look as though they didn't want to be there," she added thoughtfully, her frown sincere. "But who knows? One certainly has no business rushing all over the wharves near the Tlatelolco causeway at night, not school boys at any rate." Her scowl deepened. "Upon reflection, your lover did seem to have a black eye. It was difficult to see, as there was no sun and I was not that near, but he looked as though he had been in a fight."

Chantli's heart slipped yet lower down her stomach. "I must let Ahuitzotl know!"

"Ahuitzotl? The Water Monster?"

But she stopped listening, trying to think fast. Quetzalli had seen them a short time ago, and maybe if she hurried, she could still find the sight of them, somehow. Oh, but why didn't she listen to her friend right away instead of playing at being a role-model of a good girl, working on the stupid loom, picking quarrels with her dangerous half-brother?

Beyond the patio, the clamor of many feet invaded the relative tranquility of their alley. Firm, sandaled footsteps. Incredulous, they watched the warriors bearing down on them, in pairs or trios, progressing between the patios and the neat rows of vegetables, spreading alongside those.

"Move, girls," tossed one of them curtly, turning into their patio, signaling a few of the others. "Go inside and stay there."

Numbly, they obeyed, the urge to run inside prevailing regardless. It was always safer to move out of the warriors' way. They had been taught that since deep childhood. Yet, this time, it didn't help. Two of the warriors followed them through the doorway, scanning the main room quickly, their eyes narrowed into slits.

"Where is the owner?"

"Out, out there." Shakily, she motioned toward the patio again. "In the workshop. Why?" After all, it was her father's house, wasn't it? She had the right to ask what those people wanted.

Their spokesman paid her no attention. "Go fetch the man," he tossed toward one of his followers.

"What is happening?" This came from Quetzalli, a swift speech for a change, with no singsong pouting. A relief.

She pressed her friend's arm with her fingers, trying to reassure. "Quetzalli does not live here. She must go home now. Her family will be worried."

"Keep quiet, girls, and out of the way," was their curt answer, the man's broad back blocking the doorway, peering into the dimness of the night, the last of the twilight gone by now, replaced with the deepening darkness. The clamor outside grew stronger, a well-controlled activity. Aghast, she listened to the sound of more footsteps clattering past their patio, hushed voices distributing orders, more warriors evidently spreading, invading the neighboring houses as well. *What was going on?*

The question echoed, repeating itself, now in Father's unusually agitated voice. They were pouring through the doorway, herded in by other warriors – Father, Mother, her youngest brother openly frightened and wide-eyed, Acatlo closing the procession, his eyes still blazing.

"What's the meaning of all this?" Father demanded again, his face and hair soot-covered and smeared, reeking of sweat, not very presentable.

"Keep quiet, craftsman," repeated the first warrior, returning to his doorway duty the moment it was clear of indignant owners, peering outside, shielding his eyes as though it would help him against the darkness. "Stay quiet and out of the way, all of you."

From the outside, voices of warriors and probably protesting owners poured softly, blending with the night. The neighborhood was oddly alive, yet with no usual shouting and clattering.

"I need to go home," called out Quetzalli, but the dour glare of one of the warriors cut her protests short, made her retreat toward the inner doorway.

"Go inside, girls," Mother was whispering, edging toward their side, her touch welcomed, reassuring. "Stay there until we know what is happening. Go!"

"What do you think it is, *nantli*?" breathed Chantli, pulling her friend alongside when Quetzalli seemed to resist, pitying her. She would have felt terrible if caught in such a situation while at Quetzalli's home, in the midst of their quarrelsome family. "Why are those warriors here and not letting us out?"

"I don't know, little one." Mother was busy dragging her resisting youngest along. "There are plenty of warriors out there, entering other dwellings. All over our alley and maybe the rest of the neighborhood as well."

"They look as though ready for battle." Quetzalli did not sound as stressed as before, her color and usual spunk returning. "Do you think it has to do with Tlatelolco and their troubles?"

Chantli drew in a sharp breath. Tlatelolco; oh, but what did it mean? Would the pushy neighbors actually try to invade Tenochtitlan? No, it couldn't be! And yet, the warriors were spreading around the neighborhood so close to the old causeway, and maybe other districts as well, witnessing what Quetzalli was telling them, about the strange sensation out there on the streets, with too many men out and about, loitering. Could it be? And then there was Necalli. What was happening to him? Where had he and Miztli been taken? The nagging worry was back, gripping her stomach. Oh, but she had to find a way to discover what was happening, to help them if they needed help.

CHAPTER 14

The suite of the former royal Chief Wife looked so colorful, so richly decorated, it hurt the eye. Too many precious stones and gilt glaring from all around, sparkling viciously, assaulting one's vision. Tasteless, was Tlemilli's disdainful conclusion as she proceeded to fake disinterest, holding her head high, glancing around not at all.

The lack of elegant grace belonging to Citlalli's rooms, with their exquisite ornaments and refined delicate patterns that pleased the eye so, encouraged her, gave her more spirit. She had to do that, she just had to, and what would one expect from the quarters of the showy princess with illustrious ancestry going back to the beginning of all Five Worlds and beyond it?

She tried to stifle a snort. This woman was nothing to her and yet here she was, doing the unspeakable, betraying it all, her city and her people, or at least Father and his policies. However, he was worse than the ugly Tenochtitlan snake, much worse. Twenty time worse. No, twenty times twenty. And how hadn't she seen it before?

"What are you doing here?"

The harsh question had her snapping from her brief reverie, forcing her to concentrate, to push the doubts away. She was here and that was that. She had made her decision, hasty or not, which hadn't been easy to implement, to put into practice. Yet after Father, every action seemed worthwhile and possible, the danger in it better than her previous meaningless existence.

"I came to talk to you," she said, withstanding the freezing, openly hostile gaze, an easy feat compared to what happened in

Citlalli's rooms, no effort at all. "Send your maids out. We can't talk unless alone."

The exquisite eyes were widening in a genuine fashion. "How dare you burst into my suite of rooms, unbidden and uninvited, then proceed to give me orders? Just who do you think you are, girl? Your father or not, you are nothing but—"

"If you keep screaming, people will come and then I won't be able to tell you what you need to know." But was it her speaking, in this measured, crisp, frosty voice, so cold, so unperturbed? It didn't seem possible, still here it was, her words, harsh and sharp and matter-of-fact. "Send your maids away because we don't have much time."

And that was the sight worth seeing, she decided, grimly amused, still outside herself, watching with detached interest. The woman's face presented an unseemly vision, the gaping mouth, the round eyes. They all should have beheld the haughty princess now. Yet it wasn't the time for amused observations.

"What I came to tell you is important. So you either send your maids away in a hurry, or I go back where I came from."

The gaping eyes narrowed. "Where did you come from?"

"My sister's quarters."

The face closed again. "The Emperor's lusty toy!"

She swallowed hard. "Do not talk about my sister."

"Did you come here to demand that?"

"No, but I do demand that."

The eyes slitted again, taking much of the woman's beauty away. Truth to be told, she wasn't a fat, ugly fowl. Not on the outside.

A single wave of the imperial hand sent the serving women out, scampering. "Does your sister know that you are here?"

"No." She paused to lick her lips. "And neither does my father."

Any trace of amusement was gone. "What does your father have to do with it?"

"Everything."

For a heartbeat, silence prevailed, interrupted by the regular sound of the afternoon Palace and the gardens outside the open shutters. Tlemilli took a deep breath, willing the dizziness away. The annoying buzz in her ears was back, just like after that first time, when Father's palm crushed against the side of her face, a stunning sensation. It made her head buzz and her limbs feel weak, out of control. Just like back then.

"Sit there on those mats." The woman's voice came a little too faintly, as though muffled by an invisible screen. "If you hadn't made me send my maids out, you would have been served a drink, maybe. Pour yourself some if you want to."

Tlemilli shook her head and remained where she was. "We don't have time for any of that."

The generous mouth pursed. "Then start talking."

"I... I had a conversation with my father, not long ago."

"And came out of it looking like this?" This time, the full lips twisted in a hint of a grin. "I can imagine it wasn't a peaceful conversation."

No, it wasn't, she thought, her stomach tightening so painfully she almost doubled over. But how could she have guessed, how? She was never close to Father, never had to face him or even talk to him until the day after the competition, when his interrogation was scary but not painful, resulting in no physical violence, besides some yelling and the threat to execute Tlaco. The moment she had told him all he needed to hear, he had been done with her, storming away, spending no more time on a useless daughter, one of many, more worthless than the rest but not by much.

Yet, upon reflection, she should have known, shouldn't she? He had beaten that other Tenochtitlan boy on the shore, helpless and held from both sides, unable to resist. He had terrified *him* too, and she had never asked what it actually was, what Father did to him to make him so nervous and afraid. Come to think of it, he looked beaten enough on that day on the Plaza, like someone who had been through physical violence, plenty of it, and somehow now she knew it had been connected to Father. Had to be!

Citlalli should have known Father better, with her living in the important side of the Palace, being the Emperor's woman and Father's tool. Surely Father stopped to talk to the Emperor's wife, his own daughter, from time to time. And yet, when Father bore upon them back on the royal patio next to the lavishly decorated staircase, Citlalli had tensed and shivered, and held her breath for a moment, looking like an animal frozen before a predator, contemplating a desperate flight. Frightened as though caught doing something wrong. What?

She remembered her thoughts concentrating mainly on this, too scared to try and deal with the imminent interrogation, with the open disgust the menacing eyes radiated. So cold, so threatening. She knew she would have to tell it all, like the previous time. There were too many means to make her talk, Tlaco's life, and maybe even Citlalli's, she had realized, going rigid with fear. Still, she didn't think that her own life might be in danger as well. It was ridiculous to assume something like that. But apparently, Father didn't think it was.

Straightening her gaze to meet the stare of the woman she hated, she forced her hands to remain still, not to stray toward her swollen cheek, still pulsating with pain, knowing that she must be looking the strangest of sights, with her smelly, messed-up clothes and hair, the reminder of the last night's adventures, and her glaring cheek and the bleeding lip, still salty to the touch of her tongue, curiously tasty.

"He knows about your meeting with that boy. He knows everything."

The color drained from the exquisite face all at once, in a frightening manner; one moment smugness, even if wary, and a healthy hue, the other haunted, dismayed, staring. Tlemilli wondered if it was time to offer the woman that drink that was mentioned before. If the princess fainted, it wouldn't do any good, would it?

"What do you mean?" Instead of fainting, the woman jerked back to life with a sudden lurch, straightening abruptly, her back exaggeratedly upright, leaving the coziness of her cushioned arrangement with what looked like little regret.

Tlemilli felt like taking a step back. Would the snake try to attack now? She was in no position to deal with any more physical assaults. Or was she? It didn't even matter at this point.

"I told you already," she repeated, marveling at the sound of her voice; dull, detached, even bored. "My father knows about your spying. He will bring this matter before the Emperor, the matter of your lack of loyalty, that is. He is determined to execute you. Always wanted to." She felt her shoulders lifting indifferently, moving as though on their own, a painful gesturing as they hurt too at the place when she was made to crash against the prettily painted wall. "He won't be talking to the Emperor tonight, but you can be sure that tomorrow—"

"You told him that, you filthy little snake, didn't you?"

Tlemilli frowned, startled by the trivial, unnecessary question. "Yes, of course. I wouldn't be here if it wasn't I who had told him."

There was a pleasant novelty to this numb indifference that governed her since that dreadful interview with Father, since the moment he had slapped Citlalli, then threw her, Tlemilli, against the wall when she tried to interfere. Until that moment, she had been horrified, shocked, frightened for real by the unfamiliar sensation of helplessness and pain most of all. From the first vicious shake that finished the ice-cold cutting harangue about ungrateful children and traitorous-by-nature little snakes, she had been terrified, bereft of words or action. However, the moment he backhanded Citlalli, it was as though she popped out of her own skin, became indifferent, a changed person. She had told it all to him in a clear, cutting voice, then let him know that if he ever, ever touched her sister again, she would find ways to get back at him, frightful, torturous ways. And it didn't matter that he proceeded to discipline her by slapping her yet harder, throwing her against the wall, then dragging her by the hair into the hall and alongside it, oblivious of the terrified servants, to be locked in a small adjacent suite until he decided what to do with her. It didn't matter, because even then, she knew that he had been afraid of her, maybe a little, but he was. He wouldn't be treating her threats lightly. He wouldn't touch Citlalli again.

"Then why are you here?" The blazing eyes, the twisted face; no more haughtiness or conceit, no more smugness. "To sneer? To taunt?"

How silly! She stood the burning gaze, noting the cornered glint to it, the perfectly groomed fingers clutching the fan they held so tightly she wondered when the sound of cracking would ensue. Also, why were they wasting their time on this childish talk? Who told on whom? As though it mattered at this point.

"You are as implicated." The voice was gaining a shrill tone, raising unpleasantly, assaulting the ear. "And you evidently didn't fare well for your ill-advised badmouthing. You are as involved with this boy, and I will make sure to tell the Emperor, and then neither your father nor your mealy-mouthed sister—"

She pressed her fingers to her temples, her headache getting worse with each shrilling word. A glance toward the previously indicated podium informed her that, indeed, there were flasks there and cups, and a plate of red tomatoes and some other smaller fruits. The drink would do her nothing but good. She only hoped it was not one of those sweetened beverages favored by her stupid half-sisters.

"We don't have time for all this," she said, pouring from the half-empty flask, disgusted to discover that the water was honeyed to the point of being barely liquid, rolling rather than dripping, annoyingly thick. "You must leave before Father talks to the Emperor. It should happen tonight."

The woman was on her feet, staring, wide-eyed. Tlemilli tried to drink the thick liquid despite the nausea it brought, grimacing. Was there no water around these quarters at all?

"What is your game, girl?" This came in a relatively normal voice, no strident shouting.

She put the cup back in its place, her hands remarkably steady, just like her mind; cold, uninvolved. It was a good feeling.

"My father will prevail upon the Emperor to have you executed for treason. You should leave this Palace, return to Tenochtitlan. You must have ways to do that."

"And why would I listen to the advice of the little snake who spied on me and betrayed me, turning even the messengers of my brother against me, hurrying to inform her vile monster of a father in order to implicate me?" Again, the climbing tones.

Tlemilli shook her head tiredly. "You don't have to trust me or like me or listen to me," she said, wondering where this patience to talk and elaborate was coming from, she who had always been notoriously renowned for impulsiveness, for childish tantrums and hasty deeds. Now it was as though she had been a grown-up person, with everyone, from the shrill princess looking as though about to throw her pretty pottery cup at her, to helplessly weeping Citlalli, to Father who was lashing out with no care, beating his own daughters in front of the entire Palace or attacking the invincible city with not much thought or even a much-necessary declaration of war; to the uncertain Emperor even, afraid of omens but unable to stand up to his forceful adviser. Oh, but didn't they all behave like children, with no discretion and no sense?

"I came to warn you because I have my reasons to do that. I hate you as much as I did before, as much as you hate me." A shrug came with difficulty, the memory of *his* worried admonition to keep away from that dangerous woman and their devious politics threatening to shatter the walls of her newly found, wonderfully numb indifference, the memory of *his* voice and *his* arms. She clenched her fists tight. "But what I tell you is true. My father will talk to the Emperor against you, will bring evidence of your disloyalty. And if the night attack on Tenochtitlan succeeds, the Emperor will be forced to execute you with no fear of reprisal."

Oh, but this came out so well. She marveled at the sound of her short speech, so neatly composed, so eloquent. The woman was staring at her as though she had sprouted another head or limb, like this old water monster in one of Tlaco's stories. Briefly, she wondered if her maidservant was still in her old quarters, not harmed by Father already. Later, not now.

"The night attack?" The princess's lips lost much of their pretty coloring, turned as pale as her face became. Their movement was barely noticeable and the words they produced difficult to hear. "But he said he won't do it."

She remembered Citlalli's stories. "Yes, the Emperor doesn't believe it will bring us victory, but it will be done all the same. It will happen this night."

Actually, she wasn't certain about that, having no information besides Citlalli's reported conversation with the Emperor. Still, Father wanted it to be done this way. He had schemed, planned, and prepared, tunnels with weaponry and the rest. *His tunnels.* Another wrong turn of thought. She forced her gaze to concentrate on the woman in front of her. Not a haughty, hostile, dangerously mean fowl, not anymore. Lost, frightened, staring, the full lips having no color, almost invisible, opening and closing, emitting no sound.

"It will happen tonight and then you will not be safe in this Palace and this city." She kept listening to herself, her thoughts crystal clear, like her words. "Should we win or lose, it will not make difference to your safety here. Yours and your son's. You should try and sneak away before nightfall. You must have enough faithful servants and others to help you with that."

Another heartbeat had passed. The woman in front of her was changing again. She saw the lips pressing tighter, gaining no color but somehow turning strong with decision. The eyes lost their haunted spark, turned resolute. The cup in the royal hand – obviously a chocolate drink, such a heavy sweetish aroma – made a soft clanking sound as it touched the surface of the reed podium, not crashing at it, fallen with no will, but being put there with much care. The woman straightened up, her eyes still boring, piercing, but now probing rather than accusing, willing to listen.

"What do you want from me in exchange for your warning?"

Somehow, she knew it would come, a straightforward question requiring a straightforward answer. No flowery speech of high nobility, not in such a moment.

"I want you to deliver a note from me, a message."

"Whom to?" The high forehead creased slightly, in genuine puzzlement.

"That boy. The one who was spying for you."

This time, the pensive eyes opened too wide again, then deepened, flickered with a feminine glint. A twisted grin tugged at the corner of the full lips. "Is that so?"

Tlemilli just nodded, beyond caring.

"Can't you send him messages of your own?"

"No, I can't. I wouldn't have asked you if I could, would I?" Again, that marvelously cold tone, so even, so in control. But to be able to stay like that forever!

"No, you wouldn't." The uneven grin widened, and she thought that she detected a spark of an appreciative interest somewhere in the openly mocking depths. The annoying self-assured princess was back, not missed in the least. "What is your connection to this commoner?"

"I don't have to tell you." She held her head high, her gaze as unwavering, as determined as she felt inside, or so she hoped. "When you reach Tenochtitlan, will you give him my note? Without reading it?"

The woman shook her head, now certainly in as tight control as of yore. "You are as insolent as always, young girl," she said coldly. "How can I be sure that your information is true and not just a ruse, a scam to make me act stupidly, to flee without a true need, making a fool of myself?"

Tlemilli collected her thoughts hastily, having no clear advantage now of being the only calm person among the two of them.

"You can choose to disregard my warning, but what I say is true. The Emperor will attack Tenochtitlan tonight, and he will hear about your dealings with the enemy because my father is determined to be rid of you. He made me tell him all I know about your meeting with this boy. Here in the Palace and on the Plaza, on the day of the completion as well," she added on the spur of a moment, seeing the flicker of panic again, pleased by it.

"The slimy piece of commoner dirt has been working for both sides!" This came out with frightening viciousness.

Tlemilli shuddered against her will. "He did not," she said hurriedly, some of the blissful detachment gone. "He was not the one to tell me. He... he didn't help my father or anyone here. He is not like that."

The eyes were narrowing into slits again. "Then how do you know?"

She gathered her senses with the desperate effort. "It doesn't matter now. I came to warn you. This is something I'm willing to do for you, a favor." She drew a deep breath. "This boy was spying for Tenochtitlan and for you, but it doesn't matter now. I want to send him a note. That is all I ask in return."

"Nothing more?" That came outright mocking.

"Nothing more."

"You are a deep little thing." The pursed lips parted slightly. "Give me your note, then leave. If you betray me with your information now or anything else later on, this boy will suffer the consequences of your betrayal before you or this pitiful town of yours do."

"My *altepetl* is no pitiful town," she began hotly, then remembered her purpose. The new Tlemilli, cold and calculating, was a better fitting person than the old childish one. "I don't have a note. I need to write it."

The arrogantly held head shook in clear exasperation, as though expecting so much inefficiency. The well-groomed palm rose, indicating the smaller alcove. "You'll find papers and sharpened coals there. Don't be tempted to touch the colors. Write your note quickly and be gone. I won't promise to deliver it, so don't hold your hopes high. However, who knows? It may reach its destination in the end." The veiled gaze didn't waver.

Still, she cringed inside. "I need it to reach him!" Then the old Tlemilli was pushed back again, an unwelcome interruption. "I can be of help to you later on as well. You should remember that."

A twisted smile. "I will, girl, I will."

Another manicured palm came up, joining the previous one in order to clap several times, which brought the eager maids in, running, bursting with curiosity. Tlemilli went toward the indicated alcove, her legs surprisingly light, head on fire.

CHAPTER 15

It was hard to believe that the attack was actually happening. Pressing against the wall of peeling plaster, Necalli caught his breath, the stone swishing next to his ear, crushing against the crude construction, shot from the roof of another warehouse, he knew. Or probably just thrown with a lot of force, but not much care as to the accuracy of the throw, or rather the necessity of it.

"Stop shooting, you stupid halfwits," he yelled into the darkness, unable not to, sweat pouring into his eyes, the moon nothing but a mere glint in this part of the city, behind the marketplace and the workshops. Too many warehouses, too densely tucked. The wind whirled viciously in the narrow passages, adding to the confusion and maybe even fear, truth be told. Its wailing was certainly unnerving, as though it had already been mourning – the invaders' or the defenders' deaths? On this account, the darkness had its advantages. Less possibilities to see, yes, but less chance of being detected and shot at. The people on the rooftops, mainly the locals, the enraged dwellers of the invaded neighborhoods, did not always know how to take good aim, not helped by the fact that none of the warriors wore any insignia or carried banners like in a real battle. It made them all look alike, the defenders and the invaders.

"Stop throwing stones!" he shouted again, then motioned to the workshop boy, and together they dove into the darkness, hoping for the best.

Their destination lay beyond the cluster of warehouses and other such buildings, the plaza-like square with the pond that he remembered so well from the previous day's adventures with

Chantli, who should be safely at her father's home now, he hoped, protected. She had to be, didn't she? Who would let the girl out on such a night? Not even the filthy craftsman with deceitful ways, surely.

"Keep low," he breathed, then decided to charge on into the flickering darkness without pausing. The corner they had reached and the passageway spreading ahead looked promisingly quiet.

"Wait!" whispered his companion, but he rushed on, half bent and ready to duck, probing with his senses. Miztli's steps rang dimly beside him and he reflected again what reliable company this one was, quick and trustworthy, encouraging with his mere presence. Since what happened on the road to Acachinanco, he had trusted this boy's judgment and not only his loyalty and shooting skills.

Another corner. The vast square was lit more generously, enlivened with flickering torches and an occasional fire. At its far end, near the shimmering mass of the pond, silhouettes were darting, accompanied by sounds that had become familiar by now – shouts and thuds and worrisome groans.

"They'll be there," whispered Necalli. "The pond will give us plenty of cover."

"Wait!" This time, the hand shot forward, grabbing his upper arm, arresting his leap with the most inconsiderate abruptness, making him sway.

"What are you doing, you stupid lump—"

A swishing stone cut the darkness, crashing into the cobblestones where he might be crossing the open space by now, followed by another missile, then another. Heart pumping madly, Necalli stared at the once again peaceful darkness, then leaned against the wall.

"How did you know?"

As expected, the silhouetted shoulders lifted briefly. "It was too peaceful out there. Too much space without cover to run."

Necalli rubbed the sweat off his face. "We'll go around, circumvent this square, come closer to the pond from the other side, if they are so opposed to us crossing it. Stupid commoners!"

"Maybe it's Tlatelolcans shooting."

"Mere stones? Wouldn't happen. Their warriors would be pelting us with darts or those clay balls you are so fond of." Grinning, he motioned his companion into the darkness of the narrow pathway. "They should have put you on a roof and give you a sling, and let you to shoot them all, one by one."

He could hear the quiet chuckling. "I wouldn't mind."

"And part with your pretty new toy?"

The club from their high noon adventures was still there, carried stubbornly, never leaving the workshop boy's side, a source of Necalli's envy. He himself was still weaponless, aside from his knife, a lawful possession, Father's gift, not a spoil of war like the club. Not that he wished to fight with such common weaponry. Obsidian sword was his desire and aspiration. Still, the working boy got his club while fighting, taking it from the enemy he bested. An impressive achievement that even the Emperor commented upon amusedly, asking questions. While he, Necalli, sported no spoils. What aggravation! But for a chance to come out of this night carrying something like that.

Peeking out carefully, having reached another corner, this one not as quiet as the previous one, relating a story of people rushing about, he tried to see without letting their presence be known. No more rushing out without thinking. The workshop boy was right at stopping him. An annoying realization.

The wider alley ahead rustled with shadows. Their people or Tlatelolcans? Warriors or just agitated commoners? The elite fighters at the wharves had sent them to reach this marketplace square in order to let the leader of the forces responsible for this part of the city know of the situation and ask for reinforcements. Not that it looked as though it was peaceful here or abandoned. The Tlatelolcans, even though ambushed and made to fall into their own trap, did manage to surprise with their numbers and their spirits, so determined, so unafraid. Not the pitiful islanders from across the causeway. Anything but!

He remembered the dusk and the thrill of moving along with the best fighting force of the entire empire, the Eagle Warriors. Oh, but how quickly they moved, how silent and confident, determined, lethal, every step a correct one, dedicated to the general plan. When smaller, he always dreamed of joining the Jaguar Warriors, their clothes so vivid and their name so spectacular, their hall large and glorious, situated in such close proximity to the Great Pyramid, declaring its importance. Father had taken him there once, himself a former member of this powerful caste. Yet now, Necalli could think of nothing else but the thrill of moving around along with the elite force of beaked helmets even though they didn't wear any insignia this time, nothing to tell them apart from other people or warriors, and yet everything about them different, proclaiming of might, their swords adorned with plenty obsidian blades on each side, their movements these of weathered fighters, forceful and careful at the same time, aware of their surroundings, listening to their senses and not only their ears. If the invaders were sneaking into the city disguised, unwilling to be detected until the time to attack came, well, so did the defenders, preparing to surprise the surprising. To be part of such a force, even if running mere errands, was a thrill beyond his wildest imagination.

Excited to no end, he had treasured every heartbeat, making desperate efforts to keep the right pace, to blend and not to be just a burden, a bother, a child sent to show the way. Oh, but how carefully they spread around the abandoned temple, how efficiently they signaled the ones who were already there, how forcefully a few warriors commandeered the first canoe they had found near the wharves, with so much compelling efficiency the stunned owner of the vessel didn't manage to say a word before they were in the water, rowing vigorously.

The sail toward the tiny island brought back memories he didn't cherish, that pitiful floundering of a market interval ago that resulted in the dive in the nightly lake. Not to mention the encounter with the water monster. Still, with elite warriors in the lead, there was no chance of anything like that happening, even though they had taken a long detour, approaching the island not at all, trying to observe it without being noticed. The activity that went on all around it warranted such a precaution. The small piece of land wasn't deserted, not anymore. If anything, it seemed to be livelier than the Tlatelolcan market on a market day. Which made the warriors busy, sending for reinforcements to be placed around the temple in question, the destination of the island's arrivals, surely, and around the relevant piers. Even the nearby neighborhoods filled with armed fighters. It had puzzled him briefly, the question how they were to conceal such an amount of warriors until the time to attack or to repel one came, but this dilemma was answered shortly, when on their way back they had seen the fighters entering people's dwellings, demanding to be hidden there. Simple and brilliant! The invaders would not see it coming.

Also, the busy warriors showed no signs of sending their young escorts away. Unlike the imperial guards on the road to Acachinanco, the weathered veterans evidently appreciated their charges' willingness to stay and be of help. A wonder! No one tried to shoo them back to school, not at all. Instead, they had been made to run errands, pass words between various leaders and their men, to make the spreading of people smoother with quickly passed information. And when the actual attack came and its bloodcurdling war cries emanated from everywhere, a part of the effort to frighten, Necalli suspected, his heart fluttering even so, they were sent all the way to the further-up squares, delivering requests for reinforcements while bringing back word of the situation in those other parts of the city.

According to what they managed to overhear and deduce, the Jaguar Warriors were responsible for the wellbeing of the Royal Enclosure along with the Central Plaza and the noble neighborhoods adjacent to it. However, by now it was clear where the enemy centered their major assaulting efforts. Not the noble parts of the city.

"Think we can chance running this side of that square?" His companion's whisper tore Necalli from his reverie, made him take his eyes off the fighting at the edge of their alley. Behind the shadowed part of the enclosure, the sounds cleared off and disappeared.

"Go around that side of the tented area. It'll bring you straight to the pond," he breathed, remembering running there with Chantli. "Wait for me there."

"Where will you be?"

He motioned toward the alley. "I'll see if that leader that we are supposed to find is here, somewhere around that fighting. He is bound to be in either place, so it'll be sensible to split up. If you find him by the pond, relay our message to him. Then wait for me there."

For a heartbeat, the workshop boy seemed to hesitate, then he nodded briefly and slunk into the darkness without a sound. Impressed, Necalli took a deep breath, then broke into a run up the narrow alley, his knife clutched tightly, slippery in his sweaty palm.

Lights danced in small passageways between patios and inside the dwellings, shy and as though reluctant to draw attention. And why would they? He remembered sneaking into a similar-looking alley, eavesdropping on the stinking smugglers. Had it happened only a day before? It seemed as though a whole market interval passed, or maybe even two. The worry was nagging again, pestering. Was she well out there in her father's house? Was any fighting in her district occurring? And what if the invaders tried to break in? What was to stop them besides the defenders who might not be around yet, busy elsewhere?

The people burst upon him out of the darkness, two hurried forms, clutching what looked like clubs or maybe even swords. Instinctively, he swayed out of their way, his heart beating fast. They didn't pause to look at him, but those who rushed after them did. A larger group, five men in all, heavily armed. One of them leaped closer, but Necalli's legs took him away and along the wall, making him dive into the meager bushes adorning the pathway into the nearby patio. Through the following heartbeat, the night exploded with blows and gasps, loud exclamations, and panting breaths.

His knife out and ready, he tried to squeeze past the clashing forms, almost successful but for another figure springing from his projected destination, practically falling on him. This one carried a torch, an almost extinguished affair, barely alive. In its meager illumination, he could see that the man was tall and broadly built, his head adorned with a warriors' topknot, but of what forces he couldn't tell, his free arm sporting a spear. His torch flickered wildly, smelling of cheap oil. For a heartbeat, they just stared.

"What are you doing here, boy? Go away!" the man breathed in the end, turning around and toward more silhouettes that kept materializing out of the darkness. By now, the narrow alley was literally crammed with people, groans and cries, and worst of all, disgustingly cracking sounds and thuds.

Pushing the wall away, Necalli tried to propel himself toward any possible opening, his knife and warlike intentions forgotten, craving to reach an open space with no sweating bodies pressing from all around, determined to squash him. No, this was not how he imagined his first battle.

The man with the torch was beside him again, shoving the pressing forms away, using his spear as though it was made for this purpose. To keep close to this one seemed safe. Necalli tried to make his mind work, elbowing someone away from himself, a squirming body. The knife was again in the forefront of his mind, but now, as it cleared enough to think of participating, he didn't know against whom to turn. The warriors, they all looked alike in the darkness, undistinguished in their plain clothing. Who was who?

Jumping away from the creaking thud that exploded next to his ear, a disgustingly wet sound, he wasn't quick enough to avoid mighty push or to hold the weight of the body that was suddenly upon him, pressing him down, impossible to hold on against. It shoved him back toward the wall, but the hard stones helped, propping him from behind, not letting him fall.

Pushing the limp form away, using all his strength to do that, his mind panicked again, he felt the sturdy shaft brushing along his thigh, hurting with its hard splintered surface. His free hand clutched it without thinking, his body twisting in order to do that, to wrestle it from its lifeless owner's hands, let this one fall without it. A quick shove of his knee, and he was still there, still standing, but now armed with a spear, a long heavy affair, reassuring in its sturdiness. Blinking, he tried to understand.

People were cramming the narrow space, waving their clubs or knives or even their unarmed fists. The man who must have taken the spearman down was shoving his way toward him, obvious in his purpose. With not enough space to even spread his legs wider, let alone try and achieve the correct stance while fighting with a spear, either intending to throw it or to use it as thrusting device, like they were taught back in school, Necalli let his instincts take over, pushing his assailant with the helpfully long shaft, balancing it between his outstretched arms. It worked surprisingly well, this improvised strategy. Not only had his attacker been shoved away, stumbling backwards and into the milling people, but some of the others were thrown off balance as well, struggling to stay upright. The small opening this momentary confusion offered was too good not to use, and he charged into it, clutching his newly acquired weapon, his senses weak with relief.

Away from the melee, he could see that the skirmish he burst out from was not a huge one, just crowded. Pausing momentarily, he turned back in time to see a club charging toward him, a dark menacing form. To thrust his spear in the way he had been taught in school became easier now that he wasn't pressed from all sides. Already balanced in his hand in the correct way – when did that happen? – held perfectly in the middle, it settled in his palm, ready to pounce. To sway away from the descending club was easier with its owner suddenly wavering, groping the air. In another heartbeat, the man had gone down and sideways, taking Necalli's spear away with him.

Panicked again, he fought not to let it go, himself wavering, then losing his balance, crashing into the revolting mess of foul odor and flailing hands. The man was screaming so loudly! Forgetting the initial fight for the spear, Necalli rolled away frantically, pushing with the aid of every limb, oblivious of reason. Just to get away from this horror, the stench and the screams, so terrible, high-pitched, so full of agony!

A sturdy hand was clutching his shoulder, dragging him up and away. He tried to resist its pull, his eyes catching sight of the discarded club, rolling in the dust. The attempt to grab it did not crown with success, and now his mind raced in panic, thinking about his knife. Where was it? In desperation, he kicked, but the man jerked him up with little ceremony, his face smeared but calm, even amused, his hair sporting a familiar lock, highly reassuring.

"What is a boy like you doing in the middle of this?" the man asked, steadying Necalli as he wavered, firm, uncompromising. "Come. This is not a place for school boys."

"I..." He tried to talk reasonably above the wild pounding of his heart, now out of tempo and threatening to jump out of his chest. "We were looking... looking for Honorable Cuauhixtli. The leader of the group of warriors responsible for... for this side. We were sent to find him."

The man halted abruptly. "Who sent you?"

"Honorable Tecuauhtli." He licked his lips, still craving to rush back and retrieve the club, or better yet, his lawfully gained spear. "He told us to find Honorable Cuahixtli and his men, to ask him to send reinforcements to the wharves." His heartbeat was calming and it was a good feeling. "There is much fighting there. Near the old causeway."

"Come with me!"

There was no more amusement in the man's voice, only matter-of-fact decisiveness. Necalli shot a last glance into the darkness of the alley where the fighting seemed to calm down or maybe subdue for good, with only the groans of the wounded left and the wandering silhouettes of those who tended to them or maybe just killed them off, the badly wounded enemy mainly. Would the man agree to let him off in order to get that club or the spear? He knew the answer to that, nothing positive.

However, after another pause, with other warriors catching up with them, also clearly belonging to Eagle Forces judging by their topknots, now disheveled but still easy to recognize, their new destination turned out to be the alley itself, now nothing but a slew of slippery stones and thrown around bodies, the man he had impaled still there, sprawled on his side with his limbs stretched unnaturally and his hands frozen around the spear that was still protruding from his body, a terrible sight. Revolted but determined, Necalli forced his legs to detour, holding his breath against the smell – such a terrible stench!

The need to bend in order to grab the shaft had him gagging.

He pulled with the last of his strength, the cough impossible to hold in, choking him, the fouler odor his action released not helping. He clenched his teeth so tight he could not feel them anymore, grateful for the fact that the spear slipped out smoothly, not stuck or resisting his pull. He wouldn't be able to fight for it, he knew, not in this foulness. The plopping sound it made was enough to send his nausea into unbearable heights.

On his feet again and with the spear clutched so tightly he wasn't sure he would manage to let it go ever, he watched the warriors' backs, again nothing but dark silhouettes, hurrying up the alley and toward the open square, the man who had talked to him before glancing back briefly, motioning him to catch up. He did so with indecent haste, his legs wobbly but supporting, as eager to get away.

"Some warrior this boy is," commented the man as the moonlight greeted them on the edge of the open square. "Saw him using that spear too. Not badly at that."

Another man chuckled, slowing his step. "How did you get to be the carrier of Honorable Tecuauhtli's messages, boy?"

Necalli swallowed. "We were sent by the Emperor to guide the honorable Eagle Warriors to the wharves and tunnels with hidden weaponry there."

Now they all seemed to pause. "By the Emperor?"

"Yes." He licked his lips, suddenly dead thirsty. "The Emperor, he wished us to show the tunnels, and then, then they let us stay. Honorable Tecuauhtli thought that we could be of use, bringing his messages and orders."

"What district's school do you attend?" The warriors hastened their step again upon reaching the open space, glancing around pensively.

"*Calmecac.*"

The man who had dragged him away from the skirmish nodded thoughtfully, then put his attention to the surrounding roofs. Necalli did the same, enjoying the fresh nightly air with no stench worse than that of too many bonfires.

"Large conflagrations," commented someone. "From the lake side, I'd say."

"The wharves?"

They all nodded sagely.

"Take this *pilli* and find Honorable Cuauhixtli. He carries a message from those same areas, asking for reinforcements."

"He is there, by the pond."

The mention of the pond reminded him of Miztli, making him halt abruptly, then force his legs into renewed pacing. He would do better reaching that Cuauhixtli first, before starting to run around in a frenzy, looking for his lost companion. Did the workshop boy fare better in reaching the man they were looking for? He most sincerely hoped that it was the case. To look for his friend all over this dark, hostile, stinking plaza was not a pastime he would pick, given a choice.

No warfare seemed to plague the dark mass of the pool and the walled stone construction that brought the water to it, now closed for the night, not trickling. Still, too many silhouettes dashed all around, talking and shouting, waving their weaponry, mainly the spiked swords. Necalli clutched his spear tighter, reassured. The obsidian swords meant the elite warriors, the defenders in most probability. Who else?

"Come." His guide motioned him with his head, parting from their group, heading toward the tented area. The men congregating there turned to greet them, then they were hastened away and around and, in no time, none other than the workshop boy's sturdy form rushed toward him, breaking into a run.

"Are you all right?"

Necalli just nodded, relieved, watching his previous escort talking to the tall man in a full eagle armor of breastplate and leggings even though lacking in the typical headdress, just like the man who had sent them. "Is that Honorable Cuauhixtli?"

The workshop boy nodded in his turn. "A nasty piece of work." This came out in a quiet whisper, barely audible.

"Why?"

The generous lips were twisting with atypical crookedness, but before more whispering answers came, the impressive man in the armor bore upon them, bestowing Necalli's companion with a dark look.

"Who are you, *pilli*? What's your family connection and who are your *calmecac* teachers?"

Necalli straightened hastily. "My name is YoloNecalli, my father is Tlilocelotl, a Jaguar Warrior and one of the former leaders of this glorious force."

"Who is running your *calmecac*?" demanded the man, unimpressed.

"Honorable Yaotzin."

This time, the nod held a satisfied quality, not thawing but turning less foreboding. "What did the Honorable Tecuauhtli ask you to tell me?"

"He asked for reinforcements to be sent to the wharves and the old causeway."

"How many?"

He tried not to quail under such inimical interrogation. "As many as you can spare, Honorable Leader. Those were his exact words."

The pursed lips didn't relax. "Do you know this other boy?"

"Yes. We were sent together to deliver the message."

"Then you may wish to stay together while doing this, *calmecac* boys. Follow your orders more closely next time!" This came as an open reprimand. "Wait here, then follow the command of the warriors who will be sent back along with you."

He dared to let out his breath only when the cloaked back was upon them, swishing with displeasure.

"What was that all about?" he breathed when certain that the irritable leader was busy with shouting orders, creating waves of agitation between his men, sending many away and on the run.

"I told you, this one is a nasty piece of work." The workshop boy's mouth was twisting in an unappealing way.

It was easy to compose the picture of what happened. "Didn't want to listen to you, did he?"

The deeply set eyes rolled tellingly. "Did he? If he told me to be off and stop bothering him it would not be that bad. But he turned all nasty, asking questions, getting suspicious. He told his men to keep an eye on me and not to let me go, and just as I needed to run back and check on you, find out what was happening to you, why you didn't come." The air burst angrily, escaping through widening nostrils. "I suppose I'm lucky that he didn't tell them to cut me into pieces with those vicious-looking spiked things of theirs. He got really mad when I tried to argue."

"Why didn't he believe you?"

A shrug. "I didn't remember the name of that teacher, the one who takes you to play ball and tells you all what to do."

Necalli tried to hold in his chuckle. "No wonder he suspected your story, *calmecac boy*."

An angry grimace was his answer. "He could have told me to scamper away and be gone."

"Or he could have tortured you to find out where you got your story from, the names of the prominent Eagle Warriors leaders and such."

"Go jump you know where! Why did you take your time to come here?"

Necalli grinned with relief, pleased to have this boy's company again. Oh yes, that angry leader was right; they shouldn't have parted.

"I got busy getting this thing." He thrust his spear forward, pleased with how much better and more impressive it looked here in the moonlight, a truly invested affair of carved wood and decorations, its spike wide and vicious, two palms long, studded with ragged obsidian and of an impressive size. Not a regular spear but *tepoztopilli*, an awesome piece of weaponry! "Put your pitiful club to shame, that thing, eh?"

His companion's eyes widened. "Where did you get it?" He saw the fleeting glance traveling his face, then his chest, taking in the dry blood sprinkled all over his cloaked shoulders, something he had become aware of only now as well. "Did you get it in battle?"

"Sort of." He tried to be humble about it, as appropriate, not successful on this score. "I didn't kill its owner, but I killed someone with it, some stupid brute with a club." The mere memory of the body back there in the narrow alley made the inappropriate wave of pride subdue, replaced with the previous wave of nausea. "Anyway, it's my lawful spoil. Even the warriors said that."

His friend was eyeing him, still wide-eyed, clearly impressed. It made him feel better.

"Stop staring at me like that. You got your club in a battle too, you conceited piece of meat. Thought I wouldn't manage?"

The twisting lips curled in uncontrollable laughter. "You are wild."

"Didn't you run into any fighting on your way here?" He watched the warriors gathering in organized groups, shouting to each other. Twenty in each smaller unit, he knew, having listening avidly through the lessons concerning warriors and their organization. Less so with the classes teaching laws or religious matters, hard put not to snore when made to pore over calendars and books.

"There was some. By the pond they were fighting the hardest. When I was trying to ask for that Cuauhixtli yeller, I got attacked a few times."

"Did you fight with your club? Did you kill any?"

His companion made a face. "No. I was busy trying to deliver our message." A shrug. "It was easy to escape those who tried to attack me. They were all just rushing around like mad coyotes. Striking everywhere. Our and their people. Difficult to tell from each other. How do they manage?"

Oh yes, he remembered that feeling. "They are fighting with their units, their peers, so they know each other well enough." He made a face, not wishing to offend but needing to say it. "Don't talk like that with anyone else, even me. Don't tell them you were trying to avoid a battle, a hand-to-hand, things like that. I know you have plenty of courage, but you will be accused of cowardice and thrown out of school and whatnot if you keep talking like that."

"Like what?" Again the wide-open eyes, wary, apprehensive, those wavering expressions – to laugh or to get offended?

"You said it was easy to avoid those who attacked you. Never say it again, even if it happened. Just hope that no one saw you doing it."

The indignation won. "What's wrong with that?"

"Everything is wrong with that! You have much to learn yet, so just don't talk too much until you do. I know your worth, and so do Axolin and Ahuitzotl. And the Emperor too. But you still need to learn the correct way of behaving. If you want to stay in *calmecac* and become a great warrior, that is. If your workshop life makes you wistful, then by all means go on and brag that you managed to avoid the challenges of battle when in the middle of it."

"I did not—" began his companion hotly, but the warriors were already upon them, grim and out of patience.

"Hurry up, boys!"

They fell into the stride, still tense, aware of the burning smell that increased, spreading through the alleys, getting stronger and more pronounced as they went, the distant glow of the sky disturbing. Fires were raging out there, near the wharves probably, and maybe the neighborhoods adjacent to it, the cane-and-reed houses of the poorest, the easiest to catch fire of course, and what if...

"Chantli! Where does she live?"

"What?" His companion glanced at him from under his brow, still seething, not over the previous offense.

Necalli didn't care. "Chantli, your craftsman, his family; where do they live?"

"Out there." A noncommittal nod.

"In what sort of a house, you stupid thickhead?"

"Leave me alone with your stupid—"

"Stop bickering, you two." One of the warriors snarled at them angrily.

Necalli tried to gather his senses. "Where exactly by the wharves?"

"Near the old causeway."

"What sort of house do they live at?" he repeated when the warriors drew away, hastening their step. "Reeds or adobe?"

"Adobe."

Good. He breathed with relief.

"But near the causeway?'

"Yes."

The worry returned. No, he didn't like that smell, he just didn't. Too many things were burning out there, houses or squares. He eyed the warriors' cloaks swaying at a considerable distance now. Clearly they didn't need any more of their dubious guidance.

"Take me to that workshop, where Chantli lives."

His companion looked at him darkly. "Why?"

He didn't hurry to pick a fight, not this time, too worried to do that. "She might be in danger. There is plenty of fighting going on out there and if the fires, or the enemy for that matter, get out of control..." He stiffened at the very thought. "What's to stop the warriors from getting into the houses? I saw it happening up there in that accursed alley."

The workshop boy's eyes widened. "Yes, we better hurry."

CHAPTER 16

The smoke was everywhere, billowing, surging, stinging one's eyes, making one's throat hurt. Blinking fiercely, Chantli tried not to trip, rushing on with a pot full of water, splashing and threatening to spill out, every precious drop needed desperately. Mother was yelling to get more rags, cloths, anything, but she hoped Quetzalli was carrying that, or maybe her little brother, or anyone really. She couldn't do it all alone, could she?

Since that fire arrow got into the house, thwacking viciously into the pole supporting the entrance, with so much strength no one had managed to pull it out as yet, since that moment, she had been the calmest of them all, watching the flames licking the wooden beam hungrily, thinking fast. Even Mother panicked for a moment, let alone Quetzalli and her youngest of siblings, both gaping at the pretty show of billowing flames, transfixed. It was she, Chantli, who had rushed toward the water bin – luckily, they had filled it to the brim only this afternoon, before the warriors came – grabbing the nearest pot from the cooking facilities, shouting for them to do the same. That brought Mother from the state of unseemly staring, but not the rest of them.

By that time, no warriors were inside, and not even Father or his older sons, with the fighting out there turning into a familiar sound, ghastly but something they had grown used to by now, all those dreadful shrieks and thuds, and bloodcurdling screams of suffering. She couldn't even bring herself to imagine what was happening out there, none of them could. However, Father had ventured out in the end, to Mother's shrill protests. How could they leave their women and children alone and unprotected?

Father claimed that no one would enter the actual dwelling of people; how could they? The warriors entered it quite freely, protested Mother in this same shrill voice, looking as though about to throw something at her husband, her eyes blazing and not entirely sane. The same warriors who were bent on protecting them, reasoned Father, his face closed in atypical stubbornness, reminding Chantli of her little brother when he insisted on unreasonable things, knowing that his claims were hollow and pointless. Did Father understand that his duty was to his family first and not the stinking workshop? Probably, but after Acatlo was gone for some time, he went out and away all the same, promising to come back as quickly. But he didn't. Instead, the wandering fire-arrow came!

Coughing against the smoke, the pole that had caught fire turning blacker by the moment, the tongues of flames trying to climb up, the *petate*-mats tucked in the nearby corner flaming merrily, threatening to make the entire floor ignite, the flames small but persistent, spreading embers, determined to reach the kitchen area and the tempting abundance of wooden objects there, Chantli splashed the contents of her pot on the blazing mats, then stomped out what she dared with her sandals, too enraged to be afraid while doing this. A dash back toward the water bin told her that they were dangerously low on this vital supply.

"Mother!" she yelled.

But the older woman was busy carrying her brother out and toward the smoking entrance, holding him tightly against the fierceness of his resistance.

"Chantli, Quetzalli, follow me," she screamed, her voice drowning in the outside cacophony, having a hysterical tone to it. "Come out and follow me. Now!"

She could feel her friend's hand clutching her upper arm, hurting it in the desperation of her grip. "Come, Chantli, come," the girl was whimpering, pulling without much strength. "You must."

"No, I'm not. The entire house will burn if we'll leave." She yanked her arm in order to free it, but the insistent fingers wouldn't let up, clinging to her, panic-stricken.

"Come, Chantli, come. We must go!"

Oh, but this refrain was annoying! She tried to free her arm again, watching the small flames of the burned pole coming to life with the draft her mother's dash for the wonders of the outside created, struggling to rush either up or down, to reach new grounds, something new to destroy, to feed on. So many temptingly flammable things, the floor strewn with reed-woven mats, the kitchenware, let alone the plentitude of mats in the inner rooms and her loom with half-finished fabric, such an easily igniting thing.

"I need to get my loom!" she yelled, struggling to break free, beyond reason now, but by then Mother was by her side as well, dragging her toward the newly ignited pole of a doorway, taking Quetzalli's side.

Outside, the air was easier to breathe, but not by much. The familiar alley was alight as though dusk was still with them. The bushes of the patio glowed merrily, sending a pretty show of embers every now and then, and the neighboring house and the one after it stuck out from the darkness, as though lit by too many torches inside. However, most of the illumination seemed to be coming from further down the street where even the sky was ablaze. The warehouses, she knew at once. All made of wooden planks and such a joy for the flames to consume.

"Out there, we'll be safe," breathed Mother, again with her youngest in her arms, but not a struggling cargo this time. The little boy must be terrified beyond reason, she thought, then forgot all about it as the eerie semidarkness enveloped her, made her heart flutter.

As though in a dream – not a dream but a nightmare! – she leaped away from the dreadful shadows that inhabited it, fast-moving forms with extended arms, darting all over, striking each other down. Like a journey through the Underworld, the third or the fourth level maybe, when the dead had to struggle through the wind-stricken desolate vastness.

Mother was yelling to keep running, but she stayed where she was, mesmerized, strangely fascinated, watching the nearby men crashing against each other, full length, one of them going down at once, emitting a funny sound. The first man hesitated, silhouetted clearly against the blazing sky, as though preparing for a ritual. His movements were slow, ritual-like too, as he brought his long, viciously spiked weapon down, cutting off the inhuman screams that had erupted in the meanwhile.

For another heartbeat, the world remained still, then broke with more rushing silhouettes. The man with the sword turned around, then, glimpsing her still standing there gaping, narrowed his eyes.

"Go away, girl," he tossed, his voice somewhat familiar, reminding her of what happened back in the house such a short time ago, when the world was still sane but going mad rapidly. "Go back into your house, quick," he repeated, then whirled abruptly at the swish of another weapon, leaping aside to avoid the touch of the descending club. Its owner was also as quick, regrouping to deliver another blow, but by that time, strong hands were grabbing her across her shoulders; sturdy, familiar hands. She didn't resist their pull or the friendly smell of smoke mixed with sweat and this peculiar scent of melted metal. Father! Whirling around, she hid her face inside his familiar warmth.

Down the alley where another one crossed it, beginning the row of warehouses that separated their neighborhood from the poorer houses spreading along the wharves, the glow was stronger and so were the heat and the smoke. Still, it was easier to breathe here; this street so much wider, offering more opportunities to keep away from the fire. Father was quite a sight, smeared with soot and scratched all over, his cloak a jumbled mess.

"Where is Mother?" she whimpered, but he kept pulling her, maneuvering their way between the darting shadows, the night inhabited by nothing but yells and screams, the warriors' cries of victory or pain interweaving with the wailing of people running around. Such terrible bedlam.

She felt like breaking into screams herself. Where were Mother and her brother and Quetzalli? To crane her neck or strain her eyes, didn't help, even though Father seemed to be searching too, twisting his upper body, making her sway with every turn of his.

In the end, she pulled away resolutely, tired of this mere dragging along. At that very moment, a deafening creak exploded, generating from the nearby warehouse, a long one-story-high construction. Horrified, she watched it coming apart slowly, prettily, generating a show of flaming colors and sparks. Father's hands were yanking her again, hauling her forcefully, dragging along rather than pulling. But for him holding her so strongly she would have fallen, she realized. Yet before she could start protesting such rough, inconsiderate treatment, people around followed their example, scattering in a wild panicked surge, darting away from the scorching wave of heat and the avalanche of burning beams, such terrible missiles. Even the warriors darted away in as confused disarray as everyone else, pausing in their fighting, eager to escape the mutual danger first. A sensible thing.

Amidst the terrible bedlam, her eyes blurred with tears but struggling to see, she glimpsed Mother's twisted face, running toward them, her youngest dragging along in the fashion that probably resembled the way Father was towing her around. She reflected on it numbly before breaking into a mad run toward them. Mother! Mother was here! She was here and unharmed, and she would make everything right again. She had to!

"*Nantli*!" she yelled, relishing the touch of the gentle arms pressing her with too much force, not minding it in the least. "Are you good? Both of you?" For good measure, she gripped her younger brother, making sure he was unharmed and unscathed. The way he pressed against her momentarily before returning to the tightness of their mother's embrace made her heart melt. "Where is Quetzalli?"

"Back there in the warehouse, the largest one," panted Mother, clutching her with too much force. "We hid there, but then you weren't with us, and I had to..." The arms around her shoulders tightened again painfully. "We should go back there!"

"It will catch fire any moment," heaved Father, herding them toward the more open space. "We are safer here."

"No, no, the larger warehouse won't. Everyone says that. It's not near the burning ones and the wind..."

Were they going to start quarrelling again? wondered Chantli, turning her attention back to the happenings all around them, the warriors again hacking at each other, oblivious of the swarms of citizens and the fires lighting the night. Mother picked a bad time to start doubting her husband's words all of a sudden, didn't she?

Gasping, her eyes caught sight of a nearby man bringing his club down on another's head, missing as his victim twisted away, parrying the blow with his own weapon, the spiked sword again. But how many warriors armed with the weapons of the elite forces were here? Against her will, she watched, fascinated, secure in the knowledge that one didn't need to attend school to know that obsidian swords were used by the best fighters, *calmecac*-trained warriors and those of the highest military orders, Jaguar and Eagle warriors, and only a few others.

As expected, the owner of the sword made quick work taking down his opponent. Her breath caught, she watched his victim twisting in the dust, unable even to scream. Yet, as the victor bent to deliver the finishing blow, tugging at his weapon that was still entangled in the depths of his opponent's body – somehow she knew that it was exactly what the man was doing, her instinct whispering, soothing in a way, fascinating, taking over the most appropriate sense of pure horror – another man leapt toward the warrior's unprotected back, his club high and already descending. Like in a dream, she watched the collision, her ears absorbing the muffled thud, satisfied to hear it, expecting it. The way the sword's owner went down was also intricately slow, many heartbeats per each movement – the half turned form, the broad sway of one of the arms, the thump of the stretched back upon the gravel, not as loud as that of the club but as definite, impossible to miss.

Mother was screaming, pressing her youngest's face against her belly, shielding him. Then the terrible moment shattered as the man with the club whirled toward them, his eyes wild and ferocious, not very human or sane. The way it focused on Father made Chantli snap back to reality, took her forward and toward the already-rising club.

"No!"

She heard the scream and wondered about it for a moment, clashing full length into the man, making him sway. Was it she who had screamed? The club wavered and when it hit its target, it slid against Father's shoulder, with no terrible thud accompanying the previous blow, sending him down nevertheless, to fall like a drunken man. Somehow, her mind managed to register all that, her hands still clinging to the man she assaulted, clutching him tenaciously, with true desperation. He could not be allowed to raise his club again. He wouldn't be surprised into missing, not this time.

His smell was terrible, the odor of the lake mixed with sweat, much of it, and as he shook her off, whirling toward her wildly, so terribly strong, she thought about it for a fraction. Was he coming from the tunnel and the island under the causeway?

Another fierce shake made her grip slip and she flipped her hands in the air, trying not to fall. A futile gesture. The dusty gravel met her with eagerness she didn't expect. Gasping with pain and the unexpectedness of it all, she stiffened, her fear sudden and overwhelming. The warrior, was he going to strike her down now?

Her mind kept urging her to scramble back to her feet, her mother's screams not helping, the thought of the thud, this disgusting smacking sound, the expectation of it, causing her limbs to go into paralyzed stupor. No point in trying to see it, was there? Still, she struggled to turn around, to see the club descending, every movement an eternity, twenty heartbeats on the effort to strain her neck into turning, another twenty on the shift of the head. When the expected thump exploded, it came accompanied with no pain but just more of the muffled sounds clearly belonging to a struggle. She tried to make sense out of it, pushing with her hands now, half upright and blinking.

Legs were moving next to her, quite a few. Then her mother's arms were there again, enveloping her, pulling with surprising strength. Leaning against the familiar warmth, she strained her eyes, watching in wonder. Father was still on the ground, half sitting half lying; however, the clubman did not give his previous target any attention, engaged in a new struggle against a silhouette armed with a long sturdy shaft. A spear, her numb mind told her, noting the details, knowing at once who it was somehow, not surprised in the least. Oh, but she should have expected it, shouldn't she?

He looked nimble and sure of himself, hunched forward, careful of movement, the impressive weapon balanced easily in his hands, breathtakingly handsome, easy to see *that* in the smoldering semidarkness. Another familiar figure was poised nearby, holding a club, ready to come to the *calmecac* boy's aid, his eyes darting toward the rushing by forms but returning to the duel, their concentration on display. Oh yes, the village boy did look impressive, just like Quetzalli said, his wide, muscled frame fitting the short cloak it sported, his pose straight-backed and proud, not cornered or wary or soot-smeared and exhausted, not anymore.

Wide-eyed, she returned to watch Necalli in time to see him swinging his spear in a sort of half a circle, landing its flat side against his opponent's head as though it was a club. It made the man waver and fall and remain motionless, trampled under someone's running feet.

For a heartbeat, no one said a word, then his eyes focused, sparkling in an unabashed manner, so familiar and adored. "I knew you would be out there and fighting." All his teeth seemed to be flashing in the wideness of his grin. "I just knew it!"

"I..." She tried to make her mind work, resisting the pull of her mother's arms, who seemed to be trying to steer her backwards and away, toward the darker side of the alley, maybe, and its lively clamor of huddling people and their shouts. There seemed to be no fighting there. "I... Where did you come from?"

To free her shoulders from Mother's grip felt natural. Like back in the tunnel or Tlatelolco, she wasn't about to leave the safety of his side, not now that he had found her and saved her again. In the corner of her eye, she saw Father springing back to his feet, wavering but holding on, his mouth pursed grimly, legs wide apart, not about to move anywhere.

Her breath caught. The village boy! Oh, but what would Father do now? And where were her elder brothers, both of them? A furtive glance around reassured her that no familiar hulking forms were ready to join the family drama. No fighting seemed to take place along the burning alley, not anymore, only rushing around people, some carrying vessels with water and sand. Necalli and the village boy exchanged glances.

"Are you all right?" By now, he was probably aware of Father's ominously silent presence as well, his smile having a more reserved quality to it. "You… you didn't seem in such good shape before?"

"I… I wasn't, yes." She tried to gather her senses, wishing Father would disappear for some time, until they could talk properly. "I… I thank you. You saved me!"

He shrugged with one shoulder, his smile as uneven, twisted mischievously. "It's nothing. We were worried about you. Wanted to come and see if you were all right. The workshop boy…" Then he fell silent quite abruptly, glancing at her father with quick but unmistakable wariness, atypical for him. "We wanted to see that your houses didn't catch fire…" His voice trailed off under Father's glare, which shifted again to his companion, turning yet stonier.

"What's the meaning of this?"

The village boy said nothing, only stared back, still an impressive sight, with his cloak and the club clutched tightly, balanced well in his massive hands, as though he would use it if need be, as though he knew how. His face was as well defined as she remembered but rounder now, somehow healthier, even though it was difficult to tell something like that, not in the flickering semidarkness and with all these people dashing around, shrilling at the top of their voices, talking with no restraint. There were fewer warriors, certainly not shady types armed with clubs. Was it over for good?

"You owe me an explanation, boy, don't you?" went on Father in a cutting, dead tone.

"He owes you nothing!" began Necalli hotly, but the village boy drew a deep breath.

"There is nothing to explain," he said as stonily, looking determined not to move from the spot he occupied, his pose that of a statue with no life to it, the club thrust forward. "I don't owe you an explanation. Or anything," he added less firmly, as though after a thought.

Father looked as if he would explode, but as he sucked in his breath, clearly about to break into a squashing tirade at the very least, the clamor from one of the buildings, the one opposite to the warehouse that had already collapsed, rose to impossible heights, filled the night with screams and shouts, and thuds of heavily falling objects. A billow of flame enlivened the sky momentarily, turning the night into a bright day again.

"The oil," yelled people. "The oil!"

"It caught the flames. The warehouse with the oil…"

More howls tore the shimmering darkness along with another billow, shrieks and yells and outright pleas for help, and then she knew that it was the same largest warehouse Mother said they were hiding in and the realization made her heart leap in fright. Quetzalli! Where was she?

Mother's strangled shriek told her that her trail of thoughts did not err. A wave of dread washed over her, as bad as the one when she had been on the ground, expecting to be crushed by the club, unable to escape. However, this time, her legs did obey her.

"Quetzalli!"

Forgetting all about Necalli and the village boy and Father and everyone, she broke into a wild run, her thoughts dashing in panic. Quetzalli, caught in the fire, helpless, maybe already dying. But it was impossible! And how could she have left her friend alone out there, not trying to look her up when Mother said she had lost her? Quetzalli was saucy and a survivor, yes, but in truly pressing circumstances, she tended to lose her spirits and panic. They had been in all sorts of situations together to learn that about each other.

The smoke assaulted her face as she neared, trying to shove her way in, everyone crowding but keeping a safe distance, not wishing to endanger themselves under another building liable to crush, this one so long and two stories high.

"Let me pass," she panted, pushing with all her might. "Please!"

People didn't hurry to yield her their places, glancing at her briefly, turning away indifferently.

"Please!" she pleaded. "Quetzalli… she is in there!"

Then something made the crowds part, just a little, and she breathed with relief, feeling Necalli's presence once again, so very reassuring, so welcomed in its unwavering loyalty and strength.

"Who is in there?" he asked, pushing her on, his arms encircling, shielding from the elbowing people, maneuvering their way. "What happened?"

"Quetzalli! She is in there, in that warehouse!"

His nod was hardly perceptible but there, reassuring. He would know what to do.

With no barrier of crowding onlookers, the wave of heat was hardly bearable, assaulting their faces, making them wish to look away. The narrow openings near the roof glittered merrily, lit from the inside. And so did the gaping doorway, its screen torn away, missing. People were darting around it, yelling advice. As they rushed toward it, a man leapt out, his face black with soot, clothes scorched and in tatters but seemingly unharmed otherwise, very much alive. The crowding observers received him with a deafening cheer.

Necalli leapt toward the wild-eyed survivor. "Is it bad in there?" he shouted, catching the man by his shoulder, forcing to face him.

The village boy elbowed his way toward them as well, another reassuring presence. "What happened?"

"Quetzalli, my friend, she is there!" This time, it came as a mutter, her eyes catching sight of a woman staggering out, a small child in her arms. People rushed to catch them as the woman swayed and seemed as though about to fall.

"In there?" The village boy's mouth was pressed into a thin line.

"Yes, yes. She is in there, burning!"

He thrust his club into her hand. "Just hold it and don't let anyone take it. Will you?"

Aghast, she caught his arm. "You can't go in there. It must be bad. Look at those people!"

The scorched man was still talking to Necalli, frantic and barely on his feet, but the woman sprawled on the ground, surrounded by offered help and useless advice aplenty, her child lifeless in someone's arms.

His eyes crinkled with unexpected flicker of laughter. "This fire is nothing near the real heat. No melting room this." His uneven grin held no grudge. "Just keep the club. What's the name of your friend? In case I can't see her."

"Quetzalli," she whispered, then caught his arm once again as he began turning away, ready to charge. "You... Be careful, please! I... I'm sorry about Father and everything."

He shrugged with one shoulder then he was gone, diving into the billowing smoke, swallowed by it.

"What is he doing?" cried out Necalli, reappearing by her side.

"He went in there." The feeling of the club's handle was pleasantly soothing, warm and a little slippery, reassuring in a way. He told her to guard it, didn't he? She clutched the precious weapon tighter. "Don't go in there, please!" Cumbersome, she tried to grab Necalli's arm as well, hindered by her precious cargo.

"I need to help him. He is crazy to go in there like that. He can't be left—"

"He knows how to deal with fire. This one is no melting room!"

He gave her a skeptical glance then charged toward the scorching wave, looking determined and impossibly handsome, the hardships adding to his looks and not taking from them, like back in Tlatelolco. Still clutching the heavy club, she rushed after him. No, they could not be left saving her friend all alone. It was not decent, not just.

Next to the creaking beams, it was actually easier to see, but not to breathe. She tried not to inhale the smoke, knowing that a wet cloth against her mouth and nose would be a welcomed addition, Father's teachings on the forefront of her mind, always. No child of a metalworker could grow up without strict fire regulations. The entrance into the workshop was dependent on that.

"Quetzalli!" she yelled, trying to peek inside. "Are you there? Quetzalli!"

No answer came, but she could see the village boy's blurry silhouette moving between the glimmering objects, searching the floor. Necalli tried to venture into the groaning chaos but didn't make it past the missing doorway screen, deterred by the inhuman heat. A load screeching somewhere inside generated a shower of sparks, followed by a thundering thump of what sounded like a falling beam, like that other coming apart warehouse she had seen earlier. It made her body leap away, regardless of her mind's decision.

"Miztli!" she yelled, frightened. Necalli was trying to charge inside again, his face smeared with ash but determined, eyes dark with decision. She forced her legs into action as well, but just as the suffocating sensation became unbearable, a bizarre-looking figure of too many limbs materialized out of the swelling mist, rushing out but staggering, as though drunk on *pulque*. The next thing she knew, Necalli was dashing toward it, clutching onto it, partly guiding, partly dragging them all out, Quetzalli clutched in the village boy's arms, coughing and whimpering and making funny noises.

The momentarily stunned silence held for another heartbeat, then broke with cheers and screams and pushing aplenty. Barely able to keep upright, choking on their coughs, they were hastened toward the blissful freshness of the night, leaving another bout of deafening creaking behind. She fought the urge to fall down onto the ground and stay there for all eternity, her legs wobbly, protesting the need to support her.

"There are more people in there," Miztli was saying, repeating it again and again, looking as though about to try and charge into the billowing flames once again. Glancing back, she saw that the building was still standing, glowing in outbursts of yellow and orange, enlivening the dark alley as though it was day.

"Quetzalli!" To put her attention to her friend seemed the best of solutions for now, but the girl was oblivious, clutching her savior with both arms, sobbing yet stronger, mumbling with no comprehension.

"There are other people in there," the village boy kept repeating, looking eager to dispose of his cargo now, shooting furtive glances whichever way.

"Don't even think of it!" Necalli was again the best source of reassurance and reason, his arm wrapped around her, protecting, his body tilting forward as though ready to prevent his companion's attempt of trying to storm the burning building again.

"But they are stuck there," insisted Miztli. "Unconscious or wandering like her." Briefly, he nodded toward his charge, again making a movement suggesting that he would rather put the girl down now, or place her in someone else's care. It must be difficult to hold her like that, reflected Chantli numbly, leaning toward her friend, yet not about to leave Necalli's side or the safety of his embrace.

"Quetzalli! Are you all right?"

Someone spread a cloth upon the ground, urging them to put the hysterical girl there. More helpful hands offered water to sprinkle on the coughing victim or maybe to make her drink.

"Quetzalli, here, lie here. Can you hear me? Say something."

But the girl kept clinging to Miztli and then Necalli was snickering, his soot-covered elbow making its way toward his friend's ribs in an unmistakable fashion. "You have an admirer, brother. And not a bad-looking admirer at that. What are you going to do about it, glorious hero? Run away or face the challenge?"

And as much as she wanted to tell him to shut up and stop talking about poor Quetzalli in such a way, the humorous side of it kept dawning until holding her own laughter in became increasingly difficult. Just like back on the causeway, after fleeing Tlatelolco. And as the giggle sneaked out against her will, she saw the workshop boy glaring at Necalli incredulously, opening his mouth to say something, then beginning to guffaw too, trembling with his entire body, still holding his charge but with obvious difficulty now.

"Is that another test? For the Eagle Warriors, you know?" he sputtered, then doubled over and let the girl slip onto the spread blanket despite her tearful protestations. "Am I supposed to...? Am I...?"

And then both of them were doubling over among the disapproving stares and she hugged Quetzalli and held her tight, but the laughter was trying to burst out as well, difficult to stifle. They were such wild things, both of them, such wild pieces of crazy meat.

CHAPTER 17

The perfectly polished staircase towered ahead, as beautiful and foreboding as he remembered. The first time he had ascended those stairs – was made to ascend those – happened barely half twenty dawns ago, not so many by the count of sunsets but a lifetime nevertheless. Back then, he had been too frightened, exhausted, dizzy, and downcast to appreciate its dignified beauty, the refined luxury, the work invested in carving such wonder out of the hardest of stones. The marble was to be found in his native lands, oh yes, but not sought out to collect, required in little quantities compared to other glittering stones and minerals. Who could work with such tough rocky material? Well, apparently someone could, fashioning a whole staircase out of it. A wonder!

The *calmecac* boy leapt up the first landing, hopping over a few stairs at once. Was this one ever worried about something, unsure of himself? Miztli doubted that. Truth to be told, he felt not that badly himself after sleeping for a considerable part of the morning but not before being fed and taken to the baths near the school precinct – luxurious sweat baths of a quality he had never imagined had even existed. It helped to restore his strength and wellbeing; still, the presence of the *calmecac* boy encouraged him as always, made him believe that he could manage all sorts of difficult situations if those presented themselves. A certainty when summoned to the Palace. Did the Emperor want to hear their report regarding the night battle?

Necalli was certain it was the case, glowing unashamedly since the Palace's guards came to fetch them. Not that this boy was downcast or humble while back at school, anything but! The stories concerning their nighttime adventures he regaled the rest of the boys with made the entire school buzz, seemingly offhanded accounts of battles on the city streets, blazing warehouses, special missions out there on the mainland. It turned them into heroes right there on the spot, legendary persons out of stories or near enough to that status, their newly acquired weaponry strengthening their claims. But did Necalli keep bragging about it, his own awesomely spiky spear and his, Miztli's, impressively large polished club. No one in school had earned any weaponry, no one but them, and as much as it made him cringe inside, such outright bragging, the fame it brought did have its points. Even though he didn't feel that invincible back there, on that road to the rebellious towns with pretty names or in the night fighting, for that matter. He just did what had to be done and, in some instances apparently, it wasn't good enough. Like that matter when he admitted avoiding fighting while busy delivering their message. But he still needed time to understand, to try and grasp why the *calmecac* boy was so appalled to hear that, warning not to talk in such a manner again, to dive into battles even if it went against the essence of one's mission, unless one wished to be accused of cowardice. As though he didn't display enough courage until now, coming out the owner of a club as a spoil. Didn't this same Necalli marvel at the strength and the accuracy of his shooting or his way of directing a punch, asking to teach him and his friend how to do that? And yet it all amounted to nothing the moment he said he didn't plunge into fighting readily only because he was busy doing what he was told.

Back then, he was offended deeply, angered beyond reason by the annoying even if well-meaning advice. Yet now he knew that Necalli himself was not accusing him of a possible lack of courage. Just warning him not to talk like that, or better yet, not to think or behave in this way anymore – leap into fights whenever he had a chance and even without one, then brag about it later on. So much to learn! Would he ever manage to understand these people, to think like they thought? And did he want to?

However, such questions aside, his fellow *calmecac* students were looking differently at him now, friendlier or at least more cordial, less wary of his foreign, more than humble, origins. Those who were reserved or indifferent or decidedly cold before talked to him readily through the noon lessons, initiating conversations and jokes, with even the aggressive ball player Acoatl saying nothing nasty through the length of two spear-throwing lessons and a brief mutual work time in the kitchen areas. Axolin was the only one to make his point in not talking to either of them, turning his back whenever he saw them, huddling with this same Acoatl or some of the others and making a show out of it, talking too loudly, laughing too hard. Which angered Necalli greatly, but not enough to make the *calmecac* boy slide from his cloud of euphoria that this one had been riding since they had been escorted back to school, when the sky had already begun turning grayish with light.

Not straight away from the battle, he remembered with a grin. That had ended earlier, somewhere after midnight, with the Tlatelolcans trounced so thoroughly no warfare beside people fighting to put the fires down was left. The warriors didn't send them to deliver any more messages, but had hastened them back to the better parts of the city, the Central Plaza and that hugely impressive crimson hall of theirs, to partake in a feast before being shipped back to school, a huge honor.

Leaving the wharves came at the best of timing too, as far as he, Miztli, was concerned, as by that time the girl he had managed to snatch from the fire was taken away, followed by Chantli, to be delivered to her family. Which left them in the company of old Tlaquitoc, a gloomy, menacing presence, hovering there like a bad spirit, full of threats and accusations. Oh, but what a ghastly encounter it was, not helped with the appearance of that brute of the eldest of sons, Acatlo, an addition that had him, Miztli, clutching his club with so much force he could hardly feel his fingers anymore. And yet, it was easier to return their ugly, threatening stares with the *calmecac* boy there and ready to come to his aid, whether with words or with actions. By himself, he wasn't sure he would have managed to handle this encounter with enough conviction and presence of mind to come out of it feeling victorious, avenged in a way. Yet in the end, it was the workshop owners who looked worse than kicked coyotes, slinking back into the darkness before the returning warriors, hating every moment of their defeat. The smile was becoming difficult to conquer.

"What are you beaming about?" A nudge at his ribs was familiar, to be expected. He deflected it using his elbow, more successful than of yore.

"It's pretty in here."

The splendor of the first inner hall surpassed everything he had ever seen – even the last night's peek into the Eagle Warriors' crimson hall – his memory of this same Palace's visit again only two market intervals old yet nothing but a blur. Oh, how miserable he had been back then, how lost!

"They made an effort to impress your commoner's eyes, didn't they?" Necalli chuckled, then hastened his step, following the dignified servants assigned to conduct them in, as expected. "Think we'll be allowed into an even prettier set of rooms this time? Some nicely adorned hall with a great feast laid out to honor us. If the royal family is planning to rush out and meet us again in its entirety, then they can invest into their hospitality, can't they?"

The boy's voice dropped to a mere whisper by now and Miztli was thankful for that. But they shouldn't be talking like that, not in the heart of the Palace.

"Think they'll have that haughty Lady Atotoztli in there again, the worried *nantli*?" Necalli's chuckle was loud enough to draw disapproving glances from their entourage, which was growing as they went, joined by more meticulously dressed men whom he remembered on the previous occasion lecturing them on the correct behavior in the Revered One's presence. "Will she be burying you under indignant questioning again, eager to learn what your dealings were with her precious, haughty imperial daughter?" Another snicker. "Come to think of it, this time, your story will be even more colorful. They won't bore our royalty, your new tales."

He didn't need to be reminded of *that*.

"Shut up!" This came out too loudly as well. He clenched his teeth and returned to watching the floor, the sandaled feet of their entourage a safer thing to observe than the fury of their icy glares.

"What? No tales of scattering ducks while the princess was busy throwing you into the Tlatelolcan royal pond with her own prettily groomed, aristocratic hands?" There was no stop to his *calmecac* peer now, his snickering bouncing off the magnificent wall murals. "Just think about it." Then he sobered all at once. "I wonder what's happening to this one now."

Despite his own mounting agitation, the memories of the Tlatelolco Palace bringing nothing but anguished regrets, Miztli glanced at his friend, puzzled. "What do you mean?"

Necalli's face held none of his previously mischievous mirth, his pointed eyebrows climbing high, both of them. "The night fighting, remember that? Even without Toltitlan's swords and shields, that night attack was a declaration of war. A filthy declaration at that, not a gesture worthy of a respectable *altepetl*. Think about it. They could have sent us *tizatl* and appropriate weaponry. You know, the things they send to the cities when they wish to declare war on those, all the insignias of fighting and death. That's the proper way to do it. No cowardly night attack."

The alcove they had been hastened to, gestured to wait in with no seating arrangements in sight, was cozy, offering a measure of privacy from the passing by nobles or servants. He greeted the chance to stop and think, the Tlatelolcan treachery not coming to the forefront of his mind, not until now. But what would happen to the neighboring island? A war with Tenochtitlan, surely; the enraged, betrayed neighbor, the mighty conqueror of so many places and lands, the unchallengeable ruler of the known world or too many parts of it. Oh yes, the Great Capital's retribution would be vengeful, a terrible thing. And Tlemilli was there in the Palace, a daughter of the archenemy Teconal. Oh mighty deities!

"With them attacking us like that, put in their place and about to pay for it all, eh?" Necalli's eyebrows were still arching in a half amused, half suggestive manner. "I wouldn't switch places with the haughty royal princess, not now."

He didn't care for that particular royalty, his thoughts on Tlemilli and the possible danger she might be exposed to regardless of her personal deeds or misdeeds. How to warn her? How to take her away from it all? Tenochtitlan would conquer Tlatelolco easily. One didn't need to be a great warrior or a leader to predict that. If he had had his doubts, the night fighting proved how good these people were, even if surprised and forced to improvise; how coordinated, not prone to panic or lose their heads. And yet, there must be a way to warn her, to save her, maybe, somehow. If only she would still trust him, would let him find her and talk to her. The old pain was back, squeezing his chest, leaving it empty, struggling for breath.

"They say some of the Tlatelolcans gathered around the other two causeways, the ones that lead to the mainland."

"Why?" He didn't listen or care, but it seemed as though he was called on to say something, to offer a word of response.

"To prevent us from running away and onto the mainland, some say. Imagine that!" Again, the *calmecac* boy was speaking too loudly, forgetting their lack of privacy or the dignity of this place. "The lowlifes were that sure of their success with their filthy sneaky attack. Stupid rats! Our Jaguar Warriors made smashed tortillas out of the presumptuous lowlifes. They were responsible for this other part of the city, the better parts. Not the ones we spent our night at." Then the merriment was gone again. "Chantli deserves to live somewhere around here, not in her slums, with her filthy scum of a family. There must be a way to ensure that."

He could find nothing to say to that either, having not thought of Chantli in such connotation. Her father and brothers turned out to be rotten pieces of human meat, vengeful and mean. Still, they were her family. They wouldn't hurt her or make her unhappy, would they? Who would do something like that? And yet now, upon reflection, he understood his friend's concern more. Yes, she was too good for these people, but what could they do about it?

"That smelly craftsman of yours looked as though he would start spitting blood every time you told that stupid lump of meat, the other one, to leave you alone or else. He was eyeing your club with so much helpless loathing. It was touching. I almost started to pity him." The wide grin was back, beaming. "That's one of the things you must savor into your old age. The way that stupid bulk was staring at you, wishing to strangle you there and then, unable to because of his fear of you. Must be the sweetest of feelings."

"It was."

He took a deep breath, appreciating it all, the support and the lighthearted companionship, the real friendship and mere being there for him, back on that night or in other instances. Even this talk now, making light out of it, turning it all into something of no real significance, the days in the melting room, being exploited and cheated and treated like dirt, yes, but in the past now, never to happen again, not to remember but as a silly thing, with jokes and laughter at the expense of those who made him suffer, his revenge sweet enough, not warranting his spending time thinking of these people. Oh, but he still needed to think it all through.

"I thank you," he said gruffly, taking his eyes away, glancing at the statue of a Beautiful Serpent that was glittering not far away, at the nearest end of the hall. "I'm truly grateful, you know. For your being there and making it easier... I'm not sure I would have managed. All by myself, I mean. Without you being there and ready to help, you know, it would have been bad. I know it would have!" He paused, embarrassed to no end, but needing to say it, only this once. "I will never forget, never! I will repay you, somehow. I swear I will."

But as expected, his companion's arm flailed in the air, dismissing his words with a twisted grin he had come to know so well. "What nonsense. Next you will thank me for standing here in this niche as well, breathing the Palace's air that you might have not managed to breathe all by yourself. Eh, workshop boy? Will you repay me for that as well? I'll insist on a good compensation. Let me think what it should be."

"Shut up!" He felt his face beginning to burn worse than the fires of that warehouse back on the wharves.

"What? No 'go jump into the lake' this time? But you are enriching your arsenal of curses. Good for you." Then the chuckling ceased. "Think of how to take Chantli away from that workshop. Repay me in this way."

"Repay *you*? Is she of special interest?" His embarrassment began to evaporate, the chance of getting back at his friend for plenty of teasing and needling too great to miss. Let this one change colors for once. "Want me to raid that neighborhood, kidnap her for you? That's what you warriors do when you fancy a pretty girl, no?"

Indeed, now the *calmecac* boy's eyes were shooting thunderbolts, his well-defined cheekbones taking on a darker shade. "Shut up, you stupid lump of meat. I never heard so much stupid talk in my entire life!"

At one time, he might have gotten startled, maybe even afraid or defensive. Now he just grinned and didn't take his gaze away, watching the changing expressions, from naked anger to pure indignation to a half-amused, half-irritated grimace.

"You are something else, workshop boy," was the final verdict, uttered with a grudging half a grin. "Something out of the storytellers' tales." The wide shoulders lifted briefly. "Chantli is a nice girl and a friend. Just like your friendship. An unlikely thing, but a fact now." This time, another one-sided shrug came accompanied with a wink. "Not as exotic a bird as you are, though, but still. She is one of us now and we must make sure she is not curbed by that stinking craftsman, not harmed or made to suffer in any other way."

Oh, but it was nice to have the brilliant, self-assured *calmecac* boy on the defensive. "Not like me, surely. All those curves and pretty eyes. I don't have any of that."

Again, the angry flash was softened by a grudging chuckle. "Shut up!" Then the generous lips twisted wickedly. "You were groping plenty of curves that night, dragging her curvy friend out of the burning warehouse in your arms like the most gallant of heroes. She appreciated that; one could see that easily. And you were clutching her long after there was no danger of fire or anything else all around."

Now it was his turn to change colors. "I did not!"

"Oh yes, you did. Everyone saw it. Even Chantli's father, your stinking craftsman. They were all staring at your commoner paws clutching to that pretty thing."

"She refused to lie on that blanket! I didn't hold her more than necessary. I tried to get rid of her the moment we came out!"

"Don't scream that loudly. The Emperor will hear your story soon enough. No need to interrupt his peace now."

He glowered at his friend, helpless, knowing that he had been bested somehow, hating the feeling, remembering that, indeed, this girl refused to leave his arms, clinging to him with surprising persistence, embarrassing in a way. Well, she was distraught, poor thing, frightened to death, choking on all this smoke. Of course she didn't want to leave him until sure that the fire wasn't about to harm her again.

"Want me to go and snatch that curvy thing for you, in the best of warriors' fashion, eh? As you so neatly put in your generous offer."

There was no stop to his adversary now, delighted in his newfound line of defense. They said it was imperative to attack always, to shift the fighting to offensive whenever one could. That was what the teacher from the sling and the spear-throwing lessons kept telling them, and somehow he knew that that was what his friend had been doing now, such a good pupil, launching offensive, using the same weapon he had been attacked with, same accusation, turning it against his attacker. But for the opportunity to do the same, to reverse it all back!

To his immense relief, some of their previous escorts headed toward them again, stopping the hated tirade with their mere presence, the outpour of flowery descriptions concerning the curves of the clingy fowl, and what a pleasure it must have been to hug her in the way he did. The filthy rat!

He focused his gaze on the paneled wall and the opening that, judging by the breeze, led toward the terrace and the outside. To think of the embarrassing incident in the burning warehouse hurt. Were they all assuming what that annoying Necalli implied? That he enjoyed holding that girl in his arms? Oh, what nonsense! He didn't even remember what she looked like, except being soot-smeared like they all were, sobbing and pressing too tightly, constricting his movements. She surely didn't mean anything inappropriate. And neither did he! But what if they all, including her, and maybe Chantli, and maybe her filthy father and brothers, thought that he did. Oh mighty deities!

"You will remove your sandals, and you will not look the Revered One in the eyes unless spoken to..."

The familiar stern instructions began assaulting their ears as they neared another doorway, this one decorated most lavishly with plenty of gilt. He managed to kick off his sandals as fast as his *calmecac* peer, the new gust of breeze making him play with the idea of escaping it all through the nearby opening or a terrace, wherever it was.

"You are not to come nearer than ten paces in the presence of the Revered One and you are not to look at him directly. Stay at the assigned place unless directed otherwise."

He remembered standing only a few paces away from the barely clad, sweaty ruler, with the man taking a break from the game he had participated at as one of many, with no special honors, drinking thirstily, speaking to him, Miztli, like any other person, not minding being looked at in the eye or answered before being permitted to do so. Didn't this Palace's people know their Emperor but as a foreboding statue following strict rules and never steering from those?

The sun was still strong, washing the paneled vastness, glittering against the statues, enlivening the beautiful pattern of polished tiles. A group of magnificently dressed people spilled out of another gilded opening, this one wider and grander, with a carpet of decorated mats tracing the steps of the leaving nobles. They had their sandals still on, noted Miztli, curious for no reason.

"Must be a delegation from Texcoco," whispered Necalli, apparently watching the passing dignitaries as well. "Just look at their clothing and the way they are walking, so perfect and dignified one can vomit."

"Who?" Against his will, the question came out, although he was still seething over the unwarranted accusations concerning that well-endowed fowl.

"The Acolhua, you know. The snotty filth eaters from *altepetl* of Texcoco, on the eastern side of the Great Lake. Come on, you must have heard of these folk. I won't believe that you haven't. The members of the Triple Alliance, for all the great and small deities' sake. Don't tell me you don't know any of this!"

He regretted asking in the first place, their escorts again scurrying away, motioning them to wait where they were.

"Oh man, you do have too much to learn in too little time! What did they teach you out there in this village of yours?"

"Things. Other things. Not about alliances and snotty filth eaters. It's not important to my people, none of it!"

His companion exhaled as loudly as their semi-private corner allowed, eyeing another group pouring from the same grand entrance, too richly dressed, indeed, very haughty-looking elderly men.

"Well, it's important to our people over here. Important people, you know. Those who decide things. No stinking craftsmen, but I bet even they know. On the marketplace, they certainly gossip about everything, politics and whatnot. And if you don't want to be kicked out of school by our appalled teachers, start remembering those things. Like the Triple Alliance of the most powerful *altepetl*s in this world of the Fifth Sun." The *calmecac* boy brought his hand forward, palm up, one finger extended. "We, Mexica people of Tenochtitlan, are obviously the most important members of the Triple Alliance, the leading *altepetl*. We have plenty of provinces, more than all of them put together have. Still, the Acolhua people from Texcoco will try to tell you that they are our equal partners, because when we are warring together, the spoils of war, the tribute, everything, is divided equally between the two of us. Understand?"

Against his will, he wished to hear more. "Like half you, half them?"

"Not exactly. More like two-fifths theirs, two-fifths ours."

"Two-fifths?"

"Yes, two-fifths. It's like when you take something, say this round tasty tortilla, all hot from the fire, and you cut it into five pieces, then take two of those for yourself and give me two other parts. That's our equal two-fifths. See? Tenochtitlan takes two pieces, and Texcoco takes two other pieces."

"Oh." It was actually easy to imagine this. "And who gets the last piece, then?"

Necalli's grin was one of the widest. "Sharp boy. You get it fast.

So yes, triple means three, obviously, and the third member of our alliance gets the last piece, the last one-fifth." His gaze crinkled mischievously. "That's another *altepetl*, the Tepanec city, Tlacopan. They helped us against their own overlords, the Tepanecs of Azcapotzalco, when those ruled everywhere around the Great Lake. So they got in, into our alliance. But they are not equal. They receive only this same pitiful one-fifth of the spoils and the tribute, and they are generally not as important to us as the Acolhua of Texcoco. But they are consulted in the matters like this one, with this Tlatelolco war. So I bet that their delegation is here as well. Somewhere around. Maybe about to be received, maybe being received already." A shrug. "Maybe those were the other ones who just passed by. Our Emperor will have to consult them, get their agreement."

"And if they won't agree, what then?" It was difficult to imagine the mighty Tenochtitlan ruler asking for permission to go to war. Ridiculous!

"They'll agree." The *calmecac* boy shrugged, unconcerned. "And if they won't, the Emperor will convince them. He doesn't need their cooperation or warriors or anything. Just their agreement. So why would they argue?"

"To piss him off, for one. For spite, maybe. To make him beg." It still didn't make sense, any of it – their way of breaking spoils or tribute into five parts, like a cut tortilla – why five? – or their need to ask each other if they wanted to war on someone, or even when forced to go to war. Didn't Tlatelolco declare war with their nighttime attack? "It doesn't make sense. Why can't the Emperor just go to war if he wants to do that and doesn't even ask for their help, only for stupid permission?"

Necalli was making faces. "Because he can't, you brilliant politician. This is not how it works. Why do you always argue against the obvious things?" His beam was again one of the widest. "It's good that the Emperor doesn't have to ask for *your* permission. You would argue with him just for the sake of it, eh?" His wink held again enough of encouraging amusement. "Just accept things as they are and learn. This way, you'll stay in *calmecac* until it's your time to go out there to wave your club. Or better yet, a real obsidian sword. Eh? It may happen if you do well. Those Eagle Warriors weren't greatly displeased with us. They may wish to put an eye on us, to give us a chance when our time comes. Think about it!"

The excited tirade was cut short by the reappearance of their escorts, only two of them this time, both frowning and unsettled.

"Remember, do not step closer than the edge of the mats. Do not raise your eyes until spoken to by the Revered One."

Miztli closed his ears to the annoying repetition, concentrating on his step, awed by the statues towering on both sides of the entrance, so wide four people could pass through it without jostling each other. The touch of the decorated mats spread over the polished tiles was delightful, pleasant upon his bare feet, rustling softly. He relished the soothing sensation and the new gust of light breeze that came through the opened shutters, calming, comforting in a way.

The reed seats of honor were surprisingly many, arranged in an intricate pattern, yet unoccupied besides the two lower stools next to the high imperial chair. He kept his eyes on the floor, not terrified like the first time and not even unsettled. The Emperor must be wishing to hear their report on the night fighting, to learn their impressions and observations, to know if there was something they noticed that the others did not. He was that wise, this man!

Unable not to, he peeked at the figure upon the higher upholstered chair, rewarded with the view of the imperial hand raising, stopping their progress before the edge of the mats had been reached. Their escorts shifted uneasily, and he remembered that they were to kneel now, to prostrate themselves.

"No need for the ceremony," the familiar voice declared, calm and matter-of-fact, the hint of amusement in it unmistakable. "Not this time. These boys served me well in fighting. My warriors are not required to kneel before their emperor." A light wave sent the dignified watchdogs away. "You may raise your eyes."

The arrangement of chairs and low tables was fascinating, long folded sheets of *amate*-paper scattered upon them, their edges adorned with glittering stones, to keep the sheets from unfolding.

Somehow, he knew it, having never seen this sort of documents before. Like books in *calmecac* but not quite. Other tables hosted trays with refreshments, servants standing around those, ready to rush their goods to the requesting nobles. Judging by the sight of the round plates, the previously received delegations had feasted here to their hearts' content.

"So, my Eagle Warriors found you two to be of use through the night fighting, I hear," the Emperor was saying, his voice placid, ringing calmly in the afternoon haze.

Again, the impressive man did not recline upon the cushions of his broad chair, sitting straight-backed and proud, clad in a cloak of vibrant patterns, the wideness of his chest concealed by a round breastplate, glittering gold. Miztli's thoughts strayed to a clay form required to make such a plate, with the amount of melted metal, both copper and gold powder, and bee wax to fill it beforehand. Would old Tlaquitoc's workshop manage something like that?

"And I heard that you did not disappoint my warriors and their leaders with lack of courage, enterprise, or even a display of disobedience," went on the Emperor, his usual detached, distant self, not unfriendly or threatening, not intimidating, his eyes measuring them calmly, not displeased with what they saw. It encouraged Miztli into glancing around, meeting the gaze of the man he remembered from his first visit in the Palace, the Emperor's stocky brother, close-mouthed and undistinguished, his eyes closely spaced, veiled, impossible to read. Another dignified person, an elderly man, reclined in his chair easily, radiating affable curiosity, a plate in his lap gaining some of his attention, filled with round fruit and rolled tortillas, prettily arranged.

"It was an honor to be allowed to be of use to the best warriors of the Empire." As always, the *calmecac* boy did not search for words while being addressed by exalted company, his expression one of perfect composure, not too servile or too forward. Miztli tried to ignore a small twinge of envy, meeting the curious gaze of the elderly man, at a loss as to what to do with it – to avert his or to answer with this or that humbled expression.

"It may be that you will be allowed to visit the Crimson Hall from time to time, summoned there to train or to learn, or just to watch and maybe to be of use."

This time, to Miztli's astonishment, Necalli's composure shattered all at once. His eyes widening, blinking, the *calmecac* boy gulped and said nothing for a moment, his stare unsettling in its almost touching bewilderment, like a child offered something too wonderful, afraid to reach out and try to take it as yet. Blinking in his turn, Miztli tried to understand. Did they do something bad after all? Were they to be punished for something? The *calmecac* boy's agitation was unsettling, out of place.

"Will you be up to the task?" The Emperor sounded well pleased with the effect of his previous words.

Necalli's mouth opened several times before something came out.

"Oh, Revered Emperor, I will... we will... thank you; oh, you will never regret... never! It will be such an honor, and they will not regret..."

But wasn't it his prerogative to mumble in confusion while speaking to the Emperor? This time, Miztli felt like snickering aloud, the laughter hovering nearby, somewhat hysterical. Why was ever-confident, outspoken Necalli stammering that badly now? The elderly man was smiling in a fatherly fashion, and even the closemouthed imperial brother twisted his lips in what looked like a hint of a grin, just the very beginning of it.

Then, he felt the Emperor's eyes upon him, and his heart began fluttering out of order again.

"And what do you say to this honor, young commoner with the spectacular name? Your courage was proven alongside that of your noble-born friend, and the club you managed to capture while fighting Tenochtitlan's enemies can be easily turned into an obsidian sword should you continue walking this path."

He swallowed to make his throat work, wishing Necalli would come out of his atypical fit of stammering and help him out as he always did. What was the Emperor trying to tell him? It was about the courage and the warring path, and his club that he cherished so very much now, proven twenty times over through the night fighting, even just to intimidate like in the case of that filthy tempered Acatlo. So it must be a good thing what the Emperor was talking about. He tried to remember Necalli's words before the *calmecac* boy lost his composure altogether.

"Thank you, Revered Emperor. It was an honor to serve, to be of use to the best warriors. And this great city," he added on the spur of a moment, pleased that he remembered. "It is a great honor."

That seemed to go down well with his imperial audience. He held the breath of relief in.

"It is an honor, indeed." The Emperor seemed to be still lighthearted, still amused. "But it is an honor you will work hard to earn, serving me and this *great city*. They will teach you all this and more, and you will work hard to excel in your studies and not only your training with weaponry and your readiness to serve my *altepetl*."

This he found easier to understand. "I will, Revered Emperor. I will continue to do that, to work hard. If it pleases you, that is." A cumbersome attempt at the prettier way of talking. The Emperor's eyes twinkled openly.

"One hears that as your messenger he did less successfully, Brother," drawled the thickset man, not amused. "To be an elite warrior, one needs more than courage and good aim." The well-padded shoulders lifted in a shrug. "Our *calmecac* teachers would have to work hard making this boy into what you seem to desire to turn him into."

"They will manage." The Emperor's eyes turned sterner, lost some of their affable expression. "The matter of our sister's complaints will be examined in due time. After the situation with our neighboring *altepetl* is resolved to my satisfaction. Not a heartbeat before." The last phrase rang stonily, cutting the air.

"Why don't you send for her now, Son?" interrupted the elderly man, his voice pleasantly low, ringing with pointed calm. "She asked to be present at this particular audience."

He could feel Necalli's gaze brushing past him, as though trying to warn, the *calmecac* boy's composure back, eyes measuring, returning to the royal chairs, narrowing with attention. What was that all about? Miztli felt his skin crawling. Son? So the elderly man must be the Emperor's father? And who else asked to be present in this particular audience? Whom they were wishing to send for, what complaining sister?

The Emperor glanced at the sun. "It is futile and we have no time for silly female games." The eyes returned to him, narrowed as though gauging, with no amusement to soften the stern expression. "The information you brought from Tlatelolco on the night before, the word of the swords and shields being sent to Cuauhtitlan and Toltitlan, who gave you this information, boy? Who asked you to bring it to me?"

And then he knew he was done for, the meaning of "complaining sister" becoming crystal clear, ringing with finality. Oh, but how didn't he guess it before? She had sent word, somehow, or maybe even reached the island capital – didn't the old man suggest sending for her now? – implicating him, revealing his lies.

"Was that the princess, the revered sister of our Emperor, who had given you this information?" The voice of the imperial brother rang with utter contempt, freezing cold.

He heard Necalli drawing a convulsive breath. "If you mean the information about the Acachinanco road, Honorable Tizoc," he began, addressing the stocky man, but the curt wave of the broad palm cut those words short.

"Silence, young *pilli*. My question was not addressed to you. Mind your manners."

All the while the stocky man's eyes bore into him, Miztli, making him feel as though this last reprimand was directed at him as well. He clenched his teeth tight, aware of the rising tide of anger, trying to push it back. It was not the time nor the place to lose the last of his lucid thinking, but the anger helped, rendering him much needed strength. This man was not the Emperor. He was not the person responsible for this city, keeping its citizens from harm and its streets and avenues safe, using his, Miztli's, information in order to maintain it. He was not the person he had lied to.

"Answer!"

"No," he said quietly, marveling at the sound of his own voice, so even, so matter-of-fact. His eyes did not linger on his interrogator, shifting to the Emperor instead, encouraged by the flicker of familiar light affability, faint but there. The Emperor wasn't accusing him. Well, not yet. "The Revered Princess was not the one to let me know this."

"Who did give you this information, if so?" The ruler's voice rang softly, encouraging. It was as though the man knew the answer to that.

"The girl from the Tlatelolco Palace. She was the one to let me know. The princess... she wasn't pleased with my... my connection to this girl, and she didn't give me the information you required to bring back, Revered Emperor." At least the title came to him easily this time. He reflected on it numbly, with no elation or relief.

Now the Emperor looked outright pleased. The glance he shot at his brother had a triumphant spark to it, the "told you so" in it obvious.

"I was under the impression that the warning came from my sister," he said mildly, as though wishing to finish the awkwardness. "But it may be that you didn't explain the nature of your source properly, boy. Given the unusual time of the night this interview has been conducted, you two may be forgiven for not making yourselves clear."

"We, indeed, had no time to explain in full, Revered Emperor." Mentioned even in passing, Necalli, apparently, was not about to let the opportunity go unheeded. "It was the second part of the night and we didn't wish to intrude more than we already did."

The Emperor nodded thoughtfully, the side of his mouth twitching ever so slightly. "Next time, leave it to me to decide on the necessity of this or that information or the appropriate time to deliver it." The contemplative eyes rested back on him, meditating. "Our Noble Jade Doll is, indeed, not pleased with you, boy. On your way out, you will be escorted to her quarters in order to apologize for your behavior. Do not mislead with your reports again. Unintentionally or not, it came close enough to be a lie, the origin of your reports, and such a mistake will not be tolerated again. Do you understand that?"

Miztli just nodded, bereft of words.

"It's an interesting choice of unofficial messengers you have, Son," commented the elderly man, his attention back on his plate, picking out a small tomato. "Very diverse, very unusual." The mirthful eyes flickered with almost mischievous hilarity, somehow inappropriate in such an old dignified man. "Not to say, exotic."

"Your youngest of offspring was the one to put this crew together, Honorable Father," said the Emperor with a brief smile, getting to his feet briskly, his expression turning grave again, his thoughts evidently already away. "Our high-spirited Ahuitzotl has an unlimited pool of spies, and these two are not all that he keeps in store." This time, the crinkling gaze focused on Necalli, to the immensity of Miztli's relief. "The commoner girl you came to report the Acachinanco business with, did she come to no harm through the last night? I remember you saying that she lived near the wharves and the causeway."

Necalli was nodding vigorously, his eyes alight. "Yes, Revered Emperor. Their neighborhood was damaged by fires, but she and her family came out of it unharmed." He licked his lips nervously, again curiously unsure of himself. "She was examined for our *calmecac* studies. Honorable Tecpan Teohuatzin interviewed her himself, or so Ahuitzotl says. And well, maybe she should... maybe..." The passionate words trailed off under the Emperor's suddenly chilling gaze.

"Go back to school and busy yourself with matters that concern you, young *pilli*." The bracelets rang with finality as the man brought his arms up, clapping to summon the servants. "Have this one detour through the Noble Jade Doll's quarters. Afterward, have them fed and taken back to *calmecac*." A curt wave of the imperial head nodded in dismissal. "Now go, and remember to do your best and keep on excelling as you did until now."

Kind, encouraging parting words softened the stern reprimand. Still, Miztli began breathing again only when safely outside, feeling the *calmecac* boy still tense, ill at ease, walking by his side, his steps ringing tersely. The light breeze coming from the terrace they had passed on their way into the grandiose reception hall beckoned. If reaching the outside, he could try to climb down maybe, attempt to escape through the gardens below. Anything but to meet the haughty princess again, dragged there by the imperial order this time. Their new escorts were hesitating, conversing between themselves.

"That was such a sure way to ruin it all," Necalli was muttering, boring holes in the glittering floor tiles with the fury of his gaze. "I should have kept my stupid mouth shut."

Miztli concentrated, trying to make his mind work. "What?"

A pair of brooding eyes flew at him. "He got mad at me for speaking about Chantli. Really mad!"

Oh, that. He welcomed the chance to put his thoughts on something unrelated to his looming troubles. The respectably dressed men responsible for their escorting were still talking rapidly, arguing.

"He didn't like you presuming to offer him advice, yes." A shrug came easier than he thought, his shoulders still stiff, still not over the previous fright. That other man, the Emperor's brother, was set against him, wasn't he? "But then he told us to go on and serve him as well as we did until now. He said it in so many words. Doesn't it mean that he is not angry, that he appreciates, admits that we didn't do that badly by him?"

"Well, he said that, yes." The *calmecac* boy was glancing at him from under his brow, frowning attentively, clearly listening, needing to hear.

"It was as though he was softening that previous telling off, no?"

"Maybe." A thoughtful nod, then the generous lips twisted lightly. "Yes, he bothered to say that we excelled, that he expects us to go on excelling." The smile widened. "Yes, you are right. He appreciates our achievements even if sometimes we speak too much. Or too little. Or with no titles." The wink held all the familiar mischief. "Or using dubious sources of information. But did that other one, that annoying brother of his, have to bring it up, eager to pit you against the filthy princess! I swear I got frightened for a moment. Who would have expected the haughty fowl to escape her annoying town and pop up here?" The last phrase he bothered to whisper quietly enough, to Miztli's endless relief. No, they didn't need the Emperor getting angry with them again, standing outside his highly luxurious hall, badmouthing his sister.

"Let us proceed, boys." The men responsible for them came back to life at long last. "You, follow me." Those words clearly meant him. Miztli felt like taking a step back, or maybe even did. The plaster of the wall felt pleasantly smooth against his back, warm but not reassuring.

"We are coming together. The Emperor wished us to visit his revered sister before returning to our school." Necalli's voice rang with firm decision. "Please, lead the way."

"The Revered One said to have only this one—" began one of the men, the more dignified looking among the two, a middle-aged person resembling old Tlaquitoc in his ways.

"The Revered One told us to visit the princess on our way back to school," repeated Necalli forcefully, holding his ground with an enviable ease. "He was very clear about it."

The men exchanged puzzled glances.

"If you wish to ask the Revered One, we can wait here until you do that."

That was outright cheeky. The frowns of their escorts deepened. "Follow," said the dignified man in the end, shaking his head, his lips pressed dourly, disapproving.

The *calmecac* boy's wink and a fleeting grin gave Miztli strength to leave the safety of the wall he was still glued to. Watching the ornamented tiles sweeping before his eyes, his once again sandaled feet clacking upon those in a curiously soothing manner, he tried to gather his senses, knowing that with the *calmecac* boy by his side, he might manage the dreaded encounter, might come out of it unharmed and with some of his dignity still intact. Oh, but this boy was so good to him, so kind and loyal and patient, teaching their ways, explaining, rendering help, laughing about his blunders in the way that made them look not as bad or dangerous or harmful. Would he ever manage to repay him it all?

The straightening breeze brought his attention back in time to see the towering doorway leading to the same terrace he was contemplating to escape through. Like the inside halls, it was glamorously furnished, adorned with carvings and statues, the stone parapet high, outlined boldly against the brightness of the afternoon sky.

In the generous shadow it provided, the woman sat royally upon another upholstered chair, a narrow goblet in her hand glittering gold, a feathered fan moving slowly, monotonously, managed by one of the maids. The rest stood nearby, laden with trays, ready to do the imperial bidding. Another haughty woman reclined nearby, surrounded by a similar arrangement. Miztli's heart fell some more. The imperial mother! But did he remember that woman.

"Well, well, if it isn't my brother's high-spirited messenger." The eyes watching him above the rim of the goblet crinkled in chilly, not very amiable amusement, studying him with strange curiosity, penetrating. Not the sight he remembered seeing last, twisted with rage, spitting threats, yelling like a marketplace woman that wasn't paid what had been agreed upon. Nor the other occasions, the aloof beautiful statue on the dais, far removed from the mortal crowds, or the coy over-indulgent noblewoman, complaining in the light of a flickering torch, demanding reassurance from a beaten, tied boy. This time yet again, she looked different, more beautiful than ever, her hair arranged in intricate tresses, pulled high, revealing the curve of the column-like neck, her features relaxed, glowing gold.

Not daring to stare back, knowing that he was again in danger, like anywhere when this woman was involved, he struggled to keep his fear off his face, unwilling to let the amusement in the cold eyes deepen, reflect on the depth of his fear. To look away helped. He glanced at his *calmecac* friend, briefly amused to see this one gaping in wonder. Had he never seen the famous princess before?

"Come closer, boy. Stand by that table, in front of the maids. Where the light is."

He felt Necalli following, not about to stay behind. It gave him courage to proceed without stumbling over something, so many mats and tables and smaller objects dotting the shadowed space.

"Well, what do you have to say for yourself, boy?" Again the affable tone, openly amused, toying with him and the helplessness of his situation. No pond to jump into and run away if worse came to worst, not this time. As though reading his thoughts, the woman lowered her drink, her lips quivering, twisting in a semblance of a one-sided grin. "You look more presentable now, commoner boy. Less likely to thrash in palaces' pools, I presume." The mocking grin widened. "That was a sight Tlatelolco will not forget in a hurry."

The older woman pursed her lips, not amused. "We need to prepare for the evening feast, Daughter." A light shift of the royal head summoned the waiting maids. "Have us escorted to our quarters and the *temazcalli* prepared."

"I will come in a little while, Mother," said the princess in the petulant tone he remembered well from the shed of the old nobleman. "Have my cup refilled with more chocolate." This sent some of the maids into hurried rushing about.

The older woman drew away with no additional comment, her exaggeratedly straight back and thrust out chin telling it all, boding no good for the disobedient child, princess or not. He fought the wild urge to snicker.

"Well, boy," the princess seemed to be the only one missing the currents, or maybe not caring, "tell me, does your improved appearance mean that you bettered your ways, that you will serve the nobles honoring you with their trust in a more fitting manner, and not like a lashing out savage?"

He sifted through various rude responses that kept swamping his mind, hating this woman so very much, afraid of her, despising her greatly.

"Yes, Revered Lady. Miztli has the best interest of the Tenochtitlan royal family in his heart. He has served your brother faithfully and he will continue to do so." The *calmecac* boy's voice rang clearly, with utter conviction. If he didn't know better, he might have thought that his friend actually meant what he said. The urge to laugh wildly grew.

"Who are you, boy?"

"My name is YoloNecalli and I've been serving our Revered Emperor along with ItzMiztli." Another proud response.

The woman raised her perfectly outlined eyebrows. "Have you been recruited by young Ahuitzotl as well?"

"Yes, Revered Lady. Your youngest of brothers sought out the best of our *calmecac* students worthy of the royal family's trust. Students like ItzMiztli, brave and trustworthy youths."

"Is that so?" The chiseled chin thrust forward, in a ridiculously similar way to the older noblewoman that had just left. "Did he ask his messengers to connect with the prominent Tlatelolco nobles as well? Daughters of the vile Head Adviser for one?"

He should have expected it; still, somehow it caught him unprepared. "Tlemilli has nothing to do with it!" The words shot out as though on their own. He didn't intend to resume the argument from the heart of the Tlatelolco Palace, anything but! It didn't bring him any good back then.

As expected, the woman's eyebrows flew high. "Insolent again." However, her smile didn't waver. Instead, it turned enigmatic. "Is that what she likes about you, that wild girl? I wonder." The eyes narrowed, filled with what looked like a genuine curiosity. "You worry about her, don't you? Do you like her? Answer truthfully."

"I..." He tried to find something to say, his thoughts scattering in spectacular disarray. Was she in danger? Harmed already? "She is innocent and naïve. She must be left out of it. She... she doesn't understand what she is getting into." The woman was smiling again, this time in a motherly fashion. He didn't care. "She must be left out of it."

"Did you tell her all that?"

"I... yes, some of it." He swallowed to make his throat work, needing to say it all, hoping against hope. Maybe there was a way to protect her somehow? This woman held so much power in this other palace. And what was she doing here in Tenochtitlan, anyway? "She wouldn't listen. She is like that, can't be stopped. But she should be made to keep away from it all. Her father is a terrible man; and the others too. She doesn't understand. She doesn't think she can be in danger."

"Oh yes, that she does." The smile was still there, holding curious affability, an expression he never saw on this dazzling face before. "You understand that bizarre girl too well; more than anyone, maybe. Which makes one wonder." The perfectly groomed palm rose, summoning the maids. "Escort me to the baths, and make the maids responsible for my hair ready." Standing there in all her majesty, her draperies light, rustling with the breeze, reflecting different shades of blue, from the sky-bright to the deep nearly black hue, the woman stretched, then motioned him to come closer. "That girl went to great lengths to have you receive this." The brownish piece of paper was small, folded hastily, in no pretty manner. "Strange as it may be, I wish her to come out of this dismal city's attempt of supremacy unharmed. Her of all people. How strange."

Another exaggeratedly dramatic shake of the proud head and she was gone, followed by the hurrying maids, a whole army of those. The terrace emptied as though by a gust of strong wind. Only the light breeze remained and the sunlight, delightfully soft, warming gently. The piece of paper was still there, scorching his palm. He glanced at it numbly.

"That was one strange encounter." The *calmecac* boy's voice made him blink, his hands trembling slightly, unfolding the paper. "What was this all about?"

"I don't know," he mumbled, eyeing the drawings, hastily sketched forms with no coloring, smeared in places, some more invested, some barely there.

"What's this thing?"

Instinctively, he drew his arm away, pressed it to his chest, protecting. It was a note, a letter, just like the one they had taken from the people upon the mainland, with their swords-and-shields messages. The naughty princess said that she went to great lengths to have him receive this. Oh mighty deities! He clutched the precious paper tighter.

"I'm not trying to peek into your love letters, you breaker of female hearts." Necalli's eyes were challenging, their laughter spilling. "Only trying to understand what just happened here.

What were you two talking about after you did manage to find your tongue? What made that haughty piece of work turn all amiable and well meaning?" He rolled his eyes. "I had little hope for you in the beginning of that particular audience. And with the arrogant royal mother, twice as overbearing, oh man. But then you started to plead for that other girl. Is that the same Fire Girl that let you know about the swords and the shields?"

Overwhelmed by so many hastily arrived at conclusions, Miztli took a step back, the paper burning his palm. "I... yes, I didn't understand why she became so reasonable all of a sudden." He rubbed his face with the back of his hand. "I thought she was going to make the most of it, to get back at me for what happened back there in that accursed Tlatelolco palace." The memories flooded in, not of the pond and the gardens but of what happened here on the terrace. "I... I thank you. I wouldn't have managed without you. You talked so well! So convincing. I wish I could do that too, to talk like that. I owe you for this, I do. I won't forget."

His companion's eyes flashed mischievously. "Yes, workshop boy. It won't harm you to learn to speak properly while addressing royalty and such. You either stammer so badly one can't understand what you are trying to say or, when you manage to find your tongue, you do so with directness and manners of a marketplace scum talking to each other. No titles, no protocol, in a hurry to say your piece. The funniest sight sometimes." A healthy outburst of laughter erupted, inconsiderate of their semi-private surroundings. "That is when you are not busy giving them orders, like now that you told the illustrious princess to leave your Fire Girl alone or else. That was a sight worth seeing. One can't forget something like that in a hurry."

The twinkling eyes were challenging, provoking, annoying in their open teasing but also making him feel better, less frightened of what had happened. If it was so funny, it couldn't be too dangerous, could it? And yes, it must have been a sight, indeed, but he didn't mean to be insolent. He was just worrying about Tlemilli. Her note began burning his hand anew.

"Just look at this procession!"

The people who brought them there were bearing upon them

again, followed by servants with trays. Not a small army like that of the imperial women, but promising nevertheless, the aroma of the trays spreading, overwhelming, the most delicious of smells. Their stomachs responded in a loud manner, which made them burst into a renewed bout of snickering.

"You can read paintings, yes? Those things they draw in folded papers?" he asked after they had been directed to the mats in another alcove at the shadow of wide parapet, a low table placed between them and the contents of the trays laden upon it, making their mouths drool.

Necalli was busy grabbing the nearest tamale, hot and dripping, full of delicious stuffing, meat and something else spicy. Dunking it in a nearby bowl of thick sauce, he shoved it into his mouth in its entirety, devouring it in one bite.

"Sort of, yes," he mumbled through his full mouth. "Don't like to do that. Only when forced. When the priests shove your face into those books, you can't do much but to read the glyphs and decipher their meaning. Why?"

Miztli busied himself with scanning the contents of the smaller plates, laden with slices of meat and pieces of avocado spread on a bed of tortilla, begging to be grabbed. But for the letter, he would have attacked those as well.

"Can you... would you..." He tried to think of how to put it, or rather to avoid asking at all. How to read her note without anyone else peeking in it? Impossible. He could not recognize one single glyph. He didn't even know what they called this kind of painting, not until coming to Tenochtitlan, until entering their school. How could one paint one's words and in a way so the others could decipher those, guess their meaning?

"What are you mumbling there about?" Necalli's eyes were upon him, his hand, in the process of reaching for another tamale, waving idly, lingering. "What about those books?"

"Can you show me how to read them? How to recognize those paintings, those glyphs? I mean, this note, I don't know what's in it, and I need to... I must..."

He didn't dare to take his eyes away from the loaded plates, but after a heartbeat, the silence became annoying, wearing on his nerves. A fleeting glance confirmed what he suspected. The *calmecac* boy was staring at him, his eyes unbecomingly round, although his mouth was closed, holding its contents but apparently forgetting to keep chewing them.

"You don't know how to read glyphs?" It came out in an awkward mumble, forcing the speaker to swallow too much, not a properly chewed mass. "I mean, you can't read that tiny note?"

Miztli felt like springing to his feet and running out and away. To reexamine the contents of the trays became a necessity.

"No, wait. Don't take it wrong. I'm not laughing at you. But," his friend was apparently still staring, not returning to his assault on the loaded plates, "I mean, I can understand those calendars and old accounts; they are such a pain to decipher. But you can read simple glyphs, can't you? The most basic things?"

"No." He glared at the mound of glittering round tomatoes, arranged prettily, piled in a pyramid-like style. "I never... I don't know, we weren't taught anything like that. It's different out there. You don't have all those piles of *amate*-paper around. People do other things."

Necalli seemed to shrug before getting back to attacking the plate of tamales anew. "Oh well, it doesn't matter. Let's get stuffed with those delicious things before they take it away from us. You don't get to eat that well in school. You must have noticed that by now." The large eyes twinkled. "Then we'll see how to go about making you decipher your precious note. I hope your Fire Girl is not of a talkative type to fill that message with too many glyphs. It looks to be a large piece." One side of his mouth was climbing up faster than the other. "We'll make you read it all by yourself. It won't be difficult, unless she wrote too much or too complicated. Or unless she is a lousy painter." A quick wink held much reassurance. "After we are through with it, you'll get the idea of that glyph-reading, never fear. In the end, you will devour whole books and will turn into a scribe instead of a warrior. How about that?"

Miztli's head reeled. "You will? Oh, I'll owe you forever and then some more! You..." Unable to wait for even a single heartbeat, he unfolded the paper again, placing it on the mat, pushing one of the plates away. In the better light and with Necalli's promise of help, her note didn't look as foreboding, those clusters of paintings. They were sitting in groups, he now noticed, one above another; well, at least the two of those.

"Oh good, she isn't talkative!" the *calmecac* boy exclaimed, leaning forward, squinting against the sketched forms. "And not the best painter either. Or maybe she was in a hurry. Look at those blots. Did she try to erase those?" His eyes narrowed some more. "It's about the mainland, you know. That one in the middle," his oily finger thrust into the outline of what looked like a strange sort of a headdress with tiny strips flying above it, "this is Smoking Mountain. You can recognize that, can't you?"

Miztli caught his breath. "That one?"

"Yes. Don't you see? That fat thing is a glyph for *tepetl*, a mountain, and those small things springing out of its top mean *poctli*, the smoke. Together they make PopocaTepetl, Smoking Mountain of the Eastern Highlands. But if you put those *poctli* things above anything else, you'll get other words, like the name of our third emperor or the current Tlacopan ruler ChimalPopoca, Smoking Shield. You just draw the glyph for a shield, like the ones you saw in that message we snatched, and you put those smoking things on it and here you have it, the name of that emperor that was killed by the filthy Tepanecs before Tenochtitlan went to war against them and gained our independence and all that. Easy, isn't it?"

To draw a deep breath became a necessity. His head was buzzing too badly. "What else does it say? What are those things?" The symbolized Smoking Mountain was flanked by two crossing lines with flower-like growths on their sides.

"Forest. This glyph means *quauitl*, a forest. I suppose she meant all those woods around this same Smoking Mountain. There is plenty of it out there, they say. Real thick forests. My father fought there in the fifth emperor's campaigns, and he says we can't imagine anything of the sort over here, we just can't."

"Yes, I know," he whispered, remembering but not caring, not now. His heart was making strange leaps inside his chest, pounding too wildly, too fast. *Smoking Mountain and the forests around it, where he had promised to take her.* Was she reminding him of his promise? He didn't dare to even think about it.

"This is the weird part." Necalli was squinting against the light, leaning closer to the paper, making faces. "Those at the top are the glyphs from the calendar, but in the wrong order. There is this lizard facing a rabbit that is looking at it. The wrong direction for a glyph of a rabbit to face." He twisted his lips. "And it is a talkative rabbit too. It has three symbols of speech coming out of its mouth, see? Not one, but three! It looks like it just wouldn't shut up." He grimaced again. "Also, its ears are wrong, barely there. She is either really bad at writing, or maybe she was trying to tell you something here." A shrug. "The lizard came out perfect, though. Could copy it straight into a calendar, for the moon with the symbol of lizard on it. No talking or anything, right direction, all limbs are there. I swear I have no idea what she might be trying to say by that."

"You mean those two, above Smoking Mountain?" He had to clear his throat in order to utter this question. Still, it came out distorted, too low, croaking in a way. He didn't care. *The lizard that said nothing and the rabbit that faced it with too many glyphs of speech coming out of its mouth.* Rabbit or squirrel, it didn't matter. He knew what she wanted to tell, and the knowledge of it made his stomach tighten in a hundred painful knots and his legs fight the urge to jump up and run out, all the way across the causeway, just now, in this very moment, war or not. Oh, but she wasn't angry, not anymore. She wanted him to keep his promise, to take her all around Smoking Mountain and the talkative squirrels there, him, the close-mouthed lizard. She remembered it all and she wasn't angry. He clenched his teeth until they creaked.

"Are you trying to make holes in it with the power of your gaze?" Necalli was back at his tamales, his mouth full again, eyes twinkling. "It won't get clearer, the meaning of those glyphs, only because you stare at it your hardest."

He forced his eyes off the paper. "Thank you! I'm grateful, more than you can think of. It really is not difficult, eh? When you know how to break those paintings into parts, that is..."

"Well, it *is* challenging, because you have to memorize plenty of glyphs and some books are so full of those you have to be a true expert, a professional scribe to break so many of them apart and understand their meaning." The *calmecac* boy winked lightheartedly. "But yes, to read notes from pretty girls is not that difficult. Even though yours is a little mysterious. What's with those forests around smoking volcanoes and calendar-like stuff? A priest might have written this note to you."

"What are those here?" The last pair of glyphs in the lower part of the paper caught his attention, smaller and less significant, one of them actually easy to understand, depicting a person wrapped in a cloak or a cloth, its legs close to its body, probably squatting. "Is that a person?"

"Yes, that's a glyph for a woman. Men are done not much differently, but they are not wrapped in so much clothing, so this one is certainly a woman. See this thing she is squatting on? It's a mat and she looks silent. Maybe sad. No glyph of talking, and female glyphs usually have those. Like the one from the rabbit up there. That one took all the talking to itself, eh? Three glyphs of speech, just imagine that. But the woman got none."

His stomach was squeezing painfully again. "And the other, the last one?" he forced out, needing to be alone now, to think it all through. But there must be a way to get to Tlatelolco. Tomorrow, or on the day after. The other islanders had lost their war, got nowhere with their stupid night attack, so what could they do now but to sit back and keep quiet, lick their wounds, do nothing. No spies, no violent smugglers. Maybe to travel to that other island city might be the easiest thing now. And she would be there, like her note promised, squatting on that mat, waiting. No, not her. She wouldn't be sitting and crying, doing nothing, all sad, but she would need him to find her again, that was for certain, to reassure and to keep his promise, somehow. And to kiss, maybe; yes, if they managed to sneak away somewhere. The mere thought made his head reel so badly he had to press his palms into the mat he squatted upon in order to remain still.

"That last one near the woman is her signature, of course. The Fire Girl, eh? Field of Fire, TleMilli. Here is *tletl* for fire, those snake-like things, and that rectangle is *milli*, a field. See? Easy, isn't it? You'll learn all that in no time!"

"Yes," he muttered, his head on fire, worse than the one she drew, just a sketch, two snake-line lines and another, a shorter one. So this was how they drew "fire," and if he wanted to write something about the melting room, he would have to use this symbol, adding to it a glyph that described a room, perhaps. Or maybe something else, more complicated. So much to learn! Did she know that he couldn't even read her note when she wrote it? Would she be appalled to learn something like that? Would she turn away from him when she knew?

"You said it's not difficult? It'll take no time?"

Necalli's laughter was again too loud for the splendor of their royal surroundings. "It'll take some time, yes. But we'll have you reading faster and more accurately than the Imperial Court's scribes in the end." Attacking the smaller plate, he glanced up, his grin twisting wickedly. "But you get excited, brother, don't you? Shall we start getting organized to kidnap that fiery thing for you? What's with your suggestion of kidnapping girls one fancies; the warriors' way, you said. It'll be easy to raid that Tlatelolco now, and a warrior can take as many wives as he wants. So the clingy thing from the warehouse, then the fiery one? That makes the two of them in your collection of prospective spouses."

He stopped listening, unable to cope with it all, not up to the good-natured teasing, beyond the ability to become angered or try to get back, return measure for measure. The future beckoned, full of promise and so bright it shone. It was strange and demanding, too, so much more complicated than he could ever have thought or imagined, like a tale of a storyteller with a truly wild imagination. And yet he could try and do it, walk this path, face its challenge, best those – didn't he until now? – just like the Emperor said. Such a strong, wise, farsighted ruler, leader of warriors and people, busy keeping this enormous, gigantic *altepetl* safe, managing it and yet stopping to listen, to hear, to pay attention even to promising boys like Necalli or his own young hothead of a brother, believing in him, Miztli, a commoner boy from a forsaken village – impossible, but true. And what would Father think of it when he heard? And Mother and the rest of them, his older brothers? Oh mighty deities, but no one in his village would believe half of it, not even close. And Father would be so proud!

"If Chantli was to attend our *calmecac* lessons in the girls' hall," Necalli was musing, his forehead a study of too many creases. "It would have been easier to keep in touch with her, make sure she isn't harmed, locked inside or whatever."

Absently, he listened, his thoughts impossible to even try to organize. Was the *calmecac* boy still seeking a way to get to Chantli? And why-ever not? She was a worthy girl, courageous and kind. Very good looking too. Oh yes, it would be good to do something for her, help her to get away from the workshop as well. She did deserve better.

"Talk to Ahuitzotl," he said, his mind still buzzing but clearing gradually now, the storm of feelings and thoughts calming down, relaxing into a possible flow. Whether the war on Tlatelolco would break with vengeance or not, he would find the way to reach Tlemilli, to take her away from it all. Maybe. If she wished to be taken away. The mere thought made his head reel anew.

"About Chantli?"

"Yes. You said he was the one to know about her being interviewed by the *calmecac* priests and all that. You said it to the Emperor just now."

"Yes, I did." Necalli frowned, then brightened all at once. "You are right! Ahuitzotl can talk to the Emperor, bring this matter up again. He will find the way to do it without having the Emperor throw him out as he did with me. The young beast is capable of everything!" He snickered grudgingly. "He will be an emperor one day. Mark my words. And then Tenochtitlan will conquer every known land in our world of the Fifth Sun. It's bound to. With that wild beast in the lead, just imagine!" The smile kept widening. "And he'll force us to work hard to make it happen. I'm prepared to bet my future obsidian sword on that."

Oh yes, he would, thought Miztli, attacking the remaining tamales, very few of those, his stomach churning but his mind at peace, enjoying a long forgotten sense of tranquility, something he hadn't experienced since leaving his village all those moons ago. The huge capital was something else, impossible to measure or understand, and yet it was becoming his home, wasn't it? And he wasn't sorry about it, not in the least.

AUTHOR'S AFTERWORD

Tlatelolco, indeed, had taken a dubious course when, following the demonstrative competition upon the Great Plaza, Moquihuixtli and his adviser Teconal began sending messengers to various independent cities of the mainland, asking for help and support against Tenochtitlan and in their war preparations. Custom dictated that an offer of "shields and swords," or sometimes other weaponry of offense, constituted an invitation to participate, for the recipients of those to accept or send back according to their consideration.

Chimalpahin claims that such messages were delivered to many towns and even large *altepetls*. Even the members of the Triple Alliance – Tenochtitlan's partners, Texcoco and Tlacopan – received their share of the offered weaponry. According to his account, Chimalpopoca, Tlacopan's vigorous, warlike ruler, flatly refused to even receive the Tlatelolcan delegation and their dubious cargo – "*... as lord of Tlacopan, I am of no consequence except for my kinsman, my relative, the lord of Mexica Tenochca...*" he was reported to state.

Texcoco, on the other hand, is said to listen to the Tlatelolco messengers and then declare that they would rather stay neutral – "*... I stand on both sides... if all are to be endangered by the lord of the Mexica Tenochca, I shall go in favor of the lord of Tlatelolco. But if all are to be endangered because of the lord of Tlatelolco, I shall go in favor of the lord of the Mexica Tenochca...*" A somewhat puzzling statement in the light of many decades of mutual cooperation and closest of ties both Tenochtitlan and Texcoco maintained since 1428, when they resisted and then conquered the might of the

Tepanec Empire side by side. According to Chimalpahin, the famous Acolhua emperor Nezahualcoyotl was still alive, even though other sources state that he was dead by this time, succeeded by his son, Nezahualpilli. In the light of this puzzling reaction, I preferred to go with the claim that the old Texcoco Emperor was not alive while the aforementioned events took place. Otherwise, his response is not an easy one to understand or explain.

Having received no encouragement from the Triple Alliance's members, Tlatelolco did not steer from its warlike course. Various less important towns and settlements were approached with the offering of "swords and shields." Toltitlan, Cuauhtitlan, and several other towns of the mainland were reported to accept the offer, even though the Lake Chalco rulers went as far as arresting the Tlatelolcan messengers while sending them bound and under an ample escort to Tenochtitlan and its emperor's judgment.

Which is how, according to Chimalpahin, Axayacatl came to learn about the involvement of the mentioned above settlements and towns. The captured messengers were made to talk and so warriors were dispatched to watch the road leading to Toltitlan and Cuauhtitlan through the town of Acachinanco. Needless to say, their mission was successful and thus no positive answer reached Tlatelolco.

Not to be deterred, Moquihuixtli, at Teconal's instigation, according to Duran, devised another plan; that of a midnight surprise attack. "... *Their plan was one of treachery... they suggested that Tenochtitlan should be attacked suddenly in the middle of the night... King Axayacatl was still young, they said, and once the leading men in whom he confided were dead, there would be no need to worry about him...*"

Yet, such an enterprise demanded laborious preparations and, according to Duran, some of it managed to "leak", while alerting Tenochtitlan dwellers. There were incidents of marketplace brawls between shoppers of both *altepetls*, with the Tlatelolcan women yelling at their Tenochtitlan peers that soon they would be made to pay for their insolence, or even sell their inner parts on the marketplace of Tlatelolco – "... *so you want to sell your intestines, your liver, or your heart?...*" (Duran).

Reported to Axayacatl, such words made the young emperor suspicious, and so spies were sent to the neighboring city, to walk its markets and streets and listen to what had been said and done.

In the meantime, Tenochtitlan messengers went to the mainland cities and settlements as well, probably asking to keep away from this conflict rather than to participate in the war on Tenochtitlan's side. It seemed that Tenochtitlan was much more than a match to the smaller Tlatelolco, lacking in provinces and tributaries as it was.

Still, the nightly attack went on as planned. On the day before it happened, Moquihuixtli was reported to confide in his wife, Axayacatl's sister, who begged him not to do it, but to speak to the Tenochtitlan ruler and try to make amends. According to Duran, the Tlatelolcan ruler was having second thoughts; however, his adviser Teconal would not divert from his chosen course of warring.

Further disheartening were the omens that the Tlatelolco ruler encountered while strolling through his Palace, a man talking to a dog and being answered back, birds dancing in the boiling pot in the kitchen houses, a mask hanging on the wall beginning to "*...moan in a sorrowful way...*", the mask that the distracted ruler was reported to pick and dash against the floor. Spies sent to Tenochtitlan reported a lack of awareness on the part of Axayacatl, who was said to spend his day "*...playing ball with his noblemen... ignorant of any trouble...*". Yet, according to Duran, "*...the Aztecs had done this intentionally so as to mislead the Tlatelolcas and convince them that nothing was known of their plans...*".

Indeed convinced, Moquihuixtli put his trust in Teconal and his strategy, and so half of the Tlatelolcan warriors hid in "*... the city limits of Tenochtitlan...*". The other half was sent to block the causeways that led out of the city, and probably to attack the accessible parts of the island-capital as well.

The strategy, Tenochtitlan heard all about from its own spies, and so at midnight, while signal had been given, a surprise awaited none other than the attacking Tlatelolcans. The battle Duran reports was bloody but short, with the Tlatelolcan warriors slaughtered in great numbers, forced to retreat to their own city limits and try to barricade any possible access to it as best as they could. According to Duran, their anger was as great as the humiliation of their defeat.

In this second book of the series, I addressed the above-mentioned claims, as well as various narratives of both historians as best as I could, concentrating on the most crucial parts of their accounts for the sake of the story and its natural flow.

Again, the fictional characters along with the historical ones, had found themselves embroiled whether they wanted to be at the thick of it or not, in the right point and at the right time. However, even while exploring possible personal storylines of both fictional and non-fictional characters, I still tried to keep it as close to the narrative of both Duran and Chimalpahin, along with the described in Codex Mendoza and other primary sources regarding this famous Tenochtitlan-Tlatelolco War.

More on the history of Tlatelolco rebellion and the personal stories of various participants of it, can be read in the third book of The Aztec Chronicles, "**Heart of the Battle**".

The story continues with

HEART OF THE BATTLE

The Aztec Chronicles, Book 3

CHAPTER 1

Tenochtitlan,
1473 AD

The broom was pretty, made out of colored feathers; precious but uncomfortably short. Chantli bettered her grip on the sleekness of its handle. It had a nice touch and it murmured soothingly every time it brushed against the glossiness of the flagstones adorning the round altar.

Like in every house of worship, a heavy aroma of *copal* mixed with the typical temple's stench spread in the air, making it flicker mistily. It permeated one's breath, causing one's throat tickle and one's tongue to feel a strange aftertaste. Still, she didn't mind any of that. To be allowed into all this magnificence, to become a part of it, was beyond thrilling, the most incredible feeling.

Keeping her movements monotonously measured as instructed, she glanced around to see if there were areas she managed to miss, the floor free of dust or any other reminder of human negligence, even if dotted with dark blots, the remnants of old congealed blood gathering in the cracks between the perfectly polished flagstones.

"We are done here, I think," she said, raising the precious broom so it wouldn't drag over the floor when not in the action of doing its sacred duty. "Do you want me to help you finish with this arrangement?"

The girl she had spoken to nodded readily, struggling with the fir branches entrusted into her care, shelling the flagstones around it with soft green needles.

"They are falling apart every time I entwine them," she complained. "Those branches are not of the best quality and there are no other long enough ones in this pile. The boys who went to the mainland this morning were lazy no-goods."

"Let me try." Hiding her smile, Chantli placed the broom on the edge of the podium carefully, reverently. "I think there are a few ones that can be of use in that pile. Not very long, but enough to fit here. I'll try with those."

The intricate arrangement around the altar and various niches that hosted utensils concerning private offerings, those of the visitors and the temple's servants themselves, was easy to master, to understand its intricacy and learn to do it all by herself. The fir branches were truly so very pretty when laid against the sleekness of the stones, decorating and adding to the general grandeur. Despite her fears and misgivings, her clear lack of belonging, she had mastered this craft in a mere day of observing, pleasing the priestess who had been teaching *calmecac* girls, even making one of the more prominent priests comment. Everything concerning the temples was easy to learn and a pleasure.

Not so much the rest of the lessons conducted in the school itself, a separate spacious hall reserved for the noble girls and their learning. There she had been lost from the very beginning, not knowing where to stand or squat, or even to look, for that matter, the lessons themselves so terribly strange, unfamiliar, difficult; the art of drawing or painting glyphs beyond her, let alone deciphering that what was already painted, or adding and subtracting dots and symbols drawn on shorter sheets of *amate*-paper, multiplying and dividing. She never even heard of those rules and laws, let alone was forced to deal with them. When on the marketplace and bartering for better prices, one didn't need intricate numbers to deal with. You asked for the price, argued about it, haggled, then counted and argued some more or went away; the end of the story. Why would one use dots and symbols to represent numbers, to play with in intricate ways and according to certain rules? Shaking her head, she concentrated on the fir branches ahead of her, her fingers nimble, practiced, achieving results.

"Oh good!" exclaimed the girl beside her, her good humor returning. "Now they'll be happy enough to let us go. It is so late already. I can't believe we got stuck here for so long." Squinting against the bright spot of the entrance at the far edge of the hall, the girl shielded her eyes. "It's well into the afternoon already!"

"That floor needs to be brushed again." Shrugging, Chantli peeked at speckles of spiky green, minding neither the additional temple duty nor the less popular location of it. The temple of Xipe Totec, the Flayed One, was no less important than other principal deities, standing in the Royal Enclosure among the rest of the dazzling structures and pyramids. Growing up in the household of a metalworker, she knew all about this particular god, a patron of copper and goldsmiths, responsible for growth and rebirth of many edible fruits of the earth, flaying himself like seeds of maize before they germinate, like snakes shedding their skin. When the priest who came to greet them and elaborate on their duties talked at length, she barely needed to listen, answering every question, impressing the temple's servant into requesting her services.

"How do you know so much about gods and their duties?"

While Chantli was busy picking up the fallen needles off the floor with her hands, not wishing to mar the ritual broom with such an un-ritual task, her temporary companion stood there frowning, tapping an impatient refrain with the tip of her prettily decorated sandal, high behind the heel and around the ankle, an expensive wear of nobility. She was not the worst of companies, not like some others. A light-hearted, pouting thing named Tlazotli, prone to chatter and marked inefficiency at times, yet not mean and not snotty, not like a few other girls in this school, lavishly dressed and looking down their long noses, not pleased with the unexpectedly common addition to their class.

"I don't know that much." Glancing around, she tried to spot an appropriate container to put her refuse in. Waste or not, it was a temple's waste, after all. Could be a sacred thing or something. "It's just that my father worships the Flayed Deity. So he made us all learn whatever there is to learn. About new growth and all that." Reluctantly, she got to her feet, scooping the greenish waste with her palms, daring not to do the only sensible thing, namely tell her companion to go and bring the container, or try to be of use otherwise. One didn't order nobility about, did one? "He says that under his flayed old skin, the god is made of gold. Pure gold and not something mixed with other powders."

"That's a funny thing to say. Gold is gold. It's always shiny and pure." The girl was eyeing her with one eyebrow raised high, openly skeptical. "Your father says silly things."

"No, he does not!" She tried to get hold of her temper, knowing that it wasn't wise to pick arguments in the temple of the Royal Enclosure or to make enemies of her new classmates by telling the stupid fowl to go and bump her empty head against the nearest wall. "Gold is usually not pure. It is mixed with other metals."

"Metals?" repeated her companion as though she had used a word of an unfamiliar tongue, her second eyebrow joining the first one, arching high. "What other metals?"

"Copper and such. Silver sometimes." She cursed herself for initiating this conversation or letting it flow in such a direction, the inevitable questioning regarding her family situation looming, spelling disaster. She didn't need to elaborate on her father's line of work. Enough that they all were aware that she wasn't noble, without her going into vivid descriptions of the workshop near the wharves and the blazing braziers of the melting room. "We must find the Honorable Priest, let him know that we have finished here." To hurry off and toward the place where she could get rid of her spiny cargo helped, even though the empty-headed fowl followed, her forehead creasing in a frown, reflecting a thought process.

"You commoners worship out there in the city?"

Chantli pressed her lips tight, but the eyes that gazed at her were wide open with matter-of-fact curiosity, not haughty or deriding. She concentrated on pouring the contents of her palms into the pretty high-sided jar, then scanning the niche they had left, seeking imperfectly swept spots.

"Yes, people do worship out there in the city. They can't go all the way to the Royal Enclosure every time they wish to honor this or that deity with a private offering."

She remembered the temple dedicated to Tlaloc near the southern side of the marketplace, the low fence and the boisterous darkness all around it. The boys were not eager to enter it, to go and confess their misdeeds to the priests, face the treatment of their wounds and the general consequences of their deeds. Had it happened only a few market intervals ago, two and half, less than three? It seemed that a whole span of both rainy and dry seasons had passed since that evening and their following Tlatelolco adventures.

Even the night of the fighting and fires seemed to be in the distant past, as though not only four dawns had passed but twice, thrice that amount. She had thought that she would never forget that night, its terrors and its wonders, the thrill of being with Necalli again, next to him and involved, helping. He had appreciated that, she remembered, the memory of his arm encircling her shoulders, protecting and sheltering despite Father's ominous presence, making her insides quiver like jelly. The village boy was the one to take the real glory, saving Quetzalli, rushing into the raging flames and coming out of those against all odds, with the barely conscious girl in his arms, like the hero in stories. Still, she and Necalli were there, helping all they could, and he did come to save her before, fighting with that spear he was so proud of now, cherishing his first captured weapon. Oh, but he never tired of talking about it.

Still, even this eventful night fell into relative insignificance when two dawns later, an official of their district's council came. The entire family was busy tidying up the house and the workshop, both damaged by fire, enough to need plenty of work, new mats to be woven and new ware to be carved, let alone more substantial repairs. Plenty of work, mainly from the womenfolk of the household; however, the official cared nothing for that. In clipped, crisp tones, he related that she, Chantli, the daughter of the metalworker, was to be sent to the Royal Enclosure tomorrow with the dawn, to be interviewed by the school authorities there and be ready to stay for the first morning lessons. Just like that. No explanations; not even a polite inquiry as to the willingness of the mentioned student's father to allow her to do that. Just a curt order, a cold one at that.

She remembered her stomach going rigid with excitement mixed with fear and misgivings. The *calmecac*? She was to be admitted to *calmecac*. His school! Oh mighty deities! Was it his doing? Could he do something like that, make them demand her presence, order her father about? Oh, but for the opportunity to remain alone, to think it all through, or better yet, to run out and find him and ask. Instead, she had to endure an entire evening of Mother's frenzied chattering about inadequate wear and other needed apparel, trying to overcome her husband's thundering silence, the direfulness of his occasional glares. No, Father wasn't happy with this unusual honor, even though he had sought it out himself not very long ago, introducing her to one of the important priests of this magnificent temple, hoping to receive an invitation on her behalf. But now when it happened, he didn't like it in the least, knowing that it had to do with the cheeky *pilli* who had the gall to save his daughter on the night of the fighting; the same arrogant youth who had been taking the village boy's side against him and Acatlo. The gall! But why couldn't Father be more understanding, open to discussions and talks like he used to be?

"How is it out there in the city?" Her companion's voice broke into her musings, a welcome interruption.

Chantli blinked. "What do you mean?"

"You know, out there, beyond the Plaza and all. How is it out there?"

"Oh well, it's nice. You know, regular, like everywhere…" In the next curtained niche that hosted another of the god's effigies, a young priest was fiddling with a long-handled ladle, shaking it lightly, producing rattling sounds. "Why do you ask that?"

"You are allowed to just walk out there, aren't you? Wherever you like?"

"Yes, of course." Puzzled, she stared at her companion, discerning no malice or condescension behind the attentive eyes; only unabashed curiosity. "Aren't you allowed to walk on your own when you want something? On the marketplace, I mean, if you need to buy something…"

The girl's neatly plucked eyebrows knitted in a mix of

puzzlement and amusement. "Of course not! To walk on my own on the marketplace? Oh my, what a thought!" Her laughter rang loudly, attracting attention. The priest with the ladle shot them a disapproving glance and two men who just passed the columned entrance paused, one of them shielding his eyes, glancing in their direction. "You are so funny to say something like that, sister. They wouldn't let me walk on my own through the gardens of my father's house, let alone the marketplace filth. In those sandals and all. Too funny!"

"I didn't think that! I just asked…" She fought the urge to press her palms against her burning cheeks, hating it all, her silly company and this entire situation, with her talking too much, landing in trouble with every thoughtlessly uttered word. "We need to finish arranging this niche."

To concentrate on the vessels full of maguey thorns and round feathery balls for private sacrifice helped. The school priestess told them to rearrange those in pottery cups, didn't she? The men at the entrance still hesitated, as though reluctant to dive into the heavily scented hall. Clearly they didn't belong in this temple.

"I wish we could go home already." The pouting creature was back, complaining. Was it better to have this one cheerful but asking silly questions or moaning and of no use? "All the girls must have gone home already. Only we got stuck and in the unimportant temple, of all things!"

"You can go home if you want to. I don't mind finishing here. There are only those sacrificial cups left to arrange, unless he," she motioned toward the muttering priest, now fully occupied and paying them no attention, "plays with the idea of making us slave until the sun disappears."

As expected, a giggle was her answer. "He would, given a chance. But the Honorable Priestess would wish to see us both reporting back in the school temple." The girl's eyes were measuring her again under the arching eyebrows. "It's nice of you to offer. None of the girls would have done that. Not even the commoners."

Embarrassed, Chantli turned back toward the wooden platter. "Are there any other commoners in *calmecac*?"

"Of course. There are always a few of them in this school." Squinting, the girl turned to study the newcomers, who in the meanwhile began progressing in their direction, clearly heading for one of the curtained niches, about to make an offering. "Gifted commoners, you know. Enough of those flooding the *calmecac* halls, at all times. My brother says they should open a school for all this gifted scum, because it's—" Abruptly, the girl turned back, her eyes brushing past Chantli, gauging. "Well, I didn't mean it that way. That is, he didn't mean it, I think. It's just that there are plenty of students in this school and, you know, not enough room, you see?"

Chantli hid her resentment as best as she could. "I haven't seen much of the school yet."

"Oh, you won't see much of it anyway. We are not allowed outside our hall. Too many boys out there, you know." Her companion's wink held a clear measure of relief and for some reason, it touched her. That girl, while silly and terribly snobbish, didn't wish to offend her and wave her humble origins before her face.

"My cousin was examined by *calmecac* authorities," she related, arranging the cups with thorns while noticing one of the visiting men disappearing behind the curtain of the niche, his bearing forceful, warrior-like, his cloak flowing self-assuredly down his shoulders, sporting rich patterns and unfamiliar insignia.

"Was he accepted? Is he gifted, your cousin?"

She put her attention back to the tools of offering, her imagination painting strange pictures of the man in the nearby niche offering of his blood. What would he be piercing? Earlobes or upper arms and thighs were the most accepted places to draw one's blood from, but sometimes people would go for more daring feats of bravery, piercing their tongues, even their private parts. Appalled by such frivolous, not to say inappropriate, thoughts, she frowned.

"My cousin, yes, he is very gifted. He can read at a glance, without taking time to think before interpreting what is written. And he is always correct, always!"

"Oh, then he'll be put to study the priestly duties, or maybe the trade of the imperial scribes." The girl was glancing toward the niche that concealed the newcomer as well. "Not like that new boy whom the Emperor himself put in our *calmecac*." Her gaze returned to Chantli, flickering with excitement. "Imagine that! A real commoner. Not like you, *pillis* from traders' families, but truly a commoner. They say he is put to train with weaponry and such, but not in any other classes. I saw him a few dawns ago, bringing fir branches to the main temple. He does look like a commoner, so very broad in his limbs and face. Good looking too. But really, you can see that he is a commoner. Acoatl says he can't even read or write or do any ceremonial stuff. Only to fight, they say. But the Emperor put him in our *calmecac*, so they can't kick him out. Imagine!"

"Who is Acoatl?" asked Chantli, not truly curious but wishing to conceal her thoughts. It was clear that the chatty thing was talking about Miztli, who, indeed, even with his pretty school cloak and his newly gained spells of confidence, did carry himself like the villager he was, someone out of the fields, fit to carry heavy loads, lacking that forceful elegance of a warrior that Necalli displayed in abundance. A pity the snotty nobles could see it as well, and much too easily. Poor Miztli!

"Oh, Acoatl is a cousin of mine. A nice boy and the best ball player in the entire school. So handsome too. You should look at him. I'll show him to you tomorrow when they train out there. There is this place where one can peek into the courtyard when they are training." The girl giggled. "He can barely read either. So he can't really complain about the illiterate commoner, can he?" A conspiratorial wink. "But his bloodline is impeccable. His father is related to the royal family through his aunt, who has been given to the fifth emperor as his second wife. Not so very shabby, to be a second wife of the emperor, eh? Not a poor concubine or some minor unimportant wife."

Absently, Chantli nodded, stretching her back in relief. It had been a long day. "We can go back now, I suppose."

"About time!" The girl beamed. "Come, let us hurry. If they aren't waiting for me with their litter out there, we may linger at the temple until the boys come out. Then I'll show you my cousin.

Or maybe we'll run into our good looking YoloNecalli, eh?" The long-lashed eye winked again. "You talked to him yesterday. We saw you, Cuicatl and I. Beneath the temple's stairs."

With another wink, the girl whirled around, the sleeves of her prettily decorated *huipil* swaying. Perturbed, Chantli stared at the curtain of the other niche, her thoughts in a jumble. Yes, it would be wonderful to run into Necalli, and so very accidentally at that. Yesterday, they managed to meet only briefly, under those wide temple stairs, yes, to talk excitedly about her joining his school and about their plans but only in passing. He had to hurry back to this or that class, being sent to the temple only to deliver a message from the schoolmaster. Still, he had promised to find a better opportunity, and soon, to meet in the city and wander off, or better yet, to take her around the Great Plaza now that she had been allowed here officially, a part of the place. Such a thrilling promise, but she didn't know they had been watched by silly, gossipy fowls. An aggravation.

The curtain of the other niche moved as they passed by it, revealing the visitor, even more impressive looking from closer proximity, wiping the blood off his mouth with the back of his palm, his face strong and well defined, handsome even if slightly disfigured by a strange-looking scar running down his left cheek, splitting into two intricate lines. His eyes, large and widely spaced, were piercing, forcing them to drop their gazes and fast.

In another heartbeat, he was gone, his steps ringing strongly down the flagstones. They exchanged glances.

"Who is that warrior?" whispered Chantli, unable not to inquire. There was something about this man, something strange and unsettling, something foreign, making her think of different lands.

"How should I know?" The girl's eyes were on the drawing away cloak as well, narrowed thoughtfully. "He wears symbols of the Acolhua royal warriors. Must have come with their delegation."

"Acolhua of Texcoco? Why did they come here?"

Tlazotli's eyes sparkled, this time with regular playfulness. "We can't war on our treacherous neighbors without our esteemed partners' agreement, can we?" Shrugging, the girl turned toward the paneled columns behind which the impressive visitor disappeared already. "They may want to participate; to add to our forces, to make us stronger. Take some of the spoils for themselves as well, eh?" The softness of her chuckle bounced off the plastered walls, the entrance close now, the temple's courtyard awash with sunlight, hosting quite a few warriors. "It'll be easy to take our despicable neighbors down, my father says. The Emperor should have done it long ago, before they attacked us. Did you know that they burned out half of the city? All those commoner parts out there. By this or that causeway and some shores, Father says. You can walk there without detouring, just stroll through, because all their buildings burned down. Imagine!"

"It's not that bad," muttered Chantli, the memory of the fires making her stomach cramp. It was terrible back then, the smoke and the heat, so vicious, so eager to hurt; and the people, warriors killing each other, and the rest just running around, but some of the fighters eager to hurt the unarmed citizens too. Like that man with the club that tried to strike Father down and which but for Necalli... The familiar cold wave was gripping her insides, making her chest hurt. She had tried to save Father and Necalli came to save her, but Father wasn't grateful to any of them, his anger stronger than any other feeling. And why was he so furious anyway? The village boy might have "scampered away," the way her brothers had put it, using stronger words of cursing that Mother had forbidden to utter in the house, but Necalli had nothing to do with it. And neither did she! But it seemed that Father blamed her somehow. Why?

"Look, he is still here!" Tlazotli's palm wrapped around her wrist, arresting her progress down the wide staircase. "Over there, with the other Acolhua. See?"

To shield her eyes became a necessity, the sun too strong, glittering against the mosaic adorning the outside columns and the vast patio's floor, blinding. The visitor's cloak, indeed, now intermingled with likewise wear all around, the symbols of two flower-like things sticking out of what resembled a glyph for a mountain, or maybe some sort of a double-mountain, sported proudly on quite a few other cloaks.

"They are all from Texcoco?"

"Oh yes." The grip of her companion's hand tightened, relaying a message. "Don't stare at them. They'll notice."

Chastened, Chantli took her eyes away, only to encounter another congregation, this one near the round stone platform under construction. Those were more numerous and more agitated, warriors of high rank as well, talking rapidly, waving their hands. Their cloaks sported different patterns.

Unwilling to ask what those meant as not to come across an ignorant commoner again, she led their way down the stairs, in a hurry to reach the school's temple, out of patience. What if Necalli was looking for her, finding this or that pretext to linger around? She would be missing him and just as she needed to see him the most. The foreign delegations were of no consequence to her. If the Emperor needed to receive his allies' approval, it was his business, not hers.

"I knew Tlacopan people would be nearby," her companion chimed in, following closely, eyes everywhere. "So predictable!"

"To give their agreement too?" It was impossible not to ask, her eyes brushing past the agitated group, then drawing back toward the calmer Texcoco folk, the man from the temple still easy to tell from his peers, his grim, arrogant bearing setting him apart. He was nodding thoughtfully, glancing back toward the temple and the stairs, frowning as though directly at them. Chantli took her eyes away in a hurry.

"Well, yes. They will wash that treacherous Tlatelolco like the flood in the Fifth Emperor's days." The girl's giggle rolled down the stairs, preceding them. "But for now, I bet they are enjoying our Palace's hospitality, feasting and entertaining themselves. In Texcoco, they might boast the best of everything, food and music and libraries, but still, Tenochtitlan is the Capital of the World, not Texcoco."

"Of course!" She never thought to doubt something like that, even though they said that the Acolhua capital was magnificent, refined to the point of looking unreal. Nezahualcoyotl, their old emperor, now dead for a few rainy seasons, had built lavishly, even on the hills that surrounded his *altepetl*, channeling water for impossibly long distances, transforming the arid lands into beautiful gardens to host his palaces and places of entertainment. Still, Tenochtitlan was the *altepetl* that ruled the world, not Texcoco.

"Are those not our boys running out there?"

This time, Tlazotli was shielding her eyes against the glitter of the huge podium that separated them from the round temple, their prospective destination. From their elevated vantage point, it was easy to see how vast it was, in the process of being decorated, lined with polished stone in the form of a round platform studded with glittering pieces. What rituals will this thing serve?

Her thoughts didn't linger on these dilemmas, her eyes darting further up and toward the rushing about people, seeking the familiar short cloaks, finding those easily, two as expected, hurrying back toward the school. Her heart missed a beat, even though her eyes were not able to confirm her suspicion, not yet. Still, it must have been *him*. In the company of the village boy probably, judging by the broader frame of his companion. She fought the urge to skip two stairs at a time; no, three of them. But what could be more perfect than meeting him like that, innocently, with no beforehand preparation or intention? What could the gossiping fowls say against it?

Jumping another landing, she glanced back, relieved to see her companion close behind. A spoiled noble fowl, yes, but not too haughty to run in order to catch up with the boys. Eager to make it look as an innocent encounter too? Oh yes, one could trust any girl to be able to do that, noble or commoner.

The clamor of the Plaza enveloped them, disappointing in their lost elevated position but pleasing at the same time, animated and glamorous in no marketplace fashion and none of the pushy, violent agitation of various districts' squares. It was good to belong to such place, to walk it with confidence and aplomb.

"They must have reached our temple already." Tlazotli wrinkled her nose, glancing around warily. "Mother's servants would be on the lookout for me there. What an annoyance!"

"We still need to report to the Honorable Priestess and it

wasn't your fault you received this temple duty." It felt called upon to offer a word of reassurance, even though it was actually better that this girl, nice and not as snobbish as the rest of them, would leave her to her own devices now. They didn't need such gossipy company. Or any other company, for that matter. It would be nice if even Miztli would find something better to do elsewhere. At least for a little while. Then the inevitable twinge of guilt came. The village boy had nowhere to go, no one to seek out on the free-from-school afternoons. He needed Necalli more than she did, come to think of it. It was selfish to wish him away only because she wanted the handsome *calmecac* boy all for herself.

"Oh, here they are!"

Tlazotli's exclamation made her gaze dart, taking in the wideness of the mid-size pyramid's stairs, familiar from her first time in this Royal Enclosure, when the royal boy Ahuitzotl made her follow the corridor. Briefly, she wondered where the high-spirited *pilli* was hiding since she had entered the school.

The short-cloaked figures were standing next to the stairs, talking with marked ease, laughing loudly. Her stomach twisted with disappointment. Not Necalli and the village boy, not even remotely. Instead, her eyes recognized the taller and somewhat broader figure of the other *calmecac* boy, Axolin, unmistakable with his easy cheerful bearing. Beside him towered another boy, at least half a head taller and much broader, his school cloak looking too small for his spectacular proportions, his stance having a certain sense of challenge and defiance to it.

"*Niltze*, Cousin!" called out Tlazotli, slowing her step while raising her hand in a light indifferent greeting. There was no trace of the previously displayed excitement in the girl's movements now, neither when spotting the boys nor when talking about this same cousin of hers back in the temple. If anything, she looked offhanded, disinterested. In spite herself, Chantli hid her grin, knowing this sort of playacting too well. She, Quetzalli, and Xochi were masters of such pretense, especially Quetzalli.

The thought of Quetzalli brought another. Recovered from the shock of being nearly killed in the fire, her friend took the news of her, Chantli's, new school arrangement surprisingly well, talking about coming to meet her near the last bridge of the canal that separated the Great Plaza from the rest of the city. Was she that eager to see the Royal Enclosure and the noble school? wondered Chantli. Or had it something to do with the strange interest Quetzalli had taken in her rescuer all of a sudden, talking about the village boy a little too much and too gushingly for a few days in a row. Was he also in the same *calmecac* school? Were the girls, like in *telpochcalli*, herded into a single classroom, separated from the boys and lacking their freedom to roam about? Did she, Chantli, see him through her first days on these premises? Did he ask about her, Quetzalli's, wellbeing? A puzzling questioning, but she had no time to think about it all as yet.

"What are you doing here?"

The boys turned around, both of them. In the dimmer light of the stairs' shadow, she could see that the other one was truly outstandingly wide and muscled, his face not unpleasant but for the derisively curving lips. His eyes lingered on her for another heartbeat before shifting to his family member, who in the meanwhile smiled gloriously at Axolin.

"What are you doing here, Tlazotli?" the larger boy repeated, his grin losing its unpleasant quality, turning mischievous. "Hiding from your mother's litter-bearers?"

Tlazotli's snicker was too loud to suggest any such covert activity. "I was in the Xipe Totec temple, doing my duties, you silly one. I'm not trying to escape on wild adventures the way you do."

"I don't have to 'escape' to get your adventures," he said haughtily. "I'm a man and a warrior. I can go wherever I please."

To Chantli's certain sense of satisfaction, the girl made a face that matched her family member's in its condescending derision. "You are nothing but a *calmecac* boy, Cousin. As much a warrior as I am one of the royal Palace's wives."

"You'll never get that far," the tall boy retorted, then his eyes shifted back to Chantli. "Who is your pretty friend here? Another future imperial wife?"

Tlazotli snickered yet louder. "Rather a royal concubine." Her smile was wide, holding no guile. "Chantli is the new girl. She's just been admitted to our class and she knows everything there is to know about temples' duties. She'll be the next teacher-priestess, you just wait and see." The last phrase came out somehow defying, as though this same sharp-tongued, muscled cousin already challenged her, Chantli's, right to be here.

"You are in our *calmecac*?" burst in Axolin, speaking for the first time, atypically subdued until now.

Chantli just nodded, not thrilled to be turned into the center of their attention. She didn't need any of that. Not with the three of them being oh so very noble and well connected, with their haughtiness spilling out even without them noticing, like with the annoying fowl's concubine comment. Tlazotli wasn't too arrogant to speak and chatter and joke as though they were equals, working in the temple side by side, even though letting her, Chantli, do all the work, come to think of it. Still, deep down, the Great Plaza's girl knew that they weren't equal, not even near. And so did the rest of them. Except for Necalli, maybe. But what if he was aware of their status differences as well?

"Oh, that is a nice surprise," went on Axolin, looking anything but malicious, his smile genuine. "Necalli will be thrilled when he hears."

"Our YoloNecalli knows all about it," piped in Tlazotli. "And yes, he looked thrilled enough, come to think of it." Her beam was all innocence, clearly exaggerated this time. "Why did you say what you said?"

To Chantli's relief, Axolin just shrugged in response, but his face darkened visibly, turning stony.

"What's that piece of worthless refuse have to do with any of that?" demanded the other boy, straightening somewhat dangerously, his previous light grin gone, leaving no trace. "The stupid would-be great warrior, that one, lover of commoners, stinking piece of rotten tortilla."

Axolin said nothing while his face darkened some more.

"But you do like our Necalli, Cousin," commented Tlazotli, clearly delighted by the outburst. "All this warm feeling!"

"The only warm feeling I'll cherish for that one—"

"Don't talk about Necalli like that!" She said it without

thinking, appalled by so much venom and unfair accusations. Necalli was a great warrior already, just to witness his fighting on the night of the fires, his spear that he captured from the enemy, his bravery back in Tlatelolco and the tunnel and at the darkness of the lake, his way of saving them all. He was anything but a mere schoolboy like these two and he would turn into the greatest warrior of them all.

The tall boy was staring at her coldly. "And what is your thing with this would-be hero?"

"They like to talk a lot, these two," contributed Tlazotli readily. The filthy fowl!

Chantli hunted after something appropriate to say, something that would not sound like marketplace shrill curses she wished to heap on their heads.

"Leave her alone," said Axolin, coming back to life all at once. "She has nothing to do with any of it."

"She takes that stupid poser's side..." began his companion hotly, but Axolin just waved his hand tiredly.

"Leave her and Necalli alone."

For a heartbeat, no one said a word, then the taller boy whirled abruptly, giving Axolin a dark look of his own. "You better chose your side carefully. You can't have it all ways."

As he stormed off, Chantli began breathing again.

"What was that all about?" the girl beside her was asking, sounding all innocence and sweet naivety. "Acoatl, wait!" Her footsteps rang lightly against the clean cobblestones, the floor under the grand staircase swept into perfection as though inside this or that temple.

They watched the pair of them drawing away, the tall boy gesticulating angrily.

"Why are you going around with this one?" A glance at her current companion made her feel bad. He was frowning painfully, his forehead a study of creases. "He hates Necalli so. Why?"

Axolin's shrug held tired acceptance. "I don't know. They were squabbling always, those two, never got along without challenging each other and getting angry for real. From the very beginning of school, even though we used to run around the city all together in the beginning." Another heavy shrug joined the previous one. "But since your workshop boy came along, it became really bad. Since the very first moment!" This time, his gaze met hers, holding an open grudge. "He is not who he used to be anymore. So full of himself, bragging all the time, thinking the others to be lesser than him only because he got into a few adventures with that commoner and fought in a battle. He thinks it makes him better than the rest. But it doesn't, you know? Everyone in his place would have done the same, or at least most of us. We just didn't get the chance."

The dark eyes were peering at her, curiously unguarded and so full of hurt it made her stop the budding words of protest, keep her mouth shut; an unfamiliar feeling. What he said wasn't true, most definitely it wasn't. Not many would have done as well or as bravely, would have thought so quickly and found solutions. It wasn't Axolin they had followed back in Tlatelolco. On the contrary, this same friend of his had followed Necalli as readily as they all did, offering arguments and good-natured needling but still following and expecting him to get them out of the mess they had gotten themselves into. And Necalli was a good friend too, not bragging and making himself "bigger" at the expense of his peers. Witness his loyalty to the village boy and his continued support, not lofty or patronizing but just there; businesslike, matter-of-fact, a true friend.

"He spoke to the Emperor because the Emperor addressed his questions at him when we were brought to the Palace, after Tlatelolco. That's all. If he had asked me, I would be the one to be singled out. It was just a coincidence that he was asked first and then could help the commoner when that one couldn't manage to put two words together. He was so frightened back there!" The air hissed loudly as it blew through the widening nostrils, with much resentment. "The commoner is the one the Emperor likes to use, to send on weird errands and what not. Ahuitzotl told me all about it. He is resourceful and crazy enough to endanger himself, with nowhere to go but up anyway. A perfect tool. Also, he has no family to pacify if something happens to him, no influential nobles to answer to and explain. Not like my or Necalli's or

Acoatl's father. But Necalli somehow managed to glue himself to this villager and make the Emperor allow him to tag along. But it doesn't make him better than any of us. Just clever and around at the right time. That's all!"

Despite herself, her heart went out to him. He looked so disheartened, so sad.

"Necalli is still your friend," she said helplessly, not sure of that claim. When they talked on the day before, he said nothing about Axolin and their falling out. Until this very moment, she had known not a thing about any of that. "He still likes and admires you greatly. He talked about you only the other day."

"What did he say?" This came out a little too eagerly.

She searched for something nice but noncommittal to offer, making a mental note to bring this matter up with Necalli. "He said you are a great friend, like you always were."

"And he said nothing about me going around with Acoatl? He makes plenty of faces. Stupid faces!"

"We didn't have time to talk about it at length. Yesterday was my first day at school and he just caught me out there for a little while, to make me feel better."

The frown cleared. "How did you get here in the first place?"

She shrugged, relieved now. Maybe they could be friends again. "The district council's messenger came to my father's house and told them to present me at the *calmecac* temple before the Honorable Priestess with the dawn. And that was that." She tried to smile reassuringly. "But I was here before, once. On the day of our Tlatelolco adventures. My father brought me here back then and the Main Priest himself talked to me." She made a face. "It was scary!"

He grinned reluctantly, with one side of his mouth. "The High Priest can scare the life out of anyone." Then his smile straightened. "Well, I'm glad that you are in our school now. Don't let the stupid fowls like Tlazotli patronize or badmouth you. If you become a priestess, you'll be sort of equal to them anyway. I'll talk to Acoatl, make him understand that you are to be treated well." Another of his previously crooked grins flashed. "He has some influence among the girls of the school. Half of it seems to be his cousins, and if he thinks that you have a thing for Necalli, you are done for."

She shivered at the very thought. "The girls do what he says?"

"No, of course not." He laughed merrily, as though amused by such a silly assumption. "No noble fowl would let a boy tell her what to do or think. Not until she is given to one such in a marriage, that is. Unless a chief wife." His shoulders lifted indifferently. "But many of the girls who attend our *calmecac* are his cousins or other distant family members. They are part royal, you see? His mother is a niece once removed to Tezozomoctzin himself, our current Emperor's father. So he meets plenty of those on their family feasts and celebrative occasions. And what do they do through such boring events, do you think? Gossip about everyone and everything, the school being their favorite subject, the unusual commoner elements in it the juiciest gossip of them all, a pleasure to badmouth." He looked at her shrewdly. "And if you keep huddling with Necalli in the way you do and take his side when he is badmouthed behind his back and in front of those same vicious fowls, they will tear you apart, those snotty noble girls. The authorities may even throw you out of school if your bad name goes ahead of you and reaches the teachers' or the priestess's ears."

Her insides were nothing but a quivering mess by now. "But it would be lies, filthy lies!" she cried out, then pressed her palm to her mouth, pushing the rest of the loud outburst in. Her words echoed shrilly between the stones of the stairs and the painted plaster of the wall. "I won't be guilty of anything and they can still made them kick me out of school?"

"Or make your school life a real misery," he added levelly, not impressed by her outburst. "It is also a bad enough option."

Suddenly, the thought hit her. "This Acoatl, does he make the village boy's life a misery too?"

Axolin's broad face darkened again. "He would have but for Necalli. Your admired hero champions your workshop family member to the point of being ridiculous. As though he has a soft spot for this one, you know? Although until this time, I would have sworn that he liked girls. Not good-looking boys."

She gasped, unprepared for something like that. "He does not!"

His grin was again more crooked than before. "One wonders."

"You would slander his good name too, yes? You did it just now, like you said those girls would do to me!"

He made a face, but she could see his features twisting guiltily. "You are talking nonsense, commoner girl. Stop that. I'm trying to help you out for the sake of our Tlatelolco adventures. You were brave enough and worthy back then. That's the only reason I'm prepared to help you." His shoulders lifted briefly. "Even though you can't think straight when it comes to that bragger who used to be my friend until I saw his real face."

To bite back sharp words that were hovering on the tip of her tongue became increasingly more difficult. She took a deep breath, remembering Tlatelolco and the tunnel and the lake. This boy was there for them both as well, when Necalli had fished her from under the boat. He was the one to pull them up.

"He is your friend; he still is. You should not be angry with him for being good to the village boy. Miztli was in Tlatelolco too, remember? He was as brave as the two of you, and as loyal. He saved Necalli and Ahuitzotl, and through them, he saved you and Patli as well. You would have been found otherwise. That terrible man Teconal, he would have found and harmed you two. You should not hate Miztli for becoming friends with Necalli. He didn't take his friendship away from you." A shrug came with difficulty this time. "He just joined in."

But Axolin's face closed stubbornly. "That's what you think, pretty girl. But you don't know everything that happened. Ask him how he left me out to enjoy himself on the mainland and then later on with the Eagle Warriors. If he is not a coward, he'll tell you the truth, but I doubt that." One of his shoulders lifted briefly, desolately. "As for the commoner, I don't hate him. I have nothing for or against him. When Acoatl wanted to beat him just now, out there in the schoolyard, the two of us against him, I told him to leave him alone." Another shrug. "I have nothing against the wild villager. He is nothing to me."

Her stomach tightened violently. "Acoatl wanted to beat him?

Why?"

"For his pleasure, I suppose. Or in order to make Necalli mad." His snort was soft, rolling over the spreading shadow of the stairs. "I'm not sure he would have managed. The commoner is really very strong and clearly dangerous if cornered. But if there were the two of us against him, then he might have gotten hurt." An impassive grimace twisted his features, its placidness not in accordance with his words. "Still, I didn't do it, so you can stop making those horrified faces. Your precious village wonder is hale and healthy as yet."

She paid the barb no attention, still panicked by the very thought. "Was he alone out there? Why doesn't he make sure to be with someone if people like this Acoatl want to hurt him? What if he convinces someone else, not a good person like you, to help him next time? What then?"

He rolled his eyes tellingly. "Don't throw these panicked fits. The villager can take care of himself, you know? He is wild and has no fear, and he doesn't know his place and doesn't want to know that. Seems to me that he can take care of himself." His lips twisted as derisively as those of that vile Acoatl when they had just approached the boys. "He has been huddling all alone plenty these days, crouching with pieces of *amate*-paper and whatnot. I saw him on the day before, just before leaving the school and now as well, busy with charcoal, drawing glyphs. Maybe he is busy writing a book, telling of his Tlatelolco adventures." Another soft snort moved the air. "It looks that Necalli has been neglecting his new friend, doesn't it? Goes to tell you something. Maybe you should be careful of this boy too. Market girls didn't fare well under his tongue, not until now."

Another slight lift of the cloaked shoulders and he went away, leaving her standing there, transfixed. When her thoughts cleared enough, she had to literally force her legs to take her back into the sunlight and up the magnificent staircase, her mind in a daze, buzzing. Then she remembered Quetzalli and the promise to meet her friend by the bridge of the canal. Oh, but she had no time for any of that!

ABOUT THE AUTHOR

Zoe Saadia is the author of several novels on pre-Columbian Americas. From the architects of the Aztec Empire to the founders of the Iroquois Great League, from the towering pyramids of Tenochtitlan to the longhouses of the Great Lakes, her novels bring long-forgotten history, cultures and people to life, tracing pivotal events that brought about the greatness of North and Mesoamerica.

To learn more about Zoe Saadia and her work, please visit www.zoesaadia.com

Printed in Great Britain
by Amazon